Praise for Irene Hannon and her novels

D0890676

IRENE HANNON

The Best Gift

Gift from the Heart

Steeple
Hill®

Published by Steeple Hill Books™

STEEPLE HILL BOOKS

Steeple
Hill®

Recycling programs
for this product may
not exist in your area.

ISBN-13: 978-0-373-65131-3

THE BEST GIFT AND GIFT FROM THE HEART

www.SteepleHill.com

Printed in U.S.A.

CONTENTS

Books by Irene Hannon

Steeple Hill Love Inspired

*Home for the Holidays
*A Groom of Her Own
*A Family to Call Her Own
It Had to Be You
One Special Christmas
The Way Home
Never Say Goodbye
Crossroads
**The Best Gift
**Gift From the Heart
**The Unexpected Gift

All Our Tomorrows
The Family Man
Rainbow's End
†From This Day Forward
†A Dream To Share
†Where Love Abides
Apprentice Father
††Tides of Hope
††The Hero Next Door

*Vows
**Sisters & Brides
†Heartland Homecomings
††Lighthouse Lane

IRENE HANNON

Irene Hannon, who writes both romance and romantic suspense, is an author of more than twenty-five novels. Her books have been honored with both the coveted RITA® Award from Romance Writers of America (the "Oscar" of romantic fiction) and a Reviewer's Choice Award from *Romantic Times BOOKreviews* magazine. More than one million copies of her novels have been sold worldwide.

A former corporate communications executive with a Fortune 500 company, Irene now writes full-time. In her spare time, she enjoys singing, long walks, cooking, gardening and spending time with family. She and her husband make their home in Missouri.

For more information about her and her books, Irene invites you to visit her Web site at www.irenehannon.com.

THE BEST GIFT

The Lord is near. Have no anxiety, but in every
prayer and supplication with thanksgiving
let your petitions be made known to God.
—*Philippians* 4:5–6

To my darling niece, Maureen Elizabeth,
who came early to claim our hearts with her
sunny smile. We love you, snowflake!

Prologue

Morgan Williams glanced impatiently at her watch, then gave an exasperated sigh. "I wish he'd hurry. I have a plane to catch."

A.J. turned from the window, which framed a row of flame-red maples against a brilliant St. Louis late-October sky. "Chill out, Morgan," she said wryly. "The advertising world can live without you for a few more hours."

Morgan gave her younger sister an annoyed look as she rummaged in her purse for her cell phone. "Trust me, A.J. The business arena is nothing like your non-profit world. Hours do matter to us. So do minutes."

"More's the pity," A.J. responded, turning back to admire the view again. "Life is too short to be so stressed about things as fleeting as ad campaigns."

Morgan opened her mouth to respond, but Clare beat her to it. "Don't you think we should put our philosophical differences aside today, out of respect for Aunt Jo?" she interjected gently.

Morgan and A.J. turned in unison toward their older sister, and A.J. grinned.

"Ever the peacemaker, Clare," she said, her voice tinged with affection.

Clare smiled. "Somebody had to keep the two of you from doing each other bodily harm when we were growing up. And since I was the only one who didn't inherit Mom's McCauley-red hair—and the temper that went with it—I suppose the job had to fall to me."

A.J. joined Morgan on the couch. "Okay. In honor of Aunt Jo, I declare a truce. How about it, Morgan?"

Morgan hesitated, then tucked her cell phone in her purse. "Truce," she agreed with a grin. "Besides, much as I hate to admit that my kid sister is sometimes right, I am occasionally guilty of taking my job too seriously."

"Occasionally?" A.J. rolled her eyes.

"Enough, you two," Clare admonished with a smile.

A.J. laughed. "Okay, okay. You must whip those kids into shape whenever you substitute teach. In a nice way, of course. Their regular teacher is probably astounded at their good behavior when she gets back."

Clare's smile faded, and she looked down to fiddle with the strap on her purse. "I do my best. But I still have a lot to learn. It's been so many years since I taught…it's harder some days than others."

A.J. and Morgan exchanged a look. "Hang in there, Clare," Morgan encouraged. "We're here for you."

"It does get easier. Not overnight. But bit by bit. Trust me," A.J. added, her own voice suddenly a bit uneven.

Clare blinked rapidly several times before she looked up. "Sorry. I usually have my emotions better under control. I guess Aunt Jo's memorial service today just brought back…a lot of memories."

Her voice caught on the last word, and A.J. and Morgan simultaneously reached for their sister's hands. Clare gazed down and took a deep breath. "A circle of love," she said softly.

"The three musketeers," A.J. added, using one of their childhood nicknames as she grasped Morgan's hand to complete the circle.

Morgan squeezed both hands. "One for all, all for one."

Suddenly the door to the inner-office opened, and the sisters dropped their hands as they all turned toward attorney Seth Mitchell.

For a long moment the distinguished, gray-haired man standing in the doorway studied Jo Warren's three great-nieces, taking full advantage of the opportunity to examine them up close rather than from a distance, as he had at the service this morning. He was pleased to note that none flinched at his unhurried perusal.

A.J. was tall and lean, with long, naturally curly strawberry blond hair, too unruly to be tamed even by strategically placed combs. She seemed perfectly comfortable in her somewhat eclectic attire—a calf-length skirt and a long tunic top, cinched at the waist with an unusual metal belt—and looked at him with genuine curiosity, as if the current situation was immensely interesting to her.

Morgan, who wore her dark, copper-colored hair in a sleek, shoulder-length style, was dressed in chic business attire that spelled "big city" and "success." She gave him a somewhat bored, impatient "let's-get-on-with-this-because-I-have-better-things-to-do" look.

Clare, the shortest of the three, wore her honey-gold hair in an elegant chignon that complemented her designer suit and Gucci purse. She had hope in her eyes when she looked at him—as well as a deep and lingering sadness.

Yes, they were just as Jo had described them, Seth concluded. A.J., the free spirit who took an interest in everything around her and was grounded in the here and now…perhaps too much so. Morgan, the some-what jaded high-powered executive who might need some help straightening out her priorities. And Clare, whose double tragedy had left her in need of both emotional and financial help. Now, more than ever, Jo's legacy made sense to Seth.

He moved forward. "Good morning, ladies. I'm Seth Mitchell. I recognize you from Jo's description—A.J., Morgan, Clare," he said, correctly identifying the sisters as he extended his hand to each in turn. "Please accept my condolences on the loss of your great-aunt. She was a wonderful lady."

They murmured polite responses, and he motioned toward his office. "If you're ready, we can proceed with the reading of the will."

He didn't speak again until they were all seated, at which point he picked up a hefty document. "I'll give each of you a copy of your great-aunt's will to take with you, so I don't think there's any reason to go through this whole document now. A lot of it is legalese, and there are some charitable bequests that you can review at your leisure. I thought we could restrict the formal reading to the section that affects each of you directly, if that's agreeable."

"Absolutely," Morgan replied. "Besides, my plane for Boston leaves in less than three hours. I know Clare needs to get back to Kansas City, and A.J. has a long drive to Chicago."

Seth looked at the other two sisters. When they nodded their assent, he flipped through the document to a marked page and began to read.

"Insofar as I have no living relatives other than my three great-nieces—the daughters of my sole nephew, Jonathan Williams, now deceased—I bequeath the bulk of my estate to them, in the following manner and with the following stipulations and conditions.

"To Abigail Jeanette Williams, I bequeath half ownership of my bookstore in St. Louis, Turning Leaves, with the stipulation that she retain ownership for a minimum of six months and work full-time in the store during this period. The remaining half ownership I bequeath to the present manager, Blake Sullivan, with the same stipulation.

"To Morgan Williams, I bequeath half ownership of Serenity Point, my cottage in Seaside, Maine, providing that she retains her ownership for a six-month period following my death and that she spends a total of four weeks in residence at the cottage. During this time she is also to provide advertising and promotional assistance for Good Shepherd Camp and attend board meetings as an advisory member. The remaining half ownership of the cottage I bequeath to Grant Kincaid of Seaside, Maine.

"To Clare Randall, I bequeath my remaining financial assets, except for those designated to be given to the charities specified in this document, with the stipulation that she serve as nanny for Nicole Wright, daughter of Dr. Adam Wright of Hope Creek, North Carolina, for a period of six months, at no charge to Dr. Wright.

"Should the stipulations and conditions for the aforementioned bequests not be fulfilled, the specified assets will be disposed of according to directions given to my attorney, Seth Mitchell. He will also designate the date on which the clock will begin ticking on the six-month period specified in my will. "

Seth lowered the document to his desk and looked at the women across from him. A.J. still looked interested. Morgan looked aggravated. Clare looked uncertain.

"There you have it, ladies. I can provide more details on your bequests to each of you individually, but are there any general questions that I can answer?"

"Well, I might as well write mine off right now," Morgan said in disgust. "There's no way I can be away from the office for four days, let alone four weeks. And what is Good Shepherd Camp?"

"Who is this Dr. Wright?" Clare asked with a frown. "And what makes Aunt Jo think he would want me as a nanny?"

"When can I start?" A.J. asked.

"Let me take your questions and comments one at a time," Seth said. "Morgan, you have the right to turn down the bequest, of course. But I would advise you to get some legal and financial counsel first. Jo bought that property years ago, when Seaside was just a quiet, backwater village. The area is now a bustling tourist mecca. So her property has increased significantly in value. As for how to meet your aunt's residence stipulation—I'm afraid I can't advise you on that. Good Shepherd is a summer camp in Maine for children from troubled homes. Your aunt has been involved with the organization for many years.

"Clare, Dr. Wright is an old friend of Jo's from St. Louis. I believe she met him through her church, and even when he moved to North Carolina, they remained close friends. He's a widower with an eleven-year-old daughter who apparently needs guidance and closer supervision. As to why Jo thought Dr. Wright would be interested in having you as a nanny, I can't say.

"A.J., I'd ask you to give me a couple of weeks to tie up some legalities before you contact Mr. Sullivan. I'll let you know when it's appropriate to call."

He paused and glanced at his desk calendar. "Let's officially start the clock for the six-month period on December 1. That will give you about a month to make plans. Now, are there any more general questions?"

The three women looked at him, looked at each other, then silently shook their heads.

"Very well." He handed them each a manila envelope. "But do feel free to call if any come up as you review the will more thoroughly." He rose, signaling the end of the meeting, and extended his hand to each sister in turn. "Again, my condolences on the death of your great-aunt. Jo had a positive impact on countless lives and will be missed by many people. I know she loved each of you very much, and that she wanted you to succeed in claiming your bequests.

"Good luck, ladies."

Chapter One

It wasn't fair.

Blake Sullivan stared at the letter from Seth Mitchell. How could Jo do this to him? Okay, so maybe she'd never actually promised to leave the entire business to him, but she had certainly implied as much. After all, they'd been friends for twenty-one years. And he'd walked away from a successful career in investment banking three years ago to rescue Turning Leaves, when Jo's waning energy began to affect the business and her ongoing generosity had finally depleted her financial cushion. He'd enjoyed it so much that he'd stayed to turn the sleepy, neighborhood bookshop into a thriving enterprise. Without him, the business would have been bankrupt by now.

And what was his reward for three years of diligent labor on her behalf? She'd left half the business to her flighty, do-gooder great-niece who probably didn't know the difference between a balance sheet and a balance beam.

Blake felt his blood pressure edge up and forced himself to take a slow, deep breath. Getting worked up about the situation wasn't going to change it, he reminded himself. Maybe if he and Jo had had more time to discuss it, things would have turned out differently. But the fast-acting cancer that had struck so suddenly and taken her so quickly had left them little time for business discussions. By the time she'd told anyone about her illness, it was far too late to discuss any succession plans.

Blake fingered the letter from her attorney, a hollow feeling in the pit of his stomach. He could just walk away, of course. Let the business disintegrate in the hands of Jo's inexperienced and probably disinterested heir. But he'd poured too much of himself into the bookshop, cared too much about it to let it die.

Which left him only one option.

And that did not make him happy.

Blake watched the caller ID disappear as the line went dead. Jo's niece again. He couldn't avoid her forever, but he needed more time to think things through. Especially since he'd received Jo's brief, enigmatic letter, which had arrived a couple of days after Seth Mitchell's.

He lifted it from the kitchen counter as he waited for the microwave to reheat the cannelloni from his favorite restaurant on The Hill—a splurge that would wreak havoc with his well-disciplined diet, especially with the Thanksgiving Day triathlon looming on the horizon. But he'd needed a pick-me-up after the news from Seth.

Blake scanned the single sheet of paper once more.

Dear Blake, I know you will be disappointed by my bequest. Please understand that I fully appreciate all you have done these past three years to make Turning Leaves successful, and that my gratitude goes deeper than I can say. I have valued our friendship and our partnership, and one of my great joys has been to watch you grow into a fine man.

At the same time, I feel a special obligation to my nieces. A.J. needs an anchor in her life, and I am hopeful that Turning Leaves will provide that for her. She has been drifting these past few years, for reasons that even she may not fully comprehend, but which you may eventually come to understand. I would consider it a final favor for an old friend if you would help her learn the business we both love. With great affection, Jo.

The beeper went off on the microwave, and Blake retrieved the cannelloni. He didn't understand some of Jo's comments, but he did understand the part about the final favor. And as rational thought had prevailed over the past couple of days, he'd come to acknowledge that as much as he'd done for Jo these past three years, it was he who was deeply in *her* debt.

As he poured a soft drink, he thought back to the summer when he was thirteen. It was a couple of years after Jo's husband died, and she had just opened her shop. Pure chance brought them together. Or fate. Or maybe Providence, if one were religiously inclined. But whatever it was, it had changed his life.

Blake's parents had decided to spend the summer in St. Louis, for reasons Blake couldn't recall. They were always going somewhere on a whim, for a rally or to hang out with friends or simply for a change of scene. Jo had hired his father to do some carpentry and odd jobs at the shop. Blake hadn't known anyone in St. Louis, and after thirteen years he'd learned that it didn't pay to try to make friends in a new town, because in a few weeks or a few months his vagabond parents would be on the road again. So he'd simply tagged along with his father to Jo's. And those had been some of his happiest days.

Jo had taken him under her wing, giving him odd jobs to do and regaling him with stories of her world travels and the exotic places she and her husband had visited. She'd discussed politics with him, and philosophy, as if he were an adult, which did wonders for his shaky thirteen-year-old self-esteem. He owed his love of learning and books to Jo. And so much more. Something about him must have made an impact on her as well, because she'd stayed in touch with him when his family moved on at the end of the summer. He still had her letters tucked in a shoe box in his closet. During his teenage years, she was the one stable person in his unsettled, unpredictable world, and he clung to her voraciously, sharing with her his fears and his hopes. She'd always encouraged him, and when it came time for college, she'd come through for him again, providing a significant amount of the funding for his education.

So even though he'd rescued Turning Leaves, his

efforts were small repayment for all she'd been to him. Friend. Confidante. Supporter. Benefactor. And now she had one last request. Help her great-niece learn the business.

How could he say no?

"Blake, A. J. Williams is on the phone for you."

Blake frowned and transferred his gaze from the computer screen to the flickering phone light.

"Bad time? Should I get a number?"

Slowly, Blake shook his head and looked over at his assistant manager. There was no sense avoiding the inevitable. "No. I'll take it, Nancy. Thanks."

She hesitated at the doorway. "Is everything okay?"

Blake heard the trepidation in her voice, and nodded. "I'm sure everything will be fine."

As a divorced mother with two part-time jobs, Nancy worked hard to provide for herself and her ten-year-old daughter. She'd been unsettled ever since Jo's death, clearly unsure about the future of Turning Leaves. Blake had tried to be reassuring, but he couldn't offer much encouragement since he felt the same way.

Blake looked back at the flashing light. Too bad he hadn't hung around long enough after Jo's memorial service to meet her nieces—and get a few insights about his new partner. He took a deep breath, picked up the receiver and punched the flashing button.

"Blake Sullivan."

"Mr. Sullivan, this is A. J. Williams, Jo Warren's great-niece. I believe you've heard from Seth Mitchell about my aunt's bequest of Turning Leaves?"

The voice was a bit breathless, but bright and friendly. His was cautious and curt. "Yes."

There was a hesitation, as if she expected him to say more. When he didn't, she continued. "Well, I'm getting ready to make travel plans to St. Louis and wanted to talk with you about the timing of my arrival."

Deep inside Blake had harbored a dim hope that A.J. would pass on her inheritance. From the little he'd heard about her through the years, a bookshop didn't seem like the kind of thing she'd be interested in. Now that hope flickered and died. "There's no rush from my end."

His less-than-friendly reply was met with a moment of silence. Okay, maybe his comment wasn't exactly warm and fuzzy. But it was the truth.

"Well, according to Seth Mitchell, the clock starts ticking on December 1. But I see no reason to wait until then. I can wrap things up here pretty quickly."

Now it was his turn to hesitate. But only briefly, because he wanted an answer to his next question. "May I ask you something, Ms. Williams?"

"Yes." Her reply was immediate, but cautious.

"How much interest do you have in Turning Leaves?"

"What do you mean?"

"Is this a lark for you, or do you have a serious interest in the business?"

There was a moment of silence. "Maybe a little of both," she finally said. "I'm ready for a change, and the business sounds interesting. I don't really have any long-term plans."

"Then let me make you a proposition. I happen to

care about Turning Leaves. And I do have long-term plans, which revolve around this business. So my proposal is this—I'll work with you for six months so you can claim your inheritance. At that point, you give me the option to buy your half of the business at a mutually agreeable price. That lets us keep Jo's legacy alive, and frees you to pursue your next…lark."

On the other end of the line, A.J. felt the stirrings of her Irish temper. This man was treating her like some irresponsible airhead who flitted from one distraction to another. She hardly considered her years in Afghanistan, nor the past two working in Good Samaritan, Inc. headquarters, a "lark." Nor the rigorous years of training that went into earning her M.B.A. She didn't like his inference one bit. In fact, she didn't think she liked Blake Sullivan. But she didn't have to, she reminded herself. She just had to work with him for six months. And she'd had plenty of experience working under difficult conditions with difficult people. Maybe Mr. Sullivan would even discover that she wasn't quite as capricious and flighty as he seemed to think. Starting right now. Because she wasn't about to make any promises for anything six months down the road. That was a lifetime. And a lot of things could happen between now and then.

When she spoke again, her voice was brisk and businesslike. "I'll tell you what, Mr. Sullivan. I'll agree to consider your proposal when the time comes. But I can't make any promises. I might decide to stay on at Turning Leaves. However, if I do decide to sell, I would certainly give you first consideration."

Blake frowned at the unexpected response. Her tone had cooled considerably, and he couldn't blame her. He hadn't exactly been friendly. And he couldn't argue with her counterproposal. He would have offered the same thing. So it appeared he was stuck with Jo's niece for the next six months. Unless he just walked away. But he couldn't do that. Not after pouring himself into the business for the past three years. Yet could he stand by and watch it potentially falter in the hands of an inexperienced and seemingly strong-willed partner? For once in his life he wished he was a praying man, because he sure could use some guidance.

While Blake considered her counteroffer, A.J. did pray. Because she needed the bookshop. And she needed Blake, with his years of experience, to help her run it. Though she loved her work at Good Samaritan, the spartan pay in a high cost of living city like Chicago made it more and more difficult for her to keep up with daily expenses. She had known for several months that she'd have to make a change. The options were simple: Stay in Chicago and find a better-paying job, or move on to something—and someplace—entirely new. After praying, she'd been leaning toward the latter option. So when Jo's legacy had fallen in her lap, she had seen it almost as divine intervention, a reaffirmation of her decision to pack up and move on. And even if she decided to sell after six months, the legacy would give her a financial cushion to fund whatever direction her life took.

"All right, Ms. Williams. I'll accept your terms. If you could put them in a letter to me, I'd appreciate it."

"You have my word."

"In the business world, it's better to have things in writing."

He could hear anger nipping at the edges of her voice when she spoke. "Fine. I'll put something in the mail today. Would you like it notarized as well?"

He ignored the touch of sarcasm in her tone. "That won't be necessary. When are you planning to come down?"

"I have to close up my apartment and give notice at my job. In a couple of weeks, probably. I'll call ahead to let you know my plans. And feel free to call me in the interim if you need anything."

"I think we'll be just fine."

Without you.

The words were unspoken. But the implication came through loud and clear.

Three hours.

A.J. was three hours late.

Blake glanced at his watch for the umpteenth time and shook his head in exasperation.

"I'm sure she'll be here soon," Nancy said as she passed by with a stack of books to restock a display. "It's such a nasty day out…maybe the weather delayed her."

As if to reinforce her comment, a crash of thunder shook the building.

Blake wasn't buying it. "For three hours? Hardly likely. She probably forgot what time she said she was going to arrive."

Nancy looked at him curiously as she arranged the books. "Boy, you sure formed a strong impression of her from a couple of phone conversations. It's not like you to make snap judgments."

He shrugged stiffly. "Well, let's hope I'm wrong. Look, why don't you head home? I doubt we'll have many customers on a night like this, and I can close up. Besides, didn't you say Eileen wasn't feeling well? I'm sure you'd rather be home with her than holed up here with a grouchy bookseller."

Nancy smiled. "Well, if you're sure, I'll take you up on your offer. She just has a scratchy throat, but after that bout with strep last year I'm extra cautious. Mrs. Cook takes good care of her when I'm gone, but I'd feel better if I could check on her myself."

"Go. And be careful. It's a downpour."

Forty-five minutes later, as he worked on payroll in the back office, he heard the front door open. He glanced at his watch. Quarter to eight. It was either a last-minute customer or his tardy new partner. And he had a feeling he knew which it was. His lips settled into a grim line as he quickly logged off the computer and headed out front.

Blake had no idea what to expect when he stepped into the main room, but the dripping mess that greeted him wasn't it.

A woman stood just inside the entrance as a puddle rapidly formed at her feet on the gleaming hardwood floor. Her wet, strawberry blond hair straggled out of a lopsided topknot, and damp ringlets were stuck to her forehead. He couldn't quite decide what she was wearing—some sort of long-sleeved, hip-length tunic over what might once have been wide-legged trousers. Right now, the whole outfit was plastered to her willowy frame like a second, wrinkled skin.

She doesn't even know enough to come in out of the rain. The thought came to Blake unbidden, and he shook his head.

The slight movement caught A.J.'s eye, and she glanced over at the tall man who was looking at her with a mixture of disgust and resignation. Was this Blake Sullivan? If so, he sure didn't match the image she'd created in her mind. She'd envisioned a bookish type, fiftyish, probably wearing glasses, possibly balding, maybe a little round-shouldered, sporting a paunch. A fussy, precise and stern curmudgeon.

Well, the latter qualities might prove to be true of the man standing across from her. But she'd been dead wrong on the physical description. Blake Sullivan was tall—she classified anyone who topped her five-foot-ten frame as tall—with dark brown hair and intense, cobalt-colored eyes. His crisp, blue oxford shirt, beige slacks and well-polished leather shoes bordered on being preppy, though the effect was softened by rolled-up sleeves. His attire also showed off his athletic build—broad chest, lean hips, flat abdomen. And his shoulders were definitely not rounded.

A.J. tried not to flinch under his scrutiny. She could only imagine how she appeared. No, on second thought, she didn't even want to go there. She could read enough from the look in his eyes. So much for first impressions.

With more bravado than she felt, she straightened her shoulders, tilted up her chin and gazed directly at the man across from her. "I'm looking for Blake Sullivan."

He waited a moment, as if trying to decide whether he wanted to have anything to do with the pitiful vision in front of him or simply turn around and run. Finally, with obvious reluctance, he approached her, stopping a couple of feet away to fold his arms across his chest. "You've found him."

She swallowed and extended her hand. "I'm A. J. Williams."

Short of ignoring her courteous gesture, Blake had no choice but to narrow the gap between them so he could take her hand.

At closer range, he realized that A.J. was tall. She was probably a couple of inches shorter than him, but whatever shoes she had on put them almost eye-to-eye. If she'd been wearing any makeup prior to her dash through the storm, the rain had efficiently dispensed with it, giving her a fresh, natural look that actually had a certain appeal. There was a light dusting of freckles across her small, slightly turned-up nose, and thick lashes fringed deep green eyes highlighted with gold flecks. His gaze dropped to her lips, and lingered there a moment too long before he reached for her extended hand.

Given her height, he was surprised to discover that her hand felt small and delicate in his. But her grip was firm. At least it was until he felt a tremor run through it—and then throughout her body. He frowned.

"Are you okay?"

"A little ch-chilled. I'll be okay once I ch-change out of these wet clothes." She withdrew her hand from his self-consciously.

"Don't you have an umbrella?"

"Of course. Somewhere in the U-Haul. Along with my coat. It was sunny and warm when I left Chicago. It generally gets nicer when you head south. But obviously not today. Then I had to park down the block because all the spots in front of the shop were taken. Which is why I'm sporting the drowned-rat look."

Blake pointedly glanced at his watch. "It was quite a bit warmer here earlier. When you were supposed to arrive."

A.J. flushed. "I'm sorry about that. But I didn't plan on running into major road construction. Or having a flat tire. I'm a little out of practice, so it took me a while to change it."

And she'd paid a price for doing so. Even before the blowout her hip had already begun to throb from her long hours confined behind the wheel. Dealing with the tire had only intensified her discomfort. She shifted from one foot to the other, trying in vain to alleviate the ache that she knew only a hot bath would soothe.

"You could have called," Blake responded.

"Not without a phone."

He looked surprised. "You don't have a cell phone?"

"No." Her budget barely allowed for a regular phone.

"It might be a good idea to get one…for emergencies."

She felt her temper begin to simmer at his condescending attitude, but she wasn't in a fighting mood tonight. Better to save her strength for the battles that she was beginning to suspect would surely follow in the days and weeks ahead. So, with an effort, she moderated her comments. "I'll consider that. But I'd hardly classify today as an emergency. And I already apologized for being late." Another shiver suddenly ran through her, and this time she made no attempt to hide it. "Look, can we continue this discussion on Monday? I came directly here and I'm cold and wet and hungry."

Blake had to admit that she did look pretty miserable. The puddle at her feet had widened, and there was definitely a chill in the shop. The heating system in the older building hadn't quite caught up with the sudden, late-afternoon plunge in temperature. So if *he* noticed the coolness in the air, she must be freezing.

"Monday is fine. Shall we say nine a.m.? That gives us an hour before the store opens."

"Fine."

He stuck out his hand. "Until Monday, then."

She seemed surprised by his gesture, but responded automatically. And his assessment was confirmed. Her fingers were like ice. He frowned, good manners warring with aggravation at her tardiness.

"Look, can I offer you a cup of tea first? We keep some on hand for the patrons."

Again, surprise flickered in her eyes—followed quickly by wariness. He supposed he couldn't blame her. He hadn't exactly been welcoming—or hospitable—up till now.

"Thanks. But I think a hot bath is the only thing that will chase the chill away."

His gaze scanned her slender form, and she suddenly realized her once loose-fitting outfit had become plastered to her skin. Her face flushed a deep red, and with her free hand she tried to pry the fabric away. When that attempt was unsuccessful, she tugged her other hand from Blake's and took a step back. "I'll see you Monday at nine." Her voice sounded a bit breathless.

"Do you have somewhere to stay tonight?"

"Yes. And a real estate agent lined up tomorrow to look at apartments."

He nodded. "Can I loan you an umbrella? It's still pouring."

She backed toward the door. "There's not much point now, is there?"

He glanced at the puddle on the floor in the spot she had just vacated. "True."

The crimson of her face went a shade deeper and her step faltered. "Oh…I'm sorry about that. I can clean it up, if you have a mop or…"

"Ms. Williams," Blake cut her off, but his tone was cordial. "I'll take care of this. Why don't you follow your own advice? Take a hot bath and have a hot meal. We'll make a fresh start on Monday. Okay?"

A.J. studied him for a moment. Did she detect a softening in his manner, a slight warmth in his tone? Or was it resignation? Or perhaps pity, because she was cold and wet and hungry and had a trying trip to St. Louis? Or was it pity for himself, because he'd been saddled with a partner who would need to be guided every step of the way?

If he thought the latter, he was in for a big surprise come Monday. But for now, she *was* cold, wet and hungry—and definitely not at her best. So she needed to exit. As gracefully as possible.

With a curt nod, she turned toward the door. And tried not to run.

Chapter Two

$\sim$

At precisely nine o'clock Monday morning, A.J. knocked on the door at Turning Leaves. It was a gloriously sunny Indian summer day in mid-November, and as she waited for Blake to let her in, she surveyed the scene with a smile. Though Maplewood was a close-in suburb of St. Louis, this section had a small-town feel. The tree-lined streets and mom-and-pop shops hearkened back to another era, and morning walkers were already putting in their paces.

The door rattled, then swung inward as she turned back toward the shop. Blake stood on the other side, his clothes similar to what he'd worn on Friday except that he'd exchanged his blue oxford shirt for a yellow one, and his sleeves weren't yet rolled up. His hair was damp, as if he'd showered very recently.

"Good morning." She glanced at her watch. "You said nine o'clock, right?"

Blake ignored her question. If she expected him to compliment her punctuality, she would be sorely disappointed. It was the least he expected. Besides, he was still trying to reconcile the woman standing across from him now with the bedraggled waif who had dripped water all over his floor Friday night. Her hair was lighter in color than he remembered, and her top-knot of natural curls was firmly in place. A few rebellious tendrils had fought their way out of the confining band to softly frame her face, which still seemed to be mostly makeup free. A touch of lipstick, perhaps some mascara, maybe a hint of blush—though the color in her cheeks could well be natural, he concluded. The sparkle in her eyes certainly was, enhanced by her open, friendly smile. It suddenly struck him that A. J. Williams was an extremely attractive woman. Not that he cared, of course.

When he didn't respond to her greeting, she turned again and made a sweeping gesture. "Isn't it a glorious day?"

Blake glanced around the familiar landscape. He'd jogged his usual eight miles before coming to work, but in all honesty he hadn't paid much attention to his surroundings. He'd been thinking about his training schedule for the upcoming triathlon, a late order that he needed to follow up on at the shop, invoices that needed to be reconciled…and a myriad of other things.

"Just look how blue the sky is," A.J. enthused. "And the sun feels so warm for November! I guess you haven't had a hard freeze yet, because the geraniums and petunias still look great."

Blake looked at the sky, then glanced at the flowers in the planters along the street. He wouldn't have noticed either if A.J. hadn't pointed them out. And for some reason her comment made him feel as if he should have. Which aggravated him. He didn't need any guilt trips. What he needed was time to brief his new partner before the shop opened.

"If you're ready to come in, we can get started," he said shortly.

A.J. turned back to him and tilted her head. "No time to smell the flowers along the way, Mr. Sullivan?"

"I have work to do." His voice sounded unnaturally stiff even to his own ears.

"I think God would appreciate it if we took a moment to admire His handiwork, don't you?"

"I'm sure God has better things to think about. If He cares at all."

A.J. raised one eyebrow. "Do I detect a note of cynicism in that comment?"

Blake shrugged. "Whatever. Let's just say I haven't seen much evidence that God cares."

A.J.'s eyes grew sympathetic. "That's too bad. Because He does."

Blake frowned impatiently. "Look, can we just get down to business? Because we've only got an hour before the shop opens, and I'd like to show you around before the customers start coming."

"Absolutely. I'm ready whenever you are."

He stepped aside, and as she swept past he caught a faint, pleasing fragrance. Not floral. Not exotic. Just…fresh. It seemed to linger even after she moved away.

A.J. took a moment to look over the shop, something

she hadn't done Friday night. As she completed her circuit, her gaze returned to Blake. He was still at the door, and he was staring at her. She couldn't quite read the expression in his eyes, but it looked as if he'd found something else to disapprove of. Her chin lifted a notch.

"Anything wrong?" She tried to keep her tone mild, but a note of defiance crept in.

Blake studied her attire. She wore a white peasant-type blouse in some wrinkly fabric, and a funky bronze cross hung from a chain around her neck. An unusual metal belt cinched her impossibly small waist. Her skirt, made of several progressively longer layers of what appeared to be a patchwork of fabrics, brushed her legs mid-calf. If his attire bordered on preppy, hers could well be described as hippie. Which did not evoke happy memories.

"Mr. Sullivan, is something wrong?" she repeated more pointedly.

He frowned. "I haven't seen clothes like that in a long time."

She looked down and smoothed her skirt over her hips. "Probably not. They're from a vintage clothing store I discovered in Chicago. Pretty cool, huh?"

Actually, he had another word for her attire. But he settled for a less judgmental term. "Interesting."

The look she gave him told him very clearly that she knew exactly what his opinion was. And that, in turn, she had judged him to be stuffy, uptight and conventional. "Very diplomatic. I wasn't sure you had it in you." Before he could respond, she turned back to the shop. "So, how about that tour?"

Blake thought about responding to her comment—then thought better of it. He had to work with this woman for the next six months, and it would be to both their advantages if they made an effort to get along.

"Sure. Let's start with a walk-through."

The shop wasn't huge, and A.J. only made a few comments as Blake showed her around. There was a small area for children's books, and sections devoted to books on travel, cooking, fiction, gardening and general nonfiction. There was also a reading nook, with four comfortable chairs, and a coffee and tea maker tucked in a back corner. A small stockroom and tidy office were behind a door marked "private." Two big picture windows flanked the front door, and each featured displays of the latest releases. The older building was well-maintained, with a high ceiling and hardwood floors, and A.J. felt comfortable in the space immediately. Just as she'd felt comfortable in the tiny apartment she'd found Saturday. It, too, was in an older building, in a neighborhood that had obviously seen better days. But it was safe and in the early stages of renewal, the real estate agent had assured her.

When the tour was over, Blake waited for her to say something.

"This is a great space," she said, choosing her words carefully. "It's sunny and bright and inviting. There's a nice selection of books. And the layout is… interesting."

She'd borrowed the word he'd used earlier to

describe her attire, and Blake gave her a suspicious look. "What does that mean?"

She lifted one shoulder. "We might want to think about rearranging a few things."

He frowned. "Our customers seem to like this setup. We do quite well."

"Yes, that's what Seth Mitchell said. Which reminds me, I'd like to spend some time going over the accounts with you."

A flicker of amusement crept into his eyes. "That could be a little tedious. It might be better if I meet with your accountant. Or, if you don't have one, I'm sure Mr. Mitchell can recommend someone. But I'll be happy to answer any questions you might have today."

The condescending tone was back, but this time A.J. was ready for him. "That's kind of you," she said sweetly. "I do have a few."

"Shoot," he said amiably.

"Okay. Let's start with some basics. I'd like to get the details on return on capital, net profit, blue-sky value, inventory turnover rates, payroll expenses and any major debt. I'd also like to get some breakdowns on customer demographics, sales by book category, store traffic patterns and volume, and repeat customers. That's just to start, of course."

The dazed look on Blake's face was totally satisfying. As was the lengthy time it took for him to recover from her barrage of questions.

"I'm not sure I have all those answers at my fingertips," he said slowly. "It might take me a couple of days to pull the data together."

"Okay. I jotted down some other questions, too." She fished in her purse and withdrew two pages of additional typed questions and handed them to him. "You might as well work on these at the same time."

He scanned the list quickly, frowning, and when he looked back at her she could read the question in his eyes. She answered it before he could ask.

"I have an M.B.A. From Wharton. I chose not to pursue a business career for a variety of reasons. But I have the background. And it's kind of like riding a bicycle. You never forget."

Blake felt his neck grow warm. Jo had long ago taught him not to judge a book by its cover. Yet that was exactly what he'd done with A.J. She didn't look like a businesswoman. At least not his image of one. So he'd assumed she had no business skills. He felt suitably chastised—but he didn't like being made a fool of. "Why didn't you tell me?"

She shrugged. "You seemed to have your mind made up about me from our first conversation. So I figured I'd wait and play my hand when the time was right. Which turned out to be today."

So A.J. *wasn't* some ditzy airhead after all, he conceded. She had business savvy. Quite a bit of it, if the questions she was asking were any indication. But it was only textbook knowledge. She might be able to analyze the balance sheet, but she had no practical experience. And he did. He knew the book business. So she needed him. Which meant he still had some leverage. And some control. That knowledge gave him some comfort. Because ever since Jo's death and A.J.'s first phone call, he'd been watching his control erode. And it was not a good feeling.

When the silence lengthened, A.J. sighed. "Look, I'm sorry if you jumped to conclusions about me. Obviously, I have the financial background to run this shop. But I don't have practical experience. I guess Aunt Jo hoped you'd teach me. And I'm willing to learn. So can we just start over? Otherwise it's going to be a long six months."

Blake couldn't argue with that. "Maybe it would help if we set some ground rules."

She made a face. "Why don't we just take it a day at a time? Make up the rules as we go along?"

"You mean wing it?"

"More or less."

"That's not the best way to run a business." Or a life, as far as he was concerned. He liked rules and structure. He'd had enough of "winging it" to last a lifetime.

"We're not a Fortune 500 company, Blake. We can afford to be a little flexible."

That was another word he hated. Too often "flexible" became an excuse for not honoring commitments.

At his grim expression, A.J. grinned. "Loosen up, Blake. Life's too short to sweat the small stuff."

"I don't consider Turning Leaves small stuff," he said stiffly, sounding uncharacteristically pompous and self-righteous even to his own ears. This woman just brought out the worst in him.

"I didn't say it was. I was referring to your ground rules. I don't want to get hung up on making a lot of guidelines that may not be necessary. Let's just work things out as we go along. And before you know it, the six months will zip right by."

The bell jangled over the door, and A.J. turned her attention to the customer who had just entered. "Oh, look at that darling little girl!"

Blake glanced at the young mother and her child. The toddler looked to be about four, and she was clutching a glazed donut. Which translated to sticky fingers—and sticky merchandise. He started forward, then stopped. The house rules said no food in the shop. But he had a feeling the house rules were about to go out the window.

Blake sighed. It was going to be a long six months.

"I'd like to start closing the shop on Sundays."

Blake stared at A.J. as if she'd lost her mind. Their first week as partners had been remarkably smooth. She was an eager learner, and Blake was beginning to think that maybe this arrangement would work out after all. Until she'd dropped this bombshell.

"Excuse me?"

She looked up from the catalog of new releases she was perusing. "I'd like to close the shop on Sundays."

"Why? We're always busy on Sunday."

"I've studied the traffic and sales data. We do have a lot of window-shoppers on Sunday. But it's not one of our bigger sales days. And we're only open for five hours, anyway. I don't think we'll notice much impact on our bottom line."

This was exactly the kind of impetuous action that Blake had been afraid of. Out of the corner of his eye he caught Nancy observing the exchange, and he took a deep breath before responding.

"I don't think changing the hours is a good idea. Everyone else on the street is open on Sunday. Our customers will be disappointed."

"We can change our phone message and have a sign with our new hours made for the window. People will adjust."

He raked his fingers through his hair. "Why is this such a big deal? Sunday hours are convenient for our customers and we always have enough sales to justify being open."

A.J. closed the catalog and looked at him steadily. "My main reason for wanting to close has nothing to do with sales or with customers. Sunday is the Lord's day. A day of rest. A day to keep holy. A store like ours that sells non-essential items doesn't need to be open."

Blake stared at her. "You're kidding."

Her gaze didn't waver. "Do I look like I'm kidding?"

He tried a different approach. "Jo was very religious. And *she* was open on Sunday."

"When did she start opening on Sunday?"

"A couple of years ago."

About the time he took over the day-to-day management of the shop. Neither voiced that thought, but it hung in the air.

"Did she work in the shop that day?" A.J. asked.

"No."

"Who did?"

"Nancy and I alternated."

A.J. glanced over at Nancy. She didn't know the

part-time worker very well yet, but she'd learned enough to know that the divorced mother had a tough life, that she juggled two part-time jobs just to make ends meet, and that she was a churchgoing woman with a quiet, deep faith.

"How do you feel about it, Nancy?" A.J. asked.

Nancy looked uncertainly from A.J. to Blake, then back again. "I need the job, A.J. I'll be happy to work whatever hours you and Blake give me."

A.J. smiled. "I already know that, Nancy. That's not what I'm asking. How do you feel about working on Sundays?"

"Well, the money is nice." She hesitated. "But it's always a rush to get here after church, and then I have to leave Eileen with Mrs. Cook all afternoon. I guess, if I had a choice, I'd prefer to have Sundays off so I could spend a little more time at church and with my daughter. Six days of work ought to be enough for anyone. Even God rested on the seventh day."

Blake stared at Nancy. "You never said anything to me about not wanting to work on Sundays."

"I didn't think it was an option."

He expelled a frustrated breath. "Okay, fine. I don't mind working. We can surely find someone to fill in every other weekend for those few hours."

"I'm sure we can, Blake," A.J. replied calmly. "But that's not the point. I'm talking about principles here. And if you're worried about losing sales, I'm sure we can find a way to make up the difference."

"Such as?"

"I'm working on it."

He looked at her, and the determination in her eyes told him that she was dead set on this. He didn't agree, but he wasn't sure it was worth waging a major battle over. Yes, they'd lose some sales. But she was right. The decision wouldn't make or break the shop. Besides, he suspected there would be bigger battles to fight down the road. Maybe the best strategy was to let her win this one.

"Okay. If that's what you want. I just hope you don't regret it," he capitulated.

"I don't waste my time on regrets, Blake. They're all about the past. I try to focus on today and make the best decisions I can."

"Well, it wouldn't hurt to think a little bit about tomorrow, too."

A shadow crossed her eyes, so fleeting that he thought perhaps it was just the play of light as she turned her head. "Tomorrow has a way of surprising us, no matter what we plan," she said quietly.

Blake didn't know what to make of that comment. So he simply turned away and headed back to the office.

Nancy watched him go, then moved to the counter beside A.J. "I applaud your position."

A.J. turned to her with a rueful smile. "I'm glad someone does."

"Don't mind Blake. It's been a hard transition for him. He and Jo went way back, and he took her death pretty hard. Plus, he's more or less run the shop for the past couple of years, so having a partner is a big adjustment for him. But he's a great guy when you get to know him. He's really conscientious, and you won't ever meet a kinder, more considerate person. He even came over to my apartment one night last winter at three in the morning when I was worried about Eileen, and then drove us to the emergency room."

A.J. frowned. Were they talking about the same Blake? She didn't doubt the conscientious part, but kind and considerate? She hadn't seen much evidence of those qualities.

When A.J. didn't immediately respond, Nancy smiled knowingly. "You'll find out after you get to know him. But what I really wanted to ask was if you'd like to join me for church on Sunday. After your comments about closing, I figured you must be in the habit of attending church, and since you're new in town I wasn't sure if you'd had a chance yet to find a place to worship. We have a great congregation, and our minister is wonderful. You'd be welcomed warmly."

In fact, A.J. was in the habit of weekly worship, but so far she'd been too busy settling in to have a chance to seek out a new church. Nancy's invitation was perfectly timed. "Thank you. That would be great."

Blake came out from the office, but on his way back to the front counter, he was waylaid by a customer. Nancy glanced his way.

"I've invited Blake a few times, too, but so far I haven't had any luck," she offered, lowering her voice.

A.J. thought about his comments to her when she'd mentioned God. "He doesn't strike me as a religious man."

"I think he believes in God. But he wasn't raised in a religious environment. It's hard to convince someone who is so self-reliant that the plans we make for our life don't always match God's. Blake's kind of a loner, and he's so used to relying only on himself that I just don't think he's willing to put his life in anyone else's hands. Even God's."

A.J. looked over at the tall, dark-haired man deep in conversation with a customer. He was angled slightly away from her, and she had a good view of his profile—strong chin, well-shaped nose, nicely formed lips. Self-reliance was a good thing in moderation. A.J. knew that from personal experience. But she couldn't imagine taking it to such an extreme that she shut other people out of her life. Especially God. It would be a very empty existence.

Suddenly Blake glanced at her, almost as if he knew she was watching him. Their gazes met, and whatever he saw in hers—curiosity, sympathy, or a combination of both—brought a frown to his face. She responded with a smile. And even though he didn't physically move, she felt almost as if he'd taken a step back. And posted a sign saying Private. No Trespassing.

A.J. didn't really care if he kept his distance. Their relationship was destined to be short-lived, anyway. But she wasn't used to having her gestures of friendship so openly rebuffed. She turned back to find Nancy watching the exchange.

"Blake doesn't let too many people get close," Nancy noted. "Even I don't know much about his background, and we've worked together for almost two years."

A.J. shrugged. "I respect people's privacy. If he wants to shut people out, it doesn't matter to me."

But as she headed to the back room to check the new inventory, she realized that her answer hadn't been quite honest. Because in that brief, unguarded moment, before his barriers had slipped back into place, she'd glimpsed in Blake's eyes a stark loneliness that had touched her deep inside.

And even though they were practically strangers, even though he clearly resented her presence at Turning Leaves, even though he disapproved of almost everything she did, that loneliness troubled her. More than she cared to admit.

And she had no idea why.

"So…what do you think?"

Blake had only been gone from the shop for four days. Just a quick trip to Cincinnati to compete in a triathlon over Thanksgiving weekend. But if he'd been gone three weeks, the shop couldn't have changed more dramatically.

He stood rooted just inside the door of the office, trying to absorb the changes that had been wrought in his absence. Gone was the table of featured books and the greeting card rack that had been just inside the display window on the left. Now the four chairs from the reading nook were arranged there, and a low, square table that he didn't recognize was placed in front of them, with a small pot of copper-colored chrysanthemums in the center. Two chairs were on one side of the table, facing the window, with the others at right angles on the adjacent two sides. A couple of the chairs were occupied, and one of the patrons was helping himself to a cup of coffee from the coffee and tea maker that had also been moved to the front of the shop. Blake recognized him as a regular, though not someone who usually bought much.

"Well?" A.J. prompted.

Slowly, Blake turned to his partner. Her eyes were sparkling with excitement, but he could also sense some trepidation. She knew him well enough even after only a couple of weeks to realize that he didn't like sudden, unplanned changes.

"What happened to the display table? And the cards?"

"The table's in the back room. I moved the cards closer to the checkout counter." She gestured over her shoulder.

He planted his fists on his hips and studied the new arrangement. It was attractive enough. But it changed the dynamics of the shop entirely. And it definitely cut down on display space.

"What did you do with the old reading nook?"

"Come see."

She led him to the back corner, which had been transformed into a small enclosure complete with blocks, vinyl books and an assortment of toys. He frowned and looked at her questioningly. "What's this?"

"A play area. A lot of people come in here with toddlers and young children, and it's pretty difficult to look through books when you're juggling a little one. Now they can safely leave their children here to play while they make their selections."

He grunted in response.

"Several mothers have already commented on how much they like this." There was a slight defensive note in her voice.

"And what about the area in front? You've lost a lot of display space. That sells books."

"So does atmosphere. When people walk by and see patrons relaxing and enjoying themselves through the window, they might be more inclined to come in and look around. Besides, the other reading nook wasn't being used much. The light wasn't very good, and it was so tucked away a lot of people missed it. But it makes a perfect play spot."

Before he could respond, the bell on the front counter rang. The regular patron Blake had noticed in the new sitting area was waiting to purchase a large coffee-table book.

"Morning, folks," he said cheerily as they joined him.

"Good morning." A.J. reached for the book and started to ring up the sale while Blake retrieved a bag from under the counter.

The older man took a sip of his coffee. "By the way, my compliments on the new reading area. Never did like that one stuck back in the corner. Not enough light for these old eyes. This one is real cheerful and bright."

Out of the corner of his eye, Blake saw A.J. give him a sidelong glance, but he kept his gaze averted. "Thank you. We hope you'll come back soon."

"You can count on it. Thanks again."

They watched as the man exited, the bell jangling as

the door closed behind him. Blake knew A.J. was looking at him. Waiting for him to compliment her on what
she'd done, especially in light of the customer's unso-
licited approval. But he didn't want to encourage her.
Change was fine, as long as it was planned. And carefully thought out. And discussed. But he had a real
issue with spur-of-the-moment changes. Because in his
experience, most of the time they weren't good ones.

"I saw some new inventory in the back when I got
here. I'll log it in," he said.

He turned to go, but her voice stopped him. "Did
you have a nice Thanksgiving?"

He'd been expecting a comment on the new layout,
so it took him a moment to switch gears…and formu-
late an answer. He'd spent most of Thanksgiving Day
training for the triathlon, then he'd eaten a frozen turkey dinner at home. He'd been on the road early the
next morning for Cincinnati, spent Saturday compet-
ing, then drove home Sunday. His parents had invited
him to visit for the holiday, of course. They always
did. And, as always, he'd refused. But A.J. didn't need
to know any of that. "Yes," he replied briefly. "How
about you?"

She smiled. "I had a great Thanksgiving. I don't
know anyone here, so I joined a group from Nancy's
church to help feed the homeless downtown. And we
got a great turkey dinner in the bargain."

He frowned. Dishing up food for a bunch of down-
and-out strangers didn't sound like a great holiday to
him. It hit too close to home. His parents had never
resorted to a homeless shelter, but they'd come close

a few times. "Don't you have family?" Hadn't Jo mentioned several great-nieces? But he couldn't recall any details.

"My parents are both gone. But I have two sisters. They're too far away to visit for such a short holiday. We'll make up for it at Christmas, I hope." She'd talked to them both, of course. Morgan had actually gone to work in the morning, then out to dinner with friends. And Clare had somehow managed to wrangle a holiday dinner invitation to the same place Dr. Wright and his daughter were going. There was no stopping Clare when she set her mind to something, A.J. thought with a grin. "What about you, Blake? Any family?"

Slowly he shook his head. "No brothers or sisters. My parents live in Oregon."

"Also too far away for Thanksgiving. Maybe you can see them at Christmas."

Not likely, Blake thought. But she didn't need to know that. He started to turn away, but suddenly found himself speaking. "By the way, I like what you did with the shop."

A.J. looked as surprised by the comment as he was. He had no idea where those words had come from. He'd certainly had no intention of complimenting her. But she rewarded him with a dazzling smile. "Thank you."

Suddenly Blake felt as if he'd just hit the proverbial runner's wall. It was a familiar experience that squeezed the breath out of his lungs and left him feeling limp when it occurred at about the twenty-one mile mark of a marathon.

But the only thing racing right now was his heart.

Which made no sense.

And it made him want to run as fast as he could away from this red-haired source of disruption in his life.

———

Chapter Three

"I think I figured out a way to make up the Sunday sales."

Blake's stomach clenched. Barely a week had passed since A.J. had rearranged the shop, and now she was on to something else. Which meant more upheaval. Change seemed to be this woman's middle name. Warily he looked up from the computer screen.

A.J. shifted a large box in her arms and smiled. "Chill out, Blake. Maybe you'll like my idea."

He doubted it, and his skeptical expression told her so.

"Maybe not," she amended. "But here it is anyway." She placed the box on a chair and began pulling out a variety of items, which she lined up on the desk. "It occurred to me that people who are shopping for books are often shopping for gifts. Now, there are plenty of gift shops around. But not many that carry items like these, handmade in third-world countries. Good Samaritan, where I used to work, is starting a craft program, and a portion of the profits from the sales will benefit the artists. A lot of people in those countries are in desperate need of income, and a program like this is a godsend for them. Plus, I think it will drive traffic to our shop and more than make up for any sales we've lost by closing on Sunday. It's a win-win situation all around, don't you think?"

Blake looked at the array of items now displayed on his desk. Wood carvings, metalwork, woven placemats, pottery. Some were crude folk art. Others reflected great skill and artistry. None seemed appropriate for the bookshop. Nor was there room to display them without sacrificing space for their primary product.

A.J. spoke before he could offer his opinion. "Lots of bookstores carry small gift items," she pointed out. "And space isn't really a problem. I thought we'd intersperse a few items in the display window among the books. They'll add some visual interest. And I found out the jewelry store next door is getting new display cases. I asked Steve about buying one of his old ones to replace our sales counter, and when he found out what I was going to use it for, he offered to donate it. So we'll be able to display a lot of these items without taking any space away from the books. Isn't that great?"

Blake stared at A.J. After three years, he knew Steve Winchell, the owner of the jewelry store, well enough to say hello when they met in the parking lot. But that was about it. In less than a month, A.J. was on a first-name basis with all of their neighbors.

"Earth to Blake."

He caught her teasing tone and frowned. "This might dilute book sales."

"I don't think so. In fact, I think these items will draw new customers into the shop, and they might end up buying books as well. Plus, I bet some of our regular book customers will also buy these items as gifts. We can monitor it, though. If I'm wrong, I'm certainly willing to reconsider."

But she wasn't wrong. Within the first week, that was obvious. Blake told himself that part of the success of the new merchandise was due to the approaching holidays. It was just a gift-buying season. He suspected sales would taper off after Christmas. But even if they did, even if they only generated a modest return, it was all incremental. Because, thanks to A.J.'s creativity, the new offerings hadn't taken one iota of space away from books. Exchanging their old checkout counter for the display case had been an ingenious solution. But Blake hadn't told A.J. that. She didn't need encouragement. And he didn't need more disruptions.

But he had a feeling they were coming, anyway.

"Blake, could I speak with you when you have a minute?"

He looked toward A.J. while he waited for a customer to sign a credit card slip. She stood in the door of the office, and there was something in her eyes that made his stomach clench.

Here we go again, he thought, steeling himself for whatever brainstorm A.J. had just had.

"Sure. I'll be right with you." He finished the sale, then glanced toward the young woman restocking the cookbook section. "Trish, can you watch the front desk for a few minutes?"

"Sure, Mr. Sullivan." The perky teen who helped out a few days a week after school made her way over to the counter. She smiled brightly. "Take your time."

She'd love that, Blake thought. Trish wasn't the hardest worker they'd ever had. But front desk duty suited her to a T. She was sweet and friendly, which counted for something, he supposed.

When he entered the office, A.J. was studying a recent order, a frown marring her usually smooth brow. She looked up when he walked in.

"What's up?" he asked, willing himself to remain cool.

"I'd like to cancel a couple of the selections we've ordered."

Now it was his turn to frown. "Which ones?" When she named them, his frown deepened. "Those are sure to be bestsellers. Our customers will expect us to stock them."

"Have you read the ARCs?"

"No." He rarely had time to read the advance copies sent out by publishers.

"I took them home over the weekend. I didn't read them thoroughly, but skimmed through enough to know trash when I see it."

"Those authors are extremely popular. A lot of people must not agree with you."

"A lot of people read trash."

He folded his arms across his chest and struggled to keep his temper in check. "So you're trying to impose your values on everyone else."

She'd wrestled with that very dilemma all weekend. How to reconcile personal values with bottom-line business decisions. It was the same conflict she'd grappled with in graduate school. And had worried about facing in the business world when she graduated. As it turned out, she'd never had to deal with it. Until now.

Blake sensed her uncertainty and pressed his advantage. "It sounds a little like censorship to me."

A.J. sighed and distractedly brushed some wayward tendrils off her forehead. "I know. But I've given it a lot of thought. I don't see how, in good conscience, we can carry books that are so blatantly sensational. I'm fine with books that deal with gritty themes or realistically portray bad situations, but in these novels all of the gore and sex and violence is just for effect. There's absolutely no redeeming social value."

"In *your* opinion."

"And God's. I talked with my pastor about this. I think this is the right thing to do, Blake. Our shop isn't that big. We can't carry every book. So I think we should focus on carrying *good* books."

Blake didn't agree with her position. But he couldn't help admiring her. She had principles. And she didn't compromise them. That was a rare trait in today's world. Jo had been like that, too. And so were his parents, he admitted grudgingly. Maybe he didn't like their principles, either. But they'd stuck with them.

"We're going to have some unhappy customers," he pointed out.

"I realize that. We'll just have to explain our position and hope they understand."

"*Our* position?"

"Okay, *my* position."

"We'll also lose sales. People who want those books will go somewhere else. There's an impact on the bottom line here."

"I know. And I realize that affects both of us, since we each own half of the business. But I feel very strongly about this, Blake. So I'd at least like to give it a try. If we take a huge hit, I'm willing to discuss it again and consider other alternatives. But I'd like to try it for a month or two. Can you live with that?"

He folded his arms across his chest. "We won't get back the customers we lose."

"Maybe we'll pick up some new ones."

Blake supposed he could fight A.J. on this. But she had taken his concerns into consideration and was willing to discuss it if things didn't work out. He supposed he could at least give her the time she had requested to test the waters. "Okay. Let's try it for a few weeks. You don't mind if I funnel any questions about this your way, do you?"

"No. It was my decision. I'll defend it."

And that's exactly what she had to do a few days later when a customer asked Blake about one of the books A.J. had canceled. A.J. overheard the question and, true to her word, quickly stepped in. She glanced down at the signature line on the credit card slip the woman had just signed.

"Mrs. Renner, I'm A. J. Williams, one of the owners of Turning Leaves. I wanted to let you know that we're not going to be carrying that title. As you can see, we're a small shop, so we have to be very selective of our inventory. Quite honestly, not all bestselling books have content that's worthy of our limited space. I've reviewed an advance copy of that book, and I'm afraid it just didn't make the cut."

The woman looked surprised. "That sounds like the philosophy at the Christian bookstore I go to. I didn't realize secular bookstores were so diligent."

"I don't think most are. But we're small enough that we can be a little more careful."

"Well, that's good to know. I have to admit, some of the novels I've read have shocked me. But you never know until you've already bought the book. It's nice to think that a secular store has some standards, too."

Not all patrons were so understanding, of course. But Blake had to admit that A.J. handled all the comments—and complaints—with grace and honesty.

Blake doubted that he and A.J. would ever see eye-to-eye on how to run the business. But, by and large, her decisions had been good ones. He glanced toward the reading nook. In its former location, it was rare for more than one chair to be occupied. Now patrons vied for the seats. Since they'd added the play area for children, young mothers and grandparents lingered longer in the shop. And they'd had to restock the glass display case regularly to keep up with the demand for the craft items, which had more than compensated for the sales lost by closing on Sunday.

Blake still didn't think this latest decision would be as good for business. But it was consistent. A.J. might be a go-with-the-flow kind of woman, but in one thing she was very predictable. She stuck to her convictions.

He glanced toward her as she helped a patron select a book on gardening. Her head was bent as she listened intently to the older woman, and the late-afternoon light from the window gave her skin a golden glow. He watched as she turned to scan the selection of garden books, a slight frown on her brow, her lithe form silhouetted by the light. A moment later she reached up to select a thin volume. He was struck once again by her slender, graceful hands, recalling the night she'd arrived and his surprise when he'd reached for her hand in greeting. Because of her height, he'd been taken aback by its delicacy. And maybe he was just getting used to her funky clothes, but he was suddenly able to look past her attire and recognize that A.J. was, in fact, a lovely woman.

With a will of iron.

"A.J., do you have a minute?"

A.J. turned to find George from the Greek restaurant down the block standing at the end of the aisle. He looked agitated, and she frowned. "Sure. What's up?"

"Can I speak with you, someplace private?"

"The office is about as private as it gets around here." She headed toward the front desk. "Trish, I'll be in the back with Mr. Pashos. Stay at the desk, okay? Blake should be back from lunch any minute."

"Sure thing." The girl happily climbed on a stool behind the counter and proceeded to inspect her nails.

A.J. led the way toward the office, and motioned George to a seat. "Is everything okay?"

He sat, but leaned forward intently and shook his head. "Nothing is okay. Do you know about this thing called TIF?"

"No. What is it?"

"It stands for tax increment financing. The government can use it to help develop areas where—how do you say?—the economic potential isn't being maximized."

A.J. frowned. "Okay. So why is this upsetting you?"

George stood and began to pace. "There is a developer who wants to buy this block and put in a retail and residential development. He has already started the process."

Twin furrows appeared on A.J.'s brow. "But what if we don't want to sell?"

"That is where TIF comes in. If he can convince the city that his development will generate more revenue for Maplewood, we could all be shut down."

"But that's wrong!"

"Of course it is wrong! Your aunt, she would fight this! She was the first one to open a shop here, more than twenty years ago, when this area was not so good and businesses were closing, not opening. She believed in this area. And she persuaded others to follow. Your aunt, she was good at that. After we became friends and she found out that Sophia and I wanted to start our own restaurant, she helped us. We would not have our restaurant if it was not for her generosity and kindness, may the Lord be with her. And then others followed. Joe at the bakery, and Alene at the natural food store. Rose at the deli has been here for many years, and so has Steve. Carlos at the art gallery is the newest, but he has been here for ten years, too. We were the pioneers. We took a chance and invested in this area. And now that it is hot and trendy, what do we get? They want to throw us out! It is not right! The whole character of the neighborhood, it will change!" George's accent grew thicker as he spoke, and his agitation increased.

"There must be a way to stop this," A.J. reasoned. "Have you talked to any of the others?"

"No, not yet. I come to you first. You and Jo, you seem the same in many ways. Kind and caring. I did not think you would want your aunt's legacy to be sacrificed just so more money could be made by a rich developer. I think maybe you might have an idea."

A.J. tapped a pencil against the desk, frowning thoughtfully. "Well, I certainly believe there's strength in numbers. I guess the first thing we need to do is tell all the merchants on this block what's going on, and then have a meeting. If we all put our heads together, I'm sure we can come up with something."

"A meeting. Yes, that is a good way to start. But soon, A.J. We cannot waste time."

"I agree. Why don't we see if everyone is available

Thursday night? We can have the meeting here, after the shop closes."

"Good. I will check. And I will bring baklava. It is always good to eat when you are trying to think." He pumped A.J.'s hand. "I knew the day you came down to introduce yourself that you would be a good neighbor, just like your aunt. I tell that to Sophia when you left. Now I know even more that it is true. I talk to you soon."

A.J. watched George leave. His spirits seemed higher, now that they had a preliminary action plan. But A.J. wasn't feeling so upbeat. Fighting city hall was never easy, especially when money was involved. But she didn't want to lose Aunt Jo's legacy before she even claimed it. So if a battle was brewing, she was more than willing to do her part.

She was still sitting in the office a few minutes later when Blake walked in carrying a bag from the deli. He took one look at her face and came to an abrupt halt. "What's wrong?"

She sighed and propped her chin in her hand. "We have a problem."

Slowly, Blake set the bag down on the desk, eyeing her warily. "Does this have anything to do with more changes in the shop?"

"Possibly. But not of my making."

By the time she explained the situation, Blake was frowning, too. He pulled up a chair and sat across from her. "I don't like the sound of this."

"Neither do I. I told George we could have a meeting here Thursday, when the shop closes, to discuss our next step. He's going to let the other merchants on the block know. You've been here longer than I have. Do you think they'll be willing to close ranks and go to battle over this?"

Blake shrugged. "I don't know. I've never exchanged more than a few words with any of them."

A.J. looked at him in surprise. She'd made it a point within the first couple of weeks to visit each shop and introduce herself. Blake had been here three years and he still didn't know his neighbors?

A flush crept up Blake's neck. When he spoke, there was a defensive tone to his voice. "I don't have time to socialize when I'm at work."

"I didn't say anything," A.J. pointed out. "Well, I guess we'll find out how they feel at the meeting. In the meantime, I need to do some research on this whole TIF thing. We better have all our facts in order before we take on a fight like this."

"My next-door neighbor works at city hall. I can try to get some information from him, too," Blake volunteered—with obvious reluctance.

"That would be good." A.J. sat back in her chair and shook her head. "You know, when I came here I thought my biggest challenge would be learning the book business. I didn't expect to have to fight city hall for my legacy."

"Neither did I. And I have a feeling this could get pretty messy."

A.J. studied Blake. He didn't look any too thrilled with that idea. "I take it you prefer to stay out of messy fights?"

He shrugged stiffly. "I prefer to stay out of fights of

any kind. It's a lot easier when people can settle their differences quietly."

"True. But that doesn't always happen. And some things are worth fighting for." When he didn't respond, she stood and moved toward the door, but paused on the threshold to turn toward him. "So do you plan to come to the meeting on Thursday?"

Although his expression told her that he'd prefer to be almost anywhere else, he slowly nodded. "Yeah. I'll be there. I'm no more eager to lose this shop than you are. But this isn't my kind of thing."

"I gathered that. Thank you for making the effort. Maybe we'll come up with a way to settle this problem quietly, like you prefer."

"Maybe." But he had a gut feeling that wasn't going to happen.

And he suspected A.J. did, too.

As the group began to gather on Thursday night, Blake stayed in the background, feeling out of place and awkward—unlike A.J., who was mingling effortlessly with the diverse group, he noted. In the short time she'd been at the shop, she was already on a first-name basis with all of her fellow merchants and seemed to know their life histories. A few minutes before, he'd overheard her asking Rose how her grandson was doing in graduate school. And now she was talking to Joe about his wife's recent surgery. She had a knack for making friends and putting people at ease, something Blake had never mastered. Probably because he'd never been in one place long enough when he was growing up to learn those social skills, he thought.

They'd supplemented the seating area in the reading nook with folding chairs, and now A.J. moved to the front of the makeshift meeting room. "Okay, everyone, let's get started. I know George and Sophia have to get back to the restaurant as soon as possible, and Carlos is getting ready for an opening at the gallery tomorrow. So we need to keep this as brief as possible. George has already filled all of you in on the background, so the meeting tonight is really just a discussion to see how everyone feels about this."

"I think it stinks." Everyone turned toward Alene, who ran the natural food store. "We've all been here for years. Long before this area was hot. We put our blood, sweat and tears into these businesses, and we didn't get any help from city hall. If it wasn't for people like us, this area would never have revived. I say we fight it."

"I agree," Steve concurred. "When I opened my jewelry store, I had a tough time getting insurance. And for years, my premiums were elevated because of the crime rate in this area. I almost left once. But Jo convinced me to stay. She said if we stuck it out, eventually people would rediscover this place. And she was right. I'm not about to let some developer with dollar signs in his eyes take advantage of the turnaround at my expense."

Joe stood. "But what can we do? There are only a few of us. And if this means more money for Maplewood, the city won't care about us. They'll brush us aside."

"Not if we get more people behind us," Rose spoke up. Despite her gray hair and frail appearance, her clear blue eyes were steely. "The kind of development George described will ruin the neighborhood feel of this area. I don't think the residents will like that. I've already been talking to people about this when they stop in for their morning coffee and bagels. I bet the residents will stand behind us."

"I think we need to find out more," George said. "Like, who is this developer? And what has he done so far?"

Blake cleared his throat, and A.J. glanced his way. "Blake?"

"I was able to get some information from a pretty good source that might answer a few questions," he said. Seven pairs of eyes turned in his direction. "The developer is MacKenzie Properties. They've done this sort of thing in a number of municipalities in the area. They're very quiet and very successful, and if there's been any opposition, it's been squelched at a pretty early stage. Stuart MacKenzie is the principal and has been the primary contact at this preliminary stage with the Maplewood city hall."

"So what does he have in mind?" Alene asked.

Blake turned toward her. "George's information about the development plans is correct. MacKenzie is looking at a combination residential and commercial development over this entire block that would consist of high-end condos, office space and small shops. In the past, he's managed to get a TIF ruling, which means that existing residents are paid a predetermined sum for their businesses. In some cases, space is available in the new development for current merchants, but generally at a substantially higher cost. I believe most of us currently own our space. Under the new scenario, we'd have to lease space."

"What's the timing, Blake?" A.J. asked.

He looked her way. She seemed impressed by the information he'd relayed, which he'd only managed to gather this evening when he'd gone home for an early dinner and finally caught up with his neighbor. There was something in her eyes—warmth, gratitude…something—that made him feel proud of the little he'd done. "This is still in the very preliminary stages. MacKenzie will be presenting proposals to the city in mid-January, and there will be a public hearing in early February. It's unlikely a final ruling will be made before March or April. And I'm told that public opinion will factor heavily into the decision."

"It sounds like our work is cut out for us," Steve said.

"We need petitions," Alene added. "And press coverage."

"My nephew works for Channel 2. I can call him," Joe offered.

"Let's start with the petitions," A.J. said. "We can develop a form and ask our customers to begin signing them when they visit our businesses. We have almost six weeks until the public hearing in February, so we should be able to gather a lot of signatures. And maybe we can enlist local customers to circulate petitions in their neighborhoods, too."

"I can draw a form up for everyone to review," Steve volunteered.

"Thanks. That would be great. Let's meet again in mid-January and see where we stand. Does that sound good?"

There was a rumble of agreement at A.J.'s suggestion.

"And now everyone must have some baklava," George said. "It is just made today."

As the shop owners moved toward the coffee and pastries, A.J. made her way over to Blake, who still hovered in the background. "Thanks for digging up that information."

"It wasn't hard."

"So are you going to have some baklava? Or do you avoid sweets, too?"

He frowned at her. "What do you mean, 'too'?"

She shrugged. "Well, you don't mingle much. I found out recently that Carlos didn't even know you."

"I'm not into contemporary art."

For a moment she looked as if she was going to say something more on the subject, then changed her mind. "I think it was a good meeting."

He nodded. "But there's a lot of work ahead."

"Everyone seems willing to pitch in, though. And I'm sure Aunt Jo would have been leading the charge if she was here."

Blake couldn't argue with that. Jo had felt passionate about the shop and the neighborhood. So did the other merchants. And like it or not, he was in as deeply as everyone else. He still didn't want to get into the middle of a fight, but he'd found out enough to know that's probably where they were headed unless they rolled over and played dead. And much as he disliked confrontation, he wasn't ready to do that.

Yet.

Chapter Four

"Hi, A.J. Did you have a good time in North Carolina over Christmas?"

A.J. turned toward Rose with a smile as she recalled her visit with Clare. "Yes. It was wonderful."

"Did your sister Morgan make it down?"

"Unfortunately, no. She couldn't get away from work for more than a couple of days, so she went to Aunt Jo's cottage in Maine instead. But we all talked by phone. How about you? Did that grandson of yours make it home?"

"He sure did. He's still here, in fact. Goes back next week." She held up a stack of papers. "I've got another batch of petitions."

"That's great! I'll add them to the pile."

"So how many signatures do we have so far?"

A.J. did a quick mental calculation. "About five hundred, I think."

"Not bad. And I've been sending the form home

with some of my patrons to circulate in their neighborhoods. Is our meeting still on for next Thursday?"

"Yes. Same time, same place."

"Well, I'll be here. I'm not going to let some fancy developer run me out of here." Rose looked over A.J.'s shoulder. "Hi, Blake."

"Hello, Rose." He came up beside A.J. and glanced at the sheaf of papers in her hand. "Looks like you've been busy."

"I figure it's gonna take a lot of work from all of us if we want to win this fight. Now I gotta get back to the deli. See you both Thursday."

They watched her leave, then A.J. turned to Blake with a grin. "I hope I have half her energy and spunk when I'm that age."

"Why do I think that won't be a problem?"

She tilted her head and looked at him warily. "I'm not quite sure how to take that remark."

A smile tugged at the corners of his mouth. "Let's just say you have energy and spunk to spare."

"Why do I think that's not necessarily a compliment?" she replied.

He shrugged. "There's never a dull moment when you're around, that's for sure."

She studied him. Considering that Blake liked things predictable and well-planned, she figured that his comment was not a compliment. Which bothered her for some reason. But she shrugged it off and turned toward the office, waving the petitions at him. "I'm going to file these with the rest. Watch the desk, okay?" Without waiting for a response, she disappeared into the back room.

Blake watched her go, trying to remember what it had been like before the human tornado named A.J. had swept into his life. It had been much quieter, no question about it. And more orderly. Not to mention organized.

In other words, he realized with a jolt, it had been dull.

And to his surprise, dull wasn't nearly as appealing as it once had been.

"Okay, so we know the proposal has been presented by MacKenzie to the Board of Aldermen and the public hearing is scheduled for February 10. Is everyone planning to be there?" A.J. looked at her fellow merchants. Everyone was nodding assent. "Great. Now, let's talk about our plan for the meeting."

"I think we need a spokesperson for our group," Joe said.

"Good idea," Rose concurred. "I vote for you, A.J."

A.J. looked at her in surprise. "But I'm the new kid on the block. It might be better if one of you represented the group."

"But you're Jo's great niece, and she was the first one to come here. Now another generation is taking over. So you can speak for her and for yourself. I think you're the perfect choice," Steve replied.

"Steve is right," George agreed. "Jo would be our leader if she was here. So you should speak for us."

A.J. looked at the rest of the group. "How does everyone else feel about that? Carlos, Alene?"

"I'm fine with that," Carlos said.

"Me, too," chimed in Alene.

A.J. turned to Blake. He was still in the back, but at least he was sitting with the group this time. "Blake?"

"I agree with the consensus. I think you'd be great. And it would be a nice tribute to Jo."

"Well, if you're all sure…" A.J. looked down at her notes. "I think we need to have some residents speak, too."

"I already spoke to Mark Sanders, one of my regulars," Rose said. "He's an attorney, lives a couple of blocks away. He said he'd speak on our behalf."

"And I talked to Ellen Levine about it, too," Steve offered. "She grew up here, and she feels passionately about preserving the character of the area. And she's very grateful to people like us, who helped revitalize Maplewood. So she's willing to speak."

"A lot of people are planning to attend, too," Alene offered.

"Great. It sounds like everything's under control. If everyone will get me their petitions before the meeting, I'll present them when I speak. Anything else?" No one spoke, and A.J. nodded. "Okay. T minus twenty-one days and counting. Keep your fingers crossed!"

"Excuse me, miss. Could you tell me if Liam is working today?"

A.J. glanced up from the cash register and smiled at the woman with cobalt-blue eyes who was standing on the other side of the counter. There was something familiar about her, but A.J. couldn't quite put her finger on it. She appeared to be in her early-to-mid-fifties, and her long brown hair was pulled back into a single braid. A man with a nicely groomed salt-and-pepper beard stood behind her. It looked as if he could stand to lose a few pounds, but it was hard to tell because of their bulky winter coats.

"I'm sorry, there's no one here by that name," A.J. said. "Are you sure you have the right shop?"

"Jan, he doesn't use that name anymore, remember?" the man said.

The woman looked sheepish. "I know. But I always think of him that way. It's hard to… Liam!"

At the delighted look on her face, A.J. turned to follow her gaze. Blake stood in the doorway to the office. Shock was the only word to describe the expression on his face.

"How are you, son?"

Even after the man spoke, it took Blake a few moments to recover. "What are you doing here?"

"Paying you a surprise visit," the woman said, her delight undiminished by Blake's abrupt greeting and lack of enthusiasm.

"We're on our way to a convention in Chicago and thought we'd make a little detour, stop in and see how you are," the man spoke again.

Blake finally recovered enough to move forward, but he kept the counter between himself and his visitors. "You could have called first. I would have been more prepared."

"Then it wouldn't have been a surprise," the woman replied brightly.

Though A.J. stood mere inches away from him, Blake seemed oblivious to her presence. And unsure how to proceed. So A.J. took charge. She stepped forward and held out her hand.

"Welcome to Turning Leaves. I'm A. J. Williams, Blake's partner."

The woman took her hand first. "I'm Jan Sullivan. This is my husband, Carl. We're Liam's...sorry, Blake's...parents."

"Nice to meet you," Blake's father said as he gave her hand a hearty squeeze. "You must be Jo's great niece. We were sorry to hear of her passing. She was a wonderful lady."

"Thank you." Since Blake still wasn't speaking, A.J. filled in the gap. "Did you just arrive?"

"Yes. We'd hoped to spend a couple of days in St. Louis, but we took an interesting detour or two on the way here that delayed us," Carl said. "So we'll need to leave tomorrow if we want to get to Chicago for the whole convention. But we couldn't come this close and not stop in to see Blake."

A.J. recalled that Blake had once told her his parents were from Oregon. She looked at Blake's father in surprise. "Did you drive all the way from the West Coast?"

"Yes. We love road trips. But we haven't had time to take many these past few years."

"This sure brings back a lot memories, doesn't it,

Carl?" Blake's mother was looking around the shop, a smile of recollection on her lips.

"Yes, it does. That was a good summer for us. I see you've made some changes."

"When were you here last?" A.J. asked.

"Oh, it's been several years. I love the reading area in the front. It's so inviting," Jan said.

Finally Blake spoke. "Do you need a place to stay tonight?" The question was clearly prompted only out of a sense of obligation. He hadn't moved from behind the counter, and A.J. suspected that a whole lot more than a glass display case separated Blake and his parents.

"No, thank you, son. We already checked into a hotel."

Blake's relief was almost palpable. A.J. looked at him curiously—and with a certain degree of censure. His parents had obviously made a special trip to see him. Whatever their differences, surely he could afford to be hospitable for one night. And if he couldn't, she could, she decided.

On impulse, she spoke. "I don't want to impose on family time, but if you don't have any other plans for the evening, I'd be happy to offer you a home-cooked meal." She looked over at Blake. "You're invited, too, of course."

Blake stared at her as if she'd lost her mind.

"Why, thank you!" Jan replied. "But it's such short notice…I'm afraid it would be too much trouble."

"Not at all. Sometimes impromptu parties are the most fun."

"We couldn't agree more, right, Carl?"

"Absolutely."

"Unless Blake has other ideas, I think that sounds lovely," Jan said.

They all turned to Blake expectantly. It was clear he had no ideas at all.

"Blake, would you prefer to go out to dinner somewhere with just your mom and dad?" A.J. prompted when the silence lengthened.

If looks could kill, A.J. would be history. But she tilted her chin up and steadily returned his glare.

"Dinner at your place sounds fine." Blake ground out the words through clenched teeth.

A.J. ignored Blake and turned back to his parents with a cheery smile. "Terrific. Let me write down the directions for you. I'm sure you're tired, so we'll make it early."

After exchanging a few more pleasantries, A.J. stepped away to help a customer, leaving Blake alone with his parents. She glanced his way a couple of times, but he never moved from behind the counter. And even from a distance, his stiff posture spoke eloquently. Had she made a mistake by inviting them all to dinner? There was clearly no love lost on Blake's side. Yet his parents obviously cared for him. She could see it in their eyes. So what was the story? Had she stepped into the middle of something she'd regret?

But it was too late for regrets. She'd told Blake once that she didn't waste time on them. Which was true. Better to think about the dinner to come.

Then again, maybe not, she admitted as she glanced back at the three people standing at the counter. Considering the obviously strained relationship between parents and son, this could prove to be a very long evening.

A.J. put a match to the final wick, taking a moment to enjoy the soft, warm glow from the flickering candles placed throughout the living room. On a cold January evening like this, a fireplace would be perfect. But apartments like hers didn't come with such amenities.

Still, she was pleased with what she'd been able to do with the small space. She'd supplemented the few things she'd brought from Chicago with garage-sale finds, and the overall effect was warm and inviting. A small dinette set stood in the eating alcove next to the galley-style kitchen, and she'd covered the table with a handmade woven blanket she'd brought back from the Middle East. More candles of various heights stood in the center.

The small couch in the living room was draped with a colorful throw, and she'd turned a small trunk with brass hinges into a coffee table. A bookcase displayed favorite volumes as well as small pieces of sculpture. The final touch had been a fresh coat of off-white paint, which had brightened the dingy tan walls considerably and offered a great backdrop for some of her native art.

With a satisfied nod, she went back to the kitchen to check on dinner. She hadn't made this couscous-based dish in quite a while, but for some reason she had a feeling that Jan and Carl would appreciate it. She wasn't so sure about Blake.

She frowned as she stirred brown rice into the pot. She wasn't sure about him in a lot of ways, actually. He'd avoided her the rest of the afternoon, busying himself with customers in the shop or calling patrons whose orders had come in. She wouldn't have been surprised if he'd backed out of her invitation. In fact, when she finally cornered him to tell him she was leaving a little early to get dinner started, she was fully prepared for him to say he wasn't coming. But he didn't. He just gave her a curt nod and turned away.

If she'd made a huge faux pas, she was sorry. But she had taken an immediate liking to Jan and Carl. And in the face of their son's lack of hospitality, she'd felt compelled to step in and show some Christian charity. After all, they'd made a big detour to visit Blake. If he chose not to appreciate it, that was his issue. At least *she* could be friendly.

The doorbell rang, and A.J. put a lid on the pot, then wiped her hands on a towel. Let the games begin, she thought with a wry grin as she went to welcome her guests.

Despite Blake's buttoned-up style and obsession with punctuality, she'd half expected him to show up late for dinner in an attempt to shave as many minutes as possible off the evening. But instead she found him waiting on the other side of the door.

At her surprised look, he glanced at his watch. "Am I early?"

"No. Come in, *Liam*." She hoped her kidding tone would lighten the mood, but it had the opposite effect.

He didn't move. "That's not funny."

The teasing light in her eyes faded. "Sorry. Guess I hit a nerve."

"I don't use that name."

"Why not?"

"It's…weird."

"No, it isn't. It's very popular."

"It wasn't when I was a kid."

She eyed him thoughtfully. "When I was a kid, there was a little girl in our class named Maude. She got teased a lot. Is that what happened to you?"

"Worse. Boys aren't that nice."

"Surely your friends stood up for you?"

He looked at her for a moment, as if silently debating how to respond, but in the end ignored her comment. "Blake is my mother's maiden name—and my middle name. I've been using it since I was twelve. Now, do you think I could come in? It's a little drafty out here."

"Of course." She stepped back, instantly contrite, and ushered him in. "Let me take your coat."

He shrugged out of his leather jacket and handed it to her.

"Make yourself comfortable. I'll be right back."

She disappeared down a hall, and Blake took a moment to look over the tiny apartment. He didn't live extravagantly, but her living room, dining area and kitchen could easily fit into his great room, with space left over. And her decor—eclectic was probably the kindest word to describe it. Nothing seemed to match. Yet, oddly enough, it all blended. There was a slight Middle Eastern feel to the room, but he couldn't say exactly why. Maybe it was the artwork that hung on the walls, or the patterns in the fabrics. But he had to admit it was pleasant. And comfortable. And homey—which was not a word he could use for his own house. It might be bigger, and the furniture might match, but even after two years it didn't feel like a home.

A wife and children might help. And they were certainly in his plans. Had been for some time, in fact. He just hadn't met the right woman yet. But he knew exactly who he was looking for. June Cleaver. He wanted a homemaker—in the best sense of the word. A woman who made her family a priority, who might work outside the home but never forgot that home was what counted most. Someone who understood the importance of settling down, building a life in one place, becoming part of a community. He was not interested in returning to the vagabond, gypsy lifestyle he'd once known.

"Can I offer you something to drink?"

Blake turned as A.J. reentered the room. Speaking of gypsies, she kind of looked like one tonight. She was wearing something…different. So what else was new? he thought wryly. The full-length garment was made of a shimmery, patterned fabric in shades of green, purple and royal blue. It was nipped in at the waist with a wide belt, and swirled gracefully around her legs as she walked. It wasn't exactly his idea of dine-at-home attire. But it did look…festive. And suddenly he felt underdressed.

"I didn't have time to change," he said, half-apologetic, half-defensive.

She gazed at him. He'd obviously come directly

from the shop, though it was clear he'd taken time to freshen up. His clean-shaven jaw showed no evidence of afternoon shadow.

A.J. shrugged. "No need. It's just a casual evening."

"You don't look casual."

She grinned. "I probably look weird to you."

He felt his neck grow warm. "I didn't say that."

"You didn't have to. I've worked with you practically every day for almost two months, Blake." He noted that she was careful to use his preferred name. "I quickly realized that you're a pretty conventional guy."

"You mean stuffy."

"I didn't say that," she parroted his words back to him.

"I've worked with you for almost two months, too. I think I have a pretty good idea what your opinion is of me," he countered.

"Really? You might be surprised."

"I don't think so."

"No? Okay, try this on for size. I think you are an extraordinarily capable and bright guy. I have no doubt Aunt Jo would have been in bankruptcy long ago without your help. Your attention to detail is fantastic, and you're absolutely one hundred percent reliable. You don't like change, but in our current situation that's probably a plus. Since I know you'll question anything I propose, I think things through even more carefully than I otherwise might. You're very disciplined and regimented, which are good things in moderation. But if you'll pardon one editorial comment, you might enjoy life a little more if you added a dash of spontaneity. So how did I do?"

Blake stared at the woman across from him. She'd pretty much nailed him. And been diplomatic in the process. She'd complimented his good points, and even put a positive spin on the qualities she clearly didn't admire.

"Not bad," he acknowledged grudgingly.

"Come on, Blake, admit it. I was right on the money," she teased. "Now it's your turn."

"What do you mean?"

"Tell me how you see me."

"I didn't say I wanted to play this game."

"Too late. I took my turn. Now it's yours. And then I'll tell you how close you came."

Blake felt cornered. But it was clear A.J. wasn't going to let him off the hook. She'd settled into a corner of the couch, tucked her leg under her, and looked prepared to wait as long as it took for him to take his turn.

"You aren't…what I expected," he hedged.

She shook her head. "Not good enough. Try again."

"You're…different."

"Different how?"

He raked his fingers through his hair and jammed his other hand into the pocket of his slacks. "Look, I'm no good at this let-it-all-hang-out kind of thing."

She considered him for a moment. "Okay, then let me give it a try, and you can tell me if what I *think* you think is actually true. How's that?"

Did he even have a choice?

"At first, you thought I was going to be some airhead without any business sense. The M.B.A. surprised you. And made you a little more comfortable.

But you still consider me somewhat of an intruder, and you feel like I've invaded your turf. Although you haven't liked the changes I've made, you've had to admit that they've paid off—for the most part. Which bothers you. You think I have weird taste. And I most certainly do not fit your image of the ideal woman. How's that?"

She was good. He'd give her that. "Close."

She rolled her eyes. "For a man who deals with the written word, you sure don't communicate much. Which might be a problem if you ever do find that ideal woman."

He glared at her. How had the conversation suddenly taken such a personal turn? "How do you know I haven't?" he retorted.

"Haven't what?"

"Found the ideal woman."

She shrugged. "Just a guess."

Before he could respond, she made a move to stand, but for a moment she seemed to have trouble getting the leg she'd tucked under her to cooperate. When she finally got to her feet, she winced slightly and took a moment to steady herself on the back of the couch.

Blake frowned. It wasn't like her to be so awkward. Even though she was tall, she always moved with a lithe grace. "Is something wrong?"

She shook her head. "No. I know better than to sit like that. It was my own fault. So, can I get you that drink now?"

What was her own fault? That she had to struggle to stand? And why had she struggled? The question was on the tip of his tongue, but he bit it back, recalling how he'd balked when she'd gotten personal. She would have every right to do the same. After all, they were only business associates. Short-term, at that. So he let it pass.

"A white soda, if you have it."

"Of course. I'll be right back."

He watched as she made the short trip to the kitchen, noting that her gait didn't seem quite normal. But she was clearly doing her best to hide it.

Blake knew he should just put her personal problem out of his mind. He needed to worry about making it through this evening with his parents, not about A.J.'s physical difficulties. She was an independent woman, clearly capable of taking care of herself. She didn't need his concern. In fact, she might even resent it.

But as Blake looked around the cozy third-floor apartment and recalled the three sets of stairs he'd had to climb to reach her door, he couldn't help but wonder if she was having trouble negotiating them. Especially juggling bags of groceries. Or a basket of laundry. And if she was, was there anyone she could call on for help?

Blake didn't think so. Her two sisters were far away. And though she'd made many acquaintances since arriving in St. Louis, those were all new friendships. Not the sort of long-established relationships where one felt comfortable asking for favors. And she'd never mentioned a boyfriend—or even a close female friend—that she'd left behind in Chicago.

So maybe he and A.J. did have something in common after all. Though their philosophies of life might be radically different, and they might disagree on pretty much everything, it seemed they shared one trait.

They were both alone.

Chapter Five

"**A.J.**, this is fabulous!" Carl helped himself to a second serving of the main dish.

"Thank you. But I'm glad I didn't know your background this afternoon. I would have been too intimidated to invite you."

"You can cook for me any day. And I'm hoping I can wrangle this recipe out of you. It would be a perfect dish to feature in one of our cooking demonstrations."

"I'll be happy to share it. After all, I wouldn't have it if someone hadn't shared it with me. But tell me more about your store. How long have you had it?"

"It seems like forever, but actually it's only been fifteen years. It took us quite a while to find our niche, but better late than never, I guess," Jan chimed in with a laugh. "We'd always had an interest in good food, so opening a natural food shop just seemed…well, natural."

"My grandfather was a chef, so I already had a lot of training in food prep," Carl added. "But I went to culinary school while Jan got her credentials as a dietitian.

Then the whole thing just took off. Besides running the shop, Jan does seminars on the principles of healthy eating and I do the hands-on cooking demonstrations that put those principles into action. It's a lot of fun."

"And a lot of work," Jan added. "Especially since we opened a second shop a few months ago."

"You have two shops now?" Blake spoke for the first time since they'd gathered at the table. His tone was incredulous.

"We're as amazed as you are," Carl affirmed. "We got into this business because we thought we'd enjoy it. We never expected to make a lot of money. But we've been successful far beyond our wildest dreams."

"The only trouble with success is that it eats into your flexibility and freedom," Jan said with a sigh, helping herself to a second slice of homemade whole grain bread. "We used to love to take road trips. But this is the first time in years that we've been able to get away for any length of time."

Out of the corner of her eye, A.J. saw Blake reach for a second helping of the entrée to supplement the meager first serving he'd taken. When she'd presented the unusual vegetarian dish, she could see the wariness on his face. You'd think she'd been asking him to eat worms, she thought wryly. The man's eating habits were obviously not adventurous. He was clearly as cautious with food as he was with people. And maybe with life.

"So tell us where you got this recipe, A.J.," Jan encouraged.

"In Afghanistan."

That got everyone's attention.

"You've been to Afghanistan?" Blake shot her a startled look.

She nodded. "I lived there for almost three years."

"Good grief! And we thought *we'd* lived in some exotic places," Jan said.

"What were you doing there?" Carl asked.

A.J. hesitated. "It's kind of a long story. And maybe not the best dinner conversation."

"We'd really like to hear it, A.J. And we have all evening," Jan assured her.

A.J. looked at the faces around the table. Jan and Carl seemed genuinely interested. Blake seemed a bit stunned.

"Well, I can give you the highlights," she agreed.

And for the next hour, as they finished every last bite of the main dish and put a good dent in the Middle Eastern honey-based puff-pastry dessert that followed, she regaled them with tales of her time in Afghanistan as they plied her with questions.

A.J. told them of her work in two small villages and at a clinic. Of the kindness of the people, despite their abject poverty. Of hardships almost beyond comprehension. Of the lack of warmth and shelter and food. Of malnutrition and starvation. She described one young child, eighteen months old, who was just twenty-seven inches long and weighed only eleven pounds when she was brought to the clinic.

"She was starving to death," A.J. said, her voice slightly unsteady. "She was the youngest of six children. Their parents had both died, and their grandmother took care of them. They lived with dozens of other families in the skeleton of a bombed-out building. The grandmother did her best, but she had to rely on begging to put food on the table, and she wasn't always successful.

"If she had waited two more days to bring Zohra to the clinic, the little girl would have died. But even though her grandmother got her there in time, we were understaffed and had very limited resources. So in order for Zohra to have any chance at all, her grandmother needed to stay and give her routine care, like bathing and feeding. But there were five other children to take care of, too.

"We put a call in to Good Samaritan, and they were able to provide enough funding to cover Zohra's hospital stay and pay someone to stay with the other children while Zohra's grandmother cared for her at the clinic. That story had a happy ending…but so many others didn't."

A.J. grew silent, and Blake saw her struggling to control the tears that suddenly welled in her eyes. For some strange reason, he wanted to reach for her hand. Comfort her. Enfold those delicate fingers protectively in his. Which made no sense. They were co-workers. Nothing more. So he stifled the impulse and kept his hands in his lap.

His mother was less restrained. She reached over and laid her hand on A.J.'s. "That is an incredible story," she said in a hushed voice. "How did you deal with it, day after day?"

A.J. drew a deep breath and gave her a shaky smile. "Not every day was that emotional. It was very hard work under very primitive conditions, but the people had a great capacity for joy even in the face of tragedy and sorrow. And they were so grateful for our support. Most of the artwork you see in my apartment was given to me as thank-you gifts. It was an incredibly rewarding experience."

"But weren't you ever frightened? Afghan-istan isn't the safest place," Jan said.

"No. I really wasn't. I'd prayed a lot about the decision before I went, and by the time I actually got on the plane, I knew with absolute conviction that that was where God wanted me to be at that point in my life. So I just put my trust in Him."

"I take it Good Samaritan is a Christian organization?"

A.J. turned to Carl. "Yes. But not blatantly so. By that I mean that we didn't focus on converting anyone to Christianity. We answered questions, of course, if people asked. And they knew we were Christian. But our witness to our faith was more through actions than words."

"Which is the way it should be," Carl affirmed. "Wasn't it Francis of Assisi who told people to spread the Gospel, and to use words only if all else failed?"

Blake stared at his father. "Since when have you been interested in religion?"

Carl glanced at Jan. "We've been going to church for a number of years, Blake. Another thing we discovered a little later in life."

"That's one of our regrets, actually," Jan said. "God wasn't part of our lives when you were growing up. We didn't give you much of a foundation for faith."

While Blake was trying to digest this news, Jan turned back to A.J. "So what made you leave? Did you eventually burn out?"

"No. I got a pretty serious intestinal parasite that just wouldn't respond to treatment. So I had to come back for medical care. It actually took months to get rid of the pesky thing. At that point Good Samaritan was reluctant to send me back because they were afraid my health had been compromised. I was fine, and the doctors all gave me a good report, but the organization preferred I stay in the States and work out of its Chicago headquarters. That's where I was before I came to St. Louis."

Carl shook his head. "That's an amazing story. It kind of puts our adventures to shame, doesn't it, Jan?"

She nodded. "I admire you, A.J. What you did was so selfless. You got right into the thick of it, took an active role in trying to make the world a better place. Even in our activist days, we just attended rallies, marched and asked people to sign petitions."

"That's more than a lot of people do," A.J. reassured her. "In fact, we're sort of engaging in that kind of battle right now with the bookshop."

"Why? What's going on?" Carl asked.

After A.J. explained the situation, Jan leaned forward, an expression of concern on her face. "Is there anything we can do to help? Jo worked so hard to keep the character of the neighborhood intact, and to revitalize the area. So have all the merchants. I'd hate for that to change."

"I appreciate the offer. But everyone's very committed to telling our story and supporting our cause. I think we've done everything we can so far. We'll turn out in force at the Board of Aldermen meeting in a couple of weeks. And if that doesn't work...well, we can always take more dramatic measures. One of the merchants has a contact in the media."

"Media coverage is always good," Carl said with a nod. "Don't be afraid to use it. But you'll need to have an event of some kind to catch their interest—a protest march or something."

A.J. risked a sidelong glance at Blake. The look of distaste on his face was almost comical. "We'll keep that in mind," she told Carl.

"Well, if you need us to do anything, let us know. We used to get involved in these kinds of things all the time."

"I will. Now, would anyone like more coffee?"

Carl glanced at his watch regretfully. "I'd love some, but if we're going to get an early start tomorrow, we ought to call it a night."

"A.J., we can't thank you enough for this wonderful evening," Jan said warmly.

"It was truly my pleasure."

She retrieved their coats, then followed them to the door. Blake stood slightly apart, his hands in his pockets.

"Drive safely," A.J. said.

"We will."

There was a moment of awkward silence, then Carl held his hand out to Blake. "Take care, son."

Blake stepped forward and took it. "You, too."

Jan moved toward him and held out her arms. He hesitated, then returned her hug awkwardly. "Will you stay in touch?" There was a wistful quality in her voice that tugged at A.J.'s heart.

"Of course."

When she turned back to A.J., her eyes looked damp and her smile was a little too bright. "Thank you again for a lovely meal."

Impulsively A.J. stepped forward and gave each of them a hug. "You're very welcome. Please stop by any time you're in St. Louis."

She waved them off at the door, then turned. She'd also retrieved Blake's coat, expecting him to follow closely on the heels of his parents. But he was still standing in the same place, a frown marring his brow. She hesitated a moment, but when he made no move to leave, she closed the door.

"Can I offer you something else, Blake?"

"No." Actually, that was a lie. She *could* offer him something—answers. Starting with how she had managed to create a better rapport with his parents in the first thirty minutes of their visit than he had in thirty years of life.

"Well, go ahead and make yourself comfortable. I'm just going to blow out the candles on the table and put away the perishables. Then I'll join you."

When A.J. returned, cradling a mug of tea, Blake had claimed one of the side chairs. She sat at right angles to him on the couch, but he noted that she was careful not to tuck her leg under her this time. She'd mentioned the intestinal parasite. But had she been injured in some other way in Afghanistan that she hadn't shared? Or was the leg injury more recent?

"Your parents are great, Blake," she said, forcing him to refocus his thoughts.

"I'm glad you think so."

She looked at him curiously. "Obviously you don't."

"I didn't exactly have an ideal childhood."

"By ideal do you mean typical? Or perfect?"

"It was neither."

"Tell me about it."

He shrugged. "You've met my parents. And you're good at that mind-reading game you were playing earlier. I'm sure you can put two and two together."

Thoughtfully she took a sip of her tea. "I have a feeling your parents might have been hippies in their younger days."

"Give the lady a gold star."

At his sarcastic tone she tilted her head and looked at him. When she spoke, there was no censure in her tone. "Is that a bad thing? Were they into the drugs-and-free-sex scene?"

"No. But they were always fighting for some cause. Attending rallies, going on marches, the whole nine yards. Or they were trying out alternative lifestyles. We even spent one summer in a commune. You know how most people think of a certain place when they hear the word home? I don't. We were never in one place long enough."

"I guess I've always thought of home not so much as a place, but as simply being with the people you love," A.J. said mildly, without reproach.

"That's easy to say if you weren't the one uprooted every few months." There was bitterness in his voice now. And anger, simmering just below the surface. As if it had been there a long time. "I was in a new school practically every year—sometimes twice a year. I was never in one place long enough to make friends. To join the Boy Scouts. To play on a soccer team. It's a pretty lonely life for a kid."

And for the adult that kid became, she thought. The effects of his isolated childhood were clearly evident in the man across from her.

"But your parents seem to love you," she pointed out.

He sighed. "They do, in their own way. But I think I was very unplanned, and they just decided early on that my arrival wasn't going to put a crimp in their lifestyle. So they dragged me all over the country with them. They picked up odd jobs wherever they went, but it was always hit or miss. They had an easy-come, easy-go attitude that seemed to suit them. I was always the one who worried about whether we'd have enough food on the table. Or a place to spend the night. Even as a little kid."

"Did you? Have enough food, and a place to spend the night, I mean."

He thought about the time they'd almost gone to a homeless shelter, but at the last minute his dad had found work. "Yes. But it was always feast or famine, depending on whether my parents were working. I never knew where our next meal was coming from. Or where I'd be sleeping. And I hated that."

Which explained a lot, A.J. thought. Now she better understood Blake's dislike of change, his need for predictability. "So how did you meet Aunt Jo?"

His face relaxed, and a slight smile lifted the corners of his mouth. "We were in St. Louis one summer, right after Jo opened the shop. I don't even remember why we were there. Anyway, she hired Dad to do some work. I went with him every day, and she sort of took me under her wing. For that one summer at least, there was stability in my life. She was the best friend I'd ever had. And we never lost touch. So when the shop was on shaky ground financially three years ago, I was happy to come and help out."

"What were you doing before that?" Blake was always so close-mouthed about himself that A.J. wondered if he'd take offense at her question. But he answered easily.

"Investment banking. In Chicago."

She raised her eyebrows. "You gave that up to run a bookstore?"

"Initially, I just took a leave of absence. I wasn't sure I'd stay. But I was getting tired of the international travel and the long hours, even though the money was great. After I was here for a few weeks, I discovered I liked the book business. And St. Louis. So I stayed."

It made sense to A.J.—St. Louis, with its Midwestern values and small-town feel, was surely a world away from the nonconformist lifestyle he knew as a child. And the town also held happy memories for him. "I'm sure Aunt Jo was very grateful for your help."

He shrugged. "It was small repayment for all she gave me. Including that great summer in St. Louis. That was the first time in my life that I felt like I belonged somewhere. She gave me more of a sense of family than my parents ever did."

The bitter edge was back in his voice. A.J. finished her tea and set the cup on the chest. When she spoke, her voice was sympathetic. "I can see how growing up like that would be tough," she said.

Blake looked at her warily. "I'm surprised you're not rushing to my parents' defense. You got along with them famously."

"They seem like great people," she affirmed. "But they're probably different now than they were twenty-five years ago. We all learn and grow and change. Maybe they'd do things differently if they had a second chance. Maybe not. Maybe they thought the life they gave you was the right one at the time. But in any case, you can't change the past. And it seems to me that they'd very much like you to be part of their future."

"It's a little late."

"It doesn't have to be. They obviously love you, Blake. I think they'd like to reconnect, if you'd just let them in."

Deep inside, he knew that A.J. was right. His parents did love him. Maybe they hadn't demonstrated that love the way he'd needed them to as a youngster, but he'd never doubted that they cared for him. And he knew that with a little encouragement they would welcome him back into their lives. He was the stumbling block. His resentment ran so deep, and the chasm between them was so wide and of such long duration that he wasn't sure it could be breached. For a recon-

ciliation to work, he'd have to find a way to forgive
them. And in all honesty, he wasn't sure he was up to
the task.

A.J. sat quietly, watching him, her eyes telling him
silently that she understood his dilemma. She had certainly disproved his first impression of her as a ditzy
airhead, he admitted. Instead, she was smart, insightful, empathetic—and beautiful. He'd been noticing
that more and more lately. Hers wasn't a dramatic,
model-like beauty. It was quieter than that. And deeper. It was the kind of beauty that gave a face dimension
and character and soul. When you looked into A.J.'s
eyes, you knew that she was a strong woman. A survi-
vor. A woman with deep convictions who would stand
beside the people she loved. In good times and bad.

A startled look flashed across Blake's face. Now
where had *that* phrase come from? He certainly didn't
think of A.J. in that way. True, he'd never met anyone
quite like her. She was…interesting. And she was easy
to talk to. He'd never told anyone as much about his
past in one sitting as he had tonight. She would definitely make someone a good wife. But not him.

Blake stood, and A.J. seemed surprised by his
abrupt movement. She quickly followed suit, and he
was relieved to note that she didn't struggle this time.

"I need to leave. It's getting late."

"Okay." She reached for his coat, studying him
while he shrugged into it. He'd been quiet for so long
after her last comment that she was beginning to think
she'd overstepped her bounds. He wasn't a man given
to personal revelations, and she'd pushed him pretty

hard tonight about his parents. His jaw was set in a firm line, and twin furrows still creased his brows. He definitely did not look like a happy camper. Maybe she needed to make amends.

"Blake, I'm sorry if I said anything to offend you."

He gazed at her, his cobalt-colored eyes guarded. "You didn't."

She put her hands on her hips and studied him. "Why am I not buying that?"

He turned up the collar of his jacket and sighed. "Look, A.J., this is the first time in years that I've spent a whole evening with my parents. I'm still trying to process everything that happened. Cut me some slack, okay?"

"Sure."

She walked with him to the door, where he turned. "Thank you for dinner."

"You're welcome."

Her tone was more subdued, and her eyes looked troubled. He felt an urge to reach out and touch her, just as he had at the dinner table. Again he stifled it, jamming his fists into the pockets of his jacket. "I mean that. Everything was really good."

The ghost of a smile whispered around her lips. "I thought you were going to have a fit when you found out the main dish was vegetarian."

His own lips lifted in a smile. "I probably shouldn't have been surprised. Knowing you. But I enjoyed it."

"See? Sometimes it pays to take a chance and try something new."

"Maybe," he conceded.

"Be careful on your way to the car," she cautioned.

He was glad she'd brought that up. Though signs of turnaround were evident, he hadn't been impressed by the run-down neighborhood.

"I will. This isn't the safest area."

She frowned. "I was talking about the ice."

"Oh. Well, I'll watch for that, too. But this isn't the best part of the city. I hope you're cautious, as well, especially at night."

"I spent three years in Afghanistan, remember? Caution is my middle name. Besides, this area seems fine to me. The Realtor said it was turning around."

"It still has a long way to go."

She tilted her head. "Let me guess. You live in suburbia, in a house with a white picket fence."

At her accurate conclusion, he felt hot color steal up his neck. "I don't have to defend my lifestyle."

She shrugged. "Neither do I. This suits me fine. And it suits my budget even better."

How did this woman continually manage to outwit him? He'd always been good at thinking on his feet, but she was even better. Especially now, when his brain was reeling from all he'd learned this evening— about his parents' second shop, A.J.'s sojourn in Afghanistan and his own feelings about his childhood. It was time to call it a night.

"I'll see you tomorrow, A.J.," he said, suddenly weary.

"See you, Blake."

As the door shut behind him and he started the trek down the three flights of steps, he realized he still didn't know what had caused A.J. that awkward, obviously painful moment as she rose from the couch.

And he also realized that he hadn't asked the one question he'd been most interested in during her stories about Afghanistan. She'd spent several years earning an M.B.A. from one of the toughest schools in the country. She'd obviously intended to pursue a business career.

Why had she scrapped those plans to go to Afghanistan?

"What time does the bus leave, A.J.?"

A.J. glanced at her watch before responding to Nancy. "Not until four. We should arrive by nine in the morning."

"I wish I could go."

"You have a little one to take care of here. God understands."

"I'll be with all of you in spirit."

"We know. And thanks for filling in for me tonight."

"It's the least I could do."

"I have all my stuff in the car, so I don't need to leave until three."

"Don't put yourself in a bind. Go whenever you need to," Nancy assured her.

Blake overheard the last part of the conversation as he arrived at the front counter. He turned to A.J. as Nancy went to assist a customer. "You're leaving early?"

"Yes. Is that a problem? Nancy will be here. And tomorrow is my Saturday off."

"I wanted to go over the list of new releases before I placed the order."

"Can it wait until Monday?"

"I guess it will have to."

A.J. knew he was aggravated that she hadn't told him of her early departure. But it had been a last-minute decision. She hadn't been sure she could force herself to make another church-sponsored bus trip. In the end, though, she'd felt compelled to go because the cause was so important. "Sorry for the short notice on this, Blake. I didn't decide about this trip until yesterday."

"You're going on vacation?"

"Hardly. I'm going with a church group to Washington for the annual pro-life march. A lot of area churches are sending buses."

He frowned. "You're going to a protest?"

She studied him. Her trip probably reminded him of the rallies and marches his parents had participated in when he was a child. "It's not exactly a protest. It's just a peaceful march to let our legislators know that a lot of people have serious concerns about abortion."

He glanced out the window, at the bleak January landscape. "It's going to be cold in Washington."

"My body may be cold. But my heart will be warm."

"Is it really worth going all that way just to make a point?"

She looked at him steadily. "Not everything is worth fighting for, Blake. But when it comes to saving innocent lives, I want my voice to be heard."

A customer came up just then, and A.J. turned to

assist him. Blake watched her walk away, chatting animatedly with the man, then glanced out the window once again. He couldn't think of anything more unappealing than riding all night on a bus, marching for hours in the cold, then riding home on the bus again. He'd rather compete in two marathons back-to-back than do that.

But A.J. wasn't doing this because it was comfortable. She was doing it because she believed that it was right. He'd never met anyone with such sincere convictions. His parents had always been rallying behind different causes, and they'd been passionate about them at the time, but then they'd moved on to something else. Their passions were fleeting. And more on the surface. A.J.'s went deep. And seemed to be long-lasting. And completely unselfish.

Blake admired that. But it also made him a little uncomfortable. Because somehow he didn't feel that he measured up. Sure, he had causes that he believed in. That's why he was the treasurer for a local homeless shelter, why he served on the board of directors of the local Big Brothers organization. But he didn't have to get his hands dirty to do that. He wasn't in the trenches. He hadn't made a personal investment, like A.J. was making this weekend. Or like she'd made in Afghanistan. Maybe his convictions just weren't as strong as hers.

And there was no question about the strength of her conviction about abortion. He'd never really thought about the issue too deeply before. It was easier to buy into the woman's-right-to-choose opinion. It was easier not to get involved. It was easier not to take a stand.

But A.J. didn't go for the easy way out.

And maybe he shouldn't, either.

Blake looked around the shop, which had been transformed since A.J.'s arrival. She'd rearranged so many things. Including his life.

And he had a feeling she wasn't done yet.

Chapter Six

A.J. groaned and fumbled for the alarm clock, intent on stilling the persistent, jarring ring. It couldn't possibly be Monday morning already! But when she squinted bleary-eyed at the clock, the digital display confirmed that it was.

With a sigh, she sank back against her pillow and stole a few extra moments under the downy warmth of the fluffy comforter. In the past seventy-two hours, she was lucky if she'd managed more than twelve hours of fitful slumber. She hadn't been able to find a comfortable sleeping position in the bus on the way to Washington. But she'd figured she'd be so tired after standing for hours in the cold that she'd have no problem sleeping Saturday night on the way home.

However, that theory was never put to the test. Because only a couple of hours into their return journey they'd had to pull into a truck stop when light snow suddenly turned into a blizzard. And they'd been stuck there until Sunday morning. They hadn't gone hungry, but sleep was difficult. When they'd finally resumed their trip, many of the people were so exhausted that they slept all day. But by that time, A.J.'s hip was feeling the effects of the march, the cold and the confined conditions. She'd had to keep standing to prevent her muscles from cramping.

A.J. didn't normally think much about the accident and its aftereffects. But today it was hard not to, when her hip was throbbing so painfully. Carefully, she turned over and scrunched her pillow under her head. Even after eight years, the nightmare was still vivid in her mind. She closed her eyes, swallowing as the memories engulfed her, willing her frantic pulse to slow.

Dear Lord, please stay with me, she prayed. *Please see me through this dark moment, like You always do. Help me to feel Your care and Your love. To know that I'm not alone. Help me to be strong and to accept Your will, even when I don't understand it. To trust in You and not be afraid. Help me deal with the pain and the loneliness. Let me feel the warmth of Your presence, especially today, when I am hurting and the memories are so vivid.*

Slowly, A.J.'s breathing returned to normal and she gradually released the comforter that was bunched in her fists. It had been a long time since the pain had been so stark. Not just the pain from her hip, but the pain of loss. For a few moments it had felt so fresh, so intense, so raw. Prompted, she was sure, by the bus trip this weekend and the blizzard. But she'd get through this. God hadn't deserted her before. He wouldn't now. She might be exhausted and hurting and shaken by the flood of memories, but she'd been through worse. Far worse. She could make it through today.

And tomorrow would be better.

By Wednesday, A.J. had caught up on some sleep, and the burning pain in her hip had diminished to a dull throb. She was beginning to feel human again.

But Blake didn't see it that way. He'd been watching her since her return, and she didn't look good. There were dark smudges under her eyes, and she was limping. But she'd brushed off his careful questions, assuring him she was fine. Obviously, she wasn't going to talk.

But he figured Nancy might. A.J. confided in her. So she was his best source for information.

"Blake, when you have a minute could you help me move that box in the back that just came in? I need to check on a special order for a customer, and it's blocking the computer."

He turned to Nancy. Perfect timing. "Sure. Be right there."

When Blake joined her, she gave him an apologetic look. "Sorry to interrupt you while you were with a customer. Normally I would have asked A.J. But I didn't want to bother her. She still looks so tired."

"Yeah, I noticed. What happened?"

"Didn't she tell you? They ran into a snowstorm on the way back to St. Louis and had to spend Saturday night in a truck stop. So they drove all day Sunday to get home. I doubt she had much sleep from Friday morning to Sunday night."

That explained the dark circles under her eyes. But what about the limp?

"Did she hurt her leg on the trip?"

"Not that I know of. Why?"

"Haven't you noticed her limping?"

"No. Is she?"

He shrugged. "Maybe it was my imagination."

But it wasn't. The limp had been pronounced on Monday. However, Nancy had been off that day. By Tuesday, A.J. was managing to hide it pretty well. Today it was hardly discernible. Most people wouldn't notice. But he could see it. As well as the fine lines of strain around her mouth that told him she was in pain. And that bothered him. A lot.

By Friday, A.J. not only still looked tired, she had a doozy of a cold. Her nose was red and running, her cheeks were flushed and she had a hacking cough. Twice he urged her to go home. Both times she refused.

"I'll be fine," she said. "I'm not going to let a little thing like a cold slow me down."

And she didn't. She made it until closing, through sheer grit and determination. Blake admired her spunk—but not her stubbornness—and told her so. And for the first time in their acquaintance, he saw evidence of her Irish temper.

"Just leave me alone, Blake, okay?" she said angrily. "I've taken care of myself for years. I know what I'm capable of. I don't need any advice."

He was so taken aback by her abrupt tone that for a moment he was speechless. Then he felt his own temper begin to simmer. "Fine. Suit yourself." He turned on his heel and left.

A.J. was immediately sorry for her rudeness. And she was even sorrier when she woke up on Saturday morning. It was her weekend to work, but she didn't even have the energy to get out of bed. Calling Nancy wasn't an option because she was throwing a birthday party for Eileen. Which left Blake.

A.J. groaned. She doubted whether he would be very receptive to her request after her curt behavior yesterday. But when her temperature registered a hundred and one, she knew she had to try.

He startled her by answering on the first ring. At his clipped greeting, she hesitated.

"Hello?" he repeated, this time with an edge of impatience.

"Blake, it's A.J. Have I caught you at a bad time?"

He frowned. If she hadn't identified herself, he would never have recognized the thin, raspy voice on the other end of the line. "I was just heading out the door. What's wrong?"

She took a deep breath. "You were right yesterday, and I apologize for my short temper. I should have gone home. Because now I'm worse. Listen, I know this is really short notice, and it sounds like you already have other plans, but is there any way you can fill in for me at the shop today? Or part of the day? I'd call Nancy, but she's busy with Eileen's birthday party."

Blake glanced at his watch. He was due at a finance meeting for the homeless shelter in half an hour, and he had a Big Brothers board meeting at one o'clock.

There was no way he could get out of those commitments. Both groups were counting on him.

"I'm sorry, A.J. I can't. I'm already running late for
one meeting, and I have another one after that."

Her heart sank. But what did she expect? Blake
lived a structured life. Flexibility wasn't in his vocabu-
lary. Last-minute changes would wreak havoc with his
carefully made plans.

"Okay. I understand. I wouldn't want to disrupt
your schedule. Thanks anyway."

"I'd help you out if I could."

"Like I said, I understand. Have a good day."

Before he could respond, she hung up. A muscle in
his jaw twitched, and he put his own phone back in its
base with more force than necessary. Her implication
had been clear. He was too rigid to adjust his schedule
to accommodate an emergency. She'd judged him without even asking the details of his refusal, which made
him mad. So, fine. Let her deal with this predicament on
her own. She'd brought it on herself, anyway, with her
impromptu trip to Washington. She'd told him yesterday
she could take care of herself. Well, today she'd have to.

Except that he couldn't get her out of his mind.
Twice at the finance meeting he'd had to ask someone
to repeat a question. And at the Big Brothers meeting
he looked at his watch so many times that the president
finally made a comment about it—and he was only half
joking. By the time the meeting ended at three-thirty,
Blake had made up his mind. He had to relieve A.J. at
the shop. If she looked half as bad as she'd sounded that
morning, she was probably about ready to drop.

In fact, she looked worse. After entering the shop from the rear, through the office, he paused on the threshold of the main room. A.J. was checking out a customer, but she was sitting behind the counter on a stool, not standing as she always did. And when she reached for a bag, he could see her hand shaking.

In several long strides he was beside her. He took the bag from her almost before she realized he was there, and when their hands brushed briefly her fingers felt hot and dry. She gazed at him blankly, her eyes dull with fever.

"I'll finish up this sale," he said close to her ear. "Stay put."

A.J. didn't argue. Which told him that she was really sick.

He dispensed with the customer as quickly as he could, then turned to her. Her shoulders were drooped, and her face was flushed. "I got here as quickly as I could. Did you take your temperature this morning?"

She nodded.

"What was it?"

"A hundred and one."

He muttered something under his breath, then spoke aloud. "Why didn't you tell me that when you called?"

She tried to shrug, but the effort seemed to require more energy than she had. "Would it have made a difference?"

He expelled a frustrated sigh. "I'm not even going to answer that. Did you call the doctor?"

"It's just a bug."

He thought about another bug…the persistent parasite from Afghanistan. Which might have weakened her immune system, made her more susceptible to other bugs. He doubted she should take any chances. He considered arguing—then thought better of it. She was probably right, and he was probably overreacting. It was most likely just a virus. But if she wasn't a lot better in a day or two, then he'd argue. Right now she needed to rest. "Fine. I'll get your coat."

"Why?"

"I'm taking you home."

"There's no one to watch the shop."

"I'll put a sign in the window."

She stared at him. "We've never closed the shop in the middle of the day before."

"I guess there's a first time for everything."

"But…we might lose customers."

"They'll come back."

Suddenly she frowned. "You can't drive me. My car's here."

"You're in no condition to drive."

"Blake, I appreciate the offer, but I can get home on my own."

As if to demonstrate her point, she stood. Then lost the argument when she swayed. He grabbed her upper arms to steady her, and she closed her eyes.

"Maybe…maybe you better drive me after all," she said faintly.

When she lifted her eyelids, Blake's intense eyes were riveted on hers. There was concern in their depths—and in that brief, unguarded instant, an unexpected tenderness that made her breath catch in her throat. She was only inches from his solid chest, and his strong arms held her steadily, protectively. For a fleeting moment, A.J. wanted to step into his embrace, to lay her head on his broad shoulder, to feel his arms enfold and hold her. It was a startling impulse, surely brought on by her weakened condition. To counter it, she tried to step back. But he held her fast, and their gazes locked.

Blake stared at A.J. Despite her attempt to move away, he didn't want to let her go. He wanted to protect her. It was a primitive instinct, one he had never before experienced. He'd dated a fair amount, but no one had ever elicited this response. It was…weird. Especially since he and A.J. were simply business associates. They hardly liked each other.

Someone cleared his throat, and Blake and A.J. turned to find a customer waiting to be checked out. Reluctantly, Blake released her, but not before he gave her one more quick, searching gaze. "Are you steady enough to go get your coat?"

She nodded mutely. For some reason her voice had deserted her.

"Okay. I'll meet you in the back in five minutes."

As A.J. waited for him, she tried to figure out what had just happened between them. It was almost like…attraction. Which was crazy. They were nothing alike. In fact, they were completely opposite. And they clashed all the time. There was no basis for any chemistry. Oh, sure, Blake was a nice-looking guy. In fact, as Morgan would say, he was a hunk. But he wasn't

her type. Whatever had happened out there had to be a
fluke. Maybe it had something to do with her fever.

But that didn't quite ring true. Because based on
what she'd seen in his eyes, A.J. was pretty sure that
Blake had experienced the same thing.

And he wasn't sick.

Someone was using a hammer. In the middle of the
night. A.J. pried her eyelids open and squinted at the
clock. Seven o'clock. Okay, so maybe it wasn't the
middle of the night after all. But it sure felt like it was.

The pounding started again. This time it was
accompanied by Blake's voice, which had a slightly
desperate edge.

"A.J.? Open the door! I'm calling the police if
you don't!"

She struggled to her feet, favoring her hip, which
had started to ache again. She limped to the door and
fumbled with the locks in the darkness. When she
finally pulled the door open, she caught a glimpse of
Mr. Simmons, her elderly neighbor, peering through a
crack in his door across the hall.

"Everything all right, A.J.?" he asked.

"Fine, thanks, Mr. Simmons. Sorry to bother you,"
she said hoarsely.

She stepped back, and as Blake came in she did
some mental arithmetic. It was still an hour to closing.
"Who's at the shop?"

"I called Nancy. The party ended at five-thirty and
she came in." He flipped on a light and studied her.
"How are you?"

"I took some aspirin. And I've been sleeping."

Which didn't answer his question. But her appearance said it all. Her eyes were watery and her face still looked flushed. "Have you taken your temperature lately?"

She shook her head. "Like I said, I've been sleeping."

"Why don't you go do that while I reheat this soup?"

She stared at the bag in this hand. "You brought me soup?"

"I figured you probably hadn't eaten all day. Rose said chicken noodle soup was perfect for a cold. And she told me to tell you to get a lot of rest and drink a lot of water. She said we need you in fighting form for our battle with city hall, and made me promise to report back to her that you were taking care of yourself."

A.J. could imagine Rose issuing those instructions. What she was having a hard time imagining was that Blake had gone to all this trouble on her behalf. She looked at him quizzically. "Why did you do this?"

Blake had been asking himself the same question all the way over here. And he hadn't come up with a good answer. Or at least one he was willing to live with. "Let's just say it's Christian charity."

"I might buy that if you were a religious man."

He gave her a frustrated look. "Are you going to stand here all night, or are you going to take your temperature?"

She certainly didn't feel like standing here all night. In fact, she didn't feel like standing, period. She was starting to get light-headed again. Instead of responding, she just headed for the bathroom to retrieve the thermometer. Then she sat on the edge of the bed and stuck it in her mouth. She heard Blake rummaging in her kitchen, heard him open the microwave, heard the beeps as he programmed it. He hadn't really answered her question about why he was here. And she was too weary to try and figure it out today. But whatever the reason, she was glad he'd come.

A.J. was still sitting on the edge of the bed, thermometer in hand, when Blake appeared at her door holding a lap tray with a large glass of water and a bowl of soup.

"May I come in?"

She almost smiled. It was so like him to ask a question like that. After all, it was the conventional thing to do. "Of course. Where did you get the tray?"

"Rose had it in the back of her deli and insisted I borrow it. So what's the verdict?" He nodded toward the thermometer.

"One hundred."

He frowned. "Not good."

"It's a little better than before. The aspirin must be starting to work."

"Do you want to get back into bed? It might be easier to balance the tray."

She nodded. With an effort she scooted back and swung her legs up. A chill went through her, and she reached for the comforter.

"Are you cold?"

The man didn't miss a thing. "Chills and fever go

together." She tried to keep her teeth from chattering as she spoke.

"Maybe the soup will help." He leaned down to place the tray on her lap, and as he settled it in place their gazes met. A.J. stared up into his eyes, only inches from her own, and it happened again. She wanted to reach out to him, to pull him close, to take comfort in his strong arms. The impulse scared her. She didn't want a man in her life. Not now. Not ever. She'd been down that road once. It was not a trip she wanted to take again. Especially not with this man. But she couldn't quiet the sudden staccato beat of her heart at his nearness.

Blake's gaze flickered down to the pulse beating frantically in the hollow of her throat, and when he looked back up his eyes had darkened in intensity. A.J. had a feeling that he knew exactly the effect he was having on her, and the flush on her face deepened. She tried to look away, but his compelling gaze held hers. Suddenly his eyes grew confused, and a slight frown appeared on his brow. He stood quickly, and when he spoke, his voice had an odd, appealingly husky quality. "Eat your soup."

A.J. didn't even try to speak. She just averted her gaze and picked up the spoon. When she finally ventured a glance in his direction, he was standing near the doorway watching her, his hands in his pockets, the frown still on his face.

"You ought to leave, Blake. I don't want you to get sick, too," she croaked.

"I don't get sick."

"I don't usually, either."

"Except in Afghanistan."

"That was a fluke."

"Was the leg injury a fluke, too?" The question was out before he could stop it.

Slowly she raised her gaze to his. "What leg injury?"

Too late to backtrack now. "There's nothing wrong with my eyesight, A.J. I've seen you limping."

She swallowed and averted her gaze. "That's not from Afghanistan. It's an old injury. Most of the time it doesn't bother me."

He waited, but it was clear that she wasn't going to explain further. And much as he wanted to know the story behind the injury that clearly *did* bother her on a fairly regular basis, he knew she wasn't up to discussing it today. Her eyelids were growing heavy again, and weariness was etched on her face. At least she'd eaten most of the soup. He moved toward her and lifted the tray.

"There's more soup in the fridge. And some quiche. Take it easy tomorrow, okay?"

She looked up at him, grateful he hadn't pressed her about her injury. "Thank you, Blake."

"You're welcome. Nancy and I can cover the shop on Monday if you're still not feeling well."

She nodded gratefully. "Okay."

He turned to go, pausing on the threshold to look back at her once more. A.J. stared at him, her green eyes wide and appealing. She'd lost some weight in the past week, and the fine bone structure of her face made her look almost fragile. Somewhere along the way the band that tamed her unruly curls had disappeared. Now her strawberry blond hair tumbled around her shoulders loose and soft. She looked innocent. And sweet. And very, very appealing.

A voice inside him urged him to stay.

But he was afraid.

So he listened to the other voice, the one that told him to run.

As far and as fast as he could.

A.J. took Blake up on his offer and stayed home Monday. The Board of Aldermen meeting was Tuesday, and she needed to be in top form when she made her appeal. Fortunately, when she woke on Tuesday, she felt well enough to go to work. There was just one little problem.

She had no voice.

A fact she didn't discover until she walked into Turning Leaves and tried to return Blake's greeting. She opened her mouth. She formed the words. But no sound came out. Her eyes widened in alarm.

"What's wrong?" Blake asked.

She raised her hands helplessly and pointed to her throat, then walked behind the desk and pulled out a sheet of paper. She wrote, "My voice is gone," and pushed it toward him.

He read it and frowned. "You can't talk?"

She shook her head. And suddenly felt tears welling in her eyes. Talk about rotten timing! The rest of the merchants were counting on her to make an impassioned plea tonight. She'd carefully prepared her remarks, practiced them, prepped for possible questions. What were they going to do?

Blake studied her face, his perceptive eyes missing nothing, then took her hand and led her toward the back room. He passed Nancy on the way. "Cover the front, okay?" he said over his shoulder.

When they got in the back he gently pressed A.J. into the desk chair, pulled up a chair beside her and turned on the computer. "Okay. Let's try communicating this way. You're worried about tonight, right?"

She nodded and typed, "Everyone is counting on me! What are we going to do?"

"Can't someone else speak for the group?"

Her fingers flew over the keys. "But no one else has had time to prepare. And it's a lot to dump on someone at the last minute. I could give someone my comments, but who could deliver them?"

Blake steepled his fingers, rested his elbows on the desk and stared at the computer screen. A.J. had shared the draft of her comments with him, so he knew what she planned to say. Her remarks were eloquent and touching, but also hard-hitting. No one could deliver them as well as she could. And none of the others were accustomed to standing in front of a group and making a business presentation. Except him.

Blake knew he was the logical choice to take over. He'd worked side-by-side with Jo for years, so he could talk about her commitment to the area with authority. And he'd done his homework on TIF. He understood how it worked and why the city was inter-

ested from a financial standpoint. But he also understood why using it wasn't necessarily in the best long-
term interest of Maplewood.

Finally Blake turned and looked at A.J. And read in
her eyes exactly what he'd just been thinking. Yet she
hadn't asked him to step in. Because after meeting his
parents, after the dinner in her apartment, she knew
how he felt about getting publicly involved in causes.
Even one this close to his heart. And she wasn't going
to pressure him.

Maybe if she had, Blake would have resisted. But
because she didn't, because she had taken his feelings
into consideration and refrained from asking him to
put himself in an uncomfortable position, Blake felt an
obligation to offer. A.J. had poured herself into this
effort, as had the other merchants. He'd just attended
the meetings and contributed on a peripheral level.
Maybe it was time he pulled his weight.

He drew a deep breath and slowly folded his arms
on the desk in front of him. "Okay. How about if I
speak for the group?"

Gratitude filled her eyes, and then she turned back
to the monitor and typed rapidly. "It would mean a lot
to me. And to Aunt Jo, too, I know."

When their gazes met a moment later, there was a
softness in A.J.'s eyes that Blake had never seen
before. And suddenly he found it difficult to breathe.
He cleared his throat, and scooted back slightly. "Why
don't you give me your notes and I'll use them as a
basis for my own comments. Can you and Nancy
cover the shop part of the day while I prepare?"

She nodded. Then she laid her hand on his arm and mouthed two simple words. "Thank you."

The warmth of her touch seeped in through the oxford cloth of his shirt. And somehow worked its way to his heart.

The turnout for the meeting at city hall was better than any of the merchants had hoped. The seats were all taken twenty minutes before the proceedings were scheduled to begin, and several staff members scurried around setting up extra chairs. Even then, there wasn't enough seating. Attendees lined the walls and spilled out into the hall. By the time the meeting was called to order, the room was packed.

Routine business was dispensed with first. Then Stuart MacKenzie presented his proposal, and the floor was opened for comments and questions. A.J. glanced at Blake and gave him a thumbs-up sign. He shot her a quick grin, then stood and made his way to the microphone.

"Good evening. I'm Blake Sullivan, co-owner of Turning Leaves, a bookshop in the block that Mr. MacKenzie is targeting for his development. I represent the seven merchants on that block. I also represent Jo Williams, the original owner of Turning Leaves, who passed away a few months ago.

"I mention Jo because she was the first merchant to open a business in what twenty-some years ago was a blighted area. I'm sure some of you were around back then and remember that Maplewood wasn't exactly prime real estate. But Jo believed in the area and was convinced that with the right nurturing, it would some-day rise again. The other merchants on the block felt the same way.

"Ladies and gentlemen, I don't hesitate to call these people pioneers. They courageously took a chance on an area many had written off as too far gone to be saved. They invested their time, their energy and their finances in Maplewood, and they did it with no con-cessions from city hall.

"Today, Maplewood is a thriving community. I sub-mit to you that without people like the loyal, hard-working merchants in this room tonight, the incredible rebirth that this town is enjoying would never have happened. I also submit to you that one of the reasons this area is attracting new investment and renewed residential growth is because of its character, which has remained largely intact.

"Mr. MacKenzie's proposal is quite impressive. And I don't quarrel with his numbers. I'm sure the pro-jected revenue he discussed tonight is sound. But this type of development will change the very character of Maplewood that has attracted renewed interest. Independently owned businesses, like those represent-ed here tonight, will give way to franchises. The town will become homogenized. And in doing so, it will lose its unique appeal and charm. In the long run, I believe that will hurt, not help, the city.

"Ladies and gentlemen of the board, as you consid-er this proposal, I ask you to weigh the immediate financial gains against the long-term effect on this community. And I ask you to factor in the human element. Because in the end, people are what make up a town. There are good people in this room tonight. People who fight for what they believe in and work hard to make their dreams come true. And they are also people who will probably be forced to leave if this development goes through. That will be a great loss to this town. I present to you tonight signatures of more than two thousand residents who agree with this position and are against this development.

"As I said at the beginning, Jo Williams was the first to take a chance on this area. She's gone now. But her legacy lives on in the lives of the people here tonight and the businesses they have built. I hope that you don't let this legacy slip away. Thank you."

For a moment after Blake finished speaking, there was silence in the room. And then, almost as one, everyone rose and applauded wildly. But as he made his way back to his seat, Blake hardly heard the ovation or felt the hands that slapped him on the back. He just wanted to get back to A.J. Because the only reaction he really cared about was hers. He knew she'd counted on him to deliver an impassioned plea. Knew that a great deal rested on his ability to convince the board of the value the current residents added to the community.

When he reached his seat he glanced at her—and almost went limp with relief. Her face was shining, her lips tipped into a smile, telling him he'd done okay. Maybe more than okay. As he took his seat beside her, she reached over and rested her hand on his arm. And though her voice was gone, her eyes were eloquent, filled with gratitude, admiration…and something else he couldn't quite identify. But whatever it was made his throat suddenly go dry.

Only with great effort did he finally tear his gaze away and focus on the rest of the meeting. The other speakers, area residents, were also very good. The board appeared impressed, but it was hard to say what the outcome would be. Dollars spoke loudly, and in the end the board might not be able to ignore their voice. But the merchants and residents had certainly given it their best shot.

As the meeting wrapped up, A.J. nudged him and quickly jotted down a few words. He leaned over to read them. "What next?"

He wished he had a better response. "We wait."

She gave him a disgruntled look, wrote again, then turned the paper so he could read it. "And pray."

Blake studied the words. He didn't put much faith in the power of prayer himself. But he wasn't about to dissuade anyone who wanted to ask God for help.

Because it sure couldn't hurt.

Chapter Seven

"I don't feel right about leaving."

A.J. turned to Blake. "Why not? You've been planning this trip for weeks. Didn't you tell me this annual ski weekend in Colorado with your college buddies is an inviolable tradition?"

"Yeah. But you're barely back on your feet, and something could come up with the MacKenzie project."

A.J. planted her fists on her hips. "First, I'm feeling much better. Second, nothing is going to happen in the next five days with MacKenzie. The meeting was only last week. Didn't you say that your initial research showed there probably wouldn't be a decision until March or April?"

"I know, but…"

"No buts. Everyone deserves a vacation, Blake. Nancy told me you haven't taken one in over a year, other than a few long weekends. So go. Relax. Enjoy. We'll be fine."

He studied her for a moment, debating. She still looked pretty peaked to him. But he knew he'd never hear the end of it from Jack and Dave if he bailed out at the last minute. "Okay. You convinced me. But call if you need anything."

"Don't worry about us. Just have fun."

The fun part was no problem. Dave and Jack would see to that. But not worrying…that was something else entirely.

Because even though he was trying desperately to keep his business partner at arm's length, A.J. was beginning to get under his skin.

So not worrying was *not* an option.

"Hey, Jacko, what's with all the phone calls to the little woman?" Dave teased.

Jack grinned at Dave. "Don't ever let her hear you call her that. She'll deck you."

Dave chuckled. "Yeah, yeah. I know. Bonnie would do the same to me. But hey, on our annual guys' weekend, anything goes, doesn't it? What we say here stays with just the three of us. Right, Blake?"

Blake unceremoniously dumped his ski boots in the hall and grabbed a soft drink from the fridge before joining his two college buddies. "Absolutely."

Jack propped his feet on the coffee table, gazed at the crackling fire and gave a contented sigh. "Ah, this is the life."

"Yeah. But only for one long weekend a year," Dave groused good-naturedly. "Then it's back to bills and stopped-up toilets and diapers and the nine-to-five routine."

"You guys wouldn't change a thing," Blake said, dropping into one of the condo's easy chairs.

"That's true," Jack admitted, taking a long swallow of soda. "So when are you going to get with the program? I thought you'd be the first one married."

"Yeah," Dave concurred. "You were the one who wanted to settle down with the Leave-It-To-Beaver wife, raise two-point-five children and have a house with a white picket fence. What happened?"

"I've got the house," Blake said.

"So where are the two-point-five kids?"

"I think I need the wife first."

"Not these days, you don't."

"Mr. Conventional would," Jack declared with a grin.

"I didn't see either of you guys deviate from the norm," Blake pointed out.

"Guilty," Jack admitted. "So when are you going to take the plunge? Met anyone interesting lately?"

An image of A.J. flashed through his mind. In fact, she'd been on his mind a lot during the trip. As he'd maneuvered tricky moguls with expert skill, he'd thought again about her unexplained limp. And he kept picturing her when she'd been sick, looking so uncharacteristically fragile and helpless.

As the silence lengthened, Dave glanced at Jack and leaned forward with sudden interest. "I think he's been holding out on us."

Jack nodded. "Yeah. Okay, Blake, spill it. Who is she?"

Blake frowned. "Who?"

"The woman you're thinking about right now."

"What makes you think I'm thinking about a woman?"

Dave chuckled. "Because we've been there. We know the look."

"What look?"

"The I-don't-know-how-this-happened-but-I-think-I'm-falling-in-love look."

Blake's frown deepened. "You're nuts."

"Yeah? Are you going to tell me you weren't thinking about a woman just now?"

"No. I was. My partner."

Jack's eyebrows rose, and he looked at Dave. "His partner," he repeated knowingly.

Dave nodded sagely. "Sounds logical to me. My wife's my partner. How about you, Jack?"

"Yeah. Makes perfect sense."

"Come on, you guys, cut it out. I'm serious. She's my partner at the bookshop. I thought of her when you asked if I'd met any interesting women. She certainly falls into that category. But she's not my type."

Jack took a long swallow of his soft drink. "Right."

"How old is she?" Dave asked.

"I don't know. Thirtyish, I guess."

"Is she married?"

"No."

"What's her name?"

"A.J."

"Different name. What does it stand for?"

"I don't know."

"Hmm. Is she pretty?"

"Yeah."

"Do you think about her all the time?"

"No." Which was true. He didn't think about her *all* the time. Just most of the time lately. "Look, what is this? The third degree?"

"Maybe. If you won't talk, we have to ask questions," Jack said. "Like in the old days, when we first met. Man, you were a clam back then. Dave and I almost gave up on you."

"But persistence paid off," Dave interjected. "And we're not about to let you regress. So spill it."

"There's nothing to tell. Trust me, you guys will be the first to know if I ever meet the right woman."

"And this A.J. isn't it?"

"Not even close."

"Why not?"

"I told you. We're completely different. She's too unconventional and spontaneous for me. When I'm around her, I never know what to expect next. It's totally frustrating. We're at odds most of the time."

Dave glanced at Jack. "What do you think?"

Jack finished off his soft drink. "He's a goner."

Blake stared at his two best friends in the world. They grinned back at him smugly. He considered arguing the point. Then thought better of it. He'd be vindicated when nothing ever happened between him and A.J.

But for some odd reason that thought didn't give him a whole lot of satisfaction.

"What are you doing?"

The sound of Blake's voice startled A.J., and she almost lost her balance on the ladder. Blake was beside her in an instant, his hand on her arm. She turned and looked down at him, noting that he was tanned from his days of skiing. And he looked rested. Which was more than she could say for herself. They'd been exceptionally busy while he was gone, and since she wasn't back to full strength yet, the extra workload had taken a toll. Not to mention that her hip was hurting again.

"Welcome back," she said wryly.

Blake studied her face, noting her pallor and the fine lines at the corners of her eyes. She looked tired. "Are you okay?"

"Yeah, I'm fine. But don't sneak up on people like that. You scared me!" she complained.

Which was only fair, since she'd scared him. When he'd walked into the stockroom and found her wielding a heavy box while balancing on the second-highest rung of the ladder, he'd panicked.

"So what are you doing?" he repeated.

"Isn't it obvious? I'm putting a box on the shelf. Like I've done a million times since I've been here."

"I can do it for you."

She frowned. "I don't need you to. I can do it myself."

He recognized the stubborn set of her jaw, the slight tilt of her chin. She was prepared to do battle over this, but he took a different tack. "What are you trying to prove, A.J.?" he asked, his tone almost gentle.

Her eyes widened in surprise at his unexpected response. Then they grew wary. "What do you mean?"

"Why won't you let people help you?"

"I let people help me."

"When?"

She tried to think of an example. "I let you take me home the day I was sick."

"Not by choice. You'd have preferred to stick it out. If you hadn't almost keeled over, I think you would have told me to get lost. Try again." He folded his arms across his chest.

She couldn't come up with another example, so she took a defensive position. "What's your point?"

"I just want an answer to my question. What are you trying to prove by tackling a job like this when you have a bad leg and you knew I'd be back today."

"I don't have a bad leg," she said tersely. "And I wasn't trying to prove anything."

"I think you were. I think you were trying to prove that you don't need anyone, that you can handle things on your own."

"I *can* handle things on my own."

"Not all the time. And not everything. Now will you please get down off the ladder and let me put the box on the shelf?"

She glared at him. "No."

A muscle twitched in his jaw, but when he spoke his tone was mild. "Fine. Then I'll at least hold the ladder for you."

A.J. did *not* want him hanging around while she struggled with the heavy box. And she certainly didn't want him around when she descended the ladder. Climbing it hadn't been her most graceful moment. Getting down would be worse. But from the resolute look in his eyes, it was clear that Blake wasn't going anywhere. He was prepared to wait her out. So she might as well get this over with.

Gritting her teeth, A.J. turned back to the storage rack and hoisted the heavy box toward the top shelf. Much to her dismay, she missed the edge and had to make a second attempt. All the while she felt Blake's scrutiny boring into her back. Since when had he taken responsibility for her welfare? And what was with all those questions just now about trying to prove something, about not needing anyone? Why would he ask such a thing? And more importantly, why did the questions bother her?

A niggling voice in the back of her mind whispered back, "Maybe because he's hitting too close to the truth," but she shut it out. She didn't want to go there. At least not right now. Not when she still had to negotiate the rungs of the ladder.

A.J. knew her descent was awkward. And slow. And that Blake missed nothing. It took all of her will-power to turn and face him when she was at last back on level ground. She wanted to say, "See, I told you I was perfectly capable of doing this myself," but she couldn't tell such an obvious lie. She'd struggled with both the box and the ladder. And he knew it.

A.J. expected Blake to make some snide comment. But he surprised her.

"I'll put the ladder away," he said quietly.

She stepped aside without protest. His comment held no rancor, but she knew he was upset. On one level, she was touched that he cared enough to worry about her welfare. On another, she was troubled by his unsettling questions. She knew by now that Blake's instincts were generally sound and his insights keen. What had he seen in her to make him ask those questions?

A.J. didn't know the answer.

And she wasn't sure she wanted to. Because she had a feeling that it might change her life. Again. And that scared her.

Big-time.

"Well, it looks like the weather people were right for once."

A.J. looked up from the front counter and followed Nancy's gaze. Snow had begun to fall, and there was already a fine covering of white on the sidewalk.

"Seems odd for this time of year," she commented.

Nancy shrugged. "Some of our worst storms have been in early March. The good part is the snow never stays around very long."

A.J. didn't pay much attention to the weather as darkness fell. But when Nancy came back from an early dinner break, A.J. took notice of her worried expression.

"This is going to be bad," Nancy said. "The streets are already turning to ice, A.J. Maybe you should go home. You have the longest drive. Blake and I only have to go a mile or so."

A.J. walked over to the window and peered outside. Several inches of snow were already on the ground, and the streets had a slick sheen to them. She fought down a wave of panic. Ever since the accident, she'd hated driving in the snow. But there would be no way around that tonight. Even if she took Nancy's advice and left now, driving would be dangerous.

She turned back to find Blake watching her. Since their exchange in the storeroom a few days before, they'd largely avoided each other. They were polite. They were professional. But they didn't get personal. Their conversations focused on business and the weather.

She didn't have to say a word for Blake to know that she was nervous. He could feel waves of tension emanating from her body, could see the stiffness in her shoulders. He could also see the subtle, stubborn, defiant tilt of her chin as she gazed at him. So he knew his next suggestion wouldn't meet with a favorable reception. He also knew he was going to make it anyway.

"Why don't you let me drive you home?"

Before she could voice the refusal that sprang to her lips, Nancy spoke up. "That's a good idea, A.J. His car is a lot heavier than yours. It will be safer in this weather."

A.J. frowned. "But you'd be here all by yourself," she stalled.

Nancy shrugged and looked out the window. "In this weather, I doubt we'll have many customers."

"But you'll have to drive home alone, too," A.J. pointed out.

Nancy laughed. "Yeah, but I've got Bertha. She's a real heavyweight. Nothing stops her. She's solid as a rock. Besides, I don't have far to go."

A.J. thought of Nancy's older, sturdy, midsize car. She couldn't argue that it was safer than her economy subcompact.

When A.J. finally ventured a look at Blake, he was just watching her, waiting for her decision. He hadn't argued his case, though she suspected he'd been prepared to. But Nancy had done it for him.

A.J. took one more glance out the window. The snow was coming down even harder now. She could maintain her independence and refuse Blake's offer. Or she could admit that she wasn't up to the task, use common sense and accept his help. She thought about what he'd said to her in the storeroom. She hadn't let herself dwell on it until now because it was too disturbing. But given her reaction tonight, he'd obviously been right. She did have a hard time asking for help or relying on other people. Maybe it was time to break the pattern.

Slowly A.J. turned back to Blake. "All right. Thank you."

Though Blake's casual stance didn't change, she could sense his relief in the subtle relaxing of his face muscles and the merest easing in his shoulders.

"Good. I'll go clean off the car. Give me five minutes."

By the time A.J. stepped out of the rear door of the shop, Blake was just putting away his ice scraper. He looked up when the light spilled from the doorway.

"Wait there," he called. "It's really slippery."

A.J. did as he asked. The last thing she needed was to ignore his advice and fall flat on her face. Besides, now that the ache in her hip had subsided, she didn't want to do anything that might bring it back.

Blake joined her moments later, completely covered with snow. The storm seemed to intensify with every minute that passed. "Take my arm and hold on. This lot is like a skating rink."

Again she didn't argue. Slowly they made their way to his car, and even before they were halfway there, A.J. knew she had made a wise decision in accepting his offer. She could barely walk on the slippery surface, and driving would be a nightmare. Just riding in a car would be bad enough.

Blake helped her into the passenger seat, then came around to his side and brushed himself off before sliding behind the wheel. He looked over at A.J. Snowflakes still clung to her strawberry blond curls, and he smiled. "You look like you have stars in your hair," he said.

She tried to smile. "Better than in my eyes, I suppose."

He focused on those green eyes for a moment. No stars there. Instead he saw fear. He watched as she swallowed convulsively, then nervously brushed back a stray strand of hair with shaking fingers. She was absolutely terrified, he realized with a start. Not just a little nervous about driving in bad weather. But terrified. This time he followed his instincts. He reached for her hand and gave it a squeeze.

"Hey, it will be okay. I'll get you home safely," he said gently.

For a moment she seemed surprised by his action. But she didn't pull away. Again, she valiantly tried to smile. And failed. "I just don't like driving in snow," she said.

There was more to her terror than that. He wanted

to ask what it was, but didn't. This wasn't the time. "Just relax. You'll be home before you know it."

But he was wrong. It took them ten minutes just to go six blocks, slipping and sliding the whole way. It was so bad that even Blake, who never minded driving in bad weather, was getting worried. When they skidded dangerously close to a parked car as he maneuvered one corner, he pulled to the side and turned to A.J. She hadn't said one word since they'd left, and he'd been so busy trying to navigate that he hadn't looked at her. But now he realized that she had a death grip on the dashboard, and in the light from the street lamp he could see that the color had drained from her face.

"This isn't looking good, A.J." When she didn't respond, he reached over and laid a hand on her arm. He could feel the tremors running through her body. "A.J.?"

With an effort she tore her gaze away from the street and stared at him, her eyes wide. "Wh-what?"

"I said this isn't looking good."

"I kn-know." The catch in her voice spoke eloquently of her fear.

"Look, I don't think we should try to make it to your apartment. I have a guest room, and I'm only half a mile from here. Would you consider staying there tonight?"

"At your place? You mean…just us?"

"I'll sleep next door. My elderly neighbors are on a cruise and they gave me a key to their house."

"I don't want to put you out of your own home."

"It's not a problem, A.J. They have a huge couch in the family room. I'll be fine for one night."

She took a deep breath and slowly nodded. "Okay."

"Good. Hang in there. It shouldn't take us long to get to my place."

By the time Blake pulled into his attached garage twenty minutes later, even he was tense. He'd driven in some pretty bad weather, but the icy conditions he'd just encountered ranked right up there with a raging blizzard he, Dave and Jack had once encountered on a drive back to the Denver airport from one of their annual ski trips.

"Sit tight. I'll get your door," he told A.J.

A moment later, he pulled it open. When she didn't move, he leaned down. "A.J.?"

She was still staring straight ahead, gripping the dashboard, and he could tell that a single tear had slipped from her eye and left a trail halfway down her cheek. He leaned in and gently touched her shoulder. "It's okay. We're home. Everything's fine," he said soothingly. "Come on, I'll help you out."

Automatically she swung her legs out of the car. When she faced him her eyes were slightly glazed and she seemed almost to be in shock. He took her hands and urged her out of the car, shutting the door with his hip. And then, for the second time that night, he followed his instincts and pulled her into his arms.

A.J. didn't protest. In fact, she went willingly, letting him wrap his arms around her and hold her close. She laid her head on his shoulder, and her own arms went around him. He could feel her trembling, and he stroked her back with one hand, letting the other move up to cradle her head.

"Everything's okay. You're safe," he murmured softly near her ear.

A.J. knew she should step out of Blake's embrace. Knew that her acquiescence was completely out of character and that he would eventually want an explanation. But she couldn't help herself. As she'd stared out the window of the car on the drive to his house, watching the snowflakes beat against the glass, her nightmarish memories had replayed themselves in her mind for the second time in a couple of weeks. Once again, their vividness had taken her breath away. Even now her heart was pounding and her breathing was erratic. She needed something solid and sure to cling to. Namely, Blake. In his arms, she felt safe and protected. It was an illusion, of course. She knew that. But it felt good. And for just a moment, she let herself pretend that it was true.

A.J. wasn't sure how long she remained in Blake's embrace. But finally, when her trembling subsided, she took a long, shuddering breath and made a move to disengage. He let her step back, but continued to hold her upper arms as he searched her face in the dim light of the garage. She was still pale, and the freckles across the bridge of her nose were more pronounced than usual.

"A.J.?"

"I—I'm okay, Blake. Sorry about this. Storms freak me out."

There was a brief hesitation before he spoke. "Okay. Let's get inside where it's warm."

He kept his arm protectively on the small of her back as he fitted the key in the lock. When the door swung open, he ushered her into a small mud room.

"Let me take your coat."

He helped her take it off, then shrugged out of his own and hung both on hooks. "I'll show you the guest room and let you settle in while I get a fire going."

He led the way through a cozy kitchen/breakfast room combo, across a small entry foyer and down a hall to a door near the end.

"This is really part office, part den," he apologized as they stepped into the room. It was furnished with a modular desk and computer, and a couch stood against one wall. "The sofa is a sleeper. It's not the most comfortable bed around, but it works pretty well for emergencies."

"This will be fine for one night, Blake."

When he spoke, it was almost like he hadn't heard her. "I'll tell you what. Why don't you take my room tonight? It has a real bed, and it would be better than…"

"I'm perfectly fine with the sofa sleeper," she interrupted.

He could tell from the stubborn tilt of her chin that arguing wasn't going to get him anywhere. So he decided to save his persuasive powers for other discussions. Like finding out why she was so terrified of snowstorms. And why she sometimes limped.

"Okay." He walked over to the sofa, quickly dispensed with the cushions, and in one lithe movement pulled the bed open. "There are blankets in the closet in here," he said, nodding toward the other side of the room. "And I have extra sheets in the hall closet."

She followed him into the hall, reaching for the bedding as he withdrew it. "I can handle this. I'd rather you spend your time getting that fire going," she said.

He handed them over without resistance. "The bathroom's right across the hall," he told her, nodding toward an adjacent doorway. "There are fresh towels under the sink. There's also an extra toothbrush under there."

She gave him a small smile. "I see you're always prepared for guests."

He looked at her, and paused for a moment as if debating his next words. "No one's ever spent the night here before," he told her quietly.

Her grin faded. A.J. had been joking. Blake wasn't. He was telling her in no uncertain terms that he didn't have overnight guests. And that he didn't believe in casual intimacy.

A.J. had no idea how to respond to this revelation. So she didn't. "Well, I—I guess I'll go make up the bed," she stammered.

And before he could respond, she headed for the den.

Blake watched her go. Now why had he told her that? The statement had been true enough. He didn't believe in one-night stands or living together. When he met the right woman, he would make a commitment to her. Publicly. Formally. That was the only way intimacy had any meaning. And for some reason he'd wanted A.J. to know that. He wasn't sure why. But tonight wasn't the time to figure it out. Not when he had a fire to make and a dinner to prepare.

As A.J. made the bed and freshened up, she thought about Blake's comment. It was something you might say to a woman you were interested in having a relationship with. But they were just business partners. Maybe her receptiveness to his embrace in the garage had prompted the disclosure. But there had been nothing intimate in his touch. She had felt only caring and comfort and friendship. So she didn't think that was why he'd said it. There was something more. But tonight wasn't the time to figure it out. Her nerves were already shot from the drive here. They couldn't take much more.

She opened the closet and spotted the blankets. But her attention was diverted by trophies that shared space on the same shelf. Curiously, she stood on tiptoe to read the inscriptions. There were several for running and biking events, and even one for a very good finish in a triathlon. All were of fairly recent vintage. She stared at them, impressed. She'd known Blake was in good shape, known that he was a runner and cyclist. Nancy had mentioned it. But she'd thought his interest was purely recreational. She'd had no idea he was competitive in either sport. Or that he was a swimmer.

Thoughtfully she withdrew a blanket, and as she turned back toward the sofa she noticed a couple of framed certificates near the desk. On impulse, she moved closer to examine them. One was an acknowledgment of Blake's work with a local homeless shelter. The other recognized his contributions as a board member to the Big Brothers organization. Her glance fell on the three-month calendar under a clear mat on his desk, and her gaze was drawn to the Saturday she'd been so ill, when he'd refused to sub for her at the shop. There were meetings listed for both organizations.

A.J. took a deep breath. She'd learned more about Blake in the past few minutes than she had since they'd met. In the garage, she'd learned just how caring and compassionate he was. She'd learned he had strong moral principles when it came to relationships. That he was a superb and disciplined athlete. And that he believed in helping those less fortunate. His choice of organizations to support was also clearly a reflection of his own upbringing.

When they'd met, A.J. had written Blake off as a stuffy, inflexible, stick-in-the-mud loner. But as she was beginning to discover, there was a whole lot more to this complex man than met the eye. He might not be the most spontaneous guy in the world, but there were some very good reasons for that. And he was able to bend when necessary. His willingness to step in and speak in her place at the Board of Aldermen meeting was clear evidence of that. And also of his kindness and compassion. She knew he hated confrontation and anything that reeked of protest. But he'd put himself front and center in that situation anyway. For her, and for their cause. And she deeply admired—and respected—him for that.

As A.J. thoughtfully made her way to the kitchen, she peeked into a darkened room as she passed. It was empty except for a weight set and a racing bike. More evidence of his training regime. He skied, too. It was telling that all of his sports were solitary, she reflected.

When she got to the kitchen, she found him chopping onions. "What can I do to help?"

He turned toward her. Her face had more color now and the tension had eased. "Why don't you just go in and enjoy the fire?" he said with a relieved smile.

"I'd like to help."

"I think I have everything under control. But I'm not doing anything as exotic as the meal you made. Just meat loaf and mashed potatoes. I hope that's okay."

"I eat normal food, too," she teased. "If you have some fresh vegetables, I could make a stir-fry. And I could probably put together a salad if you have some lettuce."

He nodded toward the refrigerator. "Help yourself to anything you can find."

A.J. peered into the refrigerator and rummaged around a bit. "There's plenty of stuff here for both," she said, her voice slightly muffled. She began withdrawing items and set them on the counter beside Blake. "Where are your spices?"

He reached past her and pulled open a cabinet, his rolled-up sleeve brushing her face. She couldn't help but notice the sprinkling of dark hair on his forearm. Or the subtle masculine scent that invaded her nostrils. Her pulse suddenly tripped into double time, and she drew a sharp breath.

Blake looked at her. "Are you okay?"

She forced herself to nod, but that was a lie. She

hadn't had such a visceral reaction to a man since Eric. And she'd forgotten how to deal with it. So she focused her attention on the spice rack. "Do you have a paring knife?" she asked when she could finally speak.

He rinsed off the one he'd been using and handed it to her. "Ask and you shall receive."

She smiled. "Don't tell me you're quoting the Bible!"

He shrugged. "I have a passing acquaintance with some of the more common scripture passages. One of my college roommates was a pretty devout Christian, so I learned a few things from him. He even dragged me to services a few times."

"I take it you weren't impressed."

"Not enough to go on my own."

"Hmm. I guess it's different if you aren't raised in a Christian environment. My faith has always been so much a part of my life…it's gotten me through some tough times."

"Such as?"

A.J.'s hand stilled for a moment. "Well, the deaths of my parents, for starters," she said quietly. "My dad died of a heart attack when I was eleven. My mom died four years ago. Even though I still miss them terribly, it's a great comfort to know that they're in a better place. My sorrow when they died was for me, not them."

"But how do you reconcile a good and loving God with what you witnessed in Afghanistan? The hardship and deprivation and violence and starvation?"

"I guess that's what faith is all about. It's accepting

the things we don't understand, knowing that God does. And He gave us free will. A lot of the bad things that happen in the world are because people make wrong choices, and then innocent people suffer. That's not His choice. It's ours."

"What about natural disasters, like floods and earthquakes? Those aren't caused by human choices, and thousands of innocent people are hurt."

"I don't know the answer to that, Blake. Only God does. And I wouldn't presume to try and understand the mind of God. It's far beyond our human capacity. It all comes down again to faith. But you only have to read the salvation story to know how deeply God cares for all of us. He gave us His own son. And He suffered, too, while in human form. Suffering is part of life."

Blake slid the meat loaf into the oven. "That's probably the best explanation I've ever heard to those questions," he said, turning to face her.

She shook her head. "Then you haven't been talking to the right people. I can't give you a lot of theology. I can only tell you what's in my heart. But if you're ever interested in learning more, the minister at my new church is wonderful. I'd be happy to introduce you."

"I'll keep that in mind. Shall we sit by the fire while the meat loaf cooks?"

"Sure."

"Go ahead, and I'll join you in a minute."

A.J. made her way into the living room. The decor was conservative, but comfortable, which didn't surprise her. The only unexpected thing in the room was a crudely carved folk-art statue on the coffee table. It was of a small boy, running exuberantly, his hands joyously stretched toward the sky. The child's expression reflected absolute contentment and happiness, and perfectly captured what childhood should be all about. A.J. recognized it immediately. It was from the Good Samaritan collection at the shop. She knew it had sold, but she didn't know who had bought it. She wondered if Blake saw, in the carving, all that he'd missed in his own childhood.

When he joined her a moment later, he was carrying two crystal goblets of sparkling cider.

"Fancy," she said. "Looks like a special occasion."

"Maybe it is."

She glanced into his warm, caring eyes, and suddenly found it difficult to swallow. Tonight had been special in many ways. She'd learned a great deal about the man across from her. She'd recognized that at some point she'd have to deal with the questions he'd raised about her unwillingness to rely on other people. She'd realized that the romantic part of her heart hadn't died with Eric, after all. And she was now facing a whole evening alone with the man who had reawakened those feelings in her. Feelings she wasn't yet ready to face. Not with any man. And certainly not with this man.

But as she gazed at him, she was forced to acknowledge that, ready or not, she would have to deal with those feelings soon.

And as Blake handed her a glass, then sat beside her, she realized that the storm raging outside couldn't hold a candle to the storm that was suddenly raging in her heart.

Chapter Eight

"That was a wonderful meal, Blake." A.J. dipped a tea bag in a cup of hot water as she spoke. "How did you learn to make such great meat loaf?"

"After I'd been working a couple of years, I got pretty tired of fast food and frozen dinners. So I bought a beginners' cookbook, and I actually learned a lot. Nothing to compare with that couscous dish you made, though."

She shrugged his compliment aside. "It's not hard. The people in Afghanistan have learned to prepare simple meals with inexpensive ingredients. It's the spices that make the difference. The dish I served your parents is one of my favorites."

"I can see why. Shall we go back in by the fire?"

"Sure." A.J. stood and moved toward the living room, pausing to gaze out the window as she cradled her mug in her hands. "It still looks terrible out."

She felt Blake come up behind her to look over her shoulder. His breath was warm on her ear, and her own breathing seemed to speed up. She half expected him to put his hands on her shoulders. It would somehow have seemed natural. But he didn't.

"I doubt this is going to stop anytime soon. It's a good thing we didn't try to make it to your place."

She felt him move away, and when her breathing was more or less under control, she turned and made her way back toward the fire. Blake was sitting on the couch, one arm casually draped across the back, an ankle crossed over a knee. He was sipping a cup of coffee, and looked completely relaxed. And oblivious to her unexpected reaction to his nearness. She considered sitting in the chair next to the fire instead of joining him on the couch, figuring that if she put a little distance between them her nerves might settle down. But she also figured that might raise questions. After all, her reaction appeared to be entirely one-sided. Blake had been nothing more than friendly all evening. Even the earlier embrace that had played havoc with her emotions seemed to have left him completely unaffected. It was her own reactions she had to worry about. Not his.

She sat beside him, careful to keep a respectable distance between them, but not so much that it would seem odd.

"How's the tea?" he asked.

"Comforting. Especially on a cold night."

"My mother always liked tea."

"How are your parents doing?"

"Fine, I guess."

"I take it communication is sporadic, at best."

"Yeah."

"That's too bad, Blake."

He shrugged. "That's how it's always been since I left home."

"You could change that."

"Meaning you think I should?"

She lifted one shoulder in response. "You have to make that decision for yourself. I'm just suggesting that I think they'd be receptive."

As usual, A.J.'s instincts were accurate. Blake knew his parents would welcome a reconciliation. They'd made overtures through the years, which he had ignored. The ball was in his court. And lately, he'd been toying with the notion of initiating some contact. He just wasn't sure how to begin after all these years.

"It's not that easy to start over," he said quietly, studying his coffee.

She was silent for so long that he finally looked over at her. She was gazing into the fire, and there was such raw pain in her eyes that his throat constricted with tenderness.

"What are you thinking?" he asked, his voice a shade deeper than usual.

With an effort, she pulled her gaze from the flames and looked at him. "I was thinking about what you said. I agree. Starting over is never easy. But it can be done."

He took a sip of his coffee. His impulse was to reach out and take her hand again. But he'd done enough of that for one night. He was about to ask some pretty personal questions, and he didn't want to scare her off.

"You sound like you've had experience at that," he said carefully.

She turned away, and he saw her swallow convulsively. For a moment he thought she wasn't going to answer. But finally she spoke, her voice so low it was almost a whisper. "Yeah."

He waited a beat. "Is it something you want to talk about?"

A.J. drew an unsteady breath, then turned back to him. There was nothing but kindness and compassion in his eyes. He wasn't pushing her to confide, but it was clear that he was willing to offer a sympathetic ear. She didn't share her trauma with many people. It was part of her philosophy of putting the past behind her and making the most of today. But for some reason, she wanted to tell this man her story.

"I haven't told a lot of people," she ventured, her voice tentative.

"I'm a good listener. And you certainly have a captive audience tonight," he said, flashing her an encouraging smile.

A.J. took a deep breath. Blake had shared with her some of his issues with his parents. It seemed only right that she share some of her past with him. And he seemed genuinely interested. "Did Aunt Jo ever tell you much about me?"

"No. Family was a painful subject for me. She mentioned her great-nieces a few times, but to be honest, I never encouraged her to talk about you or your sisters."

"That's what I thought. If you'd known about the

accident, you probably would have put two and two together and figured out why I sometimes limp."

He set his mug on the table and angled his body toward her. "So the accident has nothing to do with Afghanistan?"

"Only indirectly. It was one of the reasons I decided to go." She tightened her grip on her mug and stared into the fire. "It's so hard to know where to start."

"The beginning is always a good place."

She tried to smile, but couldn't quite pull it off. "We could be here all night."

"I'm not planning to go far, anyway."

"Okay. Then I'll give you the condensed version of the A. J. Williams life story."

"Start with the A.J."

She frowned at him. "What do you mean?"

"What do the initials stand for?"

"Oh." She made a face. "Abigail Jeanette."

"Pretty."

"Not for a tomboy. Abigail Jeanette is such an old-fashioned, ladylike name. I was always tall and lanky and athletic. It didn't fit. So I shortened it to A.J. early on."

Blake didn't agree with A.J.'s assessment of her feminine charms, but he let her comment pass for the moment.

"Anyway, thanks to my mom and dad, I was totally comfortable with who I was. They always encouraged me to do my best, and I did. I excelled at basketball and soccer, and I also did well academically. Frankly, I intimidated a lot of the guys in high school because I could compete with them pretty much on their own terms and often come out the winner. Which was okay, because they respected me and considered me one of the guys. But on the other hand, when it came to dating, I wasn't even a contender. Besides, I was taller than a lot of them. So they just didn't think of me in those terms.

"Because of that, I didn't date in high school. Since I couldn't do anything about my height, and I wasn't about to play the coy, incompetent, demure type just to get men interested in me, I figured dates in the future would be few and far between, too. Not many guys have egos strong enough to handle an extremely independent woman.

"So I focused on preparing for a career that would provide a comfortable living. Since I'd always been good with numbers, I majored in business and then got into an M.B.A. program. That's where I met Eric. He was in his last year when I started."

A.J. paused to swallow painfully, and Blake leaned closer. He'd never heard her mention that name before. But the man had obviously been important to her. He found himself wondering who Eric was, and if he'd hurt her.

"We dated for a year and a half, while I was working on my M.B.A.," A.J. continued. "And when he asked me to marry him, I thought I could never be any happier. We decided to go on a ski trip with a church group over spring break to celebrate. We had a great time, and we made some wonderful plans for our future. I'll remember that trip as long as I live."

A.J. paused, and Blake saw her swallow. He knew she was getting to the traumatic part of the story, and he wanted to reach out to her. But he held back, knowing she was not yet ready for his comfort. When she spoke again, her voice was flat and lifeless.

"The…the accident happened on the way back. A couple of hours after we left the resort. I remember that it was quiet on the bus. We were all tired, and a lot of people were drifting off to sleep. I had my head on Eric's shoulder, and I had this wonderful feeling of deep contentment and happiness. It was pitch-dark outside the windows of the bus, and huge snowflakes were beating against the glass. But I felt insulated from the storm—warm and protected and safe."

She drew a ragged breath and reached up with shaking fingers to brush a stray wisp of hair off her forehead. Her gaze was fixed on the fire, but it was clear that she was seeing something else entirely, something far away and long ago.

"M-my memories after that are sketchy. I heard the brakes slam. And there was a sudden jarring, like the bus was trying to stop. There was an odd sideways motion. And then…the world tilted. People screamed. I grabbed onto Eric, and he reached for me. W-we looked at each other, and I remember the fear and… and the panic in his eyes. And then e-everything went black."

A single tear slid down her cheek, and a sob caught in her throat. "I f-found out later that our bus slid off the road. We went over an embankment. A lot of people were killed…including Eric."

Blake sucked in a sharp breath, and she turned to him. Her eyes were dull with pain, her voice mechanical now, almost clinical. "I survived, but my hip was crushed. It took three operations to restore a semblance of normalcy and two long years of therapy before I could walk properly. During that time I reevaluated my career plans. I'd lost interest in the business world. It just seemed so meaningless. I felt a need to do something more important with my life. That's when I discovered Good Samaritan. You know the rest."

Blake stared at the woman beside him, his face a mask of shock. So many things made sense now. Her independent spirit, forged from hardship. Her limp, not only a permanent physical impairment but a constant reminder of the tragedy that had stolen her fiancé and turned her world upside down. Her fear of driving in snow. And perhaps her vagabond lifestyle. Jo had hinted as much in her letter to him. Had suggested that even A.J. didn't fully understand why she'd never put down roots since the accident. But suddenly Blake did. If you'd made plans and prepared for a certain kind of life, only to have it snatched away, who wouldn't be afraid to make those kinds of plans, those commitments, again? Many people wouldn't survive the kind of loss A.J. had suffered even one time; twice would be unthinkable. In her mind, it probably wasn't worth the risk.

Another tear slid silently down A.J.'s cheek, and Blake's gut clenched painfully. Gently he reached over and pried the mug out of her fingers. They were ice cold, as was her tea. He set the mug on the coffee table and then turned back to her. She looked fragile. And haunted. And so alone.

He'd refrained from touching her before. He didn't now. Without stopping to consider the consequences, he closed the distance between them and pulled her into his arms, cradling her slender body against his solid chest. He could feel the rapid thudding of her heart, could hear her uneven breathing. For a moment she went rigid, and he was afraid she'd pull back. But then she relaxed against him, and he heard a stifled sob as she buried her face in his neck.

"It's okay, A.J. I'm here. Just hold on to me," he said unevenly, his voice tattered at the edges. He felt the tremors run through her, felt the evidence of her silent tears in the erratic rise and fall of her chest. And as he stroked her back, it suddenly occurred to him that in light of all she'd been through—the pain and suffering and loss—his own childhood trauma seemed petty. If she could rebuild her life out of the ashes, surely he could find a way to reconnect with his parents. To put the ghosts of his childhood to rest once and for all.

He held her for a long time, and gradually he felt her sobs subside. But she didn't move out of his arms immediately. And he was in no hurry to let her go.

Finally, though, she drew a deep breath and pushed back. When she looked at him, her face was flushed and she seemed embarrassed. "Sorry about that."

"About sharing your story?"

"No. Sorry I fell apart."

"You're entitled."

She sniffled, and he reached into his pocket and held out a handkerchief. "I always have a spare," he told her when she hesitated.

A ghost of a smile flickered across her face. "You would."

"Is that an insult?"

"No. I'm beginning to appreciate your ability to always be prepared." And other qualities as well, she acknowledged silently.

He reached over and traced the course of a tear down her cheek. She went absolutely still at his touch. "A.J., I'm so sorry."

He didn't need to say any more. She could see the depth of compassion in his eyes. "Thanks. It w-was a really hard time."

"How did you make it through?"

"My mom was still alive then, and she was incredibly supportive. So were my sisters. That's why I think it's so important to make sure family ties are strong. My faith helped sustain me, too. Those were the reasons I survived."

"I think there might have been a dash of fortitude and determination thrown in, too. Not to mention discipline and strength."

She shrugged. "Those things alone wouldn't have gotten me through without my family and my faith."

Suddenly she yawned, and Blake glanced at his watch. "It's getting late. And you've had a long and emotionally draining day. Why don't you make it an early night?"

"I want to help with the dishes first."

"Not tonight."

"But it's not fair to…"

"Not tonight," he interrupted, this time more firmly. "I know you're used to doing things for yourself. After hearing your story, I understand why that's so important to you. I also understand something else." He paused, and his gaze held hers. When he spoke again, his voice was gentle. "Did it ever occur to you that maybe one of the reasons you don't like to let people help you is because you don't want to begin to rely on someone again who might not be around tomorrow? That maybe you're afraid to make plans for a future that might not come to pass?"

She stared at him, momentarily speechless. Was she afraid? Not only of letting people help, but of settling down, putting down roots, making plans? But fear wouldn't be consistent with her faith. She believed in relying on God, of putting her trust in Him. So she couldn't be afraid. That had nothing to do with being independent, of taking care of herself. And as for not making plans or putting down roots, well, that was easily explained. She simply didn't want to be tied down by material things or commitments that could make her less open and available to God's call.

Those explanations had always worked for her before. Yet forced to examine her motivations under Blake's discerning eye, they suddenly didn't seem to ring quite true. But she didn't want to deal with that tonight. So she ignored his questions.

"Okay. I'll go to bed." Eager to escape both the man

and the doubts he'd raised, she stood abruptly. Too abruptly. Because she momentarily lost her balance.

Blake was on his feet instantly, his grip firm and sure on her arms, steadying her. What A.J. saw in his eyes made her heart stop, then race on. Concern. Compassion. Respect. And something more. Something powerful and compelling. Something she wasn't yet ready to deal with. She needed to put some distance between them. Quickly. But she seemed unable to move.

Blake stared at the woman who was mere inches away, their eyes almost level. Her story had resonated deeply with him, touched a place in his heart that had never been touched before. He'd known A.J. was a good person with a kind heart. He'd learned, over time, that she was smart and savvy and had great instincts. He'd also known she was strong. But until tonight, he hadn't known just how strong.

In the past, he'd used the word interesting to describe her. That term still fit. But so did intriguing. And absorbing. And exciting. Not to mention appealing. Very appealing. Too appealing.

Blake had been attracted to other women. More than a few, in fact. Something about each of them had caught his fancy, made his pulse accelerate. The difference with A.J. was that *everything* about her was beginning to make his pulse race. He liked her spunk. He liked her spirit. He liked her kindness and compassion and intellect. He liked that she challenged him to think differently, to take some risks, to reevaluate long-held opinions. She kept him on his toes. She made him smile. On top of everything else, she was beautiful. And he was having a harder and harder time imagining his life without her.

That scared him. But not enough to suppress the yearning that sprang to life as he stared into her eyes. Only the faint crackle of the fire broke the stillness in the room, and he felt a warmth that didn't come from the dying embers in the fireplace a few feet away. Suddenly he longed to run his fingers through her soft hair. To hold her close, so close that she forgot the past and the future and became lost in the moment.

But this wasn't the time. She was too vulnerable. And things could get out of hand. He already had enough regrets in his life. He didn't want to add one more.

With a supreme effort, he released her arms, stepped back and shoved his fists into his pockets. "Sleep well," he said huskily. "I'll lock the door behind me when I go next door."

Her only response was a jerky nod. And then she fled.

Blake watched her go. And when he reached for their mugs a moment later, he discovered that his own hands were trembling.

He stared at them and frowned. There could be a number of explanations for his reaction. But in his heart, he knew that fear was the primary culprit. Because Jack's words in Colorado now seemed prophetic. Maybe he *was* a goner. Which was not good. Because despite all her good qualities, logic told him that A.J. wasn't his type at all.

But his heart wasn't listening.

* * *

The fragrant aroma of freshly brewed coffee greeted Blake when he stepped inside the front door of his house the next morning, and he made a beeline for the kitchen. Obviously A.J. was up already. He certainly hoped she'd slept better than he had. By the time he'd finally drifted off, after tossing and turning for hours on his neighbor's uncomfortable couch, it had been close to three o'clock in the morning. Right now he needed a shot of caffeine.

He saw she wasn't in the kitchen, so Blake poured himself a cup of strong, black coffee and headed for the bathroom to shower. Normally he slept in on Sunday, then ran or biked for a couple of hours, followed by a swim at the nearby gym. However, given the storm, he doubted he'd be going anywhere today. Except to take A.J. back to the shop to get her car. And he was in no hurry to do that. He was looking forward to a leisurely morning with his unexpected house-guest.

When he emerged from the bathroom a few minutes later, he sniffed appreciatively and followed his nose to the kitchen. A.J. was at the stove now, intent on turning what appeared to be a fluffy omelet, her lower lip caught in her teeth, a slight frown marring her brow. Her focus was absolute, her concentration intense. Blake's gaze flickered to the table. Two places were set—a first for him at breakfast. He was used to grabbing an energy bar or stopping to pick up a bagel somewhere. He definitely preferred this.

He waited until she'd successfully flipped the omelet before he spoke, in a voice that was still slightly roughened by sleep. "Good morning."

She turned abruptly, then felt her face grow warm. She'd never seen Blake in such casual attire. Worn jeans outlined his muscular legs, and a T-shirt hugged his broad chest and revealed impressive biceps. His damp hair was slicked back, and as he stood there, one shoulder propped against the door frame, his hands in his pockets, her pulse began to race. She'd struggled late into the night trying to get her emotions under control. And thought she'd succeeded. But one look at Blake disproved that theory.

She turned back to the stove and made a pretense of checking the omelet. "Yes, it is. The road crews have been through, and the sun is shining. We're no longer marooned," she said brightly.

Blake didn't think that was particularly good news, but he'd come to the same conclusion himself as he walked home from his neighbor's house. Driving would be manageable today, except on secondary roads.

"Breakfast is ready," A.J. said over her shoulder.

He waited until she'd deposited their plates on the table, then held her chair for her. When she looked surprised, he gave her an endearing grin. "Mr. Conventional. Sorry," he said.

She smiled. "You don't have to apologize. A lot of conventions are nice."

"This looks great, A.J. You didn't have to go to all this trouble." He helped himself to some toast.

"It wasn't any trouble. I don't bother much with

breakfast during the week, but I try to do something a little nicer on Sundays. I usually eat it alone, though, so I have to admit the conversation is much better today."

He chuckled, a pleasing sound that rumbled deep in his chest. "So what else do you do on Sundays?"

"Go to church." She glanced regretfully at her watch. "But I don't see how I can make it today. The last service is at ten. By the time you drop me at the shop to pick up my car, timing will be pretty tight."

"Would you like me to take you?"

A.J.'s hand froze, her fork halfway to her mouth, astonishment written on her face. But she didn't look any more surprised than he felt. Where in the world had that come from? He hadn't been inside a church in years.

"You mean drop me off? Or stay?" she asked cautiously.

She'd given him an out. He could just leave her at the door and come back for her later. But for some reason, he hated this interlude with A.J. to end. If going to church would buy him another hour or two with her, it would be worth the sacrifice. Besides, he still needed to sort through his feelings about his houseguest, and maybe a visit to church would help him do that. Churches were supposed to be good places to think, weren't they?

"I could stay."

A.J. stared at him. "Why?"

He felt his neck grow warm. "Why not?"

"I don't know. It's just that...well, you told me you didn't really practice any religion. I'm just...surprised.

But of course, you're welcome to come with me. Our minister is great. You might even enjoy it."

He doubted that. But he had to admit he was a little intrigued. First his parents had told him they were attending church. They were the two most unlikely candidates he could think of to practice organized religion. Yet when they'd spoken about it briefly during dinner at A.J.'s, he'd seen a look in their eyes that told him they'd found something special. And there was no question that A.J.'s faith was the foundation of her life. It had seen her through some tough times, given her stability and security when everything else in her world had fallen apart.

If Christianity was powerful enough to win over his parents, and to sustain A.J. through all of her trials and tribulations, maybe it was worth exploring.

Brad Matthews was a great speaker. No question about it.

Blake hadn't really planned to listen to the sermon during the service. He'd figured that would be a good time to mull over the situation with A.J. But the minister at her church had grabbed him with his opening line and never let him go. The man spoke in simple, but compelling, terms. And oddly enough, his message seemed to be directed at Blake. He'd used the story of the prodigal son as the basis for his sermon, and talked about the difficulties—and importance—of reconciliation. And his concluding words really struck home.

"As we leave this place of worship and return to our daily lives, it's easy to leave the Lord's message behind, too. But that's not what He wants us to do. He wants us to take His words and apply them to our lives. To live the words He spoke, not just read them on Sunday.

"The story of the prodigal son is about a young man who made mistakes. Who left his family behind, cut off all contact, and isolated himself from the people who loved him the most. Yet his father welcomed him back. The parallel between this story and our relationship with God is obvious. But there are lessons we can apply in our own human relationships as well. It doesn't matter who the wronged party is. It doesn't matter who left and who stayed behind. It doesn't matter if it's a parent, a spouse, a child or a friend who is estranged. All that matters is that someone take the first step to mend the rift. And that the other person be receptive.

"If there are relationships in your life that need mending, remember the lessons of the prodigal son. It requires courage to take the first step, to initiate a reconciliation. Because it usually means we have to admit we've been wrong. Or that we have to forgive someone. Pride is a fault we all share, and it often gets in the way of reconciliation, whether we're the wronged party or the one who did wrong. On our own, we may not be able to overcome the hurdles that stand in the way of mending fences with those we love. But God can help. Call on Him. He's waiting for you. And with Him by your side, all things are possible.

"Now, let us pray…"

The congregation rose, and Blake followed suit. As

he did so, he saw Nancy and Eileen a few rows away. His gaze connected with Nancy's as she turned to say something to her daughter, and the look of surprise on her face was almost comical. Her mouth actually dropped open. Blake nodded, but even after he looked back to the minister, he knew she was still staring at him.

He couldn't blame her. She'd tried a number of times to convince him to attend services with her. He'd always adamantly refused. So he knew he'd have some explaining to do tomorrow.

Of course, his presence at church would be easy enough to justify in light of the snowstorm. He could just say that A.J. seemed disturbed about missing the service, and he'd volunteered to take her. Nancy would probably buy that.

But it would be harder to explain if he came again.

And that's exactly what he was thinking about doing.

Strange. His attendance today had been prompted by a desire to spend more time with A.J. But that wasn't why he was considering returning. It was more fundamental than that.

The fact was, for some odd reason, sitting in the church today, listening to the music and hearing the word of God spoken and discussed, he felt almost as if he'd come home. And for the first time in a long while, he'd felt at peace.

Blake didn't understand why he'd experienced those feelings. But he wanted to.

And he figured this was the place to find the answers.

Chapter Nine

The bell jangled over the front door of the bookshop, and A.J. and Blake simultaneously looked up. George was bearing down on them, still wearing his white apron. And he looked upset. A.J. glanced at Blake, then turned toward the older man.

"What's wrong, George?" she asked.

"I hear something today that is not good," he said, huffing as he tried to catch his breath.

"Let's go in the back," Blake suggested. He signaled to Nancy, and she relieved them at the front desk.

George followed them, and Blake waved him to a chair. "What's up?"

George wiped his hands nervously on his apron. "I hear a patron talking about MacKenzie and the development. So I stayed close by and listened. He said that the city is going to use the TIF after all."

Blake frowned. "Do you know who this man is, George?"

"No. I never see him before. But he had on what you call a…power suit. Expensive. He sounded like he knew what he was talking about."

A.J. gave Blake a worried look. "What do you think?"

"I think I better talk to my neighbor and see what I can find out."

"You will do that soon?" George asked.

"Tonight."

"And you will let us know what you find?"

"Of course. Let's not panic until we get some solid information. Maybe the man you heard was just speculating and nothing has actually happened."

But later that night, after talking with his neighbor, Blake found out otherwise. Apparently the city had been swayed by dollar signs after all and was preparing to side with MacKenzie. Blake punched in A.J.'s number and waited impatiently for her to pick up. When she did, he dispensed with the formalities and got right to the heart of the issue.

"A.J.? Blake. Looks like what George overheard is correct. My neighbor tells me that the board is prepared to proceed with TIF and give MacKenzie the green light to develop."

"Oh, Blake! We can't let that happen!"

He heard the dismay in her voice. "I'm not sure we can do much more," he said, his own voice tinged with discouragement.

"Well, at least we can have another meeting to discuss options. I'll call everyone tonight and see if we can get together tomorrow after we close. Aunt Jo wouldn't want us to give up without doing everything we can. And I feel the same way."

So did Blake. But he was beginning to think it was a lost cause.

"But how can they do that? Everyone was on our side!"

Somehow Blake had found himself up front with A.J. at the meeting, and he turned to respond to Rose. "Unfortunately, it's not being put to a vote. The alderman for this ward supports our cause, but the others apparently don't."

"I think it's time to call my nephew at the TV station," Joe said emphatically.

A.J. recalled the advice Blake's parents had given them at dinner. "But they won't come unless there's an event of some kind to cover."

"Then we make an event!" George declared.

"I think we should organize a protest," Alene said.

A.J. glanced at Blake. His jaw had tightened, and he was frowning. Which didn't surprise her. This had to be like a flashback from his parents' hippie days. The days he had hated.

"That's a good idea," Steve chimed in. "I know we could get a lot of the area residents to join us."

"The sooner the better," Carlos added.

"So, is everyone agreed on this course of action?" A.J. asked. Everyone nodded except Blake. "Okay, it looks like we have a consensus. Let's try to set this up for next Saturday. Can we pull it off that fast?"

"I think we have to," Rose said.

"Then Saturday it is. Now let's work out the details and the assignments."

By the time the meeting broke up half an hour later, they had a solid plan of action in place. As everyone filed out and A.J. locked the door, she turned around to find Blake watching her, a troubled expression on his face. Slowly she walked toward him. "I'm sorry, Blake. I know this isn't your thing."

He raked his fingers through his hair and shook his head. "I'm not sure I can do this, A.J. I want to save Turning Leaves as much as you do, but this… it's just not me."

"I know."

He shoved his fists into his pockets and gave a frustrated sigh. "I want to support what the group is doing. But the idea of marching around with a sign and having a TV news camera shoved in my face…I just don't know."

A.J. moved behind the desk and perched on the stool. She rested her elbows on the counter and propped her chin in her hands. Her eyes were sympathetic when she spoke. "You have to do what's right for you, Blake."

He looked at her. "Do you want to do this?"

"Not particularly. But this will certainly get the board's attention. I don't see any other way to convince them."

"I don't, either."

"You shouldn't do this if you don't want to."

"Jo would have."

"I know. But she didn't have your issues."

Blake studied A.J. for a moment. "How will you feel if I don't go?"

She was surprised by the question. "Does that matter?"

Like it or not, Blake realized he cared what A.J. thought. And he didn't want to disappoint her. "Yeah, it does."

A.J. considered the question. "I'll understand," she said finally.

"The others won't."

She shrugged. "We're all products of our past, Blake. So we shouldn't be too quick to judge what others do, or their motivations. You've worked hard on this cause, and you already left your comfort zone once—when you took my place at the meeting. Maybe that's enough."

As A.J. stood and began to turn out the lights in the shop, Blake considered her comment. Maybe she was right. Maybe he had done enough.

But deep in his heart, he didn't think that was true. Because this was the real test of his convictions. If you believed in something strongly enough, you had to take a stand. No matter the cost.

Just like A.J. had done on her trip to Washington.

The turnout on Saturday was better than anyone predicted, aided by remarkably fine weather for late March. Several hundred people milled about in front of city hall, and dozens carried signs protesting the new development.

Including Blake.

He'd spent several restless nights debating whether to participate. But in the end, he couldn't sit this one out. He'd poured the last three years of his life into Turning Leaves. The other merchants had invested many more in their businesses. Jo had believed in this area, and had worked hard to preserve its unique character and integrity. Now A.J. had taken on her cause. He had to do his part.

And oddly enough, it wasn't so bad. A number of people recognized him from the board meeting and had stopped to compliment him and offer their support. Even the presence of the news media didn't bother him. He let the other merchants do the talking on camera, but he really didn't care if his face was on the five o'clock news. Because he felt part of something important. Something bigger than himself. Something that linked all of these diverse people in a joint purpose. And it was a heartwarming feeling, one he'd never before experienced. He still had no confidence that city hall would ultimately put civic integrity above hard cash. But at least they would be able to say they'd tried their best to do the right thing. And that felt good.

"How are you holding up?"

Blake turned at A.J.'s voice, and his lips tipped into a wry smile. "My parents would be proud."

Her answering smile warmed his heart. As did the expression in her eyes, which spoke of admiration and respect. And something more, something indefinable, that made his throat go dry. "I'm sure they would," she replied softly, her voice slightly uneven. "And so am I."

She was pulled away then by a reporter, but as

Blake watched her go, he suddenly felt more alive than he had in a very long time.

The atmosphere was festive that night, almost boisterous, as the merchants gathered in the bar at George's restaurant to watch the evening news together. But silence fell when the announcer introduced their story.

The camera panned the area in front of city hall, taking in the impressive crowd. A voice-over gave the background on the development proposal, and then a number of residents and merchants spoke on camera. There was an interview with Stuart MacKenzie, followed by one with the mayor, who assured the reporter that the voices of the protesters had been heard and that the board members would take their concerns under advisement when a final decision was made.

As the anchorman moved on to the next story, George turned down the volume and looked at A.J. "So what do you think?"

"I think we did everything we could. It was a positive story for us."

"So what do we do now?" Rose asked.

For some reason, everyone looked at Blake. Maybe because he had the closest connection to city hall. He wished he could offer them more, but he could only repeat what he'd told A.J. when she'd asked that question much earlier in the process.

"We wait."

Waiting wasn't easy, however. Almost every day the merchants checked in with one another, and Blake kept in close touch with his neighbor. But one week, then two, then three passed, and still there was no decision.

In the meantime, A.J. began to realize that she and Blake were becoming a couple. She wasn't exactly sure how that had happened. She supposed it had started when he began to regularly attend church services with her, after the blizzard. That had become a Sunday ritual, followed by breakfast together. Then she had started inviting him to dinner on a regular basis. He began bringing in lunch for them at the shop. They attended several movies together that they both wanted to see. He claimed it helped them relax as they waited for the verdict from the board.

It was always Dutch treat, so it wasn't exactly dating. And there was no romance involved. But an attraction simmered just below the surface. She was aware of it. And she was sure he was, too. One day soon they'd have to deal with it. But neither seemed ready to take that step.

Though they were especially careful at the shop to keep things purely professional, Nancy was too sharp to miss the change in their relationship.

"Things seem a little…friendlier…between you and Blake lately," she ventured one day in mid-April when she and A.J. were shelving some new arrivals.

A.J. reached for another stack of books, using the maneuver to hide her suddenly flushed face. "Well, we're very different. I suppose we're finally figuring out how to work together," she replied, striving for a matter-of-fact tone.

"That's good. Where is he, by the way? He's been gone an awfully long time."

A.J. glanced at her watch and frowned. "I don't know. He said he was just going to grab a sandwich at the deli. Maybe he decided to eat at one of the tables in front." She gazed wistfully out the window. "I certainly would have. It's such a gorgeous day. Too gorgeous to waste inside."

"My sentiments exactly."

The women turned toward the back room. Blake was standing in the doorway with a wicker picnic hamper in his hand.

"What's that for?" Nancy asked.

"What do you think it's for?" He was grinning.

"Where did you get it?"

"Rose came to my rescue again."

A.J. stared at him. "You're going on a picnic?"

"Yes."

"But...aren't you scheduled to work this afternoon?"

"Nancy's here. And I called Trish. She's off from school today and can be here in half an hour. As you just said, this is much too nice a day to waste inside. The dogwoods are blooming, and the spring flowers are out in full force. I thought I'd head over to Tilles Park. Sit by the lake. Feed the ducks. Enjoy the sun."

Now it was Nancy's turn to stare. "Since when have you started noticing the beauty of nature? And skipping out on work?"

He shrugged. "I thought I'd give this spontaneous thing a shot." He turned to A.J. and gave her an engaging grin. "Want to join me?"

She continued to stare. She'd never seen him like this. "But...but I'm not sure we should just leave the shop..."

"Loosen up, A.J. The world won't end if we take the afternoon off. Nancy can handle things. Right, Nancy?"

The woman looked from Blake to A.J., then back again, clearly bewildered. "Sure."

"See? So what do you say?"

A.J. knew a stack of invoices in the back needed processing. She was also supposed to change the window display this afternoon. And she had a new shipment of merchandise from Good Samaritan to unpack. There was way too much to do today to take the afternoon off. She hesitated, torn between her responsibilities at the shop and the appeal of Blake's invitation.

"Come on, A.J. Seize the moment." Blake's eyes were twinkling, and he winked at her.

The irony of his remark wasn't lost on her. It sounded like one of the lines she'd used on him when she'd first arrived. A wry smile tugged at the corners of her mouth. "I may regret this when I have to work till midnight tomorrow, but…okay."

"Terrific!" He reached for her hand and pulled her toward the back, talking to Nancy over his shoulder as A.J. grabbed her sweater. "I'm getting her out of here before she changes her mind. You've got my cell phone number if there's an emergency, right?"

"Don't worry about a thing. Just have fun."

Once they were in the car, A.J. turned to Blake. "So what's this all about?"

"What do you mean?"

"You've never done anything like this before."

"Are you complaining?"

"No. But it just seems a little…out of character."

He shrugged. "Maybe I'm changing."

She thought about that for a moment. "Well, don't change too much."

"You mean you liked that uptight, stuffy, inflexible, conventional guy you first met?"

She flushed. "I never said you were like that."

"You didn't have to. That's what you thought. And you were right. I did need to loosen up. To be more open to change. More spontaneous. So how am I doing?"

She smiled. Actually, Blake had been slowly changing over the past few months. He was starting to let go of the tight control he'd always exercised over his life. To go with the flow a bit more. His involvement with the MacKenzie situation was a great example. He'd left his comfort zone, taken a chance, and found out it wasn't so bad after all. She was happy for him. The changes he was making would surely enhance his life.

"You're doing great. But don't lose all your good qualities along the way, too, okay?"

"Such as?"

"Well, let's see." She ticked them off on her fingers. "You're dependable. Kind. Hardworking. Practical. Thoughtful. Smart."

"You forgot good-looking," he teased.

"Let's not get carried away," she replied with a grin.

"Ouch! You sure know how to hurt a guy." He turned into the park, made the loop to the lake and pulled into a parking space. "I just discovered this park. Rose told me about it a few days ago, so I checked it out. I can't believe I've lived here for three years and never even knew this place existed. But then, there were a lot of things I never noticed."

A.J. stepped out of the car and looked at the lake. A pavilion stood off to one side, and there was a large deck that went right up to the water. Built-in benches and picnic tables were scattered around the planked surface. "Well, I'm glad you noticed this," she said, smiling appreciatively at the peaceful, quiet scene.

"Yeah, and it's all ours today," he said, nodding toward the deserted pavilion.

Once again he reached for her hand, as he had at the shop. A.J. didn't protest. She liked the way his strong fingers held hers firmly, protectively.

He led her to a picnic table on the deck, near the water's edge. "How does this look?"

"Perfect."

"Okay. Let's see what Rose has packed." He opened the hamper and handed A.J. a checkered cloth. "Hmm. I see she expects us to do this in style. A tablecloth, no less." As A.J. spread the cloth, he rummaged around in the hamper, then began handing her the food. "Chicken salad on croissants. Pasta salad. Fresh fruit. Cheese and crackers. Double fudge brownies. Bottled water. I'd say we have a feast here."

"Seems like it."

A.J. unwrapped her sandwich and took a bite. She

closed her eyes as she chewed, savoring the warm spring sun on her back and this stolen afternoon. "This is great!"

"So you don't mind playing hooky after all?" Blake teased, spearing a forkful of pasta salad.

"That's the trouble. I could do this every day. You're going to instill bad habits in me."

"I don't think that's possible."

"You might be surprised. You could turn me into a world-class loafer with no problem."

"Sorry. Don't buy it. There's not a lazy bone in your body."

"Mmm. I don't know. I feel pretty lazy today."

"That's probably because you need a day off."

"I'm off every Sunday. And every other Saturday."

"I mean a real vacation day."

She shrugged. "There's been a lot to learn at the shop. And things have been hopping with MacKenzie. Besides, who are you to talk? You don't take much time off. And I saw your calendar in the den when I spent the night at your house. Even on your free Saturdays you're busy." She turned to look at him. "I didn't know about the homeless shelter or Big Brothers until then. I'm impressed, Blake."

He dismissed her comment with a wave of his hand. "My paltry efforts pale in comparison to what you did in Afghanistan."

A troubled frown creased her brow. "Actually, I'm not sure I can take a lot of credit for that. Lately I've been doing a lot of soul-searching. In some ways, I think I was running away."

"You could have run to a safer, more comfortable place," he said skeptically.

"Maybe. But I wanted to go somewhere that didn't even remotely remind me of home."

"You picked a good place, then. And frankly, you had a lot to run away from."

She picked at her pasta salad with the tines of her fork. "Yeah, but running isn't the answer. Not in the long term," she said quietly, a touch of melancholy in her tone. She speared a forkful of noodles, and when she spoke again, her voice was more normal. "I'm not sorry I went to Afghanistan, though. We did some great work there. But I realize now that you don't have to go to the remote corners of the world to help others. You can do good work a lot closer to home. Like you do, with those two organizations."

"I'm just glad that another trip to Afghanistan isn't in your plans. Do you want a brownie?"

She grinned. "Are you kidding?"

He handed one over, then unwrapped his own. "By the way, I wanted to thank you for dragging me along to church that Sunday after the snowstorm."

"I don't recall dragging you. In fact, I think it was your idea."

"Well, maybe. But not for the most noble reasons." He hurried on before she could ask what he meant. "Anyway, I wanted to let you know that I took your advice and had a theological discussion with Reverend Matthews. In fact, more than one discussion."

She looked at him in surprise. "When did you do that?"

"The week after the storm. He was very approachable. And very informative."

"He's a great guy."

"Anyway, after that I called my parents."

She gave him a radiant smile. "Oh, Blake, I'm so glad! I bet they were delighted!"

He crumpled the plastic wrap from his brownie self-consciously. "Yeah, they were. We had a long talk. They want me to come and visit."

"Are you going to go?"

"Probably. I didn't commit, but I think it makes sense. It's hard to really connect by phone. We made a good start, though."

She reached over impulsively and laid her hand on his. "I'm so happy for you, Blake. And proud of you. It's not easy to forgive, to let go of resentment that goes so deep. Especially when you've felt that way for such a long time. But at least you've taken the first step. Started the healing process. The rest will be easier."

Blake looked down at A.J.'s hand resting on his, her slender fingers pale against his darker skin. Then he glanced at her face. Her earnest eyes reflected absolute happiness for him and her lips were turned up softly into a tender smile that tugged at his heart. The sun lit up the red highlights in her hair, and Blake drew an unsteady breath. He hadn't asked A.J. on this picnic for romantic reasons. At least not consciously. He'd simply wanted to get away from worries about MacKenzie for a few hours, and to share the beautiful day with her—as well as the news of the first steps he'd taken with his faith and with his parents. But now he realized that without her, he wouldn't even have appreciated the beauty of this day. Or considered going to church. Or initiated contact with his parents. Or found himself on a picket line. Or planned an impromptu picnic.

After meeting A.J., Blake had quickly realized that she was going to make changes. In the shop, and in his life. He'd resisted those changes every step of the way. Had feared them. But now he realized that the changes she'd made breathed new life into his mind—and his heart. And he also realized something else.

He was a goner.

His gaze returned to her face. Her smile had faded, and there was uncertainty in her eyes as she sensed the shift in his mood. He also saw fear. Which he understood. Giving your heart to someone special, then losing that person, would breed fear. And he was afraid, too. Of trusting. Of putting his welfare in someone else's hands. Perhaps that was why he'd never married. Why he'd never even gotten serious about any of the women he'd dated.

Until now.

Blake stared at A.J., a woman he had once considered the most unlikely possible candidate for a wife. Just a few months ago he had wanted to wring her neck. When had his feelings grown so serious? All he knew was that thanks to Jo—and maybe to an even higher power—this special woman had come into his life. Yes, they were different. Yes, they had disagreements. Yes, they were bound to clash. But they were both changing.

They were beginning to recognize and value the unique qualities they each brought to their relationship. And they absolutely could not deny the chemistry between them. They'd certainly tried to. But it was growing stronger every day. And they needed to deal with it.

Slowly Blake turned to straddle the bench, his gaze never leaving her face. He saw the sudden rush of fear in her eyes. But he also saw the yearning.

"Blake, I…"

His fingers on her lips instantly silenced her, and she went absolutely still. "I know. You're scared. So am I," he said huskily. "I never planned this, never in a million years expected it. But there's something between us, A.J. I know you feel it, too. I see it in your eyes."

"Th-that doesn't mean we should do anything about it."

He reached over and gently brushed a stray tendril of hair off her face. "Do we have a choice?"

She didn't respond immediately. When she did speak, her voice was choked. "I c-can't take the chance. It h-hurts too much to l-lose someone you love. I wouldn't survive…again."

With his free hand he reached for hers and comfortingly stroked the back with his thumb. "Does it hurt any less to be alone?" he asked gently.

When she didn't respond, he reached over and rested his hands on her stiff shoulders. He could feel her quivering, and he kneaded her taut muscles, realizing his own hands were none too steady.

"You know I would never hurt you, don't you?" he said softly.

"Not on purpose. Eric wouldn't have, either. That doesn't make it hurt any less when someone is gone. And life doesn't come with guarantees."

He had no response to that. Because it was true.

"Besides, w-we're too different," she said unevenly.

That was something he *could* respond to. "What's that old saying about opposites attracting?"

"I—I'm not sure I ever believed that."

"Me neither. Until now. Besides, I don't think we're as different as we once thought. And the differences we do have seem to complement each other. That's not a bad thing, is it?"

"I guess not."

"Besides, after one kiss the attraction might fizzle anyway. Then our problem is solved."

She managed the ghost of a smile. "This is sure an odd conversation."

His own lips quirked up wryly. "Well, our relationship hasn't exactly developed along conventional lines. Why start following the norm now?"

He felt the tension in her shoulders ease slightly.

"I'm not even sure I remember how to do this," she said with disarming honesty. "It's been a long time. You'll probably be disappointed."

He lifted one hand from her shoulder and traced the outline of her face with a gentle finger. "I doubt that." When he touched her lips, she drew in a sharp breath. "Come here. Let me hold you for a minute." Without waiting for her to respond, he closed the distance between them and pulled her close, cradling her head against his shoulder. It was an embrace of comfort and reassurance—but unlike the other times he'd held her, it was also an embrace of anticipation.

He stayed like that for what seemed to be a long time, stroking her back, communicating to her by his gentle but strong touch that she had nothing to fear from him. That he understood her apprehensions, and the need to take things slowly. For both their sakes. But that it was also time to begin exploring the attraction between them.

Blake wasn't sure if her trembling actually subsided, or if he only imagined it had. But finally he turned his head and let his lips make contact with her temple, then slowly travel across her forehead. When he felt her hands lightly, tentatively, touch his back, he moved slightly away and cradled her head with one hand, resting the other lightly on her shoulder. He was careful to communicate through his posture that she could move away at any time. If she kissed him back, he wanted it to be freely given.

He waited a moment, until her eyelids flickered open and he saw what he needed to see. Then, his gaze never leaving hers, he slowly closed the distance between them until their lips connected. He brushed his lips across hers, once, twice, three times, light as a summer breeze. Waiting for a reaction. Giving her a chance to pull back.

But she didn't. Instead, she pulled him closer. And Blake needed no more encouragement. Telling himself to move slowly, he tenderly claimed A.J.'s sweet lips.

After an interlude in which time seemed to stand still, Blake finally broke contact. He backed off slightly and gazed down at her, gripping her upper arms. She wasn't sure if he was trying to steady himself or her. No matter. They both needed to regain their balance.

"Wow!" A.J. whispered, her eyes wide.

"Yeah. Wow!"

She took a deep breath. "So what do we do now?"

When his eyes darkened in response and he leaned toward her, she put a restraining hand on his chest. "Not a good idea."

He sighed and backed off, flashing her a grin. "Yeah. You're right. But we can't ignore this, you know."

"I know. It's just that…" Her voice trailed off.

"You need to move slowly," he finished for her.

She nodded. "I still have issues to work through. In spite of what just happened, I'm still scared."

"I understand. I've never been a fast mover, either. Remember, I'm just starting to dabble in spontaneity. We both need time to sort things out. We'll take it slow and easy. Okay?" He reached for her hands.

She looked at him skeptically. "Do you think we'll be able to manage that?"

A smile tugged at the corners of his mouth. "We're both disciplined people. We can make this work."

"So…no more kissing?" she said wistfully.

He smiled. "I wouldn't go that far. Let's try this."

He leaned toward her, keeping her hands in his, and kissed her tenderly. It was a kiss that spoke of honor and caring and attraction.

"How's that?" he asked when he finally moved away.

She drew an unsteady breath. "This isn't going to be easy."

"I know. But we can do this, A.J. Trust me."

She gazed into his eyes and smiled. "I do."

But as they gathered up the remnants of their picnic, he hoped her confidence wasn't misplaced. Because he knew his self-discipline was about to be mightily tested. So Blake did something he'd never done in his life. He asked for help from a higher power.

Lord, I know I'm new to the fold. I don't even know how to pray yet. But I hope You'll listen to my request anyway. I'm not sure where this thing with A.J. is headed. But I know I'm falling in love with her. I don't honestly know whether that's in either of our best interests. So we need to give this time, and not get so caught up in the chemistry between us that we're blind to more important considerations. You know I've always been good at self-control. Probably too good. But I need it now. Big-time.

And Lord, I ask for Your guidance as we start down this new path. Help us both to know Your will and to make good decisions. A.J. doesn't need to be hurt again, and I don't need to make any more mistakes with people I care about. So please watch over us.

Blake had no idea if his plea was heard. But according to Reverend Matthews, God was receptive to any communication that came from the heart. And his certainly had. Because for the first time in years, he was willing to admit that he needed assistance.

Blake recalled the day A.J. was on the ladder, when he'd told her that it was okay to ask for help. He realized now that she could have thrown that comment right back at him. He was just as bad as she was in that regard, for different reasons. She refused help because she didn't want to rely on someone who might be taken away from her. Blake's self-reliance had been forged in his childhood, when he'd resolved to take control of his own destiny so that he would never again have to depend on anyone for food or housing.

But as he was slowly coming to realize, security and stability came in many forms. The material kind wasn't all that permanent and durable, no matter how well you planned. Look at his friend, Jack. He'd recently lost his job after twelve years because of a corporate reorganization. And he had two kids, a mortgage and a wife who was a stay-at-home mom. From a material perspective, his world had just caved in, his security and stability gone in the blink of an eye. But when Blake had spoken with him a few days before, Jack had been confident that things would work out. After all, as he'd told Blake, "I have my faith and my family. I'm still a rich man, buddy." Family and faith. The very things that A.J. said had seen her through the crises in her life. Maybe he'd been looking in the wrong places for security and stability all along.

He still believed self-reliance was a good thing. But maybe it was time to admit he needed other people in his life. His friends. His family. A.J.

And God.

Chapter Ten

"Thank you for seeing me, Reverend Matthews."

The minister extended his hand to A.J. "It's my pleasure. Sorry to keep you waiting. We have a very active five-year-old, and my wife needed a second pair of hands this morning. She's getting over a bad cold and isn't quite up to full speed yet."

"No problem. I hope she feels better soon."

He grinned and took a seat at right angles to hers. "There's no keeping Sam down for long." The love in his eyes when he spoke of Samantha touched A.J. She'd gotten to know the minister's red-haired wife over the past few months, and the obvious mutual affection between Reverend Matthews and his spouse always reminded her of her relationship with Eric.

"So, what can I do for you on this beautiful spring day?" the minister continued.

A.J. took a deep breath. "I could use some advice."

"I'll do my best."

Encouraged by his insightful questions, A.J. told

him her story. Of her engagement, Eric's death, her injuries, her years in Afghanistan, her work with Good Samaritan. And more recently, of Aunt Jo's legacy and her partnership with Blake.

"That's quite a story, A.J.," the minister said when she finished. "It sounds like your life is on a new and satisfying track. Your faith seems strong. So what brings you to me today?"

She glanced down and played with her purse clasp, and when she spoke her voice was subdued. "I'm not so sure about the faith part."

"Tell me about it."

She looked over at Reverend Matthews, wondering if he would judge her lacking when she admitted that she hadn't put her life fully in the Lord's hands. And how could a minister, a man of deep faith who was so happily married, understand her fears about commitment—to people or to plans?

He spoke comfortingly, as if he'd read her mind. "No one's faith is perfect, A.J."

She took a shaky breath. "It's just that…well, ever since the accident I've lived kind of a vagabond lifestyle and avoided putting down any roots. I told myself that I was trying to remain unencumbered so that I could be open to God's call and totally available to do His will. But lately, I've been thinking that maybe I've been fooling myself. That maybe…maybe I'm just afraid. Putting down roots means that you're willing to make plans for the future and to trust that no matter what happens with those plans, God will be there to comfort you and guide you. But if you don't stay in any one place long enough to make commitments or plans, you don't have to put that belief to the test."

He leaned forward intently and clasped his hands between his knees. "I can see that you're deeply troubled by this."

"I am. I always thought my faith was strong. That I had absolute trust in the Lord. Now I'm not so sure."

"Perhaps you can take some comfort in knowing that you're not alone with this struggle. Think of the story of the apostles when they were out in the boat with the Lord during the storm on the lake. They doubted and were afraid. Or the time our Lord told Peter to walk to Him across the water. When Peter's trust faltered, when he began to doubt, he started to sink. That happens to all of us, A.J. It's not a sign of weak faith. It's a sign of being human. From the story you've just told me, I'd say your faith has sustained you well through some turbulent times. So I have a feeling that your doubts are of a more recent vintage." He paused a moment. "Would Blake have anything to do with this?" he asked gently.

She nodded slowly. "I think I might be…my feelings for him are…growing every day. But we're so different. That scares me. And I'm afraid to take another chance on love. I thought I would die when I lost Eric. I'm afraid I might not survive that kind of trauma again." She gazed at him, thought of his perfect family, and sighed. "I guess that might be hard for you to understand."

A fleeting echo of pain swept across his eyes. "Actually, it's not," he said quietly. "I lost my first wife not long after we were married. An aneurysm. It took her instantly, with no warning. So I've known dark days, too—days when I doubted and was afraid. I never expected to marry again. I never even wanted to. Then Sam came into my life. We were very different people, and we both had unresolved issues. We fought the attraction, but in the end we recognized that our love was a gift. It didn't come with guarantees, but most things in life don't."

A.J. stared at the man across from her. She'd always thought he looked too young to have those streaks of silver at his temples. Now she knew what had put them there. "I'm so sorry," she whispered.

"Thank you. Loss is a very difficult thing to deal with. And it can destroy us, if we let it. But it doesn't have to. My life is happy now. Because Sam and I realized that it was better to put our trust in God and accept the gift of our love for as long as He blessed us with it than to spend the rest of our lives alone."

A.J. frowned. "Blake said almost the same thing."

"He's a wise man."

"He told me he's spent some time with you."

Reverend Matthews chuckled. "He certainly keeps me on my toes. He asks probing questions that have on more than one occasion sent me to my library to do research. But I'd rather have one believer like him, who deals directly with questions and is eager to learn about the faith, than a dozen who accept blindly. If he chooses to become a Christian, his faith will be strong. Because he will have made an informed decision. He's a good man, A.J."

"I know." She took a deep breath. "Thank you, Reverend Matthews."

"I'm always here if you need me. Shall we take a moment to talk with the Lord before you leave?"

She nodded, and he reached for her hand as they bowed their heads.

"Lord, let us feel Your presence, so that doubts may disappear. Give us the wisdom to discern Your will and the courage to follow it. Guide our steps on this difficult journey of life, and steady us when we stumble. Let us feel Your infinite love and compassion, and let us take comfort in the knowledge that You understand and forgive our mistakes. Help us to savor each day as a precious gift, and not let anxieties about the future overwhelm us. Bless A.J. with Your grace as she struggles to hear Your voice. Help her put her trust in You so that she may feel the peace that comes with surrender. And help her let go of her fear of the future so that she may live fully today. We ask this through Christ our Lord."

For a long moment, A.J. left her eyes closed. Reverend Matthews's prayer had been simple. But it had come from the heart. And it had touched on all of her fears. When she finally gazed at the man across from her, she saw no reproach in his eyes because of the doubts she'd expressed. She saw only a deep compassion and empathy that communicated more eloquently than words how well he understood exactly what was in her heart.

And if he could understand, surely so could God.

That thought came to her suddenly, like a shaft of

sunlight that streams through dark storm clouds and illuminates the world. A gentle, freeing peace stole over her as the guilt raised by her doubts dissipated, leaving her soul quiet and serene. And in that stillness, she knew God would speak to her. She had only to listen for His voice.

The doorbell rang, and A.J. smiled as she wiped her hands on a kitchen towel, then glanced at the clock. Nine o'clock on the dot. Blake may have gotten more spontaneous in the past few months, but he was still Mr. Punctuality. Which she appreciated even more since he'd told her that he thought tardiness indicated a lack of respect for the other person's time. She admired his consideration. And so many other things.

The moment she opened the door he pulled her into his arms and greeted her with a tender kiss.

When he released her, she smiled at him, her arms still looped around his neck. "You'll give poor Mr. Simmons a heart attack," she murmured, catching a glimpse of her neighbor peering through a crack in his door.

"Can't be helped," he said. "I figured it was safer to kiss you out here."

She chuckled and reached for his hand. "Come on in. I'm almost ready."

Blake followed her, and almost fell over a small, shaggy dog sitting patiently inside the door. "What's this?" he asked in surprise.

She grinned. "Blake, meet Felix. I rescued him from the pound yesterday."

"Isn't Felix a cat's name?"

She planted her hands on her hips and gave him a teasing grin. "Are you still hung up on that name thing?"

He smiled. "Touché." He squatted down and reached over to scratch the dog's head. "Hey, Felix." He looked the dog over. "What is he?"

"A mutt. He's about five years old. Apparently he'd been on the streets, just wandering around for a while. They told me at the pound that not many people want older dogs. But I thought he was perfect. Besides, he looked like he needed a friend."

"And the apartment was okay with this?"

"Yeah. For a hefty deposit. But he's worth it. I fell in love with him the minute I saw him."

Blake stood and turned to A.J. "So what prompted this?"

She shrugged. "Companionship."

"Are you feeling lonesome?" His tone was teasing, but there was something serious in his eyes. A.J. knew he was purposely letting her set the pace in their relationship. At the same time, she knew that a day of reckoning was coming.

"Not anymore. Felix took care of the problem. He's the perfect companion. And he never talks back."

"Are you telling me you like the shaggy, silent type? I could let my hair grow."

A.J. giggled. "Very funny. Let me grab a hat and I'll be right with you," she said over her shoulder as she headed down the hall.

Blake gave Felix another scratch, then wandered over to the dinette table, which was littered with notes and documents. He saw the name of their church on several sheets, and realized that the papers had something to do with the long-range plan Brad Matthews had mentioned from the pulpit a few times. The minister had said there was a committee working on a variety of projects, including a capital campaign.

"Okay, I'm all set."

Blake turned. Between the kiss and the dog, he hadn't really paid any attention to what A.J. was wearing. Now his gaze took in her calf-length dress in shades of purple, which he'd swear was tie-dyed. A macramé purse was slung over her shoulder, and she held a large straw hat. At one time, he would have thought her outfit was weird. But now he realized it wasn't weird at all. It was just A.J. And it suited her. Perfectly.

"You look very nice."

"Thanks. I found a great new vintage clothing store."

"What's all this?" He nodded to the paperwork on the table.

"Reverend Matthews asked me if I'd serve on the long-range planning committee for the church. It's a three-year term, so I wasn't sure at first. But I finally agreed." She glanced at her watch. "We'd better go or we'll be late for the service."

Blake followed her to the door, processing the latest developments. A.J. had bought a dog. Which meant she'd made a commitment to let another living thing into her life. And she'd agreed to serve on the committee. Which meant she was planning to be around for at least three years.

Blake had been asking for guidance about how quickly to proceed with A.J., praying for a sign that she was ready for what he wanted to do next. Today he'd been given two signs. It was time for the next step.

"Sorry I'm late. I got hung up."

A.J. glanced up from the computer where she was entering orders. "No problem. Did you get your business taken care of?"

Blake stuck his hand in his pocket and fingered the small box from the jeweler. He'd dropped his grandmother's engagement ring off the week before to have it cleaned and polished, and they'd done a superb job restoring the vintage piece. Blake had no idea if A.J. would like the old-fashioned setting, but he was perfectly willing to have the stones refitted if that's what she preferred. His only concern was whether she was ready to accept the ring at all.

"Blake?"

A.J. was eyeing him strangely.

"Yeah. Yeah, I got everything taken care of. Listen, what are you doing tonight?"

"Making some desserts for the church picnic tomorrow."

"Could I tempt you with dinner out instead? We could pick up something at the bakery for the church."

There was an odd electricity in the air. A peculiar tension. A.J. looked at Blake curiously. "Is something wrong?"

"No. I just thought it might be nice to have dinner

together. We don't get to do that very often on week-days."

That was true. She or Blake, or both, were usually at the shop till closing. *The shop.* Maybe that was it, she speculated. The end of their six-month partnership was looming, a fact that had hit home when she'd turned her calendar over to May yesterday. Just four weeks remained. Neither she nor Blake had talked about what would happen at the end of the month—assuming, of course, that the MacKenzie deal fell through and they still *had* a shop. But it was on her mind. A lot. She'd agreed at the beginning to consider selling Blake her half ownership. However, she had grown to love the business.

As well as the man who'd come with it.

And she had a feeling Blake felt the same way.

Maybe that's what this dinner was about, she speculated, as her heart tripped into double time. Even though no words of love had been uttered, she'd begun to let herself think about a life with Blake, to make some preliminary plans. Very preliminary. Frankly, she wasn't sure she was ready for a discussion about either their relationship or the shop, but they'd have to talk both things over sooner or later. It might as well be tonight.

"Okay. What time?"

"How does six-thirty sound?"

"I'll be ready."

And she was. Except Blake didn't show up at the appointed time. Or five minutes later. Or ten. Or fif-teen. At which point A.J. began to panic. Blake was never late. And on the rare occasion when he was delayed for some reason, even for a few minutes, he called her. Always.

The phone rang just as A.J. was reaching for it to dial his number.

"Blake?"

He heard the breathlessness in her voice, knew that she'd been worried. "I'm okay, A.J. But my dad isn't. When I called out there a few minutes ago to confirm some things about my visit next week, I found out my dad had a heart attack today."

"Oh, Blake! How bad is it?"

"Apparently pretty mild. They weren't even going to call me about it. They said they didn't want me to worry, or to cancel my trip next week because he was sick. Listen, I need to go out there. Right away. I don't know if they're telling me the whole story, and if anything happened to my dad before…" His voice grew hoarse, and he stopped to clear his throat. "I just need to go."

"Of course."

"You'll be shorthanded at the shop."

"We'll cope."

"And the whole MacKenzie deal is still up in the air."

"You said yourself there's nothing we can do now but wait. And I'll let you know if I hear any news. Just go. Don't worry about anything here."

He sighed. "I'm sorry about this, A.J."

"Don't be. This is what you do for family. You go when they need you. You support them. You show them you care. I'd be disappointed if you didn't go."

"Thanks. We'll reschedule this when I get back. Okay?"

"Absolutely. Did you call the airline yet?"

"No. That's next on my list."

"Let me know when your flight is. I'll drive you."

"You don't have to do that."

"I want to. No arguments."

He didn't even try to dissuade her. She obviously wasn't going to budge. Besides, he wanted to see her before he left.

He was on the cell phone most of the way to the airport, arranging for a rental car in Oregon, calling in regrets for a board meeting with Big Brothers, canceling an appointment he had with Reverend Matthews. She stole a few worried glances at him during the drive. He looked more harried than she'd ever seen him, and the deep creases in his brow told her just how upset he was about his father.

For safety's sake, he insisted she leave him at the drop-off area instead of parking in the garage, and she didn't argue. She stood quietly beside him as he took out his carry-on and glanced at his watch.

"You'd better go. This is cutting it pretty close already," she said.

Blake reached over and gently stroked her cheek. "This wasn't in my plans for tonight."

"You've gotten better about changing plans on short notice."

"I didn't want to change these." He studied her for a moment, as if memorizing her features, then reached over and pulled her close. For a long moment he just held her, drawing strength from her warm embrace. "I'll be back soon," he said, his voice muffled in her hair.

He backed up then, and she searched his face. The harsh overhead lights mercilessly highlighted the strain and tension in his features. Now it was her turn to touch his face.

"Take whatever time you need. I'll still be here when you get back."

"Is that a promise?"

There was more in his question than a mere confirmation that she would be physically there. And she knew it. But it didn't alter her response. "Yes."

His eyes darkened and he leaned toward her, his lips touching hers in a brief kiss.

"I—I'll be thinking about you," she whispered when he broke contact.

He took her hands in his, and his gaze locked with hers. "That's good. Because a man always likes to know that he's on the mind of the woman he loves."

Then, before she could respond, he reached for his bag and strode away.

"We appreciate your coming out, son. But you could have waited until next week, like you planned. We're sorry to inconvenience you."

Blake looked at his father and tried to swallow past the lump in his throat. He had gone directly to the hospital from the airport, mentally preparing himself for this scene along the way. But walking in and finding his robust father flat on his back and looking very frail and vulnerable had still shocked him. "It's not an inconvenience, Dad."

"Carl didn't even want me to call. But I thought you'd want to know. We didn't expect you to drop everything and come out, though."

He looked at his mother, who was sitting on the other side of his father's hospital bed, holding her husband's hand.

"I wanted to be here."

A look passed between Jan and Carl, and his mother's eyes filled with tears. His father patted her hand, then turned to Blake. His own eyes were suspiciously moist.

"I'll be fine, son. It will just take a little time."

Blake had spoken with the doctors, and while his father's prognosis was good, the heart attack had been more serious than his mother had led him to believe on the phone. Recovery would take more than a little time. Meaning that for the immediate future, his mother would be on her own to run the shops. Which he was confident she was perfectly capable of doing— under normal circumstances. But he wasn't so sure about right now, when she was worried about her husband.

"Can you stay for a few days, Li…Blake?"

He nodded slowly. "I'd like to spend some time with you. And visit your shops. Maybe I can even help out a little, since you'll be shorthanded."

Carl frowned. "This was supposed to be a vacation for you."

"We don't want to put you to work the minute you get here," his mother concurred.

He shrugged. "That's what family's for."

His mother hesitated and glanced uncertainly at Carl. "Well, second quarter closing will need to be taken care of in the next couple of weeks. Carl's always been our liaison with the accountants, but with your business background it might be helpful if you could look over their shoulder this one time."

"I can do that, Jan," Carl protested.

"I'll do it, Dad. You need to concentrate on getting better."

Jan swiped at her eyes, then impulsively reached across the bed with her free hand. Blake hesitated only a fraction of a second before he took it. And only a second more before he laid his other hand over his father's.

"I know we haven't been close," he said, his voice strangely tight. "And I know a lot of that—maybe all of it—is my fault. You've reached out to me many times through the years. I just haven't responded. And I'm sorry for that now."

"It was our fault, too, Blake. Your dad and I didn't do the best job raising you. We never realized how important stability is to a child. We thought that our lifestyle would expose you to new experiences and instill a sense of adventure in you. It was only years later, when I went back to school for nutrition and took some child psychology courses, that I realized how badly we'd failed. We never gave you the security you needed. But it was too late. You were already grown up."

His mother's voice broke, and Blake squeezed her hand.

"Mom, it's okay," he said, his own voice uneven. "I know you and Dad did your best."

"It wasn't good enough," his father said.

Blake looked over at his father. The older man's face was strained and pale, and he clearly wasn't up to an emotional scene tonight. But Blake wanted his parents to at least know that he was willing to do his part to mend the rift.

"It *was* good enough, Dad, because at the time, you and Mom thought you were doing the right thing. And it's not too late," he said, echoing words A.J. had once spoken to him. "I'm willing to start over, if you are."

Carl and Jan exchanged another look.

"It's what we've prayed for," she told Blake, dabbing at her eyes. "A second chance."

"We'll do better this time, son," his father said. "Everything will be different."

"Not everything," Jan corrected.

Blake looked at her curiously. "What do you mean?"

"We've always loved you, Blake. Maybe we haven't always shown it in the right way, or given you the things you needed, but you always had our love. You still do. That will never change."

Blake gazed from his mother to his father. The unconditional love and acceptance in their eyes made his throat tighten with emotion. Perhaps it had always been there and he'd just never noticed. Perhaps, through all these years when he'd felt so alone and adrift, he'd had a family after all, just waiting to be rediscovered.

Blake knew that the rebuilding process wouldn't

happen overnight. He needed to learn how to relate to the two people across from him, who had clearly changed and grown through the years—just as he had. He needed to learn how to share his life with them. And he needed to learn how to say "I love you."

But tonight, as they sat with hands clasped in a sterile hospital room that served as a vivid reminder that no material security in the world could guarantee tomorrow, he knew they were on the road to creating the kind of security that money couldn't buy. A security that would transcend the constraints of time and space.

The security of a loving family.

And in his heart, Blake said a silent thank-you to the Lord for giving him the courage to take this first step toward forgiveness—and reconciliation.

He knew the road ahead wouldn't be easy. That they'd all make mistakes. After all, they were very different people. But so were he and A.J., and he'd fallen in love with her. So he knew he could make things work with his parents. That with love and commitment, they could create the kind of family that would sustain them in the years ahead.

And he also knew something else. Given how A.J. and his parents had hit it off, he'd never have to worry about his wife getting along with the in-laws!

If she said yes when he popped the question.

Which he intended to do as soon as possible.

Chapter Eleven

"**A.J.**! A.J.! Have you seen today's paper?"

A.J. looked up from the sales report she was studying. George stood in the office doorway, grinning broadly.

"No. Why?"

"We won! It is over. Here. Read." He thrust the newspaper at her and pointed to a small article in the metro section, which A.J. quickly scanned.

"The Maplewood Board of Aldermen has rejected a proposal by MacKenzie Properties, a prominent real estate development firm, to use Tax Increment Financing (TIF) as a basis for the construction of a new retail/residential complex in the 1200 block of Collier Avenue.

"'The development was strongly opposed by area merchants and residents, who circulated petitions and collected thousands of signatures. They also staged a rally in front of city hall a few weeks ago, which generated significant media attention. Mayor Lawrence Russell said that this strong opposition was the key factor in the board's decision.

"'The development would certainly have been good for Maplewood from a financial perspective, but one of the reasons our town has enjoyed such a phenomenal rebirth is because we have always maintained our neighborhood feel and preserved the integrity and character of the area,' Russell said. 'We hope to work with Mr. MacKenzie on other projects in the future, but we did not feel that this particular one was in the best interest of Maplewood, nor was it endorsed by our constituency.'

"Following the ruling, MacKenzie Properties withdrew its proposal for the development."

As she read, a smile spread over A.J.'s face. So David had triumphed over Goliath after all! She couldn't wait to tell Blake!

"I think we should celebrate," George said excitedly. "Tonight, we have a party at my restaurant. Come when you close. I tell the others." He looked around. "Where is Blake?"

"His father became ill suddenly and he had to go to the West Coast. But I'll call him right away."

"I am sorry to hear that. But you will come tonight, yes?"

She grinned. "I wouldn't miss it for the world!"

Blake leaned back in his chair, giving his eyes a momentary rest from the computer screen. He'd been studying the books for his parents' stores for the past several hours in preparation for the second-quarter closing, and he was impressed.

Big-time.

They didn't just run a couple of stores. They ran a thriving enterprise that had been approached by a major corporation interested in buying them out and franchising.

Blake frowned. He was happy for his parents. They'd mentioned at A.J.'s the night she'd invited them to dinner that they'd been far more successful than they'd ever dreamed. But he'd had no idea they were *this* successful.

So successful, in fact, that it took both his mother and father working more than full-time just to keep up with the daily demands of the business. And his father was in no condition to resume that kind of work schedule. Nor would he be in the immediate future—if ever. He was home from the hospital and had started cardiac rehab, but the doctors had made it clear that he needed to permanently adopt a slower-paced lifestyle. And in light of the demands of their business, he knew that directive was weighing heavily on the minds of his parents.

And on his.

It was obvious to Blake that his parents needed more help than he could offer in a week or two. Not only because of the current crisis, but because the business was rapidly becoming more complex and growing beyond the scope of their expertise. They needed a full-time business manager. And they could certainly hire one. But Blake had the credentials, and no one would care more about the business than family. Or watch out for their interests with the same diligence. And that was important. Because as he'd looked through the books, it was obvious that while much had changed over the years, his parents still retained the sunny optimism of their youth and were always willing to give people the benefit of the doubt. Which was not a bad thing—in theory. But it had cost them on a number of occasions when fly-by-night suppliers had disappeared with their money. Blake wouldn't be such a soft touch. And unlike a hired business manager, he wouldn't just take orders; he'd watch out for the best interests of his parents, even if that meant going head-to-head with them about financially unstable suppliers or unsound business arrangements.

Blake tried to ignore the sense of duty tugging on his conscience. After all, this wasn't his business. It wasn't his problem. But a little voice told him otherwise, reminded him that if he was trying to rebuild a family, he needed to be there for his parents. Even if what that required wasn't in his plans.

And moving to Oregon to run a natural food business definitely wasn't in his plans.

Blake reached back and massaged his neck with one hand. From a practical standpoint, his parents' business was certainly more profitable than the bookshop and would provide him with more financial stability and security. But that no longer held the appeal it once had. It wasn't even a factor in his decision.

Because of A.J.

The mere thought of her brought a smile to his lips. As they'd worked side by side over the past few months, he'd learned so much from her. About priorities, about letting go, and about what really counted. And along the way, he'd fallen in love with her. Deeply. Irrevocably. Forever. He loved her enthusiasm. Her energy. The way her eyes flashed with passion when she discussed her beliefs. Her eclectic taste in clothes. Her intelligence. Her courage. Her determination. Her deep faith. And the willingness she was beginning to exhibit to once again put down roots, make plans for the future and open herself to love.

And now this. If he decided to stay and help his parents, he'd have to ask her to change direction again, to leave the shop she had come to love. Just when its future had been secured.

It was ironic, really. In the beginning, he'd backed away from the MacKenzie fight. But gradually he'd been pulled into it, and by the end he'd been fighting as hard as anyone else to stop the development. Not only to protect Jo's legacy and his own future, but because it seemed the right thing to do. He'd always figured their odds of winning were marginal, at best. That they could very well lose the shop, be forced to start over. He hadn't wanted that to happen. Now, selfishly, he almost wished it had. Because it would make his decision about his parents' situation much easier.

Blake knew that A.J. had been surprised by his somewhat subdued mood when she'd called to tell him the news. He'd tried to be enthusiastic, but his own dilemma was weighing heavily on his mind. He'd attributed his less-than-thrilled response to tiredness and concern over his father, and A.J. had seemed to buy that explanation. But it was more than that.

Because if he stayed to help his parents, he'd have

to ask A.J. to leave St. Louis and start over once more. It would be a huge sacrifice on her part. And it would have to be motivated by a deep, abiding love.

Blake knew A.J. loved him. But he also knew she was still scared. Even under the best of circumstances, making a commitment to him would require her to take a huge leap of faith.

And these weren't even close to the best of circumstances.

Lord, why does life have to be so complicated? he lamented silently. His conscience called him to do one thing; his heart, another. If he went with the call of his conscience, he knew that it would put A.J.'s love for him to the test.

And he was scared to death he would fail.

"You're offering to stay on as our business manager?" His parents' faces reflected shock, and Blake shifted uncomfortably in the wooden chair at their kitchen table. "Yes. The doctors say you'll be fine, Dad, but it will take time. You'll need some help in the meantime. And frankly, long-term as well. Because your business is getting incredibly complex. You two have done an impressive job, but I've reviewed the operation, looked at all the financials, and you're at a point where you need a full-time business manager. You could hire a stranger, of course. Or I could step into the role. I'd be happy to give you a copy of my résumé if you want to review my qualifications." He flashed them a grin, hoping to lighten the atmosphere. But they continued to stare at him, dumbfounded.

Finally Carl glanced at Jan, then turned back to Blake. "I don't even know what to say."

"Blake, are you sure? What did A.J. say about this?"

Leave it to his mom to hone right in on the heart of his problem, he thought wryly. Over the past two weeks, as he'd reconnected with his parents, she'd quickly picked up on Blake's interest in their dinner hostess. And been delighted for him, even though he'd never said exactly how serious he was about A.J.

It had taken Blake much prayer and soul-searching—and a phone call to Reverend Matthews—before he had decided to make this offer. He'd also considered talking with A.J., asking her advice, but he knew she'd tell him to go with his conscience—because she would never put selfish desires above family obligations. If there was a need, you met it. Period. So he'd made the decision on his own. He knew she would understand; he just prayed that she would find the courage to trust in their love despite the change in plans.

"Yes, I'm sure. And I haven't spoken with A.J. about this."

Jan frowned, but didn't press him on the point. She looked at Carl and reached for his hand. "It's too much to ask." The comment was directed at her husband, not her son.

"I agree." Carl turned to Blake. "You're right about us needing help, son. With the way the business has grown, we've known for the past few months that we were starting to get in over our heads. But there's no way we'd ask you to step in. We can manage."

"You didn't ask. I offered."

"And we love you for it. But it's not the right thing for you. You love the bookshop. You've fought hard to save it. And you've built a wonderful life in St. Louis," Jan said. "This business was our dream, not yours. You need to follow your own path."

Blake studied the two people seated across from him. He wanted to accept their answer. It would be the easy way out. But he knew their decision was based on consideration for him, not their own needs. So he couldn't just walk away. Because with a little convincing, he was sure he could change their minds.

"I'll tell you what. I need to make a quick trip back to St. Louis this weekend and take care of a few things. Why don't you think it over and we can talk when I get back?"

"I doubt we'll change our minds," Carl said.

"All I ask is that you think about it."

"We will. Just don't worry about us while you're gone. We'll be fine," Jan said. "And be sure to tell A.J. hello for us. She's a very special young woman. "

Blake already knew that. What he didn't know was her answer to the question he planned to ask her as soon as he returned.

"Have you heard from Blake lately?"

A.J. set down the stack of books she was carrying and glanced at Nancy. "A couple of days ago. Between helping his mom take care of his dad, plus trying to get a handle on their business, he's been buried."

"What's the latest on his dad?"

"He's doing better, but he won't be back to full speed anytime soon."

"Did Blake say when he was coming back?"

"No."

A.J. turned away to help a customer, but her mind was on Blake. Though he called regularly, her conversations with him were generally brief and fairly impersonal. And he always sounded distracted and harried. Even the good news about the shop hadn't seemed to perk him up much. And while he never failed to say that he missed her, there had been no more mention of the "L" word.

A man always likes to know that he's on the mind of the woman he loves.

Blake's parting words to her at the airport echoed again in her mind, as they had constantly for the past two weeks. In between customers at the shop, at the church picnic, lying in bed late at night, they kept replaying. He hadn't had to worry. She'd thought of little but him. And the future.

A.J. was fairly certain that she and Blake were headed down a serious path. Serious enough to end in marriage. She also suspected that things would have moved more quickly in that direction if fear hadn't held her back. She was immensely grateful for Blake's patience as she dealt with her issues, and for his understanding that those issues had nothing to do with her feelings for him. They were born of trauma and tragedy and pain, and the overwhelming fear of loss. But she'd never forgotten the words Blake had once said to her when she'd talked of those fears. He'd simply asked, "Does it hurt any less to be alone?"

Slowly, as Blake had filled her life with warmth and laughter and caring, she'd found the answer to that question. The fear hadn't gone away completely; she didn't know if it ever would. But she did know that Blake had become an important part of her life. In fact, she could no longer imagine her life without him.

So she'd begun to think of the future they might share. And to make some tentative plans. And to eagerly wait for him to return.

The bell at the entrance jangled. A.J. looked up… and stopped breathing. Blake stood in the doorway, overnight case in hand, looking weary, worn—and utterly wonderful. She smiled at him, and his intimate answering smile warmed her all the way to her toes. And did funny things to her voice when she could finally find it. "Hi."

"Hi yourself."

"Welcome back, Blake," Nancy said.

With an obvious effort he dragged his gaze away from A.J. and looked at Nancy. "Thanks. How's everything been here?"

"We missed you."

"Did you?" He looked back at A.J., and his eyes darkened. Suddenly her heart lurched into a staccato beat.

Nancy nodded. "Yeah. We've been taking on extra hours, but I'll be glad to get back to a more normal schedule. Eileen will be glad, too. She misses her mom."

Blake took a closer look at A.J. There were fine lines at the corners of her eyes, and dark circles underneath. Obviously his absence had put a strain on everyone.

"Well, if you don't need me anymore, I'm going to take off, A.J. I can lock up as I leave."

It took a moment for Nancy's words to register, then A.J. frowned and glanced at her watch. "Oh. Right. It's time to close. That's fine, Nancy. You go ahead."

"Okay. See you later. Glad you're back, Blake."

"Thanks."

They heard her set the lock on the front door, and a moment later it clicked shut.

Slowly Blake put his suitcase down and walked toward A.J. His gaze never left hers as he took her hand and pulled her into the back room, then looped his arms around her waist. His eyes were only inches from hers. "Can I get a proper welcome now?" he said.

Without waiting for her to respond, his lips touched hers. A.J. surrendered to the kiss, wrapping her arms around his broad back. There was reunion and promise in the kiss they exchanged.

When it ended, Blake pulled her close. "It feels so good to be home."

She closed her eyes. Home was a good way to describe how she felt in Blake's arms. "I missed you. A lot."

A chuckle rumbled deep in his chest. "I sort of got that impression. But I'm glad you confirmed it. Could you tell I missed you?"

Now it was her turn to smile. "Just a little."

"Of course, you do have Felix to keep you company."

"Felix is great. But he falls short in several areas."

"Such as?"

"Well, he's not a great conversationalist. And he snores."

"So snoring is a bad thing?"

She backed up and gave him a look of mock horror. "Don't tell me you snore!"

"I don't think so. But my dad's snored for years. And Mom still loves him."

Suddenly serious, A.J. studied his face. He looked exhausted. "How is he doing?"

"Better. But he still has a long way to go."

"Did you have dinner?"

"I grabbed something at the airport."

"Why didn't you call? I would have picked you up."

"I figured you'd be here. And you're already shorthanded."

"Would you like to come over to my place for a little while?"

He'd like nothing better. But he didn't want to be distracted from his plan for tonight. Regretfully he shook his head.

"I'm really beat. But I could use a cup of coffee. Is there any left in the pot out front?"

"I don't know. I haven't cleaned up out there yet."

"I'll take a look."

She restrained him with one hand. "Sit. I'll check. You look like you're ready to drop."

Blake didn't argue. Besides, he needed a moment to still the sudden pounding of his heart. He reached inside the pocket of his slacks and fingered the satin case, just to assure himself that the ring was still there. Then he took a deep breath and let it out slowly. He'd been waiting for this moment for weeks. Now that it was upon him, he was scared.

"Here you go."

A.J. deposited his coffee on the small lunch table in the back and sat beside him. He took a steadying sip, noting that his hand was trembling slightly. Which he supposed wasn't unusual when you were about to ask a woman to marry you.

"Are you going back?"

Carefully Blake set the cup on the table and looked at her. "Yes. I'm only here for the weekend. I'm really sorry to leave you shorthanded, A.J."

"Don't be. We can cope. How long will you need to stay?"

She didn't look put out. She didn't complain about the extra work at the shop. She didn't make an issue out of his extended absence. To her, it was a given. Family came first. He knew she believed that. But the strength of that belief was about to be tested.

Blake took a deep breath and reached for her hand, his gaze fixed on hers. "Possibly for a very long time." And then he filled her in.

As A.J. listened, the plans she'd let herself begin to think about slowly disintegrated and her world began to crumble. She'd been here before. And she hated it. Hated the feeling of helplessness. Of panic. Of sudden, overwhelming despair. She'd vowed once never to put herself in this position again. But she'd broken her own rule. She'd let Blake become such an integral part of her life that a future without him seemed empty and bleak. So the situation she now found herself in was her own fault. She had no one to blame but herself. She'd opened her heart to this man, and now he was going to break it and walk away.

As she looked at Blake's face, she knew that his decision had not come easily. She saw the conflict in the depths of his eyes, saw the lines of fatigue and strain at their corners, saw the deeply etched furrows in his brow. She tried to focus on his words, but as he concluded she knew she'd missed a lot.

"So I had to offer, A.J. They need me."

But so do I! she wanted to cry. Yet her spoken words were different. "I understand," she said numbly.

He stroked the back of her hand with his thumb, then made a move to stand. A.J. automatically began to follow suit, but he pressed her gently back and went down on one knee beside her. He cocooned both of her hands in his and gave her a shaky grin.

"Mr. Conventional to the end," he said, his voice slightly uneven. "I had planned to do this the night I left, in a more romantic spot with candlelight and flowers. But life has a funny way of changing plans. Besides, this is probably a more appropriate place, since the shop is what brought us together."

He paused and took a deep breath. "A.J., the life I'm about to offer you isn't the one I—or you—might have envisioned a couple of weeks ago. But it will still be good. Because we'll be together. And that's what really counts in the end. You told me once that home isn't so much a place—that it's simply being with the people you love. I believe that now. And I hope you still do, too.

"But I also know that you love Turning Leaves. I know that you're starting to build a life for yourself here. And I know that leaving all this behind, starting over yet again, will be a great sacrifice. So I want you to think about this very carefully. I don't want an answer tonight. Or even tomorrow, necessarily. Take whatever time you need."

He touched her cheek gently, then reached into his pocket and withdrew a small slip of paper.

"I spent a lot of time at the hospital while I was in Oregon, and sometimes, while my dad slept, I'd page through the Bible. I came across this passage from Jeremiah one day, and it really struck a chord with me. I wanted to share it with you." He glanced down and read in a slightly unsteady voice. "'For I know well the plans I have in mind for you, says the Lord, plans to give you a future full of hope.'" He paused, then looked back at her. "A.J., I have to tell you that you weren't in my plans. For years I'd been searching for a stereotype who fit all the conventional notions of what a wife should be. And then you came into my life and turned it upside down.

"For a long time I resented you. I liked my life just fine the way it was, and you were always changing things. But you know what? All of the changes you made were for the better. You opened my eyes to things I'd never noticed before, challenged me to rethink long-held opinions, helped me discover the joy in spontaneity. You reminded me that I should never judge a book by its cover. And in keeping with the name of Jo's shop, you helped me turn over a new leaf.

"Slowly, kicking and dragging most of the way, I came to realize that maybe my plans weren't God's plans. And that His were better. Maybe that's true for your plans, too, A.J."

Once more Blake reached into his pocket, and this time he withdrew a small satin case. He flipped it open to reveal an antique white-gold ring with a square-cut diamond in an ornate setting.

"This was my grandmother's engagement ring. I've had it for years, waiting to give it to the woman who captured my heart and filled my life with joy. You are that woman, A.J. I never thought I could love someone as much as I love you. Before we met, I thought I was living. But I wasn't. I was just moving through my days. Life before you was like a black-and-white movie. Flat and dull and ordinary. But now it's Technicolor. And it's definitely not dull!"

He flashed her a grin, but it was forced. She could see the tension in his face, feel it in his posture.

"Believe me, I know I'm getting the better end of this deal," he continued. "But while I might not always be the most exciting guy around, I'm steady. And dependable. And I honor my commitments. So when I say that I promise to love you to the very best of my ability every day of my life, you can count on it. For always."

He closed the lid of the box, placed it in her hand, and folded her delicate fingers over it.

"I know I've thrown a lot at you and that you're scared. But I would be honored if you would accept this and become my wife. Take it with you. Think about it. Pray about it. And know that I'll be waiting, however long it takes."

He leaned toward her, and his lips brushed hers, just a momentary touch before he stood. He gave her one last, lingering look, his hand cupping her cheek. "I love you, A.J. I'll call you tomorrow." And then he was gone before she could speak.

A.J. stared after him, and a moment later she heard the bell, followed by the click of the front door. Her mind was reeling as her brain worked frantically to process everything Blake had just told her. In the end, she realized that it came down to three things. Blake loved her. He was leaving. And he wanted her to go with him, as his wife.

She glanced down at the small satin box in her palm and slowly lifted the top. The diamond winked back at her, and she traced the edges wonderingly. Blake had been saving this for a special woman all these years. For her.

A.J. drew a shaky breath and brushed her hair back from her face with trembling fingers. She'd known they were heading this way. Had been prepared to put her fears aside and take a second chance on love with this special man. But she hadn't realized that he would ask her to leave everything else behind. Yet wasn't that what love was all about? She thought about the words from the book of Ruth. "Do not ask me to abandon or forsake you! For wherever you go I will go, wherever you lodge I will lodge, your people shall be my people, and your God my God." Those were words spoken by a daughter-in-law to her mother-in-law. How much more true they should be between a man and wife.

A.J. knew that leaving St. Louis wasn't Blake's preference. He loved it here. He loved Turning Leaves. And he loved her. Yet he was willing to give up the life he'd built here over the past several years, tear up roots that went deep, because of a sense of obligation to his family and a need to reconnect with parents who had been largely lost to him. She understood that. Admired him for it. And surely she could move, too. After all, she'd only been here a few months. Her roots were still new and could easily be transplanted.

But A.J. knew it was more than that. For a few moments, before he'd proposed but after he'd told her he was leaving, she had recalled with startling clarity the sense of loss and abandonment she'd felt when Eric died. Had been vividly reminded of the reasons she'd been so afraid to commit again, to make plans for the future. Blake's proposal had quickly followed, so this time the ending had turned out differently. She was being given a choice about which direction her life took. But the next time, the choice might not be hers. If she went with Blake and built a new life with him in Oregon, she had no guarantee it would last.

Slowly A.J. closed the lid of the ring box. A wonderful man had just proposed to her. Had offered her his love and fidelity for as long as he lived. Her heart should be overflowing with joy. It was a dream come true, filled with the promise of a beautiful future.

But it was overshadowed by the nightmare of her tragic past.

And until she put that firmly to rest, until she left yesterday behind once and for all, she knew that it would be impossible to move forward and embrace tomorrow.

Blake raised himself on one elbow to glance at the digital clock by his bed. Two in the morning. He dropped back with a groan and placed his forearm on his forehead as he stared at the dark ceiling.

He'd half expected A.J. to call after he'd left the shop. But she hadn't. So finally he'd gone to bed. Which was useless. He hadn't slept more than an hour, and then only in fitful spurts.

He thought about how she'd looked when he left. Shell-shocked. Wide-eyed. Confused. It wasn't the reaction he'd always expected when he finally proposed to the woman he loved. But then, not much about their relationship had been predictable.

Was there something else he could have said? Should have said? Some other way to explain what was in his heart? Had he made it clear how much he loved her? He wasn't always the most eloquent guy, despite his love of the printed word. Even though he'd given it his best shot, he was less and less confident as the hours ticked by that he'd convinced her of the depth of his feelings. And less and less confident that she'd pull up roots again and follow him to another new place.

He hadn't wanted to press her last night. Not when he'd dropped so much on her all at once. He knew she needed time to think things through. But he also knew that if her answer was no, he wasn't going to give up.

He couldn't. Because she'd become a part of him. And because he knew she loved him. They couldn't let fear rob them of tomorrow.

It might take the patience of Job to convince her of that. Not to mention racking up thousands of frequent flier miles. But if her answer was no, he would try again.

And again.

And he would keep trying, until he finally convinced her to say yes.

Because in his heart, he knew they belonged together.

Forever.

Chapter Twelve

"Hello. This is Morgan. Please leave a message and I'll return your call as soon as possible."

A.J. sighed and slowly replaced the receiver. She'd already struck out with Clare, who was having her own problems in North Carolina. Now Morgan was unavailable. She desperately needed to talk with somebody. And it was way too early in the morning to call anyone but family.

A.J. had tossed and turned all night, finally rising at 5:00 a.m. Fortunately, Trish and Nancy were scheduled for the Saturday shift, because she was in no shape—physically or mentally—to deal with customers. She poured her third cup of coffee, cradling it in her hands as the first light of dawn slowly seeped in under the window shade in her breakfast nook.

Felix padded into the room and looked up at her inquisitively. A brief smile touched her lips and she reached down and gave him a quick scratch.

"Hey, guy. Did I wake you?"

He tilted his head and wagged his tail.

"I know you need to go out. Just give me five minutes, okay?"

In response, he settled down at her feet, head on his paws. He waited patiently, but when five minutes turned into ten, he looked back up at her, this time more urgently.

"Sorry," she said, shoving aside her coffee cup and giving him another scratch. She stood and he followed her to the door, waiting eagerly while she clipped on his leash.

As they stepped outside, the unexpected mugginess of the mid-May day hit her in the face, and she hesitated. She'd heard about St. Louis's oppressive summer heat, but this early in the season? Even Felix seemed reluctant to venture out.

"Come on, boy. Let's make this fast," she told him as she started down the front steps.

He hung back, and she had to urge him with a gentle but firm tug on the leash. "Hey, this was your idea, buddy."

They headed down the street, and as they turned the corner she noticed a moving truck in the middle of the next block. A little boy was sitting on a low stone wall watching as the moving crew loaded boxes and furniture on the truck. His shoulders were hunched dejectedly, and A.J. felt a tug on her heartstrings at his obvious misery. Her step slowed as she approached him, and she stopped about ten feet away.

"Hi, there."

He looked up. She guessed he was about eight or

nine, with reddish blond hair and a healthy sprinkling of freckles across his nose.

"My mom says I can't talk to strangers."

"That's a good rule. Can you talk to me if I stay back here?"

"I guess so." He eyed her skeptically, then glanced toward her feet. "What's his name?"

"Felix."

"I wish I had a dog."

"Maybe you can some day."

He shook his head dejectedly. "Mom says not for a while. We might have to move again."

"Where are you moving to?"

"Chicago."

"I used to live there."

There was a flicker of interest in his eyes. "Yeah? What's it like?"

"It's a nice place. There are lots of things to do there. It's right on a big lake, and there's an awesome aquarium."

He pulled up one knee, wrapped his arms around it and looked at her doubtfully. "If it's so great, why did you move here?"

She was momentarily taken aback by the question. "Well, my aunt gave me a bookshop. So I came down here to take care of it."

"Do you like it here?"

"Yes."

"Are you going to stay here forever?"

She stared at him. That, it seemed, was the question of the day. "I'm not sure."

"Where would you go if you left?"

"Maybe Oregon."

"My dad was from Oregon. He died when I was five. I don't remember him much."

She felt a pang in her heart. "I'm sure he was a very nice man."

"That's what Mom says. She misses him a lot sometimes."

A.J.'s chest grew tight. "It's hard when people you love die."

"Mom says Dad wouldn't want us to be sad, though. Because he's in heaven. And she says we shouldn't feel lonely, because God is always with us. And that He's watching out for us. I thought that if we moved, God might forget where we lived. But Mom says He always knows where we are. Even if we went to China, He'd know."

A.J. struggled to swallow past the lump in her throat. "Your mom is very smart."

"Yeah. So do you think you'll move to Oregon?"

"I haven't decided yet."

"Maybe you should talk to God about it. That's what I did, when Mom told me we were moving to Chicago. I felt better after that. I mean, I'm still sad about leaving St. Louis. But Chicago sounds pretty cool. And I'll be with my mom. And God will take care of us. So it'll be okay."

"Eric! Come have your breakfast!"

A.J. sent a startled glance toward the front door of the small bungalow, then looked back at the little boy. "Your name is Eric?"

"Yeah. Listen, I gotta go. Bye, Felix."

A.J. stared after him, watching until he disappeared inside. A lot of boys were named Eric, of course. But it was…almost like a sign. A message. A.J. didn't much believe in those kinds of things. But it seemed somehow more than just a coincidence that today of all days—when thoughts of her past, and her fears, were so prevalent—that she would run across a little boy named Eric. Whose absolute trust in God reminded her of another Eric, and put her own faith to shame.

Shaken, A.J. slowly headed for home. Weeks earlier, when she'd talked to Reverend Matthews about her unwillingness to make plans for the future, and her guilt over those feelings because she thought they indicated a lack of trust in the Lord, he'd reassured her that such feelings were human, that God understood. And slowly, over the past few weeks, she thought she'd worked through her issues. That surely the tentative plans she'd made for a future with Blake indicated she'd finally put her trust in the Lord.

But she'd only been fooling herself. Because last night, when she'd been thrown a curveball, she'd realized that she hadn't really surrendered her fears to the Lord. And unless she did, unless she trusted that He would be by her side no matter where she was, through both joys and sorrows, her words of faith were hollow.

Little Eric had learned that lesson. She hoped he clung to it better than she had when his faith was tested in the years ahead. But maybe it was time now for her to relearn the lesson. To be like the little children, simple and trusting in their faith.

A.J. took a deep breath and searched her heart for the words she needed.

Lord, thank you for sending that child into my life today. His simple faith has made me realize what I've known all along. That You are with us always, to the end of time. Somewhere along the way I've lost my confidence in Your presence. I've let fear overwhelm me. Even now, when a wonderful man has offered me the gift of his love, I hesitate. Because of fear. Fear that You'll call him home, as You called Eric, and leave me alone once more. Help me banish this fear so that I can appreciate this gift, accept it, and savor it. Help me also to feel Your presence in my life, to know that You will never abandon me even on my darkest days. Give me Your grace, Your guidance and Your strength. Help me to remember always that, in this changing world, three things abide. And to joyfully accept the greatest of these from the wonderful man whose presence has blessed and enriched my life.

As she ended her silent prayer, a quiet peace came over her. Deep in the recesses of her heart, she knew that the Lord had heard her plea. And she also knew that if she put her trust in Him, He would give her the courage to leave the past behind and accept a future with the wonderful man who was waiting for her answer to his proposal.

A tug on the leash pulled her up short. Felix had stopped by the steps to her apartment, while she had blindly continued on, lost in thought. He was looking up at her quizzically, his head cocked, and she smiled, her heart lighter than it had been in years.

She'd almost passed by her apartment.

But she now knew one thing with absolute certainty.

She wasn't going to pass up her second chance for love.

The phone was ringing when Blake entered the house after clocking almost enough miles to qualify for a marathon. Usually, running was a great stress reliever. Today, it had done nothing to dissipate his tension. All it had done was dehydrate him. Even though he'd left before dawn, the heat and humidity had been heavy in the air.

But his need for water was eclipsed by his need to answer the phone. It could be A.J. His already elevated pulse accelerated as he strode toward the kitchen and grabbed the receiver. "Hello."

"Blake?"

It was his mother. His pulse ratcheted up again, this time from fear.

"Is Dad okay?"

"Yes, he's fine. He's on the other line."

"I'm here, son. And doing well. But you sound winded."

Blake closed his eyes in relief and took a deep breath. "I just got in from running."

"That would explain it. Everything okay in St. Louis?"

"Yes." It was the easiest response, but he couldn't be sure that was true until he had A.J.'s answer.

"Good. Listen, son, your mom and I have been talking about your generous offer to be our business manager. You don't know how much that means to us."

"The idea of making this a real family business is like a dream come true," his mother added, her voice catching with emotion on the last word.

"But the thing is, son, this heart attack has been like a wake-up call to us. We started this business because natural food and healthy eating interested us. We never expected it to be so successful or so consuming. It just kind of snowballed on us, and before we knew it we were caught up in the momentum. It's been a great ride, don't get me wrong. And we're grateful for our success. But we never really wanted to be business tycoons. In the past few years we haven't had much time for a lot of the other things we love. Like travel. And more importantly, each other. So we've decided to sell the business."

For a moment there was silence.

"You're selling the business?" Blake repeated when he could find his voice.

"Yes. You've seen our books and our files, so you know that we've had a good offer from a company that wants to turn the business into a franchise," Jan said. "It's a perfect solution. And it will give us the time to try some other things. Over the years we've turned down a lot of speaking invitations around the country because we couldn't afford to be away from the business. Now we can accept them. And there's a publisher that's been after us to write a healthy cookbook for some time.

"We've also been asked to consider doing a syndicated newspaper column on healthy eating," his father added. "So we're actually really excited about making this change. Selling the stores will give us a good cushion for retirement and allow us to pursue these other interests. But we would definitely welcome your help and expertise in arranging the sale of the business. That's a little out of our league."

"Are you sure about this?" Blake asked slowly.

"Yes. We talked it over. And prayed about it. I have to admit, we were tempted to say yes to your offer just because we'd get to see you a lot more," his mother said wistfully.

"But we knew that was selfish," Carl added. "You have your own life to lead."

Blake frowned. "Is that the real reason you're doing this? For me?"

"Partly," his mother admitted. "But it's also for us. We really do want to go back to a less stressful lifestyle that lets us pursue our other interests."

"We hope you won't be a stranger, though, son. You know you're always welcome to visit anytime."

The undisguised emotion in his father's voice tugged at Blake's heart. "I plan to take you up on that."

He heard his mother sniffle. "It's good to have you back, Blake. We love you."

He hadn't been able to say it in person. He wasn't quite there yet. But somehow, by phone, it was easier. "I love you guys, too."

"We'll see you next week, son. Tell A.J. we said hello."

"I will."

As they hung up, his heart suddenly light, he knew he had a whole lot more than that to tell the woman he loved.

And he hoped that when she heard the news, when she knew that marrying him wouldn't turn her world upside down after all, she would feel more comfortable accepting his ring—and his heart.

A.J. pressed the doorbell for the third time, with the same result. No answer. She turned and looked up and down Blake's street. He was probably out riding his bike or running, she speculated, as she juggled the bagels and coffee she'd picked up on the way to his house. She supposed she could wait. He had to come back sooner or later. And they could always nuke the coffee. But she didn't want to wait. Now that she'd decided to accept his proposal, she was anxious to tell him immediately. She'd delayed things long enough.

She balanced the cardboard tray on top of the banister and dug in her purse for her cell phone. He might have his phone with him, she thought hopefully. It was worth a try.

Blake pulled a T-shirt over his head and flipped off the shower exhaust just in time to hear his cell phone ringing. He made a dash for it. "Hello?"

"Blake? It's A.J."

Her voice had a breathless quality, and his own breathing suddenly went haywire. "Hi? What's up?"

"I was hoping we could get together this morning."

"I'd like that. Where are you right now?"

"On your front porch. Where are you?"

He frowned and made his way to the front door. Through the peephole he saw her balancing a tray on the banister. Her back was to him, and he quietly opened the door.

"Turn around."

There was a momentary hesitation. "What?"

He grinned. "Turn around."

She did…and stopped breathing. Blake stood in the doorway, barefoot, dressed in cutoff jeans that revealed his muscular legs and a T-shirt that hugged his broad chest. His hair was damp and spiky, like he'd just stepped out of the shower. He still looked tired—but incredibly handsome. Suddenly she felt way too warm—and she knew her condition had nothing to do with the muggy humidity.

Slowly he pushed the door open. "I was in the shower, so I didn't hear you ringing. Come in."

She reached for the tray, venturing a quick glance at him as she passed. "I brought us breakfast. Shall I put it in the kitchen?"

"Sure." He closed the door. "Give me a minute while I run a comb through my hair and shave, okay?"

"Sure."

By the time he returned, A.J. had put out plates and silverware. He also noticed the satin jeweler's box sitting in the middle of the table. Blake's grin faded, and his gut clenched. This didn't look good.

"I already put some cream in your coffee," A.J. said.

"Thanks." He dropped into the chair across from her and took a fortifying sip. Then he glanced down at the satin box between them.

"There's something I'd like to tell you," he said slowly. "I had a call from my parents this morning."

Anxiety filled her eyes. "Is everything okay?"

"Yes. They just wanted to discuss business."

She expelled a relieved breath. "I've been so worried about your dad."

"Me, too. I'd like to tell you what we talked about."

"I'd like to hear it. But I have some things I'd like to tell you first."

"It might be better if…"

She laid her hand over his. "Please, Blake. I'd like to go first. While I still have the nerve." She tried to grin but couldn't quite pull it off.

Blake felt his stomach twist in knots. He didn't even try to speak. He just nodded.

A.J. took a deep breath, and when she spoke her voice was slightly uneven. "A long time ago, that day in the storeroom when I was trying to put a box on the top shelf, you told me that I didn't want to rely on anyone, and that's why I never asked for help. Well, you were right. I was afraid of getting hurt again. I've done a lot of soul-searching these past few weeks, and had more than one conversation with Reverend Matthews. Because when I thought about it honestly, I realized that my fear about commitments, about putting down roots, about letting people into my life, reflected a lack of trust in God. It was ironic, really. I'd always thought my faith was strong. And it was, in a lot of ways. But I hadn't been able to fully put my life in God's hands."

She looked down and began tearing her bagel into little pieces. "I was a lot like you, actually," she said quietly. "Because of your experience growing up, you didn't want to rely on anyone but yourself. So you methodically set out to make sure that your tomorrows were safe and that you were in control. I set out to do the same thing, in a different way and for different reasons. But the thing is, we don't even know if we have tomorrow. All we have is today. So we just need to live each day the best we can, accept the gifts that the Lord sends our way, and trust that He will be with us if things don't always work out as we plan."

She reached for the box and flipped it open. The antique diamond blinked back at them. Blake noticed that A.J.'s hands were trembling. So were his.

"Just when I started to put down roots, to take a chance on tomorrow, you asked me to marry you and to tear out those roots, to start over again in a new place. That scared me, Blake. To be honest, it still does. But you know what scares me more? Not having you in my life. Because in these past few months, as I came to recognize what a fine and wonderful man you are, I fell in love. I didn't expect it. I didn't even want it. But it happened. And I'm glad. And very, very grateful. Because my life is so much richer because of you. So, as Ruth told Naomi, wherever you go, I will go. As your wife."

Her voice broke on the last word. The tension in Blake's shoulders eased as his heart soared. He was on his feet instantly, and when he reached for her she came willingly. He gathered her in his arms, sending a silent prayer of thanks heavenward. He knew that A.J.'s decision had been a difficult one. Because while he hadn't doubted that her love for him was strong, he'd been afraid that her fear of being hurt again, of losing someone she loved, was stronger.

But her willingness to give up the life she'd created in St. Louis, as well as the shop she loved and had fought for, and follow him to a new place, illustrated the depth of her love. It was a gift he would always cherish. And now he could give her a gift as well.

He pulled back slightly, and gently traced the path of a tear down her cheek. "I didn't plan to make you cry," he said, his own voice none too steady.

"These are tears of joy, Blake."

"Well, then I have some news that may unleash a flood."

She gave him a quizzical look. "What do you mean?"

"You know that phone call I had from my parents this morning? They're selling the stores."

She stared at him blankly. "What?"

"They're selling the stores."

She frowned. "But…why?"

"They've had a good offer. And I think they figure it's time to move on. They said the heart attack was a wake-up call. They want to travel more and write a cookbook and go out on the speaking circuit. And spend more time with each other."

Slowly the implication began to dawn on A.J. "So they don't need a business manager?"

"Only long enough to oversee the sale."

"And then you'll come back?"

He cupped her face with his hands. "Forever."

"Don't promise forever," she said softly, her voice breaking.

He stroked her cheeks with his thumbs. "Forever," he repeated firmly. "Because our love isn't tied to earthly bonds. It will continue for always."

He reached for the ring and gently eased it out of its case. "We can have this reset if you prefer something more modern."

"I like vintage things. Remember?"

He took her trembling hand in his and eased the ring over her finger, his gaze locked on hers. "I love you, A.J. Lots of things change in this world, but I promise that my love for you won't. Through good times and bad, I'll stand by your side. You can count on me."

The ring slipped over her finger and settled into place. A.J. looked down at it. "It's a perfect fit," she said softly.

"Perfect," he repeated.

When she looked back up at him, his gaze was fixed on her, not the ring. Then he sealed their engagement with a kiss filled with tenderness, joy, enduring love and the promise of their life to come.

A.J. gave herself to the kiss. But before she completely lost herself in the magic of Blake's embrace, she sent a silent, heartfelt message heavenward to the woman whose legacy had made her happy ending possible.

"Thank you, Aunt Jo."

Epilogue

❦

"This looks like an important letter."

A.J. glanced toward Nancy, who was sorting mail. "Why do you say that?"

"It's from a law firm."

A.J. reached for the letter and glanced at the return address. Mitchell and Peterson. Her aunt's law firm. Seth Mitchell had called her a few days earlier to remind her that the six-month period in Jo's will was over, and to find out whether her aunt's stipulation had been met. She'd happily informed him that not only had she and Blake carried through on their business partnership, they planned to make it a permanent—and much more personal—arrangement. He'd offered his congratulations and said he'd be in touch shortly. This must be the follow-up.

She ripped open the envelope and quickly scanned a brief note that was attached to another, smaller envelope.

"Ms. Williams: Your aunt asked that I forward this to you after the six-month period specified in her will.

My congratulations again to you and Mr. Sullivan. I wish you great happiness."

A.J. glanced at the smaller envelope, written in her aunt's flowing hand, and addressed to both her and Blake. She went in search of him, and found him in the romance section, putting a stack of books on the shelf.

"Look at this," she said, holding the letter out to him.

He set the books down and took the envelope. After a quick glance, he looked back at her, puzzled. "This is from Jo. I recognize her handwriting. Where did you get it?"

"Her lawyer, Seth Mitchell just sent it. Go ahead and open it." She handed him a letter opener she'd brought from the back.

Blake slit the flap, and A.J. moved closer as they simultaneously read Jo's note.

My dearest A.J. and Blake, please accept my congratulations on your engagement. I am overjoyed that the two of you have fallen in love. It's what I had hoped for, you know. That was the reason for the stipulation in my will—to bring you together.

Much to our regret, Walt and I never had children. So A.J., you and your sisters have always been special to me. As I grew older, I knew that I wanted to leave each of you something of lasting value. I have always found great solace in books, and Turning Leaves helped me turn over a new leaf in my own life when Walt died. It went a long way toward filling the void his absence created. I hoped it would do the same for you, and that you would come to love it as Blake and I do. But I also wanted to leave you a more lasting legacy.

I felt the same way about you, Blake. I treasured your support and guidance these past few years, as well as your friendship. You have always held a very special place in my heart.

So I wanted to give you both the best gift of all. Namely, love. I am glad that you have found this priceless treasure as a result of my bequest.

I hope that both of you will forgive an old lady for her interference in your lives. But please understand that it was done out of love, with only the best intentions. I am delighted that the ending to your story is a happy one. May your future be bright and filled with faith and love.

A.J. and Blake finished reading the letter at almost the same time. When they glanced at each other, A.J. noted that Blake's eyes were suspiciously moist. As were hers.

"Did you have any idea?" she asked softly.

"None."

"But…how could Aunt Jo know this would happen?"

He shrugged. "She was a very insightful woman. I guess she knew us better than we knew ourselves."

A.J. put her arms around Blake's neck and gave him a teasing grin. "Maybe. But I plan to get to know you a whole lot better."

Blake put Jo's letter on the shelf beside him and

then looped his arms around A.J.'s waist. "Why do I think that's exactly what Jo had in mind?" he responded with a smile.

"Then let's not disappoint her."

Blake leaned toward her, and just before his lips touched hers, A.J. caught a glimpse of the title of the new book he'd been shelving.

"The Best Gift."

Yes, she thought dreamily, that's exactly what Aunt Jo had given them.

And this time, with the Lord's help, it would last forever.

* * * * *

Dear Reader,

As I write this letter, I am in the midst of making plans for my parents' fiftieth anniversary party, and legacies are on my mind.

The dictionary defines *legacy* as a gift by will, especially of money or personal property. But a legacy doesn't have to consist of material things. Nor does it have to follow someone's departure from this earthly life. In fact, the best legacies aren't and don't. They are living things, given daily, so that the lucky recipients find themselves richly blessed with the things that matter most. The things money can't buy.

My parents have given me such a legacy. I will be forever indebted to them for magical Christmas mornings, memorable family vacations and special moments of infinite sweetness. I am grateful to them for teaching me that it's better to give than to receive. For making *home* a word to be revered and honored. And for providing a shining illustration of what marriage is all about. Their legacy to me includes the gifts of acceptance. Laughter. Encouragement. Respect. Family. And, most especially, absolute love that is unconditional. Unlimited. Forever. That is a legacy beyond price.

In this first book of my series for the Love Inspired line, SISTERS & BRIDES, Aunt Jo offers A.J. and Blake a legacy. But it is up to them to recognize it—and to have the courage to claim it. Because love doesn't always come in the form we expect. And it often requires a leap of faith. But with God's grace, with trust in His abiding presence, we can learn to overcome our fears and find our own happy endings.

Just like my mom and dad did.

Irene Hannon

GIFT FROM THE HEART

For You have tested us, O God! You have tried us as silver is tried by fire; You have brought us into a snare; You laid a heavy burden on our back. You let men ride over our heads; we went through fire and water, but You have led us out to refreshment.

—*Psalms* 66:10–12

To my wonderful husband, Tom, who supported
my decision to leave the corporate world
and follow my dream. Thank you—always—
for your gifts of love and encouragement.

HOW TO VALIDATE YOUR
EDITOR'S FREE GIFTS!
"THANK YOU"

1 Peel off the FREE GIFTS SEAL from front cover. Place it in the space provided at right. This automatically entitles you to receive two free books and two exciting surprise gifts.

2 Send back this card and you'll get 2 Love Inspired® books. These books are worth over $10, but are yours absolutely FREE!

3 There's no catch. You're under no obligation to buy anything. We charge nothing—ZERO—for your first shipment. And you don't have to make any minimum number of purchases—not even one!

4 We call this line Love Inspired because every month you'll receive books that are filled with inspirational romance. These contemporary love stories will lift your spirits with stories about life, faith and love! You'll like the convenience of getting them delivered to your home well before they are in stores. And you'll love our discount prices, too!

5 We hope that after receiving your free books you'll want to remain a subscriber. But the choice is yours—to continue or cancel, anytime at all! So why not take us up on our invitation, with no risk of any kind. You'll be glad you did!

6 And remember... just for validating your Editor's Free Gifts Offer, we'll send you 2 books and 2 gifts, *ABSOLUTELY FREE!*

YOURS FREE!

We'll send you two fabulous surprise gifts (worth about $10) absolutely FREE, simply for accepting our no-risk offer!

The Editor's "Thank You" Free Gifts Include:

- ● Two inspirational romance books
- ● Two exciting surprise gifts

YES!

PLACE
FREE GIFTS
SEAL
HERE

I have placed my Editor's "thank you" Free Gifts seal in the space provided above. Please send me the 2 FREE books and 2 FREE gifts for which I qualify. I understand that I am under no obligation to purchase anything further, as explained on the opposite page.

	I prefer the regular-print edition 113 IDL EYPP 313 IDL EYQD

	I prefer the larger-print edition 121 IDL EYPZ 321 IDL EYQP

FIRST NAME   LAST NAME

ADDRESS

APT.#   CITY

STATE/PROV.   ZIP/POSTAL CODE

Order online at:
www.ReaderService.com

Steeple
Hill®

Steeple Hill Reader Service — Here's How It Works:

Prologue

Clare Randall drew a shaky breath and reached up with trembling fingers to tuck a stray strand of honey-gold hair back into her elegant chignon. With a sigh, she transferred her gaze from the brilliant St. Louis late-October sky outside the window to the interior of the legal offices of Mitchell and Montgomery. Normally, the hushed, elegant setting would have calmed her. As it was, the tranquil ambiance created by the dove-gray carpeting, rich mahogany wainscoting and subdued lighting did little to settle her turbulent emotions.

Still, she couldn't help noticing that Seth Mitchell, Aunt Jo's attorney, had good taste. Or at least his decorator did. The Lladro figurine displayed on a lighted shelf was exquisite, the Waterford bowl beside it stunning. Yet the beautiful items left her feeling only sad and melancholy, for they reminded her of another time, another life, when her world had been filled with such expensive objects. A life that now seemed only a distant memory as she struggled just to eke out a living.

Suddenly the door to the inner office opened, and three heads swiveled in unison toward the attorney.

Please, Lord, let this be the answer to my prayers! Clare pleaded in fervent silence as her fingers tightened convulsively on the tissue in her lap.

But the distinguished, gray-haired man who paused on the threshold didn't appear to be in any hurry to disclose the contents of Jo Warren's last will and testament as he gave each of her great-nieces a slow, discerning appraisal.

Clare wondered how they fared as she, too, turned to contemplate her sisters. A.J., the youngest, was tall and lean, with long, naturally curly strawberry-blond hair too unruly to be tamed even by strategically placed combs. Her calf-length skirt and long tunic top, cinched at the waist with an unusual metal belt, were somewhat eclectic, but the attire suited her free-spirited personality. She seemed curious and interested as she gazed back at Seth Mitchell.

Clare looked toward Morgan. Her middle sister wore her dark copper-colored hair in a sleek, shoulder-length style, and her chic business attire screamed big city and success. She was looking at the attorney with a bored, impatient, let's-get-on-with-this-because-I-have-better-things-to-do look.

And how did Seth Mitchell view her? Clare wondered, as she turned back to him. Did he see the deep, lingering sadness in the depths of her eyes? Or did he only notice her designer suit and Gucci purse—remnants of a life that had vanished one fateful day two years ago.

She had no time to ponder those questions, because suddenly her great-aunt's attorney moved toward them. "Good morning, ladies. I'm Seth Mitchell. I recognize you from Jo's description—A.J., Morgan, Clare," he said, correctly identifying the sisters as he extended his hand to each in turn. "Please accept my condolences on the loss of your aunt. She was a great lady."

They murmured polite responses, and he motioned toward his office. "If you're ready, we can proceed with the reading of the will."

Clare paused to reach for her purse, glancing at her sisters as they passed by. Morgan was looking at her watch, clearly anxious to get to the airport in plenty of time for her flight back to Boston and the high-stakes advertising world she inhabited. A.J. had slowed her step to take another look at the flame-red maples outside the window.

Clare shook her head and an affectionate smile tugged at the corners of her mouth. No two sisters could be more different. A.J. always took time to smell the flowers; Morgan didn't even notice them. And their personalities had clashed in other ways, too. As the oldest, Clare had spent much of her youth acting as mediator between the two of them. Yet the three sisters shared an enduring bond, one that had only been strengthened as they'd clung together through A.J.'s tragedy.

And her own.

As Clare followed her sisters into the attorney's office, her spirits nosedived. The past two years had tested her faith—and her finances—to the breaking point. Her work as a substitute teacher barely kept her solvent, and loneliness—especially during the endless, dark nights when sleep was elusive—was her constant companion. With A.J. living in Chicago, Morgan in Boston and Clare in Kansas City, their contact was largely confined to periodic telephone chats. Which was better than nothing. But not enough. For the past couple of days, as they'd come together to mourn and pay tribute to their great-aunt, Clare had felt a sense of comfort, of love, of warmth that had long been absent from her life. She would miss them when they all returned to their own lives.

Tears pricked her eyelids again, and she blinked them back fiercely, fighting to maintain control. Crying didn't help anything. It was just a selfish exercise in self-indulgence. Especially when she had no one to blame for her situation except herself. Focus on the present, she told herself resolutely as she took a steadying breath. Just concentrate on what Aunt Jo's attorney has to say and put regrets aside for a few minutes.

Seth Mitchell waited until the three women were seated, then picked up a hefty document. "I'll give each of you a copy of your great-aunt's will to take with you, so I don't think there's any reason to go through this whole document now. A lot of it is legalese, and there are some charitable bequests that you can review at your leisure. I thought we could restrict the formal reading to the section that affects each of you directly, if that's agreeable."

Morgan quickly replied in the affirmative, making it clear that she was in a hurry. Then, as if realizing she may have overstepped, she sent her older sister a questioning look. Clare nodded her assent, struck as always by Morgan's focus on her job. Clare had enjoyed her teaching career, but she hadn't built her life around it. Nor had A.J. put success—in a worldly sense—at the top of her priority list. Clare wasn't sure why Morgan had become so focused on making the big bucks. But maybe she should take a lesson from her middle sister, she acknowledged with a sigh. Because she could use some big bucks about now. Or even some small bucks, for that matter. That's why Aunt Jo's bequest seemed the answer to a prayer.

As Seth flipped through the document to a marked page and began to read, Clare forced herself to pay attention.

"Insofar as I have no living relatives other than my three great-nieces—the daughters of my sole nephew, Jonathan Williams, now deceased—I bequeath the bulk of my estate to them in the following manner and with the following stipulations and conditions.

"To Abigail Jeanette Williams, I bequeath half ownership of my bookstore in St. Louis, Turning Leaves, with the stipulation that she retain ownership for a minimum of six months and work full-time in the store during this period. The remaining half ownership I bequeath to the present manager, Blake Sullivan, with the same stipulation.

"To Morgan Williams, I bequeath half ownership of Serenity Point, my cottage in Seaside, Maine, providing that she retains her ownership for a six-month period following my death and that she spends a total of four weeks in residence at the cottage. During this time she is also to provide advertising and promotional assistance for Good Shepherd Camp and attend board meetings as an advisory member. The remaining half ownership of the cottage I bequeath to Grant Kincaid of Seaside, Maine.

"To Clare Randall, I bequeath my remaining financial assets, except for those designated to be given to the charities specified in this document, with the stipulation that she serve as nanny for Nicole Wright, daughter of Dr. Adam Wright of Hope Creek, North Carolina, for a period of six months, at no charge to Dr. Wright.

"Should the stipulations and conditions for the aforementioned bequests not be fulfilled, the specified assets will be disposed of according to directions given to my attorney, Seth Mitchell. He will also designate the date on which the clock will begin ticking on the six-month period specified in my will."

Seth lowered the document to his desk and looked at the women across from him.

"There you have it, ladies. I can provide more details on your bequests to each of you individually, but are there any general questions that I can answer?"

Clare vaguely heard the disgust in Morgan's voice as she made some comment about the impossibility of getting away from the office for four days, let alone four weeks. A.J., on her other hand, sounded excited about the bookshop and eager to tackle a new challenge. But Clare was too caught up in her own bequest to pay much attention to her sisters' questions.

"Who is this Dr. Wright?" Clare asked with a frown. "And what makes Aunt Jo think he would want me as a nanny?"

"Dr. Wright is an old friend of Jo's from St. Louis. I believe she met him through her church, and even when he moved to North Carolina, they remained close friends," Seth told Clare. "He's a widower with an eleven-year-old daughter who apparently needs guidance and closer supervision. As to why Jo thought Dr. Wright would be interested in having you as a nanny, I can't say."

He paused and glanced at his desk calendar. "Let's officially start the clock for the six-month period on December first. That will give you about a month to make plans. Now, are there any more general questions?"

When no one responded, he nodded. "Very well." He handed them each a manila envelope. "But do feel free to call if any come up as you review the will more thoroughly." He rose and extended his hand to each sister in turn. "Again, my condolences on the death of your great-aunt. Jo had a positive impact on countless lives and will be missed by many people. I know she loved each of you very much, and that she wanted you to succeed in claiming your bequests. Good luck, ladies."

The three sisters exited Seth Mitchell's office silently, each lost in her own thoughts. When Clare had been notified that she'd been named as a beneficiary in Aunt Jo's will, she'd just assumed that her great aunt had left her a small amount of cash—enough, she hoped, to tide her over until she got her teaching career reestablished. She certainly hadn't expected a six-figure bequest. Or one that came with strings.

None of them had.

She glanced at her sisters. A.J. looked enthusiastic and energized. But then, she was always up for some new adventure, and she had no real ties to Chicago. It would be easy for her to move and start a new life. Morgan, on the other hand, looked put out. To claim her inheritance, she'd have to find a way to juggle the demands of her career with the stipulations in the will. And that wouldn't be easy.

As for Clare—she was just confused. She'd never been to North Carolina, had no experience as a nanny and had never heard of this Dr. Wright. It wasn't that she minded moving; she had nothing to hold her in Kansas City now. Yet wouldn't this man think it odd if she just showed up on his doorstep and offered to be his daughter's nanny?

But Clare needed Aunt Jo's inheritance. She had to find a way to make this work.

As the sisters paused outside Seth Mitchell's office, each preparing to go her own way, Clare's eyes teared up once more. It might be a long time before they were together again. And different as they were, they'd always been like the Three Musketeers—one for all, and all for one.

A.J. also looked misty-eyed as she reached over to give each of her sisters a hug. "Keep in touch, okay?"

"Have fun with the bookshop," Clare told her. Then she turned to Morgan. "I hope you can work things out with the cottage."

Morgan returned her hug. "I'm not holding my breath," she said dryly.

"I'll pray for all of us," A.J. promised.

That was a good thing, Clare thought, as they parted. Because they would need all the prayers they could get.

Along with a whole lot of luck.

Chapter One

Hope Creek, North Carolina

Dr. Adam Wright wearily reached for the stack of messages on his desk and glanced at the clock, then to the early November darkness outside his window. He was already late picking up Nicole, and he knew he'd hear about it. Neither his wife nor his daughter had ever had much patience with the demands of his family practice. And things had gone from bad to worse with Nicole since she'd come to live with him a year ago. Toss awakening hormones into the mix, and it was a recipe for disaster. Which just about described his relationship with his eleven-year-old daughter, he thought with a sigh.

Adam rapidly scanned the messages. Janice had taken care of all but the most urgent in her usual efficient manner, he noted gratefully. Those that remained were from patients who really did need to speak with him. Except for the last one.

Adam frowned at the unfamiliar name and the out-of-state area code. The message was from a woman named Clare Randall and contained just one word—*Personal.* His frown deepened. Janice usually intercepted salespeople, so he assumed this Clare Randall had convinced Janice that she had a legitimate reason for wanting to speak with him. But the message wasn't marked urgent, so it could wait until tomorrow, he decided. The other calls he'd return from home, after he picked up Nicole.

It would help pass the long evening ahead, in which he assumed his daughter would once again give him the silent treatment for his latest transgression of tardiness.

Nicole was out the door of Mrs. Scott's house even before Adam's car came to a stop. The older woman appeared a moment later, and even from a distance Adam could see her frown. Not a good sign. He summoned up a smile and waved to his temporary baby-sitter, then steeled himself for the coming encounter with his daughter. His stomach clenched, and he forced himself to take a deep breath as she climbed into the car and slammed the door.

"Did you thank Mrs. Scott?" he asked.

Nicole didn't look at him, and when she spoke her voice was surly—and accusatory. "Why should I? You pay her to watch me. And you're late. Again."

A muscle clenched in his jaw even as he told himself to cut his daughter some slack. She'd lost her mother just over a year ago, been forced to live with a father she'd never quite connected with, then been uprooted from her home and friends in St. Louis and plopped down in this small North Carolina town. At the time, Adam had thought the move back to his home state was for the best. He didn't like the crowd of friends Nicole hung out with, nor the fact that she often seemed to be eleven going on thirty. Day by day he'd felt his authority slipping away as his daughter spun out of control. So when he'd heard of the need for a doctor in Hope Creek, it had seemed like the answer to his prayers. He'd hoped that the wholesome atmosphere of small-town living would straighten Nicole out and help them bond.

Unfortunately, things hadn't worked out that way. If anything, Nicole resented him more than ever, and the gulf between them had widened. She had also become a master at evading questions and putting him on the defensive, he realized. But the ploy wasn't going to work tonight.

"The issue isn't whether or not I pay Mrs. Scott. The issue is politeness," he said firmly.

She ignored his comment. "So why were you late?"

He wasn't going to be sidetracked. He'd already been through half a dozen sitters. He was grateful that Mrs. Scott from church had taken pity on him and offered to watch Nicole until he found someone on a more permanent basis. But he hadn't had any luck on that score yet. So he couldn't afford to alienate his Good Samaritan.

"Did you thank Mrs. Scott?" he repeated more firmly.

Her jaw settled into a stubborn line, and she glared at him defiantly. "Yes."

He knew she was lying. And she knew he knew it. She was calling his bluff. And he couldn't back down. "That's good. I think I'll just go have a word with Mrs. Scott myself," he said evenly as he reached for the door handle. He was halfway out of the car before she spoke.

"Okay, so I didn't thank her," Nicole said sullenly.

Adam paused, then settled back in the car. "There's still time. She hasn't gone in yet."

Nicole gave him a venomous look, then rolled down her window. "Thanks," she called unenthusiastically. The woman acknowledged the comment with a wave, then closed the door. Nicole rolled her window back up, folded her arms across her chest and stared straight ahead.

Adam stifled a sigh. Nicole's response had hardly been gracious. But at least she had complied with his instruction. He supposed that was something.

"So why were you late again?" Nicole asked as they made the short drive to the house Adam had purchased the year before.

"A couple of last-minute emergencies came up." Adam had done his best to maintain a more moderate workload than he had in St. Louis, but he still rarely got out of the office before five-thirty or six. "Do you want to stop and pick up dinner at the Bluebird? It's meat loaf night." The Bluebird Café's offerings had become a staple of their diet, and meat loaf was one of Nicole's favorites. Adam's culinary skills were marginal at best, and while he could manage breakfast and lunch, dinner stretched his abilities to the limit. So they frequented the Bluebird or resorted to microwave dinners. Only rarely did he indulge Nicole's preference for fast food.

"Whatever."

He cast a sideways glance in her direction. She was sitting as far away from him as the seat belt would allow, hugging her books to her chest, her posture stiff and unyielding. As distant and unreachable as the stars that were beginning to appear in the night sky. Just like Elaine had been by the time their marriage fell apart four years ago. Now, as then, he felt isolated. And utterly alone. He didn't blame Elaine for his feelings. Or Nicole. His loneliness was a consequence of his own failings. Of his inability to connect emotionally to the people he loved. That was the legacy his own father had left him.

Adam made a quick stop at the Bluebird, and a few minutes later pulled into the detached garage next to his two-story frame house, ending the silent ride home. Nicole got out of the car immediately, leaving him alone in the dark. The savory aroma of their meal filled the car, but even though he'd skipped lunch, he had no appetite. Because he knew what was ahead.

He and Nicole would eat mostly in silence. Any questions he asked would be met with one-word answers. Then she would disappear to her room on the pretense of doing homework. A few minutes later he'd hear the music from a CD. Though they shared a house, they'd each spend the evening alone, in solitary pursuits.

Adam desperately wished he knew how to connect with his daughter, who was as lonely as he was, according to the school counselor. Apparently she'd made virtually no friends in the year they'd been in Hope Creek. *Standoffish* and *prickly* were the words the counselor had used to describe his daughter. At the woman's suggestion, they'd actually gone for a few sessions of joint counseling. But Nicole had been so unresponsive that it had seemed a waste of time.

He rested his forearms on the steering wheel and lowered his forehead to his hands, struggling to ward off the despair that threatened to overwhelm him. And, as always in these dark moments, he turned to God for comfort and assistance.

Dear Lord, I need your help, he prayed silently. *I know I'm not doing a good job as a father. And I know Nicole is unhappy. But I don't know how to get past the wall she's built between us. She hates me, and she shuts me out every time I try to reach out to her. I know I failed with Elaine. I don't want to fail with Nicole, too. Please give me strength to carry on and guidance on how to proceed. I can't do this on my own. I'm so afraid that time is running out for us. I love my daughter, Lord. Please help me find a way to make her understand that before it's too late.*

Slowly Adam raised his head, then tiredly reached for their dinner. But when he stepped into the kitchen a few moments later, Nicole was already nuking a frozen dinner. She turned to him defiantly, daring him to comment.

Adam said nothing. He just set the food he no longer wanted on the table, put her meat loaf in the refrigerator and prepared for another silent, strained dinner.

It was going to be a very long night.

Clare added the column of figures again and frowned. Not good. Even with scrupulous budgeting, six months with no income would be rough. But she could make it. She had to. Because she needed Aunt Jo's legacy.

Clare rose and set a kettle to boil on the stove in her tiny efficiency apartment. She could use the microwave, but she preferred boiling water the old-fashioned way. There was something about a whistling kettle that she found comforting. It brought back happy memories of growing up on the farm in Ohio with her parents and two sisters. Though they hadn't been wealthy in a material sense, they'd been rich in love and faith. It was the kind of family she'd always hoped to create for herself.

And she'd succeeded. Up until two years ago. Then her own selfishness had destroyed both of those precious gifts—faith and family.

Clare swallowed past the sudden lump in her throat. She wasn't going to cry. She didn't believe in such indulgences. She'd made a tragic mistake, and now she'd have to live with the results. Her family was gone. And her faith…it wasn't gone, exactly. It was too deeply ingrained to just disappear. But it had languished to the point that she no longer found any comfort in it or felt any connection to God.

Of course, she still had A.J. and Morgan. She wasn't sure what she would have done without their moral support these past two years. But while they were close emotionally, geographically they were scattered. Besides, her sisters had their own lives, their own challenges to deal with. Clare didn't want to unduly burden them with her problems. Especially her financial ones.

She hadn't communicated the sad state of her finances to Aunt Jo, either. Though she'd written to her great-aunt on a regular basis, she'd always tried to be upbeat. Aunt Jo knew that Clare and Dennis had always lived a good life, enjoying the best of everything. When Clare had moved from a lavish home to an apartment after the accident, she'd simply said she needed a change of scenery. And when she'd reentered the teaching world, she'd explained that she just needed to fill her time. So Aunt Jo had had no idea how precarious her situation was. Otherwise, Clare was sure her aunt would have made some income provision for the six months of the nanny stipulation in her will.

That reminded her—Dr. Wright still hadn't returned her call from yesterday. Clare frowned and glanced again at the figures on the sheet in front of her. It was time for another call to the good doctor.

"Adam, I've got Clare Randall on the phone again. She says it's urgent, and she's willing to hold until you have a few minutes."

Adam stopped writing on the chart in front of him and glanced distractedly at Janice. "Clare Randall?"

"She called yesterday. I left the message on your desk."

Adam frowned. "That was the one marked personal, right?"

"Bingo."

"Do you have any idea who she is?"

"Not a clue."

Adam glanced at his watch. "Do I have a few minutes?"

"Mr. Sanders is in room one, but he's telling Mary

Beth about his fishing trip, so I expect he wouldn't mind if you take a couple of minutes. I can't speak for Mary Beth, though. Last time I went by, her eyes were starting to glaze over and she was trying to edge out the door," Janice said with a grin.

Adam chuckled. "You could relieve her."

"No way. Last time he cornered me I had to listen to a twenty-minute soliloquy about the newest hand-tied trout flies he'd discovered."

Adam chuckled again. "Okay. We'll let Mary Beth handle him this time. Go ahead and put the call through."

Adam made a few more notes on the chart, then set it aside as the phone on his desk rang. "This is Adam Wright."

"Dr. Wright, this is Clare Randall. I'm Jo Williams's great-niece. I believe you and my aunt were friends?"

"That's right."

"Well, I'm very sorry to tell you that my aunt passed away two weeks ago."

Adam felt a shock wave pass through him. He and Jo had met at church when he'd first arrived in St. Louis to do his residency, and they'd been friends ever since. Even after his move to North Carolina, they'd kept in touch. In many ways, she had become a mother figure for him, and he had always been grateful for her support and sympathetic ear. He'd had no idea she was even ill. But then, that didn't surprise him. Jo had never been one to burden others with her problems.

"Dr. Wright? Are you still there?"

He cleared his throat, but when he spoke there was

a husky quality to his voice. "Yes. I'm just…shocked. I'm so sorry for your loss. Jo was a great lady."

She could hear the emotion in his voice, and her tone softened in response. "Yes, she was."

"What happened?"

She told him of the fast-acting cancer that had taken Jo's life, and then offered her own condolences. It was obvious that Adam Wright had great affection for her aunt. "Did you know her well?"

"We met more than fifteen years ago, and she became a good friend. We attended the same church when I lived in St. Louis. She was a woman of deep faith. And great generosity."

Clare took a deep breath. "As a matter of fact, her generosity is the reason I'm calling you today. As you may know, Aunt Jo didn't have much family. Just me and my two sisters. And she was very generous to us in her will. However, there is a rather unusual stipulation attached to my bequest."

When Clare hesitated, Adam frowned and glanced at his watch. He had no idea what this had to do with him, and he couldn't keep Mr. Sanders waiting much longer. He pulled the man's chart toward him and flipped it open, his attention already shifting to his next patient.

"So how can I be of assistance?" he asked.

"I understand that you have a daughter named Nicole?"

Adam's frown deepened. "Yes. What is this all about, Ms. Randall?"

"In order to claim my bequest, my aunt required that I act as nanny to your daughter for six months, at no charge to you."

There was a momentary pause. "Excuse me?"

Clare's hand tightened on the phone. "I know this sounds crazy, Dr. Wright. Trust me, I was shocked, too."

"But…why would Jo do such a thing?"

"I have no idea."

Adam tried to sort through the information Jo's great-niece had just given him. None of it made any sense—the stipulation, or this woman's willingness to go to such lengths to claim what couldn't be a large bequest. As far as he knew, Jo wasn't a wealthy woman. With her generous heart, she'd given away far more than seemed prudent to him sometimes. But maybe she'd had more assets than he knew.

Adam glanced up to find Mary Beth standing in the doorway. She nodded her head toward room one, pointed at her watch and rolled her eyes. He got the message.

"Look, Ms. Randall, I've got to go. I have patients waiting. Give me your number and I'll get back to you."

Clare did as he asked, then suggested he call Seth Mitchell. "I'm not sure he can explain Aunt Jo's reasoning any better than I can, but at least he can verify that my offer is legitimate," she said.

"Thanks. I'll do that. I'll be back in touch shortly."

When the line went dead, Clare slowly replaced the receiver. Dr. Wright hadn't exactly been receptive to her offer, she reflected. But she couldn't really blame him. She would have reacted the same way. After all, he was a doctor. He probably made more than enough money to hire any nanny he wanted. In fact, he might have one already. So why should he let a woman he didn't know help raise his daughter, even if it was for only six months?

Logically speaking, there were all kinds of reasons why Adam Wright could—maybe even should—turn her down. So she needed to put together a strategy in case he declined to cooperate.

Because Clare needed Aunt Jo's legacy.

And she didn't intend to take no for an answer.

Adam looked across the kitchen table at Nicole. Tonight she was eating the meat loaf he'd brought home last night, while he ate a frozen dinner. As usual, they were out of sync. He speared a forkful of broccoli and searched for something to say, anything that might generate a little conversation.

"So…anything interesting happen at school today?"

She gave him the look he'd come to clearly recognize over the past year. It was a look that let him know how pathetic she thought his overtures were. And even after all these months, it hurt. But he made himself try again.

"Come on, Nicole. Tell me about your day."

With a long-suffering sigh, she lowered her gaze and picked at her food. "There's nothing to tell. It's just a dumb, hick school. Everything and everybody there is boring."

It was the same refrain he'd heard over and over again. So he changed subjects. "I had some bad news today."

She looked over at him. "Yeah?"

"Do you remember Mrs. Williams, from St. Louis? She ran the bookshop and went to our church."

"Yeah. She was nice."

"I found out today that she passed away a couple of weeks ago."

Nicole looked down at her meat loaf. "Why do people you care about always have to die?"

Adam knew she was thinking of Elaine and the tragic boating accident that had taken her mother's life a little over a year ago. Nicole and Elaine had been close, and though Adam had thought Elaine was too liberal in her child-rearing practices—a frequent point of contention between them—he knew that his wife had deeply loved her daughter. And that Nicole was still grieving for her.

"It was just their time, Nicole," he said gently. "God has His reasons."

"Yeah, well, I don't think God is very nice. He lets bad things happen that just make people sad. I don't know why people are always praying to Him. He never listens anyway."

Adam frowned. Over the past couple of years, he'd been having a harder and harder time getting Nicole to go to church with him on Sunday. And it had become a weekly battle since they had moved to North Carolina. She and Elaine hadn't gone to church regularly, and he knew that the lapse in church attendance had come at a critical stage in Nicole's life, shaking her still-developing faith. It was another change he didn't like in his daughter.

Nicole put her fork down. "May I be excused?"

Adam glanced at her plate. She'd barely touched her food. "Are you feeling all right?"

Nicole glared at him. "Can't you stop being a doctor

even for a minute? I feel fine. I'm just not hungry anymore. So may I be excused?"

Adam's gut clenched. His question had been prompted out of fatherly concern, not medical interest. But clearly Nicole hadn't seen it that way. She saw him as a doctor, not a father. Which only served to underscore the problems in their relationship.

"Yes, you may be excused."

Disheartened, he watched her walk away, then reached into his pocket and pulled out the slip of paper containing Seth Mitchell's phone number. Last night he'd prayed for help with his daughter. Today Clare Randall had called with her offer. That wasn't exactly the kind of help he'd had in mind, but then, God's ways weren't always our ways. Maybe Clare was the answer to his prayer. Since he wasn't getting anywhere with Nicole on his own, and he was rapidly running out of possible babysitters in Hope Creek, he'd be a fool not to at least consider Clare's offer.

He'd been too busy to call Seth Mitchell today. But he'd make that the first order of business tomorrow morning.

Adam slowly replaced the receiver and leaned back thoughtfully in his desk chair. Seth Mitchell had just confirmed Clare's story, though he'd been unable to offer any further insight into Jo's offer. Nor much additional information about Clare herself, except that she was a widow with teaching credentials. When Adam had seemed skeptical about Jo's unusual stipulation, the attorney had assured him that it was completely aboveboard and verified that Clare Randall would expect no payment for her services.

Despite that reassurance, Adam had a hard time accepting the offer. Getting something for nothing was outside the realm of his experience. And it had been ever since he was twelve years old and asked his father for a new bicycle. To this day he vividly recalled his father's gruff response.

"There's no such thing as a free lunch, boy. You have to work for what you want."

So Adam had done just that, doing odd jobs around the neighborhood until he'd earned enough money for his bike. And that was generally the way life had worked for him ever since. Which was why he found it hard to believe that this woman's offer came without any strings attached. Despite what the attorney had said.

Still…he did need help with Nicole. And financially he wasn't in a position to hire a full-time nanny. So wasn't Clare Randall's offer at least worth exploring?

Before he could change his mind, Adam reached for the phone and punched in her number. She answered on the first ring, almost as if she'd been sitting by the phone.

"Ms. Randall? This is Adam Wright. I wanted to follow up on our conversation yesterday. I took your advice and spoke with Seth Mitchell, and he verified that your offer is legitimate."

He paused, and when Clare spoke he could hear the trepidation in her voice. "I sense a 'but' coming," she said cautiously.

"Listen, I'm sorry if I seem a little suspicious, but frankly I keep wondering, what's the catch?"

"What do you mean?"

"Well, if I accept your offer, it will totally disrupt your life for six months. I just can't understand why you'd go through that."

"I'm not going to inherit a million dollars, or anything close to it, if that's what you're asking," Clare said stiffly. "This isn't a TV reality show, Dr. Wright."

She seemed insulted by his question, but Adam didn't think it was completely out of line. She *was* a total stranger, and he wasn't entirely sure about her motivations. Something just didn't feel quite right to him. Then again, maybe it was his problem, he acknowledged. He was so used to paying his own way that maybe he was just uncomfortable accepting anything as a gift.

"Look, Dr. Wright, would it make you more comfortable if we met face to face?" Clare offered when Adam didn't respond.

He could hear a touch of impatience—or was it desperation?—in her voice. "Maybe," he conceded slowly.

"Then why don't I come down?"

He glanced again at the area code. "Where do you live?"

"Kansas City."

"That's a long trip. And I can't make any promises."

"I'm not asking you to."

If she was willing to make the effort to come down, how could he refuse to meet with her? And what did he have to lose, except an hour or two of his time?

"Okay. Let's try that."

Clare had a couple of substitute teaching assignments to fulfill, so they agreed to meet on a Saturday in mid-November.

"I'll see you then," Clare said as she hung up, already making a mental list of all the things she needed to do to prepare for a six-month absence from Kansas City.

Because even though Adam Wright seemed to have some qualms about accepting her offer, she knew one thing with absolute certainty: One way or another, she would find a way to convince the good doctor that she was exactly what he needed.

Chapter Two

Clare let her car slowly roll to a stop, set the brake and peered through the passenger's-side window at Adam Wright's house. Located at the edge of town, on the side of a hill near the end of a country lane, it was just as he'd described it—a two-story white clapboard with forest-green shutters and a large front porch. It was set on a spacious lot shaded by large trees, and a detached garage was just visible to the right, about fifty feet behind the house. When she turned to look out the driver's-side window, she saw a valley filled with fields and patches of woodland. Blue-hazed mountains were visible in the distance, their wooded slopes ablaze with fall color. It was a lovely, peaceful setting—and completely at odds with her emotional state.

Clare nervously withdrew her compact from her purse and studied her face. Despite her best efforts to artfully apply some blush, she still seemed pale. She also looked tired, but there wasn't much she could do about that. She'd driven straight through from Kansas City, arriving last night about ten. Though she'd been exhausted from the long journey, jitters about today's meeting had kept sleep at bay. She'd tossed and turned most of the night, then risen at dawn in anticipation of her nine o'clock meeting with Dr. Wright. The stress and lack of sleep had clearly taken their toll on her appearance.

After one final, dismayed look, she dropped the compact back in her purse and opened her door. This was as good as it was going to get, she acknowledged with a sigh. Maybe Adam Wright wasn't the observant type, she thought as she made her way toward the front porch.

All such hopes quickly vanished, however, when the front door opened in response to the doorbell. In the seconds before he greeted her, the blue-jean-clad man gave her a swift but thorough perusal that was insightful, assessing—and unnerving. She saw surprise in his eyes— and caution. And even before he said a word, she sensed that something about her appearance had raised a red flag. Nervously she smoothed a nonexistent wrinkle out of her skirt and adjusted the strap on her shoulder purse.

As Adam scrutinized his visitor, he struggled to keep his face impassive. Seth Mitchell had described Clare Randall as a widowed schoolteacher. But the elegant, fashionably clad woman on his doorstep was far from the older, matronly type he'd somehow expected. His prospective nanny couldn't possibly be even forty. And she was small. At five foot ten, he didn't consider himself to be especially tall, but she seemed petite beside him. It wasn't that she was short. She had to be about five foot five. But she was very slender; so slender that the fine, classic bone structure of her face was startlingly evident. She was also lovely. Her honey-gold hair was pulled back into a chignon, and her slightly parted lips looked soft. Despite her beauty, he caught a glimpse of a haunting sadness in the depths of her large, azure-blue eyes that stirred something deep in his heart.

She was dressed beautifully, as well. While he wasn't too knowledgeable about clothes, he did know quality when he saw it. His wife had always bought expensive things, so he recognized the designer touch in Clare Randall's attire. Especially the discreet Gucci logo on her handbag.

The woman obviously had money. Which made her willingness to go along with Jo's stipulation even more suspicious.

While Adam assessed her, Clare looked him over, as well. The doctor appeared to be about forty, with dark-brown hair that was touched with silver at the temples. Even though she wore two-inch heels, he was still several inches taller than her. And obviously in good shape. His worn jeans hugged his lean hips, and his sweatshirt couldn't disguise his broad shoulders or the solid expanse of his chest.

She completed her rapid scan at his eyes. They were deep brown—and they'd narrowed imperceptibly since he'd opened the door. A slight frown had also appeared on his face. Not good signs. Clare felt the knot in her stomach tighten.

"Clare Randall, I presume?" He had a deep, well-modulated voice that Clare would have found appealing under other circumstances. Now she was all too conscious of the subtle note of caution in his tone.

"Yes. Dr. Wright?"

He held out his hand, and Clare's delicate fingers were swallowed in his firm grip. "Guilty. Please come in." He stepped aside for her to enter, then nodded to his right. "We can talk in the living room."

As he led the way, Clare looked around the spacious room with an appreciative eye. It was a lovely space, with high ceilings, tall windows and a large fireplace. It had great possibilities…but unfortunately, none of its potential had been realized. While the living room was meticulously clean, it was sparsely furnished. The leather couch and chair were completely out of sync with the character of the house, and the contemporary coffee table was bare. So were the walls. There were shades at the windows, but no window treatments to soften the austerity.

"Make yourself comfortable."

Adam took the chair as Clare perched on the edge of the couch. From her rigid posture, he could only assume that she was as uncomfortable with this whole situation as he was.

"May I get you some coffee?"

"No, thanks. That's not one of my vices." She tried to smile, but couldn't quite get her stiff lips to cooperate.

Clare's obvious tension reminded Adam of patients with white-coat syndrome. The minute they stepped inside his office their blood pressure skyrocketed and they got the shakes. There was no medical explanation for it. But that didn't make it any less real. Through the years he'd worked hard to put such patients at ease, finding that casual small talk sometimes helped. So it was worth a try with his visitor. He purposely leaned back in his chair and crossed an ankle over a knee, keeping his posture relaxed and open.

"Did you have a good trip?"

"Yes. It took a little longer than I thought, but the scenery is lovely."

"When did you leave?"

"About six yesterday morning."

He frowned. "Did you drive straight through?"

"Yes. As I said, it took a little longer than I thought."

"You must be exhausted."

She shrugged. "I've been more tired."

He studied her for a moment. The light from the window was falling directly on her face, and he could see the faint shadows under her eyes—which he suspected she'd carefully tried to conceal. And despite her obviously fair complexion, she seemed pale.

"Did you have breakfast?"

She shook her head. She'd been way too nervous to face food. "Not yet. I'll get something a little later."

His gaze swept her slender figure. Make that too slender, he corrected himself. "You don't look as though you can afford to skip too many meals, Ms. Randall."

"Please call me Clare. And I've always been slender. But I'm very strong, Doctor, and certainly capable of tackling the nanny job."

He hadn't brought up her weight because of concerns about her capabilities, but clearly the job was on her mind. His attempt at small talk wasn't working. So they might as well dive right in. "First of all, my name is Adam, not Doctor. Second, I have to tell you I've never hired a nanny before."

"And I've never been one. So we're even. But I'm sure I can handle the job. I'm a teacher, so I'm used to being around children."

Adam raked his fingers through his hair and sighed. "Nicole isn't exactly a typical child. My wife, Elaine, and I separated several years ago, and Nicole spent most of her time with her mother. When Elaine died a little over a year ago, Nicole came to live with me full-time. It quickly became apparent to me that she had less-than-desirable friends in St. Louis and seemed to be heading down the wrong path. I'm originally from North Carolina, and I thought moving away from the big city might help. But it hasn't worked out as I'd hoped. She may have had the wrong friends in St. Louis, but she has no friends here. She barely tolerates me. And she hates life in a small town. So she can be very difficult to deal with. Frankly, I haven't been able to keep a sitter for more than a few weeks."

Clare frowned. The situation sounded a lot more complicated than she'd expected. But surely, at age eleven, there was still time for Nicole to turn her life around. "I'm certainly willing to do whatever I can to help."

Adam leaned forward and clasped his hands between his knees. "I guess the real question is why. Why do you want to put yourself into this situation? This isn't a happy household, Clare."

Clare swallowed. It might not be happy, but there was time to make things right. Time for a second chance. Which was something she hadn't had with her own family. Clare realized that Adam was studying her intently, and shifted uncomfortably. This wasn't the time to dwell on the past. She needed to convince Adam that she would make a capable and competent nanny. She took a deep breath and looked back at him.

"I appreciate your honesty. But from everything you've told me, it sounds like you need a nanny even more than you realize," she said.

"Maybe. But you haven't answered my question. Why are you willing to do this?"

"I need the money."

His gaze swept over her attire again, lingering on the logo on her handbag. When he looked up, she saw the skepticism in his eyes.

"Don't let my clothes fool you, Doctor," she said quietly. "This suit is several years old. The purse is even older. At one time I was in a position to buy expensive things. That's no longer the case. Aunt Jo's legacy will help me pay off some debts and get a new start. And I will do my best to earn it. I promise you that I will do everything I can to help you with your daughter. If it will make you feel more comfortable, I can supply some character references."

Adam studied the woman across from him. He had no reason to doubt Clare's story that she'd fallen on hard times. And as for a character reference, he couldn't ask for anyone better than Jo—the very person who had sent Clare to his door. But the whole thing still struck him as odd. And somehow unfair to the woman across from him. Despite his thumbnail sketch of the situation, she had no idea what a mess she was stepping into. And he had a feeling she'd already seen enough trauma in her life. The echoes of it were still visible in the depths of her eyes. Which, for some odd reason, troubled him, even though she was a stranger.

"That's not necessary," he said. "But I'd like to…"

"Who are you?"

The two adults turned in unison toward the foyer. Nicole stood in the archway at the entrance to the living room, dressed in hip-hugging jeans and an abbreviated crop top. Her brown hair, worn parted in the middle, hung past her shoulders, the ragged blond ends suggesting that it had once been dyed. She was barefoot, and her toenails were painted iridescent purple.

"It's not polite to interrupt a conversation," Adam said with a frown.

Nicole shrugged insolently. "Whatever. We're out of cereal. Again."

The tension between father and daughter was apparent to Clare even in such a short exchange. Before Adam could respond, she smiled and addressed the young girl. "You must be Nicole."

"Yeah. So why are you here? We never have company."

"I had some business to discuss with your father."

"Are you sick or something?"

Clare looked startled for a moment, then grinned. "I'm not a patient, if that's what you mean."

"Too bad. That's the only thing he cares about."

The remark was meant to cut, and if the sudden clenching of muscles in Adam's jaw was any indication, his daughter had hit the mark. But Clare knew it was also a cry for help. And her heart went out to the lonely little girl.

"Oh, I don't know. We weren't discussing medicine," she said, keeping her tone casual.

Nicole tilted her head and gave Clare an appraising glance. "So are you his girlfriend or something?"

"That's enough, Nicole."

Clare could hear anger in Adam's voice. And frustration. Her heart went out to him, too. He was clearly in over his head with Nicole and clueless about how to control a prepubescent daughter.

"Actually, we just met," Clare said mildly.

Nicole studied Clare for a moment. "I like your hair."

"Thanks. But I was just admiring yours. It's so long and full. You could do some really cool things with it."

"Really? Like what?"

Clare considered Nicole for a moment. "Well, I think you'd look terrific in a French braid."

Nicole stuck her hands in her pockets. "I don't know how to do that."

"It's not hard. But it is easier if someone does it for you. Of course, you'd have to even out the ends a little first."

"I haven't cut my hair in a long time," Nicole said skeptically.

"Well, you wouldn't want to lose any length. Just cut it enough to smooth things out." And get rid of the dyed ends, Clare added silently.

"Do you know how to do a French braid?"

"Mm-hm. I used to do them for my sister, A.J., when we were younger. I'm sure there's a salon in town that could do one for you so you could see if you liked it."

"Maybe." Nicole tucked a lock of hair behind one ear. "So…do you live here?"

"No."

"I didn't think so. Everybody here is such a hick. I bet you're from a big city."

"I live in Kansas City now. But I grew up on a farm in Ohio, out in the middle of nowhere. Hope Creek would have been a big city to us," she said with a smile. "What I've found, though, is that most people are pretty nice anywhere you live if you give them a chance."

Nicole grunted. "Not the kids at my school. They all…"

The sudden ringing of the phone interrupted her, and she turned to Adam with a long-suffering sigh. "It's going to be for you."

"Would you grab it and just take a message, please?"

She gave him a hostile look, then disappeared down the hall.

Clare turned to find Adam studying her. "Is something wrong?"

Slowly he shook his head. "I'm just trying to figure out how you managed to do that."

"What?"

"Have a longer conversation with my daughter than I've had in more than a year."

Clare shrugged. "I came without baggage. She obviously resents you, but she doesn't have any feelings for me one way or the other. Sometimes it's easier to talk to strangers."

He dropped his voice. "So what do you think now that you've met her?"

Clare frowned. "She needs friends. And she needs her father."

"The friends part I agree with. The father part… I'm

not so sure. She pushes me away every time I try to get close to her."

"She's still grieving for her mother. And dealing with a lot of anger…about a lot of things. She's probably mad at her mother for dying. Maybe she's mad at God. She might be mad at life in general because it seems unfair. You're convenient, so you get the brunt of her anger. And you're an easy target, because you're the authority figure. I'm sure she fights you every step of the way. But you know, even if kids don't like rules, they need them."

Adam sighed. "I guess it helps to have a teaching background. You're probably used to dealing with kids. I never had much…"

"I told you it was for you."

They glanced toward Nicole, who was back in the archway.

"Did you take a message?"

She walked toward Adam and thrust a slip of paper at him. Then she turned to Clare. "So will you be here for a while?"

"At least for a few days."

"Maybe I'll see you again."

"That would be nice."

"Yeah." She shoved her hands in her pockets. "Well. See ya around."

Clare watched Nicole walk away, then looked back toward Adam. He was frowning at the paper in his hand.

"Trouble?" she asked.

He glanced up. "One of my patients. I need to get back to him." He took a deep breath. "You said you planned to be here for a few days?"

Actually, she planned to stay for six months. But she simply nodded in reply.

"Let me sleep on this whole nanny thing, okay? Can I get back to you on Monday?"

"Of course."

"How can I reach you?"

"I'm staying at the Evergreen Motel." She rummaged around in her purse and handed him a card. "You can just call me there."

Adam had driven by the Evergreen Motel many times. It was a nondescript one-story building that had obviously seen better days, on the other side of town. Somehow it didn't fit with this woman's designer clothes and Gucci purse. Nor with the woman herself. Whatever her financial situation now, everything about her spelled class. She was the type who belonged at the Ritz, not the Evergreen.

As he walked Clare to the door and they said their goodbyes, he glanced toward the street. Her car—a modest, older-model compact—was yet another confirmation that she'd fallen on tough times. But why? She didn't strike him as the frivolous type. Was her late husband to blame for her current predicament? he wondered, as she made her way toward the street. If so, he had done a great disservice to his wife. Even after only a brief encounter, he sensed that Clare was a kind, intelligent, empathetic woman, who deserved far more than she currently seemed to have. The thought of her at the Evergreen Motel actually made him feel a bit sick.

Clare reached the car and paused to shift her purse

higher on her shoulder, then shaded her eyes with one hand and gazed at the distant mountains. He found himself admiring the natural grace of her movements, as well as her quiet dignity. And he wondered what she was thinking as she looked toward the mist-shrouded peaks.

When she glanced back toward the house, she seemed surprised to find him still standing at the door. And for a moment, he had a sudden, compelling urge to call her back, to offer her a place to stay. Which was very out of character. Because he was not an impulsive guy. And she was a stranger. A moment later, the fleeting impulse disappeared when she slid into the driver's seat.

Adam waited until the car was out of sight, then slowly shut the front door. Even though he'd told Clare he wanted to think about her proposal, he was already pretty sure that he would accept. Because he desperately needed help with Nicole.

And in his heart he had a feeling that Clare was the answer to his prayer.

The water stain on the ceiling in her cramped motel room was the first thing Clare saw when she opened her eyes the next morning, and she quickly averted her gaze. She didn't need luxury, but neither was she used to these kinds of conditions. Tears welled up behind her eyelids, but she refused to give in to them, focusing her thoughts instead on the good, home-cooked meal she'd had yesterday in a quaint little place called the Bluebird Café, and the long, invigorating walk she'd taken through the town. The fresh air, cloudless blue sky and

vibrant trees in their autumn finery had done wonders
to renew her spirits. She'd arrived back at her room so
tired that, despite the lumpy bed, she'd slept soundly.
So, physically, she felt better today. And even though
Adam hadn't given her a definitive answer to her
proposal, she was hopeful that in the end he would say
yes.

In the old days, Clare would have taken a moment
upon waking to speak to the Lord about her situation.
But even though she still tried to pray on occasion, the
words were dry and did nothing to quench the thirst in
her soul. So her talks with the Lord had become infre-
quent at best. She wished she had A.J.'s solid faith.
Tragedy had only strengthened her sister's relationship
with the Lord. Of course, Clare supposed she was better
off than Morgan, who seemed to have completely abandoned the faith of her youth in her pursuit of worldly
success. Still, Clare felt an emptiness that could only be
filled by reconnecting with the Lord. She just didn't
know how to go about it.

An image flashed through her mind of the small
white church in town that had caught her eye yesterday.
Set in a grove of trees, its tall steeple rising toward
Heaven, it had called out to her, offering peace and
solace. She'd gone so far as to try the door, but of course
it was locked in the middle of a Saturday afternoon.
However, Clare had made a note of the times for Sunday
worship.

She glanced at her watch. If she hurried, she could just
make the second service. Since she didn't have anything
else planned for the day, and she wasn't inclined to spend

any more time than necessary at the Evergreen, she figured it couldn't hurt to go. Maybe worshipping in a new place might give her some fresh insights that would help get her back on track in her faith journey.

When Clare pulled up in front of the church forty-five minutes later, the small lot was already full. By the time she found a parking spot half a block away and stepped inside, the service was just beginning. She had planned to simply slip inconspicuously into a pew in the back, but unfortunately, there were no empty seats in the rear. An usher motioned to her, and before she could decline he was leading the way toward an empty spot near the front. Short of ignoring his hospitality, she had no choice but to follow him.

Clare was aware of the curious glances of the congregation as she traversed the main aisle. She supposed that in a small town like Hope Creek, visitors were big news. But she'd never liked being the center of attention, so she kept her eyes looking straight ahead. Only when she murmured a thank-you to the usher did she glance at the pew across the aisle—and found Adam and Nicole watching her. Adam gave her a brief smile and nod, and Nicole peeked around him and waved. Clare smiled in response, then turned her attention to the service. Or at least tried to. But she found herself casting frequent, surreptitious glances at the doctor and his daughter.

Nicole sat on the other side of Adam, so she couldn't see the young girl very well. But she caught enough glimpses to know that Nicole was dressed in tight black hip-hugger jeans. Her top seemed to be a bit more discreet than the one she'd worn yesterday, but it was not attire Clare would have deemed appropriate for church.

Adam, on the other hand, was well dressed. His broad shoulders filled out his dark suit, and a gold tie lay against his starched white shirt. He'd looked great yesterday in jeans, and was equally handsome in today's more impressive formal attire, which gave him a distinguished air.

Clare did her best to sing the hymns and listen to the sermon, but the elderly minister was a bit dry, and she found her attention—and her gaze—frequently wandering over to the doctor and his daughter…until she found Adam staring back. For a moment they'd both seemed startled, then Clare quickly looked away as hot color stole on to her cheeks. Served her right, she thought in chagrin. She was in the house of God. That's where her thoughts should be, too. For the rest of the service she made a concerted effort to be more focused.

As the last hymn ended, however, her thoughts returned to Adam and Nicole. She was so preoccupied formulating a greeting in her head that it took her a moment to realize the woman next to her had spoken.

"I'm sorry. Were you speaking to me?"

The older woman smiled at her. "I'm the one who should apologize. You must have been deep in prayer. I'm sorry I interrupted."

Prayer had been the furthest thing from her mind, Clare thought with a pang of guilt. "No reason to apologize. I must admit that I was thinking about something I need to do after the service. But I *should* have been praying."

The woman chuckled. She had short, stylish gray hair that established her senior status, but her blue eyes twinkled with the enthusiasm of a youngster. "That's something we're all guilty of on occasion, I suspect." She held out her hand. "I'm Adele Malone."

Clare returned the woman's firm handshake. "Clare Randall."

"You're new in town."

"A visitor, actually. I'm here on…business."

"Well, I'm glad you joined us this morning. Why, Nicole…"

Clare turned. Adam and Nicole had moved out of their pew, and stood only a few steps away.

"Your hair looks lovely today!" Adele said.

For the first time Clare noticed that Nicole's hair was done in a neat French braid.

"Thank you. It was Clare's idea."

"We had to find a salon that would take Nicole yesterday afternoon without an appointment. But it was worth the effort. The style suits her." Adam's remark was directed at Clare, and she could read the gratitude in his eyes.

Adele looked with interest at Clare, then at Adam. "You two know each other?"

"We just met yesterday. On a business matter," Adam replied.

"How nice. Well, I was just going to invite our visitor to stay and have coffee in the church hall. I hope you can join us, too."

"Not today, I'm afraid. Nicole has quite a bit of homework, and I have to return a couple of pages that I received during the service."

Was there regret in his voice? Or was it just her imagination, Clare wondered.

"Another time, then. I do hope you'll stay, my dear," Adele said, turning back to Clare.

Clare almost refused. But she really didn't have anything else to do today. And if Adele knew Adam, perhaps the woman could offer a few more insights about the good doctor that would help Clare persuade him. "Thank you. I'd like that."

"Good to see you, Adele," Adam said. Then he turned to Clare. "I'll be in touch."

She nodded, and both she and Adele watched as Adam and Nicole made their way out.

"Such a nice man. And a wonderful doctor," Adele said. "Hope Creek was lucky to get him when Doc Evans retired last year. And he certainly tries hard with Nicole. But it's such a challenge raising children these days. Especially alone." She glanced down at the ring on Clare's left hand. "Do you have children, my dear?"

Clare's throat tightened. Maybe someday that question would be easier to answer. But not yet. It still hurt as much as it had two years before. "No. I'm a widow."

The older woman reached over and spoke softly as she touched Clare's hand. "I'm so sorry."

"Thank you."

"I don't suppose that's something one ever gets over. I know I'd be completely lost without my Ralph. He's home today with a cold, and it just didn't feel quite right sitting in church without him. But you have your faith to sustain you. That's such a great blessing in times of trial." She tucked her arm through Clare's. "Now come along and let's get some coffee and a doughnut. Adam's forever after me to lose twenty pounds, but honestly, I don't think one doughnut on Sunday is going to hurt, do you?"

The woman chatted amiably as they made their way to the church hall, where she took pains to introduce Clare to several members of the congregation. It became clear that Adele was quite prominent in the town, obviously active in both church and civic pursuits. When they finally found themselves alone for a moment, Clare glanced at her watch and set down her cup of tea.

"I think I've taken up far too much of your time," she apologized.

"Not at all. I enjoy meeting new people. Will you be in town long?"

"At least for a few days."

"Do you have any friends or family nearby?"

"No."

"So what are your plans for Thanksgiving?"

Clare hadn't really thought much about the holiday, even though it was only four days away. A.J. had just arrived in St. Louis, so she wasn't in a position to leave the bookstore. And the last she'd heard, Morgan intended to work most of the holiday weekend. So Clare had planned to just grab a bite somewhere by herself. Which was a far cry from how she preferred to celebrate holidays, she thought wistfully. Special days should be festive occasions filled with fun and family. But both of those things were now absent from her life. Treating Thanksgiving like any other day seemed the best way to cope without falling apart.

"I really don't have any plans," she told the older woman.

"Then you must join us for dinner."

Clare stared at her, surprised by the impromptu invitation. "But...I wouldn't want to intrude on a family celebration."

Adele waved her concern aside. "You won't be. My husband and I don't have children, or any close family. So we've always invited others to join us for Thanksgiving. The associate pastor and his wife will be there. And Adam and Nicole are coming, too. Adam's only brother lives in Charlotte, and they go to his wife's house for Thanksgiving. So Adam and Nicole will be on their own for the holiday. There will be a few others, as well. You'd be more than welcome."

Clare considered the invitation. It was certainly preferable to eating at the Bluebird, charming as it was. Besides, the café might not even be open on that day. And it would give her a chance to press her case with Adam. But more than anything, she was touched by the older woman's generosity in opening her home to a stranger on a holiday. Her invitation was truly Christian charity in action.

"Thank you," Clare said with a smile. "I'd love to come. May I bring something?"

"Just yourself." Adele opened her handbag and withdrew a small notepad and pen. "I'll jot down my address and phone number. We usually begin to gather about four."

Clare took the slip of paper a moment later and tucked it in her purse. "Thank you, Mrs. Malone."

"Adele, my dear. We aren't that formal in Hope Creek. And it's my pleasure. No one should spend the holiday alone. Or lonely."

As Clare said her goodbyes, she reflected on Adele's parting words. The woman was right, of course. And she'd apparently taken care of the "alone" part for a number of Hope Creek residents. But the loneliness was harder to deal with. Because it went deeper. And wasn't always as visible.

Adam and Nicole came to mind. They lived in the same house. They shared meals. They went to church together. So they weren't alone. Yet Clare knew they were lonely. And sometimes that kind of loneliness was worse than being physically alone. There was something especially tragic about two people living in close proximity who were unable to connect.

Her work would be cut out for her with Nicole, Clare reflected. The young girl desperately needed guidance. But in her mind, there was a whole lot more to this nanny job than simply helping Nicole get her act together.

Bottom line, Adam and Nicole needed to establish a bond. And they needed an intermediary, a catalyst— maybe even a referee—to help them do that.

It would be a challenging role, Clare knew. But she wanted to play it. Because in the short time they'd spent together, she'd felt their pain. And she wanted to help them salvage their relationship before it was too late.

For Nicole's sake, of course.

But also for Nicole's father.

Chapter Three

"Thanks for coming by on such short notice."

Clare nodded. She hadn't expected to hear back from Adam so soon, but when she'd returned to the Evergreen after church and a quick breakfast she'd found a message waiting, asking her to stop by his house at four o'clock that afternoon. She'd called back, confirming the appointment.

"Would you mind if we talked in the kitchen?" Adam asked. "I had to make an emergency run to the grocery store and I just got back. I need to put a few things away."

"Of course."

Clare followed him down a hallway toward the back of the house. At least the sunny kitchen had a little more personality than the living room. It was painted a pale blue, and a border of trailing morning glory vines had been stenciled along the top of the walls. A weathered oak table and four chairs stood beside a bay window that afforded a lovely view of the pine woods on the hillside behind the house.

"Have a seat and I'll be with you in just a minute," Adam said.

She chose a chair that gave her a view of the restful scene out the window. But instead Clare turned her attention to Adam, watching as he rapidly took items out of the plastic grocery bags—eggs, canned soup, bread, lunch meat, crackers, milk, cereal, microwave dinners. She caught a glimpse of his nearly empty refrigerator when he opened the door to put the milk inside.

"Sorry about this," he apologized. "I try not to shop on Sunday, but sometimes the week just gets away from me. Then it becomes an emergency. I thought I'd have everything put away before you got here, but it always takes me longer at the grocery store than I expect."

"Don't worry about it. I didn't have any plans today, anyway."

He glanced at the counter. "I think that takes care of all the perishables. Can I offer you something to drink?"

When she declined, he filled a coffee cup and joined her at the table. "I know I said I'd call you tomorrow, but frankly, I didn't see any reason to wait. Seth Mitchell has confirmed your story. You seem sincere. I trust Jo's judgment, and I desperately need help with Nicole." And you need Jo's legacy. He didn't voice that reason. But it had been a definite factor in his decision.

Coils of tension deep in the pit of Clare's stomach began to unwind. "Then you're willing to take me on as nanny?"

He took a sip of his coffee and looked at her steadily.

"To be honest, I'm still not entirely comfortable with this. It doesn't seem right for me to accept your services at no cost."

"That was the stipulation in Aunt Jo's will. So there's no choice. And I'm fine with it."

Adam put his mug on the table and wrapped his long, lean fingers around it. "I talked to Nicole about this. Well, I tried to, anyway," he amended. "I didn't get much more than a few grunts, but at least she didn't throw a fit. So I took that as a good sign. I don't think she'll fight you the way she has every other sitter I hired. But I could be wrong. It could be miserable. For everyone. So what I'd like to propose is that we try this for a month. If everything works out, we can commit to the remaining five months. But this will give us both a chance to test the waters and back out if things don't go well. How does that sound?"

Clare had no intention of backing out. She was determined to make this work. So she had no qualms agreeing to Adam's terms. "It seems like a sensible plan."

"Good. As for your duties, I'm open to suggestions since I've never had a nanny before. I thought you could just make sure Nicole gets ready for school on time so she doesn't miss the bus, and be here when she gets home. During the school day your time would be your own. Nicole could also use some help with her schoolwork. Even though her standardized test scores are always high, her grades have been marginal at best since she came to live with me. With your teaching background, I'd appreciate any help you could provide. Most of your weekends should be free, other than

Saturday mornings if I have patients in the hospital and need to do rounds. Ellen James, our housekeeper, comes on Thursdays. She has a key and doesn't need any supervision. Mostly I just need you to keep an eye on Nicole. Does that sound reasonable?"

"Very. And I'll be happy to do some tutoring."

"That would be great. So when can you start?"

"As soon as I find a place to live and get settled in. I hope within a few days."

Suddenly an idea began to take shape in Adam's mind. Considering Clare's current accommodations at the Evergreen Motel, her finances probably wouldn't allow her to upgrade very much when it came to a more permanent place to live. And he had a small, furnished apartment above his garage. Maybe he couldn't pay her, but there was nothing in Jo's will that would prevent her from accepting housing.

"As a matter of fact, I may be able to help," he said. "There's a furnished apartment above my garage that I always planned to fix up and rent out, but I've never gotten around to it. You're welcome to live there. It's the least I can do, considering you're providing your services free of charge."

Clare looked at him in surprise. "Well, that would certainly be convenient." And easy on her tight budget, she silently added.

"Would you like to take a look?"

"Sure."

After retrieving the key from his office, Adam led the way out the back door and down a cobblestone path toward the garage. When they reached the door, his first couple of attempts to pull it open failed. Finally, after he exerted a bit more force, the door swung out.

"I've only been up here a couple of times since I bought the place," he apologized. "The door probably needs to be sanded."

He preceded her up a narrow set of stairs to a small landing where he inserted the key in another door. This one opened easily, and since there wasn't room on the landing for both of them, he stepped inside first. He switched on the harsh overhead light—and immediately regretted his offer.

He'd known the apartment wasn't in great shape, but it was even worse than he remembered. The walls were painted a dingy, muddy beige. The green shag carpeting had seen better days. The garishly upholstered sofa sagged in the middle, and the shade on the lamp beside it was ripped. Even from the front door, he could see that the countertop in the tiny galley kitchen was badly chipped at the edges. A small wooden table and chairs in the tiny eating area were nicked and worn. And he didn't even want to look at the bathroom or bedroom. As near as he could recall, the furnishings in the bedroom included a lumpy bed and a nondescript dresser with a cracked mirror. There was no way he could offer this space to anyone in its present condition. Especially to Clare, with her obvious elegance and breeding.

"Adam?"

He knew he was blocking the door, but he didn't budge. "Listen, this wasn't such a good idea after all. I forgot that this place was in such bad shape."

"Can I at least look around?"

He hesitated. "I'm not sure you want to. This apartment makes the Evergreen Motel look good."

He heard her laugh—a musical sound that he found extraordinarily appealing.

"That bad, huh?"

At least she had a sense of humor. And she was certainly going to need it, considering what she was walking into, literally and figuratively, with him and Nicole. "Let's just say that I think a four-legged creature would be more at home here than a two-legged one."

"Okay, now I *have* to see it."

"Just promise me one thing."

"What?"

"You won't quit before you even start."

She laughed again. "There's no chance of that."

Hands planted on his hips, Adam surveyed the room once more, then shook his head and moved aside. "Okay. But trust me, you won't hurt my feelings if you take one look and run right back down the stairs."

Clare stepped into the apartment, walked slowly to the middle of the room, then pivoted, making every effort to keep her face impassive. Okay, so it was bad. But it was free. And she was pretty handy with a hammer and a paint brush. She completed her perusal of the living room and kitchen area, then peeked into the bathroom. At least it was serviceable. The bedroom, however, didn't fare as well. She would definitely take the lumpy mattress at the Evergreen over this one, which seemed to have a crater in the middle. She returned to the kitchen, opened a few cabinets, checked out the small refrigerator, silent all the while.

Adam watched Clare as she went from room to room, admiring her natural grace even as he berated himself for showing her the apartment. In her slim, black wool skirt and elegant blue silk blouse she looked completely out of place in the run-down apartment. He couldn't possibly let her live here.

"Look, this was a bad idea and I'm sorry for even suggesting it," he apologized as the silence lengthened.

"Actually, this isn't so bad," she said gamely.

He looked at her incredulously. "You've got to be kidding."

"No. I'm serious. Mostly what it needs is a cosmetic makeover. I assume the appliances and heat work?"

"Last time I checked."

She shrugged. "Why don't you let me tackle it? I think I can make this livable."

He raked his fingers through his hair as he skeptically eyed the room again. "I'm not sure it's even salvageable, let alone livable."

"At least let me try."

When he looked into her eyes, he saw determination—and spirit. He suspected she was prepared to argue the case if he withdrew his offer. She must really be strapped for cash if she was willing to take this on, he realized. He thought about just offering to pay for housing somewhere rather than let her deal with this mess, but he knew she'd refuse to take his money. It seemed he'd been backed into a corner. "All right. And I'll send Ellen over to help with the cleaning. But if things don't come together, we'll work something else out, okay?"

"Okay."

"I'll order a new mattress, too. The one in the bedroom seems pretty pathetic."

She looked relieved. "That would be great. Thanks."

"Well, do whatever you need to do. Just save the bills and I'll take care of them. I assume you'll be judicious." He tacked on that last admonition out of habit. He'd always used it with his wife, though it had never worked. That was one of the reasons he hadn't been able to save much money during their marriage. But he was immediately sorry he'd said it to Clare. Luckily, she didn't seem to take offense.

"Of course. I'll get started first thing tomorrow. If all goes well, I should be able to take on my duties as Nicole's nanny in a week. If that's okay."

"Absolutely. I'll have the mattress delivered and the door sanded. Let me know if I can do anything else to help in the meantime."

"Thank you, but I'll be fine. I've gotten used to handling things on my own."

After flipping off the light, Adam followed Clare down the steps. Her head was bent as she navigated the narrow stairs, exposing the delicate nape of her neck below her upswept hair. It made her seem vulnerable. And fragile. And it awakened a protective instinct in him. He recalled experiencing a similar feeling about Elaine early in their marriage. But it had been long absent from his life. Nor did it make any sense now, especially in relation to a virtual stranger who, he suspected, would not appreciate being thought of as either delicate or fragile.

For so many years, the only woman in Adam's life had been Nicole. Worrying about her and their rocky relationship had consumed his thoughts and energies when he was away from work. He'd rarely given any other female more than a passing glance, avoiding well-meant setups by friends and keeping all women at arm's length.

Now Clare would literally be living in his backyard. But as she'd noted moments before, it was a business arrangement, nothing more. And he would do well to remember that. Because even if he was inclined to consider her in a more personal light, that would be a tragic mistake. It was a mistake he'd made once before, with Elaine. And it was one he didn't intend to repeat. It wouldn't be fair to any woman.

Because he just wasn't husband material.

Adam glanced up at Clare's apartment as he hit the electric garage-door opener. As usual, the lights were on. She'd surprised him by moving in right away, even though he'd considered the place unlivable. And no matter what time he looked toward the garage—early in the morning as he grabbed a cup of coffee before leaving for the hospital, or late at night before he went to bed—the lights were on. A pile of debris had begun to accumulate next to the driveway—including the shag carpeting. His work schedule before holidays was always crazy, so he hadn't had a chance to stop in. But he wanted to check on her progress and thank her for assuming some of her duties early. When Clare had found out that Mrs. Scott was going away on vacation during the holiday, she'd offered to watch Nicole after school even though she hadn't officially assumed her position yet.

Adam glanced at his watch. Since Thanksgiving was tomorrow, he'd closed the office early. It was the first time he'd been home before six o'clock in weeks. And there was plenty of time to pay his new nanny a visit before dinner.

The ground-level door to the apartment opened without a problem; the carpenter he'd called had obviously paid a visit. He stepped inside, noting that the stairwell had been cleaned up, as well. The bare light bulbs at the bottom and top of the stairs had been hidden under shades that softly diffused the light. The walls were brighter, too, he noted as he made his ascent. They'd been painted in a soft eggshell color. And the wooden steps had been thoroughly cleaned.

Raising his hand to knock on the door, Adam paused at an unfamiliar sound. His daughter's laughter. His throat tightened with emotion, and he sent a silent prayer of thanks heavenward. He had known it would take a major miracle to get his daughter back on track. But if Clare could get her to laugh, she'd already worked a minor one. He hoped this was just the beginning.

His knock was answered almost immediately, and his words of greeting died on his lips as he stared at the woman looking back at him. Clare's honey-gold hair was carelessly pulled back into a ponytail, and her paint-spattered jeans and sweatshirt were a far cry from her usual designer clothes. She didn't seem to be wearing any makeup, either—unless you counted the specks of paint dotting her porcelain complexion. She looked far younger and less sophisticated than in any of their previous encounters. She also looked very, very appealing.

A faint flush rose on Clare's cheeks, and she dropped her gaze under Adam's close scrutiny. Nervously she wiped her hands on her worn jeans.

"Sorry for the way I look. I wasn't expecting company," she apologized in a breathless voice.

"I didn't mean to barge in. I just wanted to thank you for keeping an eye on Nicole this week. And to see if you needed any help with anything."

She stepped aside and motioned him in. "Actually, everything's going really well. Take a look."

Adam walked into the room, then stopped, stunned by the transformation.

The walls had been painted a sunny yellow. The couch, which seemed to have new cushions, had been slipcovered in a floral print with throw pillows tucked in the corners. A rocking chair had been added, and the ripped lampshade had been replaced. The top of the scarred coffee table was hidden by a large lace doily, and an arrangement of dried flowers stood in the middle. Attractive valances had been draped over the two windows, and the pine floor gleamed under a coat of wax.

Slowly he made his way toward the kitchen area. The blemishes on the wood table and chairs had been masked by bright white paint, and cobalt blue accents on the rungs and table legs added a whimsical touch. Even the nicks in the countertops seemed to have disappeared.

The faint scent of lemon hung in the air, and everything was spotlessly clean.

Adam shook his head and turned to Clare. "This is amazing! How in the world did you manage to do all this in three days?" he asked incredulously.

She grinned, obviously pleased by his reaction. "Lots of elbow grease. I told you I'm stronger than I look. And Ellen was great. Thanks for sending her over. I also had some other help." She nodded toward the bedroom.

He moved toward the doorway. Nicole was on a ladder, sponge painting a wall in peach tones and humming along to some song only she could hear through the earphones of her portable CD player. As she stretched toward the pan of paint, Adam instinctively took a step toward her.

"Be careful, Nicole."

Her placid expression changed to a frown when she saw him. Reluctantly she removed her earphones. "What?"

"I just said to be careful. Ladders can be dangerous."

She rolled her eyes. "I'm eleven. I know how to use a ladder."

"I did the top of the walls already. Nicole's helping me with the rest," Clare said from behind him. "She's doing a terrific job, isn't she?"

Adam turned and looked at Clare. Her eyes seemed to say, "Trust me. I wouldn't let her do anything dangerous. And give her a compliment."

Adam got the message. "This looks great, Nicole." In truth, it did. He really couldn't tell where Clare's handiwork stopped and his daughter's began.

When Nicole didn't respond, Clare glanced at her watch. "Looks like it's almost dinnertime, Nicole. Why don't you clean up in the bathroom, then you can walk back to the house with your dad."

"I'm not finished yet."

"You've already done more than I expected. You were just going to do two walls, remember? You're almost done with the third one. Thanks to you, I'll actually be able to move into the bedroom tonight."

Adam frowned. "Where have you been sleeping?"

"The couch was fine for a couple of nights," she replied lightly. "But I'm anxious to try out the new mattress. It looks very comfortable. Thanks again for ordering it."

"It was the least I could do."

"What do you want me to do with the sponges?" Nicole had climbed off the ladder and now spoke to Clare.

"You can just leave them there. I'm going to do a little more work after you leave. Just show me where you left off."

Adam glanced around the bedroom while Nicole and Clare conferred about the walls. A comforter, still in its plastic bag, stood in the middle of the bed, which had been pulled to the center of the room. The cracked mirror had been replaced with one in a white wicker frame, and a lace runner on the dresser effectively hid the scarred top. Lace curtains hung at the window, and a shade had been added for privacy. As Nicole headed for the bathroom to clean up, Adam turned to Clare.

"Where are you going to put the bed?"

"In the middle, over there," she said, pointing to one

of the finished walls. "That way, when I wake up in the morning, I can look out the window and see the fir trees on the hill."

Shrugging out of his jacket, Adam handed it to her. "Hold this for me and I'll move the bed for you."

She took the soft leather garment, which emanated a faint but very masculine scent. "I can do that," she protested.

"It's too heavy for you. This will only take a minute."

Clare thought about arguing, then decided against it. The bed *was* heavy. She'd had a tough time jockeying it to the center of the room so she could paint the walls. And it was even heavier now, with the new mattress on it.

Adam finished the job far faster than she would have. And considering the way his muscles bunched with strain under the fine cotton of his shirt, revealing impressive biceps, she was glad she'd let him handle it.

"Is this about right?" He stepped back to survey his handiwork.

"Perfect."

He slid his arms back into his jacket, then planted his fists on his hips. "Look, Clare, I appreciate all your efforts here. But the nanny position doesn't require heavy manual labor. You could get hurt trying to move something like that bed. Promise me you won't tackle any more jobs like that."

"I think I'm almost done, anyway."

"Promise me."

His deep-brown eyes were intent, and slowly she nodded. "If it's that important to you, okay, I promise. But like I told you, I'm stronger than I look."

Silently he reached for her hand, splaying the small, delicate fingers in his much-larger palm. She was so taken aback that she could only stare, first at her paint-splattered fingers against his strong, yet gentle hand, then into his intense, enigmatic eyes.

"This hand was not made for heavy labor. I'm sorry if you think that's a sexist remark, but it's the truth. You have a very delicate bone structure, and it wouldn't take much to crush these fingers. That's a medical fact, and I don't want to be paying any house calls to my new neighbor. Okay?"

Clare could manage only a one-word response. "Okay."

He held her hand for a moment longer, than slowly released it.

"I'm ready."

With an apparent effort, Adam looked over to his daughter. "I'll be right with you." Then he turned back to Clare. "If you'll give me the receipts for your expenses, I'll write you a check."

She was glad to focus her attention on something besides the quivery feelings that Adam's touch had ignited in her. "They're on the table." She moved toward the kitchen and picked up an envelope, turning to hand it to him as he followed her into the room. "That should be everything. I did an itemized list of the expenses, and the receipts are attached."

Adam withdrew the single sheet of paper, quickly scanned it, then frowned. "This is the total?"

Nervously she brushed back a stray strand of hair that had escaped from her ponytail. "Well, I can pay for the rocking chair if you like. I didn't really need that. And…"

"Whoa!" He held up his hand. "I'm not complaining, Clare. It's far less than I expected. You did all this—" he gestured around the room "—for *this* amount?"

She drew a relieved breath. "Elbow grease doesn't cost much. And I know how to live frugally. You can find some great buys at discount stores," she said with a grin.

Adam glanced again at the sum. His late wife, Elaine, would have spent far more than that on a new handbag. And she wouldn't have been caught dead shopping at discount stores. Nor would she have handled such a reversal of fortune so well.

Clare, on the other hand, seemed to have accepted whatever blow life had dealt her with grace and character. She had obviously once lived a far more luxurious lifestyle, if the Gucci purse and designer clothes were any indication. Yet she had adapted to her reduced financial status. And he hadn't heard her complain once. Not about the Evergreen Motel, nor about the dismal state of this apartment. And there had been plenty to complain about in both cases.

She was a remarkable woman, he acknowledged. And while he'd questioned her physical strength, he had no doubt that she could hold her own with anyone when it came to inner strength.

As they said their goodbyes and Adam followed Nicole down the steps and out into the chilly night air, he glanced back up at the warm glow emanating from the windows of the garage apartment. And he made another surprising discovery.

The warm glow wasn't only in the windows; for the first time in many years, it was also in his heart.

Chapter Four

"Clare's going to Mrs. Malone's tomorrow for dinner, too. Why don't we give her a ride?"

Adam looked up from the file he'd been studying. Nicole hovered in the doorway to his office, hands in her pockets, shoulders tense, her expression defiant—as it always was in his presence. He wished he knew how to make her relax around him, to elicit her laughter, to evoke even a trace of warmth, as Clare had. Already their new nanny had connected with his daughter as he never had. He was glad for Nicole's sake, of course. She needed a friend. But it only made him realize how miserably he had failed.

"You can come in, Nicole," he said gently.

She shrugged. "I have homework to do. I just wanted to ask about Clare."

Since they'd moved to Hope Creek, Adam couldn't recall a single instance when Nicole had come into his office. And she obviously didn't intend to start tonight.

But she *had* sought him out and initiated this conversation. He considered that a good sign.

He focused on Nicole's question. Clare's invitation was news to him. But it didn't surprise him. Adele Malone had told him once that no one should be alone on a holiday, and she always made an effort to ensure that everyone within the circle of her acquaintance had a place to spend the day. Obviously the older woman had taken Clare under her wing.

"So can we give her a ride?" Nicole repeated impatiently as the silence lengthened.

Adam couldn't think of a reason to say no. At least not any reason that made sense. There was no way to put into words the vague concern that fluttered along the edges of his consciousness, a subtle caution sign about crossing the line between a professional and personal relationship with his new nanny. He couldn't explain his trepidation to Nicole. Or even to himself. So he was left with no alternative. "Sure. I'll walk over later and ask her."

"I can do it."

"I thought you had homework."

Nicole glared at him. "I can take a break for a couple of minutes."

To talk to Clare, but not to him. The message was clear, even if the words were unspoken. "Okay. Let me know what she says."

A half hour passed before Adam heard the back door slam, signaling Nicole's return. A moment later she appeared at his doorway.

"She said she'd go with us. And to say thanks. Here."

Nicole stepped across the threshhold into his office and set down a plate containing four chocolate chip cookies.

"What's this?"

"Clare made some cookies. I stayed to have a couple. That's why I was gone so long. She asked me to bring you these. I gotta get back to my homework," she said, backing out of the room even as she spoke.

Adam looked down at the homemade cookies, still fresh from the oven, oozing chocolate chips. He reached for one and weighed it in his hand for a moment as the just-baked cookie warmed his palm. Then he closed his eyes and bit into it, letting the sweetness dissolve on his tongue.

It had been a long time since he'd had such a treat. Even though some of his patients had given him homemade cookies last Christmas, he'd been so new to his practice that he'd had no faces to associate with the gifts. But he definitely had a face to associate with these cookies. And more.

As Adam reached for a second cookie, he pictured Clare as he'd seen her earlier in the evening, when he'd stopped in to check on her progress with the apartment. She might be close to forty, but she looked about twenty with her hair pulled back into that ponytail, her face makeup free. Only the sadness that hovered in the depths of her eyes hinted that she'd lived longer than twenty years. Long enough to have experienced—and survived—some terrible tragedy.

Adam hadn't had time to analyze his doubts when Nicole had suggested that they give Clare a ride to

Adele's. But now he realized that they stemmed from fear. There was something about Clare that attracted him. Big-time. But it was way too soon for him to have those kind of feelings. He hardly knew her. Besides, she'd come here for one reason and one reason only— to fulfill the stipulation in her aunt's will so that she could claim her inheritance. She had no personal interest in him or Nicole. This was a job. When the six months were over, she'd leave.

In the meantime, he needed to keep his own feelings in check and take pains to encourage nothing more than friendship between them. Because Adam clearly knew his own shortcomings when it came to establishing and maintaining emotional intimacy. He'd failed miserably with both his wife and daughter. He just couldn't give the women in his life what they needed. And he had a feeling that Clare had already experienced enough hurt to last a lifetime. He wasn't going to add to her pain.

Reaching toward the plate, Adam discovered that he'd eaten all four cookies. Clare's gesture had been considerate, and he was touched by her kindness. But he suspected that thinking of others was just part of her nature. As it had been part of Jo's. Though she would only be with them for six months, Adam resolved to savor and appreciate such gestures. Because those small kindnesses, which added so much to life, had been long absent from his.

Adam glanced toward the blue-rimmed crockery dish and suddenly realized something startling. The plate might be empty. But oddly enough, his heart wasn't.

* * *

"Reverend Nichols, would you please say the blessing?"

Adele took her seat at the large, lace-covered mahogany table, and the dozen people sitting around it joined hands. Clare reached for Nicole's hand on one side and the young minister's on the other, then bowed her head.

"Lord, we thank You for this food and for the generous hospitality of our hosts, who have taken us into their home for this special holiday. We pray today for those who are not so fortunate, who are experiencing hunger or homelessness or who are alone. We ask You to always help us follow the example You set, and which our hosts so admirably demonstrate today, of offering the hand of friendship to those most in need. Give us the courage and stamina and grace to do Your work and to follow Your call, wherever that may lead us.

"Finally, Lord, we ask that You give solace to those who are troubled in spirit. As we have been welcomed into this home today, please help those who are lost know that You wait to welcome them, and help them find the path home to You. May they feel Your healing presence and know that even when things seem darkest, they are never alone. Amen."

For a long moment after the prayer ended, Clare kept her head bowed. The young minister's words had touched her deeply. It was almost as if they had been spoken directly to her. She had been feeling spiritually lost for months, going through the motions of her faith, but failing to connect on a deeper level with the Lord.

She hoped that Reverend Nichols's prayer would be heard, and answered, for everyone at the table. And she added her own brief silent prayer at the end. *Lord, show me the way back to You.*

When she finally raised her gaze, it collided with Adam's. He was sitting directly across from her, and for the briefest moment, before he shuttered his eyes, there was an odd, unreadable expression in them. Clare sensed that the minister's words had resonated in some way with him, as well. Adam's faith seemed strong, so she doubted that he felt estranged from God. But perhaps the part about being alone had touched him. Because the more she saw of Adam, the more she was convinced that he was deeply lonely. From what Adele had said, he had little family. Just a brother, who was married and lived several hours away. His marriage had fallen apart. His relationship with Nicole was strained and tense. He obviously worked long hours, which probably precluded any sort of social life. When Clare got lonely or needed to hear a friendly, caring voice, at least she could pick up the phone and call A.J. or Morgan. Who did Adam have?

The young minister spoke to her then, and she made an effort to put aside that troubling question about Adam and focus on the conversation. Reverend Nichols kept her engaged in a lively discussion, and she was pleased to discover that he would be taking over as pastor of the congregation when the elderly minister retired at the beginning of the New Year. She didn't discover the answer to her question about Adam, of course. But she suspected she knew it, anyway. Adam didn't have anyone.

And even though she had come into his life on a professional basis, as a nanny for his daughter, for some reason that answer bothered her on a personal level. She didn't know why. And she didn't want to know.

Because she was afraid the answer might scare her.

Something smelled good. Really good.

Adam paused in the mudroom, sniffing appreciatively as his salivary glands went into overdrive. He'd worked through lunch, and he was so hungry that he'd even been looking forward to a microwave dinner. But this didn't smell like any microwave dinner he'd ever eaten.

He shrugged out of his coat and hung it on a peg beside the door, then strode toward the kitchen. When he appeared in the doorway, Clare looked up from setting the table and a slight flush warmed her cheeks. Though her hair was pulled back in its customary chignon, she was dressed casually in jeans and a sweater.

"Hi." Her voice was soft and a bit uncertain.

"Hi." He glanced at the table, which had a large bouquet of chrysanthemums in the middle, then at the stove, where several pots simmered. "What's all this?"

"Dinner."

"I figured that. But cooking isn't in your job description."

She shrugged. "I don't mind. I like to be busy." Which was true. Since the accident, she'd purposely packed her days full so that she had less time for reflection. Besides, nonstop activity helped fill the empty place in her life...though not in her heart or soul, she acknowledged. "I just used what I could find in the pantry and the fridge. But there wasn't much to work with. I hope it's okay."

"If that aroma is any indication, it's more than okay. But I already feel guilty for taking your services as a nanny for free. I don't expect you to cook, too."

"I like to cook. Besides, you'd better reserve your judgment. I haven't spent much time in the kitchen the past couple of years, so I'm afraid my skills are a little rusty."

"Rusty skills are better than no skills, which is what I have," Adam said with a grin.

The corners of her mouth teased up. "I hope you don't eat those words."

"I'd rather eat that food. How did your first day with Nicole go?"

"Fine. I made sure she had something to eat before she left for school, and fixed her a lunch. I was here when she got home, and we worked on her math homework for a while. She's writing an English composition now. I'll work with her a little more after dinner. You can just send her over to the apartment when you're finished."

Adam frowned and glanced toward the table, noting for the first time that only two places were set. "Aren't you eating with us?"

She shook her head. "I don't want to infringe on your time together."

"Trust me, you're not infringing. Meals are pretty silent affairs around here. Besides, the only way I'll even consider letting you cook for us is if you stay for dinner."

For a moment he thought she was going to argue, but in the end she capitulated. "Okay. Assuming the offer still stands after you've tasted my efforts," she added with a smile. "I'll put everything out while you get Nicole."

By the time he returned, she'd set a third place and arranged the food on the table. There was a large bowl of rice, what appeared to be a chicken stir-fry of some kind, biscuits and a platter of fresh fruit.

"Wow!" Nicole said.

"I second that," Adam added as they took their seats.

Adam gave a brief blessing, and almost before he finished, Nicole was helping herself to a healthy serving of rice. She ate heartily and chatted amiably with Clare, who made a concerted effort to draw Adam into the conversation whenever possible. He appreciated her attempts to include him, but tonight he was content mostly to observe and listen to his daughter's animated voice. For the first time since they'd moved into the house a year ago, their evening meal was something to be enjoyed rather then endured. And he was savoring it. As well as the delicious food. He took two helpings of everything, and Nicole wasn't far behind.

Only later, as Clare rose to clear the table, did he notice that much of her food remained untouched. He also realized that she had grown more subdued as the meal progressed, letting Nicole do most of the talking. And in the brief moment before she turned away, he saw a suspicious glimmer of moisture in her eyes.

Adam had no idea what had distressed her. He

thought the dinner had been a great success. He glanced toward the sink and studied Clare's back. For a moment he thought he detected the faintest droop in her shoulders, but even as he watched, she straightened them. And when she turned to put a plate of brownies on the table, her smile was back in place.

"I hope you both left room for dessert."

"Wow!" Nicole said, repeating her earlier comment even as she reached for a brownie. "We never have stuff like this!"

"The meal was delicious, Clare. Thank you."

Short of ignoring his comments, Clare had no choice but to look at Adam. She glued her smile firmly in place, then glanced his way. And almost lost her composure. There was caring and concern and empathy in his eyes. So he'd picked up on her mood after all, despite her best efforts to keep her feelings at bay.

Resolutely, Clare fought down another wave of melancholy. She hadn't expected a simple dinner to affect her so deeply. But as the meal had progressed, she'd felt more and more overwhelmed by the scene, so reminiscent of the family dinners she had once known, filled with laughter and sharing and warmth. It had all served as a stark reminder that those good times were gone forever. Her powerful, painful reaction had thrown her, and long-suppressed emotions had bubbled to the surface. She desperately needed a few minutes alone to regain her equilibrium.

"You're welcome. I'm glad you liked it." She pushed her chair in and reached for the sweater she'd draped behind it. "Whenever you're ready, let me

know and we'll go over the English composition," she
told Nicole.

"Aren't you going to have a brownie?" Nicole asked,
reaching for a second one.

"Not tonight."

She turned to go, but Adam's voice stopped her.

"I'll definitely take you up on your offer of making
dinner in the future, assuming you share it with us," he
said. "That was the best meal I've had in a long time."

It was too late to take back her offer. But it would be
easier next time, Clare consoled herself. She'd be better
prepared to deal with the memories—and the regrets.
Summoning up a smile, she looked at him. "Thanks. I'll
be happy to do it."

"Just get what you need. I have an account at the
local grocery store."

"Okay."

Again she turned to go. And again his voice stopped
her.

"Clare…is everything all right?"

The caring quality in his voice almost undid her.
This time she didn't turn back. "Yes. Everything's fine."

She was lying. He could tell by the slight tremor in
her voice. But he had no idea how to help her. With his
patients, he could ask them where it hurt, and then use
his medical training to fix the problem. But that training
did him no good in matters of the heart. Dealing with
those kinds of problems required a whole different set
of skills, which he was woefully lacking. He'd learned
that with Elaine. And Nicole.

The back door closed behind Clare, shutting with a

gentle click as she walked into the darkness. Silence fell at the kitchen table as Nicole finished her brownie and then quickly exited, leaving him alone. Yearning for more. Desperately wishing he knew how to open the shutters on his heart and share the warmth he held inside, instead of always holding back.

Slowly he rose and poured a cup of coffee, then propped his hip against the counter as he took a sip. He heard the door to Nicole's room close, and looked out the window toward Clare's garage apartment. The shades were drawn, masking what was within.

Kind of like the three of us, he thought wistfully.

"Adele, where do you keep the soup containers?" Clare asked.

The older woman bustled over to a large cabinet, opened the door and surveyed the contents with her hands on her hips. "Hmm. They should be in here. Marlene, are we out of those little round containers?"

A middle-aged woman looked up from the cake she was cutting. "I think a new shipment came in. Let me look downstairs."

Adele walked over to where Clare was stirring a large pot of chicken noodle soup. "Smells good."

"Well, I've never cooked in such large quantities before. I hope it tastes okay."

"I'm sure it's fine. And our clients will be grateful. I sometimes wonder what all those people did before we started the Feed the Hungry program."

"How long have you been doing this?"

"Several years. If we can get more volunteers, we

might be able to provide a main meal more than two days a week. But people are so busy these days. I'm just glad we recruited you."

Clare shrugged. "My mornings are mostly free. I'm happy to help. It's good work."

"Yes, it is. So how is everything going with the nanny job?"

"Well, it's only been two weeks. But so far, so good."

Adele wiped her hands on her voluminous apron. "That's nice to hear. I'm sure Adam is very grateful to have you. Trying to juggle a demanding career with the challenge of raising a young daughter alone must have been very stressful for him."

"I'm sure it was," Clare agreed as she began ladling the soup into the containers that Marlene set beside her, thinking about the fine lines around Adam's eyes. They spoke of stress and a deep-seated weariness that seemed to reach right into his soul.

"Well, I'm certainly glad he found you," Adele said. "I've already noticed your influence on Nicole's clothes at Sunday services. There have been some subtle changes that are definitely a step in the right direction."

Clare shook her head. "I suspect that balancing my ideas of fashion with Nicole's will be an on ongoing challenge. How to be trendy yet tasteful. I can't believe what young girls wear these days."

"Your work is definitely cut out for you," Adele agreed. "Well, I'm heading out. I have bridge club this afternoon and I have to get ready. Will I see you at church on Sunday?" At Clare's nod, Adele patted her arm. "Good. Don't work too hard, now."

Clare absently stirred the soup as she watched the older woman circle the room, speaking a few words of thanks and encouragement to the other volunteers before she left. She did intend to resume weekly church attendance. Though her faith had been shaken in the past couple of years, and her church attendance had lapsed, she knew deep inside that the core of her faith was still there. She just needed to find her way back to it. One step on that journey was attending Sunday services. And it was an opportunity to support Adam in reinforcing the importance of church attendance with Nicole. Apparently he'd been fighting that battle every week with his daughter. Clare understood his insistence, because the foundation of her own faith had been established in childhood, when weekly church attendance had been mandatory.

She also saw it as another opportunity to act as a mediator between Adam and Nicole. Aside from dinner, it was one of the few occasions during the week when they spent time together. Adam was always gone in the morning before she arrived to get Nicole off to school, and he generally got home just in time for the evening meal. Afterward Nicole retreated to her room while Clare briefed Adam on the day, then he generally disappeared into his office. She did her best to get a conversation going between father and daughter at dinner, and she knew Adam was trying. But Nicole wasn't. So Sunday gave her one more chance to try and make some inroads.

But deep in her heart, she acknowledged that as much as she wanted to bring father and daughter together, attending church with them also gave her one more chance to spend time with the elusive doctor who seemed so alone.

"What's this?" Clare picked up a sheet of paper that Nicole had tossed on the table.

Nicole helped herself to two oatmeal cookies from the new cookie jar on the counter before she answered. "Just a dumb school project. They need volunteers to help. You can throw it away."

Clare scanned the sheet. The class was going to construct gingerbread houses for Christmas, and the teacher was looking for a few people to help coordinate the activity. The sheet was dated the week before, and the activity was in two days.

"This sounds like fun," Clare said. "My mom made a gingerbread house every Christmas, and my sisters and I always helped. Although my mother might have used a different word to describe our contributions, since we ate most of the candy she was planning to use for decorations," she amended with a chuckle. "Don't you want to make one?"

Nicole shrugged. "It sounds like kid stuff."

"Kid stuff is sometimes the most fun. Do they still need help?"

"I guess. The teacher said today she needed a couple more moms."

So Nicole's careless toss of the flyer hadn't been so careless after all.

"Would a nanny do?" Clare asked.

Nicole sent her a cautious look, but Clare could see

a glimmer of hope in her eyes. "You don't have to do it. I don't think this kind of stuff is part of your job."

"It can be if I want it to be. I'd like to come, unless you don't want me to."

Nicole chewed on her cookie. "I guess it would be okay. At least I'd have someone to talk to."

Clare took a cookie herself, poured each of them a glass of milk and sat at the table. Despite her careful questions about the social aspect of school, so far she hadn't learned much from Nicole. But the girl seemed more willing to talk today. "Aren't the girls friendly?"

Nicole lifted one shoulder. "They already have their cliques. I don't fit in. But I don't care, anyway."

Her defiant posture was directly at odds with the hurt look in her eyes.

"It's hard to break into an established group," Clare sympathized. "That's true even when you're an adult. When I got married, my husband and I moved to Kansas City. I didn't know a soul. And all the teachers at the school where I taught had worked there for years. I don't think they meant to be unkind, but I still felt like an outsider. I was too new to understand their inside jokes, and a lot of them were single and hung out with each other after work while I went home to my husband. It took me quite a while to feel at home there."

Nicole eased into the chair next to Clare. "So did you do something to…you know, make them like you?"

"Well, it's hard to *make* people like you," Clare said gently. "But most of the time, if you let people get to know you, then they decide on their own to like you. I finally figured that out, after about three months. So I made it a point to ask them questions about their lives, and to tell them about mine. Then I invited all the teachers to our house for a barbecue."

"Did they come?"

"Mmm-hmm. And after that, things got a lot better."

Nicole frowned and played with the crumbs of the cookie that had fallen on the table. "The girls at school think I'm a snob."

"Why would they think that?"

Spots of color appeared on Nicole's cheeks and she kept her eyes downcast. "I might have called them hicks once."

"I can see where that could be a problem. I'm sure that hurt their feelings."

"Yeah."

The disheartened tone of Nicole's voice tugged at Clare's heart, and she reached over and took the young girl's hand. "But I bet there's a way to make things right."

"Yeah?" Nicole looked up hopefully.

"Let me think about it, okay? And in the meantime, how about we make some gingerbread houses?"

Nicole was right. The girls in her class did snub her. Most of the time she was alone, her shoulders stiff and hunched, her back to the rest of her classmates as she worked on her gingerbread house. Clare's heart went out to her. She knew the girl desperately wanted to make friends, but her body language said Keep Out— a message the rest of the class definitely heeded. The other girls were clustered in small groups, giggling and laughing as they admired each other's handiwork, oblivious to Nicole's misery—or just ignoring it.

It didn't take Clare long to pinpoint a blond-haired girl named Candace as one of the class leaders. She flitted from group to group, a born organizer and trendsetter. Many of the girls seemed to take their cues from her. So that was where she needed to start, Clare decided. She picked up the paper containers of candy she'd parceled out for decorations and slowly made her way toward Candace, giving out candy as she went. When she reached the blond-haired girl, she paused and smiled at Candace's creation.

"That looks great!" Clare said. "I like how you used the peppermints for stepping stones."

The girl turned to her and giggled. "Thanks. But I think I ate too many of them. See, I ran out." She pointed to the abrupt end of the path.

"Well, we can fix that." Clare took a paper cup with several peppermints in it and set it beside Candace. "There's even a couple extra if you're still hungry," she said with a wink.

"Great!" Candace glanced toward Nicole, then gave Clare a curious look. "So are you really her nanny?"

"Yes."

"That must be hard."

"Why?"

Candace shrugged. "Nicole's kind of…well, prickly, you know? She always seems mad. Nobody likes her."

"That's too bad. She's had a really hard time, so she could use some friends."

After strategically placing a gumdrop on her house, Candace turned to her inquisitively. "What do you mean?"

"Well, her mom and dad got divorced a few years ago, and she lived with her mother. Then her mom was killed in an accident just before last Christmas. I bet it was a really sad holiday for her." Clare paused and glanced toward Nicole, then looked back at Candace. "Anyway, after that she went to live with her dad. But he decided to move here, so she had to leave all her friends behind. That's an awful lot of stuff to deal with. Enough to make anybody mad, don't you think? And sad, too."

Candace frowned and looked uncertainly toward Nicole. "Yeah, I guess so."

"So what are you going to do with your gingerbread house?" Clare asked.

Candace continued to look at Nicole, and when she spoke her voice was more subdued. "I'm going to give it to my mom for Christmas."

"Well, I'm sure she'll like it very much. I'm going to check and see how Nicole is doing on hers, but let me know if you need any more candy, okay?"

"Yeah, thanks."

Clare made her way toward Nicole, sending Candace a surreptitious glance as she admired her charge's handiwork. The other girl was still watching them, a troubled expression on her face.

Mission accomplished, Clare thought.

Chapter Five

"I thought I'd decorate the house tomorrow. Where do you keep your Christmas things?" Clare asked as she sliced a carrot cake for dessert.

Adam's face went from placid to troubled at the question. Other than an artificial tree, he didn't have any holiday decorations. Elaine had always handled the decorating, and she'd taken all the expensive goo-gaws with her when they'd separated. He'd never bothered to replace them. It didn't make much sense to waste a lot of time decorating when he'd lived alone and spent most of his time at the office, anyway. Then when Nicole had come to live with him shortly before the holidays last year, he'd had other things on his mind. Now, in retrospect, he realized that he should have made more of an effort to celebrate the holiday. Their Christmas last year had been a pretty dismal affair. He had tried to roast a turkey breast so they had some semblance of a holiday meal, but it had come out dry and overcooked. In the end, he'd sent for pizza from a local joint that was the only place open.

"Adam?" Clare prodded when he didn't respond.

"We don't have any," Nicole said, shooting Adam a resentful look. "Except for a dumb fake tree that's in the basement."

His neck reddened at his daughter's indictment, and Adam expected to see censure in Clare's eyes, as well. But when he finally had the courage to look at her, there was only sympathy and compassion reflected in their deep-blue depths.

"Well, I think we can fix that. Assuming your dad agrees."

"Absolutely," he concurred. "Get whatever you think we need."

"How about you and I go shopping on Saturday?" Clare said to Nicole.

"Cool!"

"And I definitely think we should have a real tree," Clare added, a plan taking shape in her mind. "There's an Elks lot at the edge of town that seems to have a good selection. And I saw in the paper that there's going to be a holiday festival downtown on Sunday, with carolers and roasted chestnuts and all the trimmings. What do you think, Adam?"

She supposed she should have discussed it first with him privately, in case he didn't like the idea. But Clare didn't want to give him the option of saying no. He and Nicole needed to spend time together in family activities or they'd never develop any kind of rapport. Fortunately, he didn't seem to object.

"That sounds good. In fact, let's make a whole day of it. We can stop after church and have breakfast, then we'll come home and change before we head out to pick a tree."

Nicole eyed him warily. "You never do stuff like that."

He gazed at her steadily. "Maybe it's time I started."

Nicole didn't respond. But before she turned her attention to the generous wedge of carrot cake that Clare placed before her, Adam saw the barest flicker of something in her eyes. Something he couldn't quite identify, but for a brief moment, it seemed a little bit like hope.

When he looked over to Clare, he saw different messages in her eyes. Approval. Gratitude. And something more. Something even less identifiable than the emotion in his daughter's eyes. But just as potent.

With a hand that wasn't quite steady, Adam picked up his coffee cup and took a sip as Clare reached down to place his cake in front of him. And as her arm brushed his shoulder and her faint, pleasing scent invaded his nostrils, he suddenly felt warm.

And it wasn't from the coffee.

They had shopped till they were ready to drop. Or at least Clare was ready to drop. Nicole seemed to have plenty of energy left, Clare thought with a wry grin as she watched her young charge veer off to check out yet another clothing display.

They'd finished their shopping for affordable decorations at the Wal-Mart on the edge of town, then Clare had suggested they head for the nearest mall—which, much to her surprise, turned out to be nearly thirty miles away, just outside of Asheville—on the pretense of helping Nicole find a Christmas present for her father.

But Clare's real agenda was broader than that. She also wanted to supplement Nicole's wardrobe with a few more age-appropriate items of clothing. She'd discussed it with Adam, and he had totally agreed that Nicole's clothing left something to be desired. But he'd had no clue how to guide her. So he'd basically ended up letting her buy whatever she wanted, only to disapprove of it when he actually saw it on her. Clare hoped to begin rectifying that situation today.

"Ooh, look at this cool top!" Nicole called, holding up an orange knit sweater that looked as if it had shrunk.

Clare tried not to shudder as she pictured it on Nicole—skin-tight and midriff baring. But she knew that if she wanted to make any inroads on the youngster's taste she needed to temper her response and use as much tact as she could muster.

Clare joined Nicole and reached out to finger the top. "I like the material," she said, keeping her tone conversational. Then she tilted her head and studied Nicole's face. "I'm not sure about the color, though. You have such beautiful deep-green eyes…let's see." She glanced around the junior department, then walked over to a display table and selected a longer crew-neck cotton sweater in forest green. "Take a look at this, just for the color," she said, positioning Nicole in front of a convenient mirror and holding the garment in front of her. The shade of green was almost a perfect match for the girl's eyes, and the effect was startling. Her French braid highlighted the developing classic bone structure of her face, and the sweater put the focus on her best asset— her large green eyes.

"Wow!" Nicole said.

"Yeah. Wow!" Clare agreed with a grin.

Nicole studied her image, then frowned as she fingered the sweater. "Too bad it's so long."

"I don't think it will look quite as long when it's on," Clare said. "Why don't you try it? And it would look great with a pair of black pants. Let's see what we can find."

Half an hour later, they left the store with not only the sweater and black pants, but a modestly short plaid skirt and black turtleneck. As well as a tie for Adam.

"Do you think my dad will mind that we bought all these clothes?" Nicole asked anxiously as they made their way toward the car.

"No. He said it was okay if you got a few new things," Clare assured her.

"It's really different than the stuff I usually buy."

"But you like it, don't you?"

"Yeah. A lot. It kind of makes me think of some of the clothes you wear." Clare was saved from having to think up a response by Nicole's next comment. "You should have gotten something for yourself."

Clare smiled. "I have enough clothes."

"But you wear the same stuff a lot."

Clare couldn't deny that. She'd left some of her clothes in storage in Kansas City, but she'd disposed of much of her wardrobe at a resale shop when she'd moved into her apartment. Dennis had frequently encouraged her to buy new things, and she'd done so because it seemed to please him. But her interest in clothes had been marginal at best, and it had completely waned with his death. So she'd kept some of the more classic, well-made things that would wear well and stay in style, and gotten rid of the rest. Besides, her new life-style didn't call for designer suits and cocktail dresses. And the money she'd made from her closet purge had come in handy.

Clare turned to Nicole and grinned. "Are you saying my wardrobe is boring?" she teased.

Nicole smiled in response. "No. I like what you wear. But new clothes are fun."

"And just where would I store them? Have you seen the closet in my apartment? It was made for a Barbie doll."

Nicole giggled. "It is pretty small."

"That's the understatement of the year," Clare said wryly as they stowed their packages in the car and settled in for the drive home. "It's a good thing I left some of my clothes in Kansas City."

"So were you always a teacher when you lived there?" Nicole asked.

For the briefest second Clare's hand froze as she fit the car key in the ignition. "No. For a while after I got married I taught, but then for a long time I didn't work outside the home." She put the car into gear and began to back out of the parking spot.

"How come?"

Clare swallowed. It wasn't that she purposely kept her past a secret. But it was so hard to talk about. And there'd been no reason to bring it up. Until now. "I—I had a baby. And I decided to stay home with him."

Nicole's head swiveled toward her and her eyes grew

wide. "Wow! I didn't know you had a baby! You never told me that. Where is he?"

"He died."

There was a long moment of silence, and when Nicole spoke again her voice was more subdued. "Dad told me that your husband died. He didn't tell me about your baby."

"He doesn't know. I don't talk about it much."

"Why not?"

Because it was my fault. And the guilt overwhelms me when I think about, Clare silently cried. But her spoken words were different. "It still…hurts too much."

Nicole turned to look out the front windshield. "Yeah. I know what you mean. I still miss my mom a lot. It's like I still kind of expect her to come back, you know? Because she wasn't sick or anything. She just went out on a boat with her friends and I never saw her again."

"That's the same way it happened for me. Only it was a car accident."

"How old was your baby?"

"He wasn't a baby anymore then. He was eight."

"What was his name?"

"David."

Silence filled the car as Nicole digested that. "It must have been really hard for you to lose two people you love. I just lost one. And at least I still had my father, even though he isn't very good at being a dad. Did you have anybody?"

"I had my sisters."

"But they didn't live near you, did they?"

"No."

Nicole sighed. "That's hard. It's like, with my dad, even though I don't talk that much to him, at least I know he's around. That helps a little, you know? But I still get lonesome sometimes."

"I'm sure your dad feels the same way."

"I don't know," she said skeptically. "He's always so busy, I don't think he has time to be lonesome."

Clare thought about the helpless, hungry look she'd seen in Adam's eyes when he watched his daughter. He desperately wanted…needed…her affection. And she thought about the other look she'd sometimes seen when he thought no one was watching, a look that spoke of deep, soul-wrenching loneliness.

"You might be surprised. Some people just hide their loneliness very well," Clare said softly.

"Are you lonely?"

"Sometimes."

"So what do you do?"

"Find something to keep me busy. Or maybe talk to God."

"Yeah. I tried that, too. But He doesn't listen."

"How do you know?"

"Because nothing ever changes."

Clare was still trying to think of a response when Nicole spoke again, this time more thoughtfully. "Well, maybe that's not really true."

Clare sent her a quick, curious glance. "What do you mean?"

"Things did change when you came. I told God that I hated my new life, and I asked Him to fix it. I wanted

Him to make my dad move back to St. Louis, so I could be with my friends again. I asked and asked for a long time, but when nothing ever happened I finally figured praying was a waste of time. So I quit. But maybe He was listening. Maybe instead of making Dad move back to St. Louis, He sent me you instead."

Nicole's insight jolted Clare. She'd often learned from her students, and today was certainly no exception. Clare thought about her own sporadic prayers, and how she'd felt much the same way as Nicole—unheard and desolate. The only difference was that Nicole had had hope when she prayed. Clare, on the other hand, had known all along that there was no way God could fix the mess she'd created for herself. Her prayers had been a nebulous plea born of desperation for something… mercy, peace of mind, strength, forgiveness. She'd never put a name to her request. And she'd never felt it had been answered.

But maybe Nicole was right. Maybe God had heard her. Maybe Aunt Jo's legacy was the answer to her prayer. Maybe, with Nicole and Adam, He was giving her an opportunity to redeem her mistake by putting her in a position to help another family get the second chance her own would never have.

It certainly wasn't the answer she'd expected. Or wanted.

But it *was* an answer.

And a challenge.

Because even though she felt she'd made some progress with Nicole, and laid some groundwork to strengthen the relationship between father and daughter, she knew there was still a whole lot of work to do before those two lonely people could be called a family.

"What do you think, Nicole?"

Nicole studied the tree that Adam was propping up for their inspection and gave a nod of approval. "It's perfect."

"Mission accomplished," Clare pronounced.

"Good! I don't know about you ladies, but my fingers are starting to turn numb," Adam said with a relieved grin as he signaled to one of the attendants on the lot and handed over the Fraser fir for bundling. "How about we go get some hot chocolate?"

"Sounds great to me," Clare agreed.

Nicole chatted excitedly with Clare as they drove back into town, and even included Adam briefly in the conversation.

"So can we put the tree up when we get home?" she asked him.

"Sure."

"Clare and I got some stuff for it. Bows and tinsel and lights and glass ornaments. You can help us decorate it, if you want."

Adam felt his throat tighten, and when he spoke his voice was a bit rough at the edges. "I'd like that."

A short time later he pulled into a parking spot in the town square and they piled out of the car. A few snowflakes had begun to drift down lazily, and the crowd—or what passed for a crowd in Hope Creek—seemed to be in good cheer as residents ambled around, stopping to sample cookies and hot cider at the shops of the various merchants who were taking part in the festival.

Carolers sang in the gazebo in the middle of the square, accompanied by a local brass band.

Adam glanced at Nicole. She seemed totally caught up in the festive scene, and her eyes were shining. He smiled and turned to Clare. She looked especially lovely today, he realized, as he tried to swallow past the sudden lump in his throat. Her dark-blue earmuffs and matching scarf brought out the azure color of her eyes. A few delicate snowflakes clung to her golden hair, and her cheeks were flushed from the cold. Her breath came out in frosty clouds through softly parted lips.

Adam felt his pulse begin to pound. He'd glanced her way to see if she'd noticed Nicole's good spirits. Instead, he'd noticed her.

Clare wasn't sure what to make of the expression on Adam's face. It had started off as merely friendly, and she'd been prepared to respond in the same way. But it had rapidly changed to something intense and more than a little unnerving. She felt her heart stop, then race on, as the warmth in his eyes enveloped her. It wasn't the kind of warmth produced by a blazing fire that boldly vanquishes everything in its path. It was more like the deeply buried, white-hot heat of a smoldering ember just waiting for the right moment, the right circumstance, to ignite it.

"Hi, Nicole."

With a supreme effort, Clare looked away from Adam and glanced down. Candace was standing a few feet in front of them with a couple of other girls. Nicole seemed so taken aback by her classmate's greeting that it took her a moment to find her voice.

"Hi."

"Is that your tree?" Candace pointed to the car behind them.

"Yeah."

"It looks nice. We got ours last week."

"We're going to decorate it later. We just stopped to get some hot chocolate."

"Ben's has a stand over by the gazebo. They have awesome hot chocolate."

"Okay. Thanks."

"See you Monday."

"Yeah. See you Monday."

Nicole watched the girls walk away, then looked up at Clare with an awed expression. "Candace stopped to talk to me," she said in a hushed voice.

"I noticed."

"She's never done that before."

Clare put her arm around Nicole's shoulder. "Maybe she's had a change of heart."

Her face alight with hope, Nicole looked back at the girls, who were quickly disappearing among the other holiday revelers. "Yeah."

Adam watched the exchange, knowing he was missing something significant. But the nuances were lost on him. He doubted they were lost on Clare, however. So he'd just have to rely on her to fill him in later.

As they made their way toward the gazebo, it suddenly occurred to him that he was beginning to rely on Clare for a lot of things. Which wasn't necessarily good. He was immensely grateful for the small but important changes that she had already brought to their lives, of course. But he needed to remember that this was not a permanent arrangement. Clare would be with them for six months. Actually, closer to five now. He had spoken about the time limit of the arrangement with Nicole when he'd told her about Clare's offer, but he needed to remind her periodically so she didn't become too attached. Otherwise, Clare's departure at the end of May would be devastating.

And he needed to remind himself, as well, he acknowledged. Or he had a feeling that Nicole wouldn't be the only one who was devastated.

"Now I remember why I hate tinsel," Adam grumbled good-naturedly as he draped a few more strands over a sturdy branch of the Fraser fir.

"Stop complaining," Clare chided with a smile. "Tinsel is what makes a tree magic. A tree without tinsel is like…like a hot fudge sundae without the hot fudge."

"We never had tinsel," Nicole offered. "And Mom and I never decorated ourselves. Some people always came and did it for us. Our tree looked different every year, too. One Christmas it was all white."

Clare couldn't imagine having a totally different tree every year, but she kept her thoughts to herself. For her, Christmas was all about tradition. About taking out treasured ornaments and sharing memories of where and when they'd been acquired, and about the warmth and caring and laughter of family holiday rituals.

"So did you always have a real tree?" Nicole interrupted her thoughts.

"Absolutely."

"I'm going to grab some cookies. Anybody want some?" Adam asked.

"You're just trying to escape the tinsel job," Clare accused with a smile.

"Guilty as charged," Adam admitted with a grin.

"I'll take a couple," Nicole told him.

"Clare?"

"None for me, thanks."

"And did you always have tinsel?" Nicole asked, resuming the previous conversation.

"Always."

"Did David help you decorate?"

At the sound of shattering glass, Adam sharply turned from the doorway. Clare had dropped one of the round glass ornaments on the hardwood floor and it lay broken at her feet. She stared down at it, her face suddenly pale.

Nicole moved beside her and gently touched her arm. "I'm sorry, Clare," she said contritely.

Adam watched as Clare struggled to compose her features, noting the tremor in her hand as she put her arm around Nicole's shoulder. "It's okay. Just chalk it up to my clumsiness."

Hardly, Adam thought. *Clumsy* and *Clare* were not words anyone would ever use in the same sentence. Nicole's question had obviously upset Clare deeply. Unfortunately, Adam hadn't really been listening very closely to the exchange as he headed for the kitchen. He thought his daughter had mentioned someone named David. But Adam was pretty sure that Seth Mitchell had told him Clare's husband's name was Dennis. So who was David?

Adam didn't have a clue. But Nicole obviously did. And he intended to get the answer to his question at the earliest opportunity.

"That was another great meal, Clare. Thank you."

"I'm glad you liked it." She smiled, but some of the light had faded from her eyes since they'd decorated the tree earlier in the afternoon.

"You look a little tired. Why don't you let Nicole and me handle the dishes tonight."

Nicole looked at him in surprise. "You never help with the dishes."

"You're right. And I'm wrong. The cook shouldn't also have to do the dishes."

"Really, Adam, you don't have to do that," Clare protested. "You work all day. And you're tired when you get home. I don't mind."

"I didn't work today. And I'm not tired tonight. You, on the other hand, look like you need some rest. Go climb into a hot tub with a good book or a cup of tea. Doctor's orders."

She managed a tired grin. "The hot tub part sounds good, anyway. Are you sure you don't mind? Just for tonight?"

Her quick capitulation told him more eloquently than words that his assessment had been correct. But he suspected Clare's exhaustion was more emotional than physical. "Not in the least." He rose and began clearing the table as if to demonstrate his point.

"Well…okay. Nicole, don't forget to finish that reading assignment tonight."

She groaned. "Do I have to?"

"Absolutely. Promise me you'll do it."

"Okay, okay. I promise," she grumbled.

Clare glanced at Adam as she passed and nodded toward Nicole.

"I'll make sure she finishes it," he said quietly.

He waited until the door shut behind Clare before he turned to Nicole. "How about you scrape the plates and put them in the dishwasher and I'll work on the pots?"

She hung back warily. "I have to finish my homework."

"It can wait a few minutes. Or I could see if Clare would come back and help. But she looks pretty tired."

His ploy worked. "I'll help."

They worked in silence for a few minutes as Adam struggled to find a way to broach the subject of David.

"The tree looks nice," he said.

"Yeah."

Silence.

"Did you have much luck on your shopping trip yesterday?" he tried again.

"Yeah."

More silence.

He closed his eyes and took a deep breath. Why wasn't there a book on how to talk to teenage daughters? None of his medical texts had ever addressed this issue.

"So did you and Clare buy some clothes?"

"I did. Clare didn't."

"Why not?"

"She said she has enough."

"Well, maybe she does."

Nicole gave him an exasperated look. "Don't you notice anything? She always wears the same stuff."

Adam couldn't argue with Nicole, because he really didn't pay that much attention to what Clare wore. He just knew that she always looked good.

"So are we going to get her a Christmas present?" Nicole asked when he didn't respond.

Adam looked at her in surprise. "Do you think we should?"

Nicole gave a long-suffering sigh. "Of course. You're supposed to give stuff to people you like. And she probably won't get anything else, except maybe from her sisters."

"Okay. What do you think we should get?"

"Clothes."

That seemed a little too personal. "I don't know. How about a cookbook?"

"Good grief, Dad. You are so out of it!"

"What's wrong with a cookbook?"

"She already knows how to cook. Real good, too. If you give her a cookbook, she might think you don't like her cooking."

He frowned. That certainly wasn't his intent. But now that Nicole had pointed it out, he could see how the gift might be misinterpreted. "You may have a point," he conceded. "So what kind of clothes did you have in mind?"

"I saw her looking at this pretty blue sweater with

beading around the top at the mall in Asheville. I think she really liked it, but it was kind of expensive."

A sweater. That didn't seem too personal. So it would probably be safe. "That sounds like a good idea. Do you want to go with me to get it some night this week?"

Nicole hesitated, and he held his breath. He knew she was debating the torture of spending time with him against the desire to do something nice for Clare.

"Okay, I guess," she said slowly. Then she sighed and went back to stacking plates in the dishwasher. "Maybe that will help me make up for upsetting her today."

Bingo. That was the opening he'd been waiting for.

"I heard her drop the ornament. What happened?" Adam kept his voice casual and continued scrubbing a pot.

Nicole paused and stuck her hands in her pockets, her face troubled. "I shouldn't have brought up David. I think she misses him a lot."

"Who's David?"

"Her son. He died in the car crash with her husband."

Adam's hands stilled, and he sucked in a sharp breath. He'd had no idea! When Seth Mitchell had mentioned that she was a widow, the man had made no reference to a double tragedy that had taken both her husband and son. Now he understood the source of the ever-present pain in Clare's eyes.

"I hope she's not mad at me."

Nicole's comment brought him back to the present, and he turned to his daughter. "She knows you didn't mean to make her feel bad. Sometimes it's just hard to be reminded of people you love when they're gone. It takes a long time to stop missing them."

Nicole's face grew sad. "Maybe you never do."

He knew she was thinking of her mother. "Maybe not," he conceded. "But it does get easier in time."

Her shoulders hunched and she dropped her head. "Yeah. I guess. But you don't miss Mom like I do."

Adam dried his hands on a dish towel and reached out tentatively to lay a hand on her stiff shoulder. He was afraid she'd pull away, but she didn't. "Your mom and I had some good times, Nicole," he said gently. "I like to remember those. And I miss them. But I wasn't the best husband. I was too caught up in my work. And I've never been very good at letting people know what's in my heart. I have a lot of regrets about the way things turned out between your mom and me. But at least one good thing came from our marriage. You."

Nicole looked up at him, and he saw a glimmer of unshed tears in her eyes. "Sometimes I feel like I just get in your way," she said in a choked voice. "Like you'd rather talk to sick people than to me."

His gut clenched, and his instinct was to reach out and pull her close. But he was afraid she'd back off. So he restrained the impulse. "That's not true. It's just easier to talk to them sometimes because I can usually help them solve their problems. But I've never been very good at solving problems for the people I love. I can't write a prescription for those."

She studied his face. "You don't always have to fix everything. Sometimes just listening is enough."

He tried to swallow past the lump that suddenly appeared in his throat. "I'll remember that."

They looked at each other for a moment, then Nicole

backed up a step. Adam let his hand drop to his side. "Well, I gotta go finish my reading." She glanced around the kitchen. "Are we done?"

"Yeah. I think so."

As he watched her leave, he realized that this was the longest civil conversation he'd had with his daughter since she'd come to live with him. And he also realized his response to her last question hadn't been quite accurate.

Because he had a feeling they weren't done. They were just beginning.

And his heart felt lighter than it had in a long time.

Chapter Six

"Okay, she's almost done in the kitchen. Should I bring it out now?"

At the sound of the excited, low-pitched voice behind him, Adam turned from the crackling fire and nodded at Nicole. "I think it's time."

As his daughter scampered away, he thought back to their outing to the mall in Asheville. Though they'd spent much of the time in silence, and their conversation had been mostly strained, there had been a few occasions when they'd seemed to connect. Those fleeting moments had given him hope that their relationship might be turning a corner. As far as he was concerned, that was the best present he could have received this holiday season. And it was thanks to Clare.

Adam leaned back in his chair and slowly looked around the living room. Spruce garlands, held in place with festive plaid bows, were draped on the mantel, around the doorways and on the stair rail in the foyer. Strategically placed white twinkle lights added magic to the setting. Sparkly snowflakes of all sizes and a collection of pine cones were displayed on the mantle, interspersed with glowing candles of varying heights. A feeling of warmth and peace enveloped the living room. And he had Clare to thank for that, too.

As well as for the early holiday meal they'd just shared. Roast lamb, new potatoes and a spinach soufflé that melted in their mouths. Not to mention the fabulous chocolate mousse. And all of it had been homemade. Tonight's hearty, delectable fare had been a far cry from the sparse, sometimes unidentifiable nouvelle cuisine and imported chocolates, fine wines and designer pastries that had been staples of the catered holiday dinners Elaine had insisted on during most of their marriage. Those meals had been stiff and formal. Tonight's had been homey and relaxing.

It had also been unlike anything he'd known as a child. Their Christmases had always been rather sober; the meals quiet affairs served by a succession of equally dour housekeepers. Tonight had reminded him of what he'd missed...and what he still yearned for.

Nicole reappeared then, diverting his thoughts. As she tucked a beribboned package under the tree, Clare appeared in the doorway carrying two presents of her own.

"Well, it looks like we all had the same idea," she said with a smile as she made her way to the tree and placed her gifts beneath the scented boughs.

It hadn't occurred to Adam that Clare would have gifts for them, as well, and he was doubly grateful for Nicole's suggestion. His daughter gave him a smug I-told-you-so look when he glanced at her, and he responded with a grin and a thumbs-up signal.

"Open ours first, Clare," Nicole instructed.

Clare flushed and sat cross-legged on the floor, then reached for the foil-wrapped box. "I didn't expect this."

"We wanted to do it. Didn't we, Dad?" Nicole prodded.

"Absolutely."

Clare tore the wrappings away, then lifted the blue, pearl-beaded cashmere sweater from the tissue. Her eyes widened, and she looked first to Adam, then to Nicole. "This is the one we saw in Asheville."

"Nicole said you admired it."

"Yes, I did, but…it's way too generous."

"So do you like it?" Nicole chimed in excitedly.

"I love it. Thank you." She ran her hands gently over the whisper-soft wool, then looked at them curiously. "Did you go together to get this?"

"Of course. Sending me to the women's clothing department with only a description would have been a recipe for disaster," Adam said with a chuckle.

"I had to show him the way," Nicole chimed in. "He almost got lost trying to find the right department, and the sweater was in a different place than when we looked at it. He would never have found it by himself."

"Well, it's a good thing you went, then."

"It was a very successful outing," Adam said. Clare saw the deeper meaning in his eyes and smiled in response.

"So can I open my present now?" Nicole asked excitedly.

"Of course. But I'm afraid mine aren't as grand as the one you gave me," Clare said as she handed Nicole a package.

The young girl quickly tore open the wrappings, then lifted out a knitted angora cap that matched her new green sweater.

"Ooh, this is awesome!" She jumped to her feet and tugged it on, then examined her reflection in the mirror over the mantel.

"I'm so glad it fits!" Clare said in relief. "The pattern was a little vague on sizes, and I couldn't exactly ask you to try it on without ruining the surprise."

"Did you make this?" Nicole asked in awe.

"Mmm-hmm."

"Way cool!" The girl admired her reflection for a moment longer, than turned to Adam. "Aren't you going to open yours?"

Clare reached for the remaining box and silently handed it to Adam. He pried the tape off and carefully eased the box out of the wrapping, then lifted the lid. Nestled in the folds of the tissue was a gray-and-black knitted tweed muffler of fine wool.

"You made this, too?" At her nod, he looked down again and fingered the subtle herringbone pattern. He couldn't remember the last time anyone had given him such a thoughtful gift, one that clearly represented a significant investment of time. His throat tightened, and he took a steadying breath. "It's wonderful. Thank you, Clare."

A warm flush suffused her face. "You're welcome."

He examined the scarf more closely, then shook his

head. "This looks complicated. So does Nicole's. When in the world did you find time to make them?"

She shrugged. Sometimes, when the nights seemed especially long, occupying her fingers—and her mind—helped pass the dark hours and kept unhappy thoughts at bay. "Here and there," she said lightly.

"I'm going to wear mine to Uncle Jack's," Nicole declared.

"What time are you leaving tomorrow?" Clare asked as she began to gather up the remnants of their early Christmas exchange.

"Right after breakfast. We should get to Charlotte by noon if all goes well. What time will your sister arrive?"

Clare was looking forward to A.J.'s visit more than she could say. She was just sorry that Morgan had been unable to get away from work long enough to make a trip south more practical. "Sometime tomorrow. It depends on how early she can leave. I wish she could stay longer, but at least we'll have three days."

"She's in St. Louis, right?"

"Yes."

"That's a long drive for just a three-day visit."

"She won't mind," Clare said with a chuckle. "She likes to travel. I think *Adventure* is her middle name."

Adam grinned. "Well, I'm glad you'll have some company while we're gone. But I'll leave the phone number in the kitchen, just in case you need to reach me. Though you'll probably be glad to have us out of your hair for a few days."

His comment was made in jest, but in fact, Clare knew she would miss the Wrights.

Both of them.

She kept that thought to herself, however, and responded instead with just a smile. Because that seemed a whole lot safer than giving voice to what was in her heart.

"Hey, bro, are you gonna share some of the couch or not?"

From his prone position, Adam opened one eye and looked up at his younger brother. "Not."

"Then I might just have to sit on top of you."

Adam groaned. "Have some mercy. I can't move after that enormous meal. How do you stay in such good shape, eating like that all the time?"

"I don't eat like that all the time. Usually we just nuke a microwave dinner."

"Jack!" His wife poked his arm playfully as she came up behind him.

He gave her a saucy grin and looped his arms around her waist. "Hey, I'm not complaining. I didn't marry you to cook. You excel at…other things."

Theresa's face turned bright red. "You are incorrigible."

"But you wouldn't have me any other way, would you?" he said cajolingly as he kissed her cheek.

She squirmed out of his embrace and turned to Adam. "I want you to know that we do not have microwave food every night. With two kids…" she paused and gave her husband a wry look, "…make that three… I try to prepare healthy, homemade meals most of the time."

Adam chuckled. "Don't worry, Theresa. I only believe half of what Jack says. If that much."

Jack planted his fists on his hips and feigned a hurt look. "I don't know if I can take all this abuse. First my wife, now my brother. And on Christmas, no less."

"Get out the violins," Adam said wryly.

"Well, you do have some redeeming qualities," Theresa conceded. "You always remember to take the trash out, and you did stay up until two in the morning last night putting together Bobby's new bike."

Jack grinned and draped his arm around his wife's shoulders. "That's not a bad start on an apology. But we'll work on a better one later." He winked playfully.

She rolled her eyes and shook her head, but her smile was affectionate. "Like I said…incorrigible."

"So how about a turkey sandwich?" Jack said innocently.

Theresa stared at him incredulously. "We just finished the dishes!"

"I hear some turkey calling my name."

"It takes one to know one," she replied pertly.

"Ooh, low blow!" Jack said with a chuckle. "Never marry a woman who talks back, Adam."

Adam smiled. "You're lucky Theresa puts up with you."

"Isn't he, though?" Theresa concurred with a grin.

Jack reached for her hand and pulled her close. "Yeah, I am," he said, his eyes suddenly serious. "Merry Christmas, Mrs. Wright." He leaned down and brushed his lips over hers.

The spell was broken a moment later when a loud crash sounded from the far reaches of the house. Theresa sighed and extricated herself from her husband's embrace. "Sounds like a new toy has bitten the dust already. I'll take care of it. You two need some guy-time to catch up "

Adam watched her leave, envying the easy give-and-take between husband and wife. It was something he'd yearned for, but had never found with Elaine.

"What's with the look?" Jack asked as he sank into an overstuffed chair beside the couch.

Adam turned toward him and shrugged. "You seem to have it all."

Jack laughed. "Yeah. Mortgages and sibling fights and a never-ending list of chores. Plus a boss who drives me nuts."

"Not to mention a wife who loves you completely and makes all those everyday problems seem incidental."

Jack cocked his head and eyed Adam speculatively. "Hey! Are you coveting Theresa?" he teased.

Adam smiled, but his voice was weary. "Maybe. Are any of her sisters still single? And good with kids?"

Jack's face grew more serious. "Still having trouble with Nicole, huh?"

"That's putting it mildly."

"Teenagers are tough. I'm not looking forward to that stage, either."

"At least you've got Theresa to help. With that and other things. I have to admit I am a little envious, Jack." He sighed, and when he spoke again his voice was quiet. "To be honest, I…I never had anything with Elaine that came close to what you have with Theresa."

"Elaine was…different," Jack said carefully.

"What do you mean?"

Leaning back, Jack stretched his legs out in front of him and jammed his hands into his pockets. "She wasn't the warmest person I ever met," he said slowly. "I don't mean to speak ill of the dead, but honestly, Adam, I never could figure out what you saw in her."

In retrospect, Adam had to admit, he couldn't, either.

"She was very beautiful," Adam offered.

"True. But that's not enough to keep a relationship going for the long-term."

"Jack? Can you come in here for a minute?"

Theresa's voice interrupted them, and Jack gave Adam an apologetic look. "Don't move. I'll be right back."

Adam watched as Jack exited the room, then sat up and leaned forward, resting his forearms on his thighs and clasping his hands as he gazed at the flickering flames in the fireplace. Jack was right about Elaine's beauty, of course. But the physical chemistry that had initially drawn him and Elaine together had been powerful. Powerful enough to sustain their marriage long after it should have ended. And powerful enough to undermine his good judgment at first.

He thought back to their courtship. Things had moved quickly. Too quickly, he acknowledged. Always an introvert, Adam had been so flattered that someone like Elaine, so vibrant and beautiful, would take an interest in him, that he'd proposed far too soon. He knew now that the proposal had been prompted by her complaint that the demands of his residency hadn't given them enough time to spend together. He hadn't wanted to lose her, and he'd figured that a proposal would demonstrate his serious intent. Once they were engaged, she'd been so caught up in the flurry of wedding plans that his preoccupation with his work had no longer been an issue. Still, her displeasure should have warned him of stormy seas ahead. Because doctors were often as busy, if not more so, than residents.

As his practice had grown, Elaine had come to hate the demands of his job, which often pulled him away from home at odd hours or made him miss social events. Soon she spent more and more time shopping and socializing with friends to compensate for his lack of attention and had run up bills that began to alarm Adam. By the end of their marriage, they'd been deeply in debt. It had taken him years to regain financial stability.

As their marriage had deteriorated, Adam had begun to wonder what Elaine had seen in him. Gradually he'd come to believe she had been more attracted to the notion of being married to a doctor than of being married to him. It gave her a certain prestige and cachet with her friends. That had been a hard pill to swallow. And it had made him even more withdrawn.

Adam leaned back and wearily closed his eyes. He knew there were a lot of reasons for the breakup of their marriage. Basic incompatibility, for one. They'd had different interests and tastes and priorities—which would have surfaced if they'd taken more time to get to know each other before rushing into marriage. Elaine's insistence that they remain in St. Louis after Adam's residency, despite his intention to return to North Carolina, had also led to resentment on both sides.

He knew they both shared the blame for the disintegration of their marriage. But he was painfully aware of his part in it. Especially his inability to allow people to get close to him. That had eventually alienated Elaine. It continued to hinder his ability to establish a rapport with his daughter. And it made him afraid to even consider a future romantic relationship. He knew that unless he found a way to unlock his heart, he was destined to remain alone—and lonely—for the rest of his life. Which was a really depressing thought for Christmas Day.

"Sorry about that." Jack dropped back into his chair. "Minor crisis in the bedroom. Bobby's foot got stuck under the dresser."

"Is he okay?"

"Yeah. This kind of stuff happens ten times a day. So where were we? Oh, yeah. You were coveting my wife."

Adam smiled. "Not really. I'm happy you found Theresa. I just wish I knew how you…" He raked his fingers through his hair. "I don't know. You two have such an easy give-and-take. Like you're always on the same wavelength at some really deep level." He shook his head in frustration. "I don't know how to explain it. Or how you do it. I wish I did."

Jack shrugged. "There isn't really a secret. You just share things. Make sure the other person always knows how you feel about stuff."

Adam sighed. "You make it sound so easy."

"It is."

"Not for me."

"You're just different than me, Adam. You know, the

still-waters-run-deep thing. A lot goes on under the surface. It doesn't mean you feel any less than I do. I'm just more up-front with my emotions."

"I wish I was." Adam clasped his hands together and looked down. There was silence for a moment, and when he spoke again his voice was halting and laced with pain. "Sometimes I think I'm becoming just like Dad."

"No way!" Jack exploded, his voice fierce as he leaned forward intently. "Don't ever think that! Dad was a bitter, resentful, unkind man who was incapable of expressing love. I'm not even sure he knew what love was. If I didn't dislike him so much, I'd feel sorry for him. I used to wonder what made him the way he was. But frankly, at this point I don't even care anymore. God forgive me, but I'm glad he's gone so my children won't be exposed to him. You are nothing like him, Adam. Nothing!"

Adam searched Jack's eyes. He wanted to believe his brother. But his fears ran deep. "Even if you're right, I'm just as bad as he was about expressing emotions."

Jack studied him. "Okay, so maybe you need a little work in that area. But the thing is, at least you feel them. He didn't. You're a kind, compassionate person. He wasn't. I'm just sorry for what he did to you. For making you feel so awkward and uncomfortable about showing affection. For making you so afraid to let people get close."

"But you lived there, too. You don't have the same problems. Maybe it's me, not him."

"Uh-uh. Don't buy it. I just have a different tempera-ment. The old man and I clashed all the time because I never cared about winning his approval the way you did. I realized early on that it was a lost cause. That's why I joined the navy when I was eighteen—to put as much distance between me and him as possible. And I never looked back."

Adam leaned back and expelled a long breath. "You were smart."

"So are you. The first step toward fixing a problem is recognizing it. You've done that."

"Yeah. But I still don't seem to be making much headway with Nicole. I just don't know how to reach her."

"She has other problems, Adam. She just lost her mom. She's in a new town. She had to leave all her friends behind. She's probably mad at life in general. That's a lot of stuff to deal with. It's not just you."

"That's what Clare says."

"The new nanny?"

"Yeah."

"Well, she's right. But if it's any consolation, I think Nicole's far less prickly now than when we visited you last summer. And the relationship between the two of you seems to be a little more cordial. That's a step in the right direction."

"I hope so. But I can't really take the credit for any positive changes. Clare's had a lot of influence on her."

"Then three cheers for Clare! And you want to know something else? I think maybe she's had a positive in-fluence on you, too."

"What do you mean?"

"Do you realize that this is the first time in our lives that you actually opened up and shared your feelings with me? I'd say that's cause for celebration. And if Clare's the reason, more power to her. In fact, let's drink an eggnog to that."

He stood, but Adam put a hand out to restrain him. "I appreciate the sentiment, but I don't like eggnog."

Jack leaned down and spoke in a conspiratorial whisper. "I'm not crazy about it, either. But Theresa says it's a holiday tradition and she won't be happy until it's all gone. So play along, okay?"

He returned a minute later with two large glasses. "How about we go out on the deck for some fresh air and have our eggnog," he said in a louder-than-normal voice.

"Sure," Adam replied with a grin.

They shrugged on their coats, and once they stepped out on the deck, Jack quickly dumped the eggnog behind a convenient bush. "Whew! Safe for another year," he said with a mock sigh of relief. Then he withdrew two cans of soda from under his jacket and handed one to Adam. "Better?"

"Much."

They popped the tops, and Jack's face grew serious as he held his can up in a toast. "To all the things that really matter. And to Clare…may she continue to fish in still waters."

Adam looked at Jack in surprise. That wasn't his brother's typical irreverent toast. But as he lifted his can, Adam couldn't think of anything he'd rather drink to.

"Okay, enough about the bookshop and the ongoing saga with my partner, Mr. Conventional. Tell me about you."

Clare grinned at A.J. Her sister had spent the last hour regaling her with hilarious tales of her escapades in Aunt Jo's bookshop, from her drowned-rat arrival in the midst of a rainstorm to the apparent chaos she was wreaking on the peace of mind of her partner, Blake, who was having a hard time coping with A.J.'s many changes to the shop. Clare hadn't laughed so much in years.

"I'm afraid my story isn't nearly as entertaining," she apologized.

"Well, lay it on me anyway. I take it you don't have to fight the good doctor every step of the way like I do my nemesis?"

"No. I think he knew he was in over his head with his daughter and that he needed help. So he's pretty much given me free rein with her."

"Excellent. And how's the problem child doing?"

"Coming around, I think. But it'll take time. She's had a lot of stuff to deal with." Clare gave A.J. a quick recap.

When she finished, A.J. frowned. "Wow! That's tough. Losing your mom, being uprooted, leaving your friends behind. No wonder she got off track."

"And, of course, Adam bears the brunt of her anger. He tries to reach out to her, but she backs off. I know that hurts him. I can see it in his eyes. Bottom line, I think they're both very lonely people who are hungry for affection and love but who live very isolated lives. Nicole is beginning to blossom, though. She just needed some nurturing and some guidance. I'm not sure what it will take to get through to Adam, though."

A.J. eyed her speculatively. "But that's not your problem, anyway, is it? You're just supposed to be a nanny for Nicole. There wasn't anything in the will about her father."

Clare stared at the miniature tree in her tiny apartment. "True. But I'd like to help them both if I could. The opportunity to create a family is such a precious gift. I'd hate to see them throw it away."

Clare's voice broke on the last word, and A.J. reached over and squeezed her hand. "I know how hard this must be for you, Clare," she murmured.

There was silence for a moment. Then Clare took a deep breath and turned to her sister. "It will be better after the holidays are over. It's just that so many of the things I did with Nicole and Adam this year made me remember the good times with Dennis and David. We had wonderful Christmases, A.J. I want Nicole and Adam to have the same thing. For a lot longer than I did."

A.J. nodded. "I understand. And I know you'll do your best to make that happen."

Clare did, too. But she didn't know if her best would be good enough to heal the immense rift that threatened to keep father and daughter from ever becoming a real family.

Clare frowned at the columns of figures in front of her. Her financial situation was precarious at best. And today it had taken a turn for the worse. Of all the rotten times to need a root canal! Even though that tooth had been damaged in a sledding accident more than twenty-five years ago, it had never given her a bit of trouble. Until now. So much for the slight cushion her rent-free situation had provided. Her dental bills were going to wipe it out. But given the pain in her tooth, she didn't have much choice. What a belated Christmas present!

A knock sounded at her door, and she looked up distractedly. Except for Nicole and, on rare occasion, Adam, she never had visitors. Especially in the middle of the day. Curious, she rose and moved toward the door. When she pulled it open, she was startled to discover Adam on the other side.

"Is everything all right?" she asked in alarm.

"I was just about to ask you the same thing."

She stared at him blankly, still trying to process his uncharacteristic midday appearance at her door. "Your tooth?" he prompted, when the silence lengthened.

"Oh! Right. My tooth. Is that why you stopped by?"

A faint flush crept up his neck. "I was on my way from the hospital to my office and had to swing by here to pick something up. I thought I'd drop in and see what Mark had to say."

Clare had been reluctant to incur the expense of a dentist visit, but when her distress had been evident at dinner last evening, Adam had insisted on calling Mark Miller, a dentist friend in Asheville. He'd arranged for Clare to see him this morning.

"Oh. Well, come in for a minute. It's cold in the hallway." She moved farther into the room, and after a brief hesitation, Adam followed. "Have you had lunch?"

"Not yet."

"I'm just heating some soup. Would you like some?"

Another brief hesitation. "Don't go to any trouble. I can only stay a few minutes."

"It's no trouble, and the soup is almost ready."

"Okay. Thanks."

"Have a seat at the table." She preceded him, and he caught a glimpse of columns of numbers on the sheets of paper she quickly gathered up as she cleared a place for him.

"So tell me about the tooth," he said as he shrugged out of his leather jacket.

She made a wry face. "Not good. I need a root canal."

He grimaced. "Ouch."

"Yeah." In more ways than one, she thought as she stowed her budget scribblings inside a drawer in the kitchen.

"When is he going to do it?"

"Friday. I figured that would give me the weekend to recover in case there are any aftereffects."

Adam frowned. "Don't wait on our account. If you need to take a day or so off, we can cope."

"I'll be fine." She ladled the soup into two bowls and put them on the table, along with a basket of crackers and a plate of cookies. "I'm afraid this isn't a very substantial lunch," she apologized.

"It's more than I often have," he assured her. "Things get pretty crazy at the office and a lot of times I just skip lunch. I'm glad I didn't today, though. This is delicious," he said appreciatively as he sampled the hearty beef barley mixture.

"I like soup for lunch in the winter. It's not hard to make, and one pot lasts me all week."

He stopped eating long enough to look at her. "You made this?"

"Mmm-hmm."

"My compliments to the chef."

She inclined her head. "Thank you."

As Adam wolfed down his soup, he realized that Clare was hardly making a dent in hers. She was eating each spoonful gingerly, taking care to avoid the tooth that needed work. "Are you sure you can wait till Friday?" he asked with a frown. "I could call Mark and ask him to fit you in sooner."

She looked up from her bowl. "No. I'm just being careful. But don't feel like you have to stay until I'm finished. I'm sure you're in a hurry."

Adam glanced at his watch. If he left immediately he'd barely get to the office in time for his first appointment. Which was his own fault. He'd only intended to make a quick inquiry, then be on his way. But Clare's unexpected invitation had been too tempting to turn down. He rarely saw her alone, and the opportunity to spend a few minutes with her had been immensely appealing.

Adam wasn't really sure why he'd detoured to the house at all. He certainly could have done without the file he'd retrieved from his home office. And a simple phone call would have sufficed to alleviate any concern he had about her dental problem. His impromptu visit had been impulsive and completely out of character, he acknowledged.

He looked over at Clare, noticing for the first time that she was wearing the blue sweater he and Nicole had given her for Christmas. He suddenly realized that it matched her expressive eyes exactly. His gaze dropped to her soft lips, lingered a moment too long, then returned to her eyes. And for just a moment he got lost in their azure depths. Lost enough to experience a brief moment of panic.

"I'm used to eating alone, Adam. So please don't stay on my account," Clare repeated, her voice now a bit breathless. "I can see you're concerned about being late."

In an abrupt move that momentarily startled her, he reached for his jacket, said his goodbyes and quickly made his escape.

Because suddenly he was concerned about far more than being late.

Chapter Seven

The midwinter cookout was a smashing success.

Clare breathed a sigh of relief as she watched the giggling clusters of girls roasting hot dogs around the bonfire, noting with satisfaction that Nicole was firmly ensconsed in the middle of one of them. Since she'd run into Candace at the Christmas festival in town, Nicole had seemed much happier. She talked about school more, and it sounded as if the girls had begun to include her in their activities. So Clare had thought a party might give Nicole another helping hand. She'd made it a point to talk to each of the mothers in advance, hoping to ensure good attendance, and her efforts had obviously paid off.

"Looks like they're having fun, doesn't it?"

Clare turned. Adam stood just behind her, holding the oversize thermos of hot chocolate he'd retrieved from the kitchen. She smiled and looked back at the group of girls. "I'd say so. It brings back memories of good times as a kid, doesn't it?"

When Adam didn't respond, she turned back to him.

He had an odd expression on his face, one that she couldn't quite identify. Instinctively she reached out to touch his arm. "What is it, Adam?" she asked softly.

For a moment he didn't answer. Then he looked down at her gloved hand, which rested lightly on the sleeve of his sheepskin-lined jacket. A different expression flitted across his eyes, and she saw his Adam's apple bob. A moment later, he nodded toward the thermos. "Where do you want this?"

He was ignoring her question. Which was certainly his right, since she'd trespassed on to personal ground. She should just let it go. But something compelled her to persist. "Adam, what's wrong?" she tried again.

Reluctantly he raised his gaze to hers, as if he were afraid to let her see his eyes. But they were shuttered now, anyway. "Nothing."

She replayed their conversation in her mind, wondering what she'd said to trigger his look. Then she briefly glanced back toward the bonfire. "This doesn't bring back happy memories for you, does it?"

A muscle clenched in his jaw, and she was pretty sure he was going to ignore her question. But he surprised her by answering. "It doesn't bring back memories of any kind," he said flatly.

She frowned. "What do you mean?"

"I didn't have the best childhood, Clare. Nothing like the one you described at Christmas. My mother died when I was six. I barely remember her. My father was a good provider, but he wasn't exactly... demonstrative. He was a hard taskmaster who expected his sons to toe the line and not be distracted by frivolous things. We never had parties like this."

Clare's eyes softened with empathy. She couldn't even imagine a childhood like the one Adam described, devoid of love and laughter. Suddenly a few more pieces of this man's life clicked into place. How could you connect to people you love if you had no experience with love yourself, no example to follow? "I'm sorry, Adam. That wouldn't have been an easy way to grow up."

He shrugged stiffly. "It could have been worse. We always had a roof over our heads and we never went hungry."

Maybe not for food, Clare thought. But his youthful diet sounded sadly lacking in emotional sustenance.

"So where do you want this?" he repeated.

She pointed toward a long table set back from the bonfire. "Anywhere over there is fine. Thank you."

As she watched him walk away, his back ramrod straight, Clare's heart ached for him. No wonder he'd had difficulty sustaining a marriage and bonding with his daughter. Being raised in a strict, emotionally cold environment would have left him ill-equipped for either task. Yet she knew that Adam craved emotional closeness. She could see the longing, as well as the discouragement, in his eyes when he looked at Nicole. He was obviously convinced that he didn't have the tools to create the kind of bond he yearned for with his daughter.

But Clare was sure he was wrong. Because she'd seen something else in his eyes, as well. A fire burning deep in their depths. A capacity to love just waiting for release. A hunger to connect. She believed with all her heart that he desperately wanted to escape the loneliness that he thought was his destiny, to fill the emotional vacuum created by his sterile upbringing.

And she also believed that where there was a will, there was a way.

It might be one of the biggest challenges of her life, but Clare was determined to help Adam find the key that would unlock his heart so that he and Nicole could finally become a family.

Clare was freezing.

As she groggily came awake, she automatically reached for the fluffy comforter, only to realize it was already covering her. She frowned and peered at the illuminated face of her clock. Two in the morning.

Shivering, she reached for her bedside lamp and flipped it on, blinking as light flooded the room. Something was wrong with the heat, she realized, as a frosty cloud of breath suddenly appeared in front of her.

Clare didn't have a clue about the heat source for her apartment. Adam had shown her how to work the thermostat when she'd moved in, and she'd never had a need to investigate further. So she had no idea how to fix the problem. She couldn't bother Adam at this hour, but she had to do something. Even if she piled every blanket in the apartment on her bed, it wouldn't be enough to keep her warm.

Taking a deep breath, she forced herself to get up. With shaking fingers she rummaged in the dresser for her heavy wool sweater and pulled it on over her nightgown. Then she slipped her arms into her velour robe. Finally, after wrapping the comforter around her shoulders, she padded out to the living room to examine the thermostat.

It didn't surprise her to find that the temperature in the apartment was thirty-nine degrees. So her next stop was the furnace, which was probably in the garage, she speculated. She didn't recall ever seeing it, but then again, she'd never really looked. As she searched in her kitchen cabinets for a flashlight, it occurred to her that even if she found the furnace, she doubted whether she could do anything to fix the problem.

But taking some kind of action beat sitting around freezing to death.

Adam wearily replaced the receiver on his bedside phone and wiped a hand across his face. Middle-of-the-night calls from his emergency answering service were one of the down sides of his job, and he'd never quite gotten used to being jarred awake so rudely. The resulting adrenaline rush always left him restless and unable to get back to sleep.

He rose and headed to the kitchen to get a drink of water before returning the patient's call. As he reached for a glass, he glanced out the window toward the garage…and his hand froze in midair. Why were the lights on in Clare's apartment?

A sudden wave of panic engulfed him, sending another surge of adrenaline through his veins. Then he forced himself to take a deep breath. Maybe she was doing the same thing he was doing—getting a drink of water, he rationalized. Just because she was up in the middle of the night didn't mean there was a problem.

But after he drank his water and jotted a few notes about his conversation with the exchange, the light was still on. For a moment he hesitated. If all was well, Clare might consider his middle-of-the-night visit an intrusion. On the other hand, he knew he wouldn't get another wink of sleep until he assured himself that everything was okay. He'd just have to risk her annoyance, he concluded, heading for his room to pull on a pair of jeans and a sweatshirt.

Adam shivered as he stepped outside, noting that the temperature had dropped substantially during the night. He wasted no time covering the ground between the house and garage, and when he reached the top of the stairs he rapped softly on the door.

A moment later he heard Clare's cautious voice on the other side. "Yes?"

"Clare, it's Adam. I saw your lights on. Is everything okay?"

Instead of a verbal response, he heard the lock sliding back. A moment later the door swung open.

Clare stood silhouetted by the light behind her. At least he thought it was Clare. But the apparition before him actually looked more like a mummy.

"Clare?"

She stepped aside, and now the light fell on her face. She was wrapped in some sort of quilt or comforter. "Boy, am I g-glad to s-see you!"

Her voice was shaky, and he moved beside her. "What's wrong?"

"N-no heat."

Adam suddenly became aware of the bone-chilling cold in the room. "What happened?"

"I wish I kn-knew. I just woke up a f-few minutes ago."

Now he could see the clouds of breath when she spoke. "Why didn't you call me?"

"I didn't want to bother you at this hour. Why are you up, anyway?"

"Patient call. Look, you can't stay here. Grab your coat and come back to the house. We'll deal with this tomorrow."

Instead of responding, she quickly dropped the comforter and pulled her coat out of the tiny hall closet. He held it while she slipped her arms into the sleeves, but her fingers fumbled on the buttons. Finally she gave up and just bunched it closed with one hand.

Adam preceded her out the door. "Be careful on the steps," he cautioned, eyeing her long robe. "In fact, let me go first."

She followed closely on his heels, and when they reached the bottom, he flipped off the light in the stairwell and opened the door. A blast of cold air whipped past them as they stepped outside, and Clare faltered. Instinctively, Adam reached for her hand, enfolding her delicate fingers in his. The iciness of her skin startled him, and without even stopping to consider his actions, he drew her closer to his body and placed a hand protectively around her shoulders as he guided her toward the house.

When they reached the kitchen, Adam didn't even pause. He continued toward the living room, eased her out of her coat, and gently pressed her into the chair closest to the fireplace. He retrieved the throw that was draped over the couch and tucked it around her, then knelt and set a match to the kindling in the

grate. As flames began to lick up the sides of the dry
wood, he returned to Clare's side. She was still shivering noticeably, and he could hear her teeth chattering. He reached for her cold hands, cocooning them
in his warm clasp.

"I'll make you a cup of tea."

"Th-thank you."

When Adam returned a few minutes later and silently
handed Clare a steaming mug, she sent him a grateful
look. "Thank you. This looks wonderful."

But no more wonderful than she did, he realized. The
flickering firelight cast a warm glow on her face, and
her eyes looked large and luminous. Yet it was her hair
that caught his attention. He had never seen it so loose
and free before. It tumbled around her shoulders in
disarray, gossamer strands of gold as fine as newly spun
silk. Another rush of adrenaline that had nothing to do
with his late-night patient call surged through him, and
he felt an almost overpowering urge to reach out and
run his fingers through her soft tresses. He stifled the
impulse by jamming his fists into his pockets. What was
wrong with him tonight?

Clare took several long sips of tea, then sighed contentedly and snuggled more deeply into the chair. "I'm
finally starting to feel my fingers again. Thank you for
coming to my rescue."

"You should have called me right away."

"I hated to bother you in the middle of the night."

"I would have been more bothered if I'd discovered
that you tried to stick it out till morning. And maybe
ended up with pneumonia in the process."

"I never get sick. I told you, I'm stronger than I look."

"Well, don't push your luck. I need to return a call to my patient. Will you be okay here for a few minutes?"

"Of course. Take your time."

Adam was gone longer than he expected, and by the time he returned Clare had set the empty mug beside her chair and fallen asleep. With her hair spilling over one cheek, and her face in repose, she looked younger than ever. And more fragile, somehow, despite her claim about being strong.

Adam felt a bit indiscreet, standing there watching her sleep, but he couldn't help himself. She was so lovely. And her loveliness went deeper than mere physical beauty. She was kind and sensitive and caring, and generous to a fault—much like Jo had been, he reflected. Despite her own pain, she had opened her heart to him and Nicole and given far more of herself than her job as nanny required. And because of that, she was making a huge difference in their lives.

Without conscious decision, Adam moved slowly toward her and tentatively touched her hair. It was whisper soft. Silky. And so appealing. Just like the woman.

Suddenly Adam was overcome by a longing so deep and intense that it took his breath away. Not just a longing for physical intimacy, but for an even deeper, more lasting connection. A connection of the heart, mind and soul. The kind that Jack and Theresa shared.

Jack had told him at Christmas that there was no secret to what he'd found with Theresa. It just required a willingness to reveal to special people what was in your heart. And Adam wanted to do that. Desperately. But the memories of his father's ridicule the few times he'd tried, as a youth, to express his feelings were difficult to overcome. How did you move past that? How did you learn to trust the most fragile of all your possessions—your heart—with another person?

Adam stared at Clare and drew a long, unsteady breath. He didn't know the answer to those questions. Nor was he sure he could find them. But unless he did, he would never make much headway with Nicole. She was his first priority. He needed to focus on their relationship, to find a way to welcome her into his heart. To open himself up and share.

Then maybe, if he succeeded with her, he would succeed with other relationships.

That was a big maybe, of course. And even if he got that far, even if he decided to explore another kind of relationship, he needed to move very slowly. He'd made impulsive decisions once, with Elaine, and the results had been disastrous. He wouldn't make that mistake again.

Adam raked his fingers through his hair. The whole notion of emotional intimacy was uncharted territory for him. And he couldn't exactly go out and buy a road map to show him the way. So he bowed his head and sought direction from a higher power.

Dear Lord, I know I've made a mess of things up till now in my relationships. But with Your help, I'd like to try and escape from the self-imposed emotional exile I've lived in for so long. You've already sent us a great blessing in Clare, and I thank You for that. I thank You, also, for the example of a good marriage that You've given me in Jack and Theresa. And for the insights of my brother, and his support. Please help me to listen with my heart to the guidance You are providing, and to recognize the opportunities to grow that You send my way.

I also ask that you let Clare feel Your healing presence in a special way. I know that You have given her a great cross to bear, and sometimes I think that her slender shoulders may not be able to hold it up. I see the pain and sadness in her eyes. She has been so good for us...please be good to her. Help her to find a way to replace her sorrow with joy.

And finally, Lord, please pass a message on to Jo for me. Tell her I said thank you.

"So how's the birthday girl?"

Clare smiled. "Hi, A.J. The birthday girl is trying to ignore the increasing number of candles on her cake."

"You're only as old as you feel."

"That's easy for you to say. You're the youngest."

"You aren't that far ahead of me. Did you hear from Morgan?"

"Yes. She called before she left for work. Woke me up at some uncivilized hour this morning. Apparently there's some crisis at the agency. Sometimes I think she should just close up her apartment and move into her office. She's never home, anyway."

"Tell me about it. Someone needs to give that girl a good talking-to."

"Someone did. Grant Kincaid, to be exact."

"The guy who inherited half of Aunt Jo's cottage?"

"None other. She tried to get him to meet with her on Christmas Eve to discuss it, and he told her to forget it. That it was a holiday and he was spending the time with his family."

"Good for him! I take it Morgan wasn't too happy about that?"

"Apparently not. It was still on her mind when she called today. And Christmas was two weeks ago."

"Hmm. Maybe she's finally met someone who can talk some sense into her. We can hope, anyway. But I called to talk about you. Any special plans for the day?"

"No. Just the usual."

There was a moment of silence. "You haven't told anyone it's your birthday, have you?" A.J. said, her tone slightly accusing.

"No. I don't want people to make a fuss."

An audible sigh came over the line. "I wish I was there. We'd go out on the town, have a great dinner, see a movie. Look. Promise me you'll do something special today. I don't care what it is. Just something."

"Such as?"

"I don't know. But it's important to mark the special days in our lives. Even if it's only for ourselves. Just do something out of your normal routine, okay?"

Clare smiled. "I'll do my best."

As she hung up the phone a few minutes later, Clare thought about A.J.'s request. Her sister was right, of course. And up until two years ago she'd enthusiastically embraced that same philosophy, making it a point to celebrate special days in ways that created happy memories that could be pulled out and relived on not-so-special days. But she'd gotten out of the habit since Dennis and David died. No day seemed special to her anymore. Which was a sign of depression. She'd learned that from the reading she'd done over the past two years as she'd searched in vain for solace and comfort.

But she'd promised A.J. she'd make an effort. Considering that it was an unseasonably warm day, maybe she could take a hike along Hope Creek. She'd seen the trail marker outside of town and she'd been meaning to explore. And a change of scene might help lift her spirits, which always took a nosedive on special days. Especially since she now spent most of them alone.

Clare paused and listened. The path had veered momentarily away from the creek, but she was sure she heard the splash of a waterfall through the trees. She struck off toward the sound, brushing aside the branches that blocked her way.

A couple of minutes later, she paused in delight as she emerged into a secluded, magical clearing. A small waterfall cascaded into a clear pool, and large, flat rocks were strewn along the edges. It was the kind of place where a fanciful sort of person would expect to find a leprechaun sitting on a boulder, hammering on his shoe.

A smile tipped up the corners of her mouth. That was more like something A.J. would dream up, she thought affectionately. Her youngest sister had always had a whimsical streak. Morgan, on the other hand, had always been all business. She'd been the one who ran the lemonade stand when they were kids and devised ways to increase sales, while A.J. drank away most of the profits. Clare had been the practical one, making sure there were enough cups and napkins for the customers Morgan hoped to entice.

But right at this moment, in this place, she didn't feel practical. She felt young. And at peace. It had to be the setting, she concluded. The mist-clad mountains rose in the distance, but the sky above was cloudless, and the wind whispered in the fir trees. She lifted her face and closed her eyes, letting the sun seep into her pores. It felt so warm, so relaxing, so...

"Clare?"

Her eyelids flew open and she gasped, jerking toward the voice. At the sight of Reverend Nichols sitting on a rock a short distance away, a book in his hand, Clare's shoulders sagged in relief.

"I'm sorry. I didn't mean to startle you," he apologized. "I was engrossed in my reading, and when I looked up there you were. At least I thought it was you."

"That's okay. I didn't see you, either," Clare reassured him as she closed the distance between them. "Then again, I wasn't looking. I didn't think anyone would be here."

"I stumbled across this spot a few months ago, and I've sort of adopted it as my private hideaway. It's a great place for contemplation."

"Then I'm sorry I disturbed you."

"Not at all. I was just getting ready to go back. What brings you out on this beautiful day?"

"I've been meaning to explore the creek. And when my sister called this morning to wish me a happy birthday, she suggested I do something different to celebrate the day. So I took her advice."

"Well, you couldn't have picked a better way than to spend time in God's glorious creation. Especially on a day like this. And I think I have a perfect verse for both the place and the occasion." He flipped through his book, which Clare now realized was a pocket Bible, until he came to Psalms. "'I lift up my eyes toward the mountains; when shall help come to me?'" he read. "'My help is from the Lord, who made heaven and earth.'" He continued further down the page. "'The Lord will guard you from all evil; He will guard your life. The Lord will guard your coming and your going, both now and forever.'"

The minister's voice echoed in the stillness, and for a moment after he finished he was silent. Then he closed the book and looked up at Clare. "What better birthday present could we ask?" he said quietly.

She blinked rapidly a few times, then gave him a melancholy smile. "That's one of my sister's favorite verses."

"But not one of yours?"

The question was gentle and held no reproach. Clare studied the young minister, debating how best to answer. "I'm not sure I've experienced that verse in my life," she said slowly.

"And your sister has?"

Clare thought about his question. A.J. had suffered plenty of trauma and tragedy in her thirty-two years. Enough to last a lifetime. The loss of her fiancé. A disabling injury. Shattered dreams. Yet her faith had never wavered, as Clare's had. She still found comfort in the Bible. Even in the verse Reverend Nichols had just read. Slowly Clare sat down on the rock across from the minister, her face troubled.

"I think so. But I'm not sure why." She recounted A.J.'s story, then shook her head. "Despite everything she went through, she never lost her connection to God, even though it didn't seem He'd been very diligent in guarding her." She sighed. "I wish I had her faith. When things got rough for me, I felt as if the Lord had abandoned me."

"Do you still feel that way?"

Clare stared at the clear stream, tumbling over the rocks a few feet away. "Most of the time. But I don't want to feel that way. It leaves an empty place deep inside that I don't know how to fill."

"I see you at church every week. Does it help?"

"More so since you became pastor. Your sermons are always wonderful. But a lot of the time I feel like I'm just going through the motions. I'm still missing the connection to the Lord that I used to have."

"Do you pray? On your own?"

"I try sometimes. But my prayers are pretty unfocused. I don't even know what to ask for, exactly."

"You mentioned that you'd had some rough times. Do you want to tell me about them?"

Clare looked over at the minister. She rarely talked about her trauma. A.J. and Morgan knew what had happened, of course. But even they didn't know about the burden of guilt she carried. She hadn't shared that with anyone. It was too painful. Too incriminating. Yet maybe she needed to talk about it, to acknowledge it, before she could let it go.

"I lost my husband and son in a car accident two years ago," she said softly.

Reverend Nichols's eyes filled with sympathy. "I'm so sorry, Clare. I knew you were a widow, but I didn't know any of the details. One tragic death is difficult enough to deal with. Two would break a lot of people. It takes great strength to endure that kind of cross. But you survived."

She didn't respond immediately, and when she spoke her voice was a mere whisper. "Sometimes I wish I hadn't."

"A devastating loss can make a person feel that way," he said gently.

"It's not just that." She hesitated. Her heart hammered painfully in her chest, and she brushed back a stray strand of hair with an unsteady hand. "It was my fault that they died."

There was a moment of silence, and then the minister spoke again. "Are you sure about that, Clare?"

She nodded miserably. "I was at a pool party…a birthday party…for a good friend. Dennis, my husband, had just gotten back from an overseas trip. I knew he had jet lag. But I didn't want to leave the party, so I—I asked him to drive our son to baseball practice, even though I was supposed to do it. We'd had a brief rain shower, and the pavement was slick. The accident report said h-he'd lost control of the car going around a curve on the wet road." She drew a ragged breath and buried her face in her hands. "How I wish I could believe that! But I know how tired he was. I'm so afraid that he fell asleep at the wheel. Or that he simply couldn't react quickly enough because his reflexes were dull from fatigue. They both died as a result of my selfishness. If only I'd honored my commitment to drive David to practice, left the party when I was supposed to, I'd still have my husband and son." Her voice broke on the last word.

For a moment only the sound of the tumbling brook could be heard in the stillness. Then Clare felt a comforting hand on her shoulder. She was almost afraid to look at Reverend Nichols, sure she would see reproach in his eyes. But when she finally did risk a glance, his eyes remained kind and nonjudgmental.

"You've made a lot of assumptions, Clare," he said gently.

"I was there, Reverend," she said, her eyes dull with pain. "I knew Dennis was tired. I should never have asked him to drive."

"Maybe not. But you don't know what really happened on that road. Maybe your husband was fully awake. Maybe an animal darted in front of the car and he tried to avoid it. Maybe when the car started to slide, there was no way to stop it no matter who was driving. Maybe if you'd been in the driver's seat, you would have been killed. Perhaps the Lord had other plans for you. Things He wanted you still to do here."

Her shoulders slumped and she looked away again. "Maybe," she said dispiritedly. "But I still feel that my selfishness was the cause of everything."

"May I tell you something, Clare? Our friendship is still new. But *selfish* is not a word I would ever use to describe you. I've seen your dedication to the Feed the Hungry program. You're at church every week, rain or shine, working in the kitchen. And I've seen what you've done for Adam and Nicole. You've put your heart and soul into the nanny job. And now that I know your story, I can only imagine how difficult that's been for you. But you're making a tremendous difference in the lives of two very lonely people who were desperately in need of help. Selfish? I don't think so. And I don't think the Lord does, either."

"I wish I could be sure of that in my heart," Clare said wistfully.

"May I make a suggestion? You said earlier that you'd tried to pray, but that you didn't know what to ask for. So don't ask for anything. Just talk to the Lord. Tell Him what's in your heart. Tell Him about your fears and your guilt and your pain. And trust that He'll give you what you need, whatever that is…release…healing…forgiveness…purpose. He'll know."

Clare looked at the minister thoughtfully. "You make it sound so simple."

"It is simple. But that doesn't mean it's easy. It can be very difficult to acknowledge that we don't have all the answers and to be open to God's guidance. In fact, we often tend to fight His direction, because it's not the path we thought we were supposed to follow. So we have to learn to listen for His voice speaking softly in our hearts, just as Elijah did in the cave. And we can't force God to respond. He always answers…but in His own time, not ours."

For the first time in two years, Clare felt hope stirring

in her heart. Reverend Nichols's words had eased her burden of guilt, and he'd given her some sound advice about how to reestablish her relationship with the Lord.

It wasn't a present Clare had expected to receive on her birthday. But she couldn't think of anything she would have rather received.

Chapter Eight

"So why didn't you tell us your birthday was last week?"

Clare shot Adam a startled look across the table. "How did you know?"

"I ran into Reverend Nichols in town today. He said you two crossed paths by the creek on your birthday."

"Your birthday was last week?" Nicole stared at her. "We didn't even have a cake!"

Clare flushed. "I don't need a cake. And I stopped counting birthdays a long time ago."

"But birthdays are a big deal! We should have had a party or something!"

"I agree," Adam said. Then he turned to Clare. "Do you have anything planned tomorrow?"

She stared at him, taken aback. Her Saturdays were generally her own, except when Adam had patients in the hospital. Then she watched Nicole for a couple of hours in the morning, as she was planning to do tomorrow. "I'll be over here in the morning while you're gone. That's about it."

"Good. Then how about we go out to lunch when I get home, and afterward take the sled to Logan's Hill? I heard we're supposed to get several inches of snow tonight, now that our brief reprieve from winter is over."

Nicole and Clare stared at him incredulously, and Adam felt hot color steal up his neck. He knew his suggestion was out of character. He hadn't exactly been Mr. Spontaneous when it came to planning family outings. But for some reason, the sledding idea had popped into his mind and he'd just run with it. Though based on their looks, maybe he should have run in the other direction, he thought ruefully.

Nicole spoke first. "What sled?"

"The one I bought on the way home tonight."

"Cool!"

At least he had Nicole's approval, he thought with relief. But he wasn't so sure about Clare. When he looked at her, he saw uncertainty in the depths of her eyes. Had his suggestion triggered some unhappy memories, he wondered suddenly? It hadn't occurred to him that sledding might make her think of similar outings with her own family. The last thing he wanted to do was cause her more pain. Maybe this hadn't been such a good idea after all.

"If you'd rather do something else, just say the word," he told her. "We could go to a movie instead."

"I like the sledding idea," Nicole declared.

"But it's Clare's birthday, Nicole. So we need to pick something she'll enjoy."

Clare looked from father to daughter. She was deeply touched by Adam's gesture to recognize her birthday, although sledding wouldn't have been her first choice. It reminded her of the childhood accident that had damaged her tooth. And of similar outings with David and Dennis. But if her goal was to help Adam and Nicole become a family, she should be encouraging them to do things like this together, not putting a damper on them. Surely she could put her own memories aside for the day.

"Sledding sounds great!" she assured him enthusiastically, hoping they wouldn't notice that the brightness in her voice was slightly forced. "But you really don't have to do anything."

"Can we get a cake, too, Dad?"

"Of course. What kind would you like, Clare?"

"Really, Adam, it's not necessary."

"She likes chocolate," Nicole told him.

"Chocolate it is, then. I'll call the bakery in the morning."

Clare capitulated with a smile. "Okay, I can see I'm being overruled here. But you have to promise me one thing. No presents."

"It's not a birthday without presents," Nicole protested.

"No presents, or I'm not going sledding," Clare said firmly.

"That's not fair," Nicole sulked.

"Hey, we did pretty good so far. Let's not push our luck," Adam told Nicole. Then he turned to Clare. "Okay. Cross my heart. No presents. Deal?"

Clare smiled at his teasing tone. "Deal."

As the dinner progressed, punctuated by easygoing conversation and laughter, Clare had the oddest feeling.

It wasn't altogether unfamiliar, but it had been absent for so long that she almost didn't recognize it. Contentment.

It didn't take her long to pinpoint the reasons for her feeling of warmth and well-being. The chip on Nicole's shoulder was slowly disappearing. The relationship between father and daughter was showing definite signs of thawing. Her pain and guilt had eased slightly since she'd begun to talk to God, as Reverend Nichols had suggested. And now she had an impromptu party to look forward to with two very special people.

So much for a quiet and inconsequential birthday, she thought with a smile.

A.J. would be pleased.

"Okay, it's Clare's turn again," Nicole said, handing over the sled.

"Just one more run, then we need to leave," Clare responded. "The sun's going down. Besides, you're starting to look like Rudolph."

Nicole giggled and rubbed her nose. "I don't care. This is fun."

"Well, we've outlasted everybody, that's for sure," Adam said, surveying the deserted hill.

Clare lay on the sled, and Adam moved behind her. "Ready?" At her nod, he leaned down and grasped the edges of the runners. A moment later he gave her a hearty push.

The cold air whipped past her face as she flew down the hill, and Clare smiled both at the invigorating ride and the success of the day's outing. They'd shared a late lunch, and Nicole had been more animated than usual in anticipation of the sledding to come. She'd even teased Adam once, which had clearly delighted him. Since arriving at Logan's Hill, it had been nonstop action. And just plain fun. An unexpectedly happy, laughter-filled interlude she suspected they'd all needed desperately.

As a sudden spray of snow crystals stung her face, Clare closed her eyes for a brief moment. She didn't even see the hard clump of ice that loomed ahead and brought the sled to an abrupt stop. All she knew was that she was suddenly flying through the air, minus the sled. She opened her eyes in alarm, then quickly shut them again as she landed in a heap with a bone-jarring thud that completely knocked the breath out of her.

For several long seconds she lay unmoving, trying to coax her lungs into working again. Just when she was about to panic, they kicked into gear, and she gasped greedily, inhaling the bracing cold air.

As she concentrated on breathing in and out, she felt the hair being brushed back from her face.

"Clare? Are you all right? Don't move!"

At the undisguised panic in Adam's voice, she struggled to turn over. But a firm hand on her shoulder restrained her. "Don't move!" he repeated, his voice strained and tense.

"Dad, is she okay?" Nicole sounded scared and close to tears.

Clare took another deep breath before she tried to speak. "I'm fine," she reassured them, her voice muffled. "Adam, please let me up. I just had the wind knocked out of me."

For a moment his hand remained in place, then gradually the pressure eased. "Okay, but let's take this slow and easy."

When he rolled her onto her back, Clare almost lost her breath again. There was still panic in Adam's eyes, though it was tempered slightly now. But she saw something else, as well. Something that made her heart stir to life. Adam's worry about her condition wasn't just driven by professional concern or even friendship. He cared about her. Deeply. Not just as a person who had come to be important in his life and the life of his daughter. But as a woman.

Oddly enough, Clare wasn't even sure he recognized the depth of his feelings. Or wanted to recognize them. Which was probably good. Because she certainly wasn't ready to deal with them. Or with her own.

"Does anything hurt?"

She blinked, trying to refocus her thoughts so she could answer Adam's question. "No."

"Did you hit your head or black out, even for a second or two?"

"I don't think so."

"Okay. Let's try a couple of things."

She flexed the limbs he requested, then waited while he examined her scalp with gentle fingers.

"Everything seems to be okay," he finally said with evident relief.

She sat up. "I told you that at the beginning."

"Well, it doesn't hurt to be cautious. Come on, I'll give you a hand up and we'll get Rudolph here out of the cold."

Clare glanced at Nicole. The girl was hovering a few

feet away, her red nose bright against her suddenly pale face. Obviously Adam had noticed how upset she was and was attempting to lighten the mood.

Clare put her hand in Adam's, and he pulled her to her feet in one swift, smooth motion. She was grateful for the support of his arm around her waist, however, because her legs suddenly felt very rubbery.

When she looked up, he studied her face assessingly. "Okay?"

"A little shaky. I'll be fine in a minute."

Nicole edged closer, and Clare reached out a hand. "Hey! Cheer up. You should be glad it was me that wiped out and not you. Now you guys can tease me about my rusty sledding skills."

Nicole took her hand. "Are you really okay?" she asked tremulously.

"Fine. Ask the doctor," Clare said with a smile.

"I expect she'll have a few bruises. But other than that, no harm done," he assured his daughter.

"Can we go home, then? I'm getting pretty cold now."

"Sounds like a plan to me," Clare agreed.

As they started for the car, Adam kept his arm around her waist and Nicole held tightly to her hand. Almost like a family.

Unfortunately, just not her family, she thought with a sudden, wistful pang.

Adam caught a movement out of the corner of his eye and looked up from the medical journal he was reading. Nicole was hovering in the doorway of his office, her face uncertain.

"Everything okay?" he asked.

"Yeah. I just finished my homework."

Adam waited while Nicole shifted her weight from one foot to the other.

"So…are you busy?" she finally said.

Adam closed the journal. "Not really. I can read this anytime."

She hesitated, then moved slowly into the room, her hands in her pockets. "I just wanted to make sure you really thought Clare was okay."

"She's fine. Just a little headache. She hit the ground pretty hard."

"Yeah. I was kind of scared for a minute."

"Me, too."

"Really?"

"Yeah."

Nicole perched on the edge of a chair, tension quivering in her body, like a child about to make her first jump off the high-diving board. When she spoke, her voice was quiet and a little shaky. "It made me remember how fast Mom died. I mean, one day she was taking me shopping, and the next she was gone. Like, with…with no warning."

Her voice broke, and Adam's heart contracted. He set aside the journal and leaned forward. "I'm sorry you had to go through that, Nicole. It's very hard to lose someone you love, especially when you're so young."

"I felt really alone after that. I mean, I know you took me in, but it kind of wrecked up your life. Like all of a sudden you were stuck with a kid living with you. At first I…I felt like you didn't want me. Like I was in the way. Sometimes I…I still do."

Adam felt like someone had kicked him in the gut.
Instinctively he stood and moved out from behind his
desk to sit on the arm of the chair beside Nicole. Tentatively he put his arm around her thin shoulders. She
stiffened, but didn't pull away.

"You weren't in the way. And I did want you," he told
her emphatically. "Even before the accident, I wanted
to be more involved in your life, but I didn't know how.
You and your mom had a special bond, and I never felt
like I fit in very well. I know a lot of that's my fault. I've
never been very good at expressing my feelings. But I'm
learning. Because I love you, Nicole. I always have. And
I'm doing my best to make us a family. I want that more
than anything."

She sniffled and looked up at him. "Really?"

"Really."

She looked down again and fiddled with the hem of
her sweater. "Sometimes I get scared that maybe…maybe
you'll go away, too," she said in a small voice.

He swallowed hard and squeezed her shoulder. "Not
if I can help it."

"But stuff…happens, you know? Like today, with
Clare. I mean, she's okay and all, but what if she wasn't?"

That thought had occurred to Adam, as well. And it
left him with a sick feeling in the pit of his stomach. So
he couldn't very well try to placate Nicole. "Then we'd
have to do the best we could. We'd have to take care of
each other. We'll have to do that anyway, when she
leaves at the end of May."

"I know. But that's months away. And we can still
be friends with her even after she leaves, can't we?"

"Of course."

Nicole frowned. "But it won't be the same. I'll miss her a lot."

Adam didn't know how to respond to that. Because he was beginning to feel exactly the same way.

Things were not looking good. Clare added the columns of figures once more—with the same discouraging results.

With a sigh, she reached for her mug of tea and took a fortifying sip. Although she was doing her best to stretch her limited resources over the six months of her nanny job, she'd already blown her budget. Living rent free helped immensely, but the root canal and some major repair work on her car had put a huge dent in her bank account. If everything went smoothly for the next three and a half months, she might be able to eke it out. But she couldn't count on that. Another emergency could easily arise.

And if it did, where could she turn for help? She couldn't ask A.J. Her youngest sister had lived on subsistence wages for years. And Morgan was having her own financial problems. So she needed to build up her cash reserves in case of another emergency.

Which left her only one option.

"I saw Clare at Wal-Mart yesterday."

Adam continued writing in Adele's chart. "Is that right?" he replied distractedly.

"She works too hard, Adam. You should talk to her. Between taking care of Nicole and cooking your meals, not to mention helping out at church and at Nicole's school on a regular basis, I'm sure she has her hands full. She doesn't need another job."

Adam stopped writing and looked up at Adele. "What did you say?"

"I said I think you should talk to her about taking on this second job."

Adam had only half listened to Adele's chitchat, but now he tried to focus on what she'd said. She'd mentioned running into Clare at…Wal-Mart. And what was this about a second job?

"I'm sorry, Adele. Did you say Clare had a second job?"

She raised her eyebrows. "You didn't know?"

"No."

"Hmm. Clare's working at Wal-Mart."

Adam frowned. "How long has that been going on?"

"Just a couple of weeks, from what I could gather. I asked why she didn't just substitute teach, but apparently she'd have to get different credentials in North Carolina."

Adam's frown deepened. Since early February, things had gone crazy at the office as a flu epidemic swept the county. He'd been getting home far later than usual, too exhausted to do anything but wolf down his dinner and head for bed. He and Clare had hardly exchanged more than a few words all month. So he had no idea what had prompted her need for a second job. But he intended to find out tonight.

"Thanks for letting me know, Adele. I'll definitely look into it."

"Good. I hate to see her wearing herself down."

Adam jotted down a prescription, then tore it off and handed it to Adele. "This should help those sinuses."

She tucked it into her purse and rose. "You're a good doctor, Adam. I'm sure this will solve my problem. Now take care of your nanny."

"Clare, could I talk with you for a minute?"

At the serious tone in Adam's voice, Clare turned from the sink. "Is everything all right?"

"That's what I'd like to find out. Is Nicole doing her homework?"

"Yes."

"Let's sit for a minute, okay?"

Clare wiped her hands on the dish towel and carefully draped it over the sink. Something in Adam's tone put her on alert, and when she joined him at the kitchen table a moment later she gingerly eased into a chair and folded her hands nervously in front of her.

For a moment he didn't speak, and she studied his face. He looked bone weary, she thought. Which wasn't surprising, since he'd put in a ridiculous number of hours over the past month. While the workload was finally beginning to abate, the pressures and demands had left their mark. The fine lines that radiated from the corners of his eyes had deepened, and the smudges beneath them spoke of late hours and interrupted sleep. The fingers he'd wrapped around his coffee cup seemed slightly unsteady, as well.

"I saw Adele today," he said at last.

"Is she okay?"

"Yes. But she passed on some disturbing information. She told me that you had taken a part-time job."

Clare frowned, momentarily caught off guard. "Yes. But I only work nine to two, four days a week. We agreed that my time was my own while Nicole was in school."

"It is. But I didn't expect you to go out and get another job."

She sent him a curious look. She hadn't purposely kept the part-time job a secret. But with Adam's hectic schedule, there'd been no real opportunity to bring it up. She wasn't sure why it was such a big deal. Unless he felt awkward about having his nanny work at Wal-Mart.

"I would have done substitute teaching if I had the right credentials for North Carolina," she said. "But since I didn't, this was the most convenient thing I could find. I didn't mean to embarrass you."

Now it was his turn to frown. "This isn't about me, Clare. You could never do anything to embarrass me. I'm more concerned about why you felt the need to take on another job. It seems to me we keep you plenty busy here at the house, and I know you help out at church and at Nicole's school. I don't mean to pry into your personal business, but have you had some sort of financial emergency? Because if that's the case, I'd certainly be happy to help."

Although she was touched by Adam's generosity, accepting such an offer wouldn't be in keeping with the spirit of Aunt Jo's will. Besides, it was important to her to be self-reliant. She drew a deep breath, then looked directly into his eyes. "I appreciate that, Adam. But there's no immediate emergency. I just want to build up a little reserve. The root canal and car repairs pretty much wiped me out."

Adam took a moment to digest that. When they'd first met, Clare had implied that she'd fallen on tough financial times. But apparently they were even tougher than he'd imagined. Which explained why she was so in need of Jo's legacy. And why she'd taken on a second, low-paying job. Yet at one time she'd obviously enjoyed a far different lifestyle. What had happened to reduce her to such a desperate state? It wasn't any of his business, of course. And she hadn't offered details. But he wanted to know.

"You can tell me to mind my own business if you want to, and I won't be offended," he said slowly. "But what happened, Clare? You obviously weren't always in such dire straits."

As she searched his kind, caring eyes, Clare was torn between the need to share her burden and the need to protect Dennis's memory. She didn't want anyone to think badly of her husband because he had left her with so little in a material sense. That's why she'd never revealed her precarious financial situation, even to her sisters. Dennis had loved his family with an intensity that had sometimes taken her breath away. He had done everything he could to provide them with the best of everything. And he'd planned to continue doing so.

He just hadn't planned on dying.

Clare blinked rapidly, then reached up to brush back a few stray strands of hair that had worked their way loose from her chignon. For more than two long years she'd carried her burden alone, struggling to make ends meet even as she dealt with her grief. There had been times when she'd been utterly discouraged, had longed for a sympathetic shoulder to cry on. Figuratively speaking, anyway, because Clare didn't cry. She hadn't shed one tear since the accident. At first she'd been too shocked even to react. Shock had been followed by numbness, which in turn had given way to an emptiness that had left her heart devoid of everything—even tears. Which wasn't the best way to deal with grief. She knew that. Tears were therapeutic. But she was afraid that if she gave in to her grief she'd sink into a pit of despair from which she would never emerge.

So she'd held her tears inside and somehow managed to find the strength to carry on alone. But she was tired of being alone. Lately she'd felt an almost desperate longing to share her burden with someone. To share what it had been like to wake up one morning and realize that her whole world had changed forever in the blink of an eye. And as she gazed into Adam's kind, warm eyes, she suddenly knew that he was the one she wanted to share it with.

"It's kind of a long story," she said.

"I have all evening."

"You may be sorry." Clare tried to smile, but couldn't quite pull it off.

"I don't think so."

"Well, I'll try to give you the condensed version." She paused for a moment to collect her thoughts, then took a deep breath. "When I was twenty-five, I met a wonderful man named Dennis. He was kind and smart and outgoing, and I fell head over heels in love. We were married a year later. And two years after that we…we had a son."

"David." At her startled look, Adam explained. "Nicole told me about him."

She nodded. "We were so happy! I gave up teaching to be a full-time mom, and Dennis's star started to rise. Within a few years he had an executive position in public relations with a major agency. I was happy for him because he'd come from a dirt-poor family where no one had ever gotten a college education, and success meant a lot to him. So did the trappings of success. We had a beautiful home in an exclusive suburb of Kansas City, and we sent David to one of the finest schools in the area. We took fabulous vacations, and Dennis lavished us with gifts. We had the best of everything, from clothes to cars to home furnishings."

Clare paused, and when she spoke again her voice had dropped. "The thing is, Dennis didn't expect to die. He was young and healthy and had many more years to work. To save. To pay off all our debts. At least that's what we thought. But the accident changed everything. In every way. They were both…" She paused and sucked in a sharp breath. "They both died," she said in a choked voice.

Adam looked down at her tightly clasped hands. He ached to reach over and cover them with his own, to comfort her for the loss of her family and her dreams. But he remained still, knowing she had more to say.

"Afterwards, I realized just how deeply in debt we were," she continued unsteadily. "We had a huge mortgage on the house, and we'd heavily financed the cars…as well as other things. Dennis had some life insurance, but it wasn't anywhere near enough to cover our financial obligations. It was clear that everything would have to go."

She raised her head and gave Adam an intent, almost fierce look. "But I didn't really care about those things, anyway. They were important to Dennis, and I understood that, given his background. I grew up on a farm, and while we never lived lavishly, we always had nice clothes and plenty to eat. So I never attached as much importance to material things. It wasn't hard for me to give them up."

It was obviously important to her that Adam understand she held nothing against her husband for not providing for her after his death. But Adam wasn't so generous. A man with a family, who chose to live so close to the edge of financial ruin, should at the very least have considered the possibility of an accident and provided for the welfare of those he loved. Adam had little sympathy for such irresponsibility. But he kept those thoughts to himself.

"So then what happened?" he prompted gently.

"I sold almost everything and moved into an apartment. I knew I'd have to go back to work, so I got re-certified as a teacher. I was just starting to substitute teach on a regular basis when Aunt Jo's legacy fell in my lap. I still have some debts to pay off, and I'd like to establish a little financial reserve. So her bequest was a godsend. I'll be fine once I can claim it, but in the meantime I need to generate some income. Things are a little…tight."

He suspected that was a gross understatement. She was clearly living a bare-bones existence, purchasing only the absolute necessities. Yet she truly didn't seem to mind.

But something didn't quite make sense, he realized with a frown. "Given your situation, I'm surprised Jo didn't provide some sort of stipend for you while you worked as our nanny. Sort of an advance against the bequest. She wasn't the type to ever leave a need unaddressed."

Clare averted her face. "She didn't know about the state of my finances. No one does."

He didn't have to ask why she'd kept that information to herself. Clare was protecting Dennis's memory. Which he admired. But loyalty to her late husband wasn't going to solve her problem. Clearly she needed a temporary job, for her own peace of mind if nothing else. And teaching was out of the question. Still, there had to be something that would make better use of her skills than clerking at the giant discount store.

Suddenly, in a flash, a solution presented itself. He wasn't sure she'd go for it. But it was certainly worth a try.

"I may have an idea," he said slowly.

She looked at him curiously but remained silent.

"When Janice has her baby, she'll be taking six weeks off. The temp I had lined up just fell through, so I'm desperate for a replacement starting next Monday. I only need someone from eight to four, four days a week. Nicole's gone by seven-thirty, and she could stay at the after-school program for half an hour. You'd still have Wednesdays free to work with the Feed the Hungry program if you wanted. You'd be perfect for the job, Clare."

She stared at him. Working as a temporary receptionist in Adam's office was far preferable to stocking shelves at Wal-Mart, but was it somehow violating the spirit of Jo's legacy?

As if he'd read her mind, Adam spoke. "Jo's stipulation about pay related to the nanny job," he pointed out. "If you don't take the receptionist job, I'll still have to fill it. I'll be paying the same salary whether it's to you or to someone else. And I guarantee you'll have a great boss," he added with a grin.

Some of the tension in Clare's shoulders eased, and she smiled in return. She couldn't argue with his logic. And it was the perfect solution to her problem. "You've convinced me. I accept. But I've never done this kind of work before. I hope you won't be sorry."

"Not a chance," he assured her.

Which was true. He already knew Clare was sharp and quick. She'd have the office routine mastered in a couple of days. It was the ideal solution to her problem. And his.

Not to mention the fact that for the next six weeks, he would get to see a whole lot more of his daughter's nanny.

Chapter Nine

"Adam, may I interrupt you for a moment?"

At Clare's slightly uncertain voice, Adam paused and glanced up from the chart he was reviewing on his way to the next examining room. "What is it?"

"There's a Mrs. Samuels on the line. I know you have back-to-back patients today, but I think you might want to take this. I checked her records and saw that she's diabetic. It sounds like she may be having problems with her insulin."

The twin furrows in Adam's brow deepened. "Pull the chart and put her through to my office."

Clare handed him the chart. "She's waiting on line three."

Adam nodded. "Let Mr. Travis know I'll be right with him."

A few minutes later, as Adam hung up the phone, he was reminded again of how quickly Clare had become a valued member of his staff. After only two weeks, she had not only learned the office routine, but took appropriate initiative and demonstrated sound judgment with patients. Like Janice, she was able to screen calls and quickly discern the true emergencies. Today she'd been right on the money in her assessment of Mrs. Samuels's condition. The woman had needed immediate attention, and Clare had recognized that.

As he strode down the hall, Adam took a moment to pause at the receptionist's counter. "Good call," he told Clare.

She gave him a relieved smile. "Thanks."

"Mary Beth, could you do a throat swab on Mrs. Reed in room four? We might have a case of strep."

"Sure thing."

The two women watched as Adam continued down the hall, then Mary Beth turned to Clare with a grin. "Congrats on the accolades. They were well deserved. I have to admit I was a little nervous about Janice being gone, but you've really picked things up quickly. It's been smooth as silk. Don't tell Janice I said that, though. She might get nervous about her job."

Clare laughed. "She doesn't need to worry. This is very definitely a temporary position for me."

"I don't know. Adam runs a tight ship, and he seems really pleased. He might not want to let you go."

Clare knew Mary Beth was just teasing, so she only smiled in response. But more and more, she was finding herself wishing that were true. And not just about the receptionist job. It was silly, of course. Adam clearly wasn't in the market for romance. Despite what she'd seen in his eyes the day of the sledding accident, he'd never done anything to suggest directly he had an interest in her beyond the jobs she was doing for him. His primary goal was to establish a close relationship with his daughter. Clare was simply a catalyst for that.

And frankly, even if he was interested in her in a more…personal way, she wasn't ready to offer him much encouragement. She was trying to work through her guilt over the accident, but it was slow going. And until she resolved that, she couldn't really mourn the loss of her beloved family. So she wasn't ready to think about the future yet, either.

But as she watched Adam interact with his patients at work and strive so diligently at home to be the kind of father he had never known, she recognized what a fine and caring person he was. His patients loved him for his empathetic and unassuming bedside manner, and Clare had been struck time and again by his warmth and patience. No matter how tired or stressed he was, no matter how many demands he was trying to juggle, when he sat down with patients they generally had his full and complete attention. He was an insightful listener who was able to quickly asses a condition and then make sound and decisive decisions. Clare now understood why the town felt so fortunate to have him. He truly was a superb doctor.

He wasn't quite as far along on the father front, but he was making great strides. Where once Clare had had to struggle to get Nicole to include Adam in the dinner conversation, the two of them now talked more easily and naturally without her intervention. And she'd noticed that, more and more, Nicole was seeking out Adam for advice. There were even occasional moments of physical affection, when Adam would put his hand on Nicole's shoulder or she would jab him playfully in the arm. While there was still a lot of room for improvement, the trend was in the right direction. And both father and daughter were blossoming because of it.

Which was good. Because with only a couple of months remaining in her nanny commitment, she was running out of time to help those two become a family.

"A penny for your thoughts."

Startled, Clare shot Adam a guilty look, embarrassed at being caught daydreaming. "They're not for sale," she told him with a smile. "Did you need something?"

Clare saw something flicker for a brief moment in his eyes, something that made her breath catch in her throat. But then he simply handed her Mr. Travis's chart. "Could you write up an order for blood work?"

"Sure."

As he walked away, she tried to quiet the sudden staccato beat of her heart. Though the look in his eyes had been brief, she was pretty sure she had identified it correctly.

Longing.

And she felt exactly the same way.

But until she dealt with her personal issues, and until Adam recognized—and acknowledged—his own feelings, there was nothing to do but wait.

"Boy, this is a great spot! The furniture's new, isn't it? Seems to me the last time we were here this porch was bare."

Adam leaned forward to lift his mug from the wicker coffee table, then settled back into the comfortable matching chair before he replied to his brother, "You get an A for your powers of observation," he said with a wry smile. "Clare found the whole set at an estate sale, including the settee you've appropriated."

Jack chuckled. "As I recall, you hogged the couch at Christmas. Now it's my turn." He sighed contentedly. "This is the life."

"I'm glad you're enjoying our hospitality."

"The amenities have improved considerably since the last time we were here. And there's actually a bed in the guest room now. No more sleeping bags."

"Clare found that at the same estate sale."

"And the food is better, too. No more take-out from that café in town for every meal."

"Clare's a good cook."

"She seems to be good at a lot of things."

Adam nodded. "She's worked wonders with Nicole."

"I've noticed. The prickly pear has been replaced by a peach."

"Clever, but true," Adam said with a smile. "And we're getting along better than ever. My only concern is what will happen when Clare leaves. I'm afraid Nicole will be devastated."

Jack eyed his brother speculatively. "And how about her father?"

Adam stared into his coffee. "I'm trying not to think about that," he said quietly.

"Why not?"

He gave a frustrated sigh and raked his fingers

through his hair. "Clare's had a lot of trauma in her life already. She doesn't need any more. And I'm just not husband material. My wife would have told you that."

"Maybe you just had the wrong wife."

"Maybe. But I had a tough time with Nicole, too. I have trouble with relationships in general. I think I'm getting better, but I wouldn't want to risk hurting Clare—even if she was open to romance. Which I don't think she is. She loved her husband very much. She still does."

"Just because she loved her husband doesn't mean there isn't room in her heart for someone else. And I've seen the way she looks at you. My guess is that her interest is more than professional."

Adam felt his heart stop, then race on. "Even if that was true, I can't risk hurting her," he said carefully. "I wouldn't want to be married again unless I could have something like you and Theresa have. But that takes a willingness to open up and to share your feelings and emotions. I'm still fighting Dad's legacy on that front."

"Let me ask you something, Adam. Do you trust Clare?"

"Of course."

Jack sat up and dismissed Adam's response with an impatient shake of his head. "I don't mean do you trust her to keep the rec . . . . . . rrectly at your office, or to tutor Nicole or to handle your household budget. I'm talking about trust at the deepest level. Do you trust that no matter what you tell her about your past, about your deepest fears and your dreams and your feelings, that she'll always treat you gently?"

Adam frowned. Leave it to Jack to ask the tough

questions. Adam turned toward the distant, blue-hazed mountains and thought back over the many examples of Clare's empathy and caring that he'd witnessed: the gifts she'd lovingly knitted for him and Nicole at Christmas, her generous work with the Feed the Hungry program, her efforts to help Nicole make friends at school, the way she'd transformed his house into a home—a place he relished returning to after a long day. He thought about her keen insights and gentle kindness, honed in the fire of adversity. About her loyalty to the ones she loved, and about the way she was miraculously transforming the lives of two lonely people. Trust Clare? The answer was obvious.

"Yes."

"Then what's holding you back?"

Jack's question was not only pointed, but valid. And Adam knew the answer, though it was difficult to articulate after years of living with a father who saw such admissions as weakness. Adam glanced down into the murky depths of his coffee and forced himself to give voice to the word. "Fear."

"Bingo," Jack concurred quietly. "And you know what? That's not a sin, Adam, despite what Dad might have made you think. It's okay to be afraid. I've been afraid. A lot of times. And Theresa knows it. That didn't hurt our relationship. In fact, it made it stronger. Being willing to admit that you don't always have all the answers, that sometimes you're afraid and uncertain, is just being human. Superheroes might be nice in the movies, but in a relationship nobody wants a perfect mate. That would be impossible to live with—or live up to. People just want someone who cares, who tries to understand their point of view, their feelings, their fears, their hopes—and who's willing to share theirs. That doesn't mean you're always perfect. It just means you sincerely try." He paused for a moment and took a deep breath. "May I tell you something else?"

Adam looked up, but remained silent.

"You're just about there, buddy. I can't believe the difference in you in the past few months. You look happier and more relaxed than I've ever seen you. And you've shared more with me in our last couple of visits than you have in our entire lives. I'd say that's progress. And my guess is that one very special nanny can take the credit for that."

Jack leaned forward, clasped his hands and rested his forearms on his thighs. "So here's a piece of advice from your kid brother, for whatever it's worth. If I were you, I'd think long and hard about renewing Clare's contract—on a permanent and personal basis."

As they settled into the church pew for the sermon, Clare glanced at the family group next to her. Nicole was on her left, with Adam beside her. Theresa was next in the row, then came Adam's niece and nephew, Karen and Bobby. Jack was at the end of the pew, on the aisle.

When Adam and Nicole had insisted that she join in the family's Easter activities, she'd hesitated, not wanting to intrude. But in the end, she was glad they had talked her into it. She'd liked Jack and Theresa immediately, and they had embraced her warmly, making her feel like part of the group instead of an outsider. Under Jack's energetic direction, there had been nonstop activity since their arrival. And Clare was glad for that. It gave her less time to think about past Easters, when she'd had her own family.

Reverend Nichols moved to the pulpit, and Clare focused her attention on him. As usual, his sermon was well prepared and articulate. And his final words touched her deeply.

"A few years ago, shortly after I was ordained, I was assisting at a church in a small town in Oklahoma," he said. "I preached what I thought was a very good sermon, and I was eagerly waiting to greet the congregation afterward, sure I'd receive all kinds of accolades.

"Well, things didn't go quite as I expected. Most people said polite, perfunctory things. But no one raved. Finally an older gentleman came along. At that point I was desperate for a compliment, so I asked him if he'd enjoyed the sermon. And I'll never forget what he said to me.

"'It was okay, young man. But if you want people to really listen, you need to speak from the heart. Facts and figures are all well and good, and I expect I learned a thing or two today about Bible history. But that's not going to make me change my life. Don't just tell me what I'm supposed to believe. Tell me why *you* believe it. What's in the heart is just as important as what's in the head.'

"Well, needless to say, my ego was pretty deflated. But when I thought about it, I realized he was right. And I took his comments to heart. But I can tell you that his advice isn't always easy to follow. Because when we speak from the heart about our faith, we take a risk. We're not just putting our theology on the line, we're putting ourselves on the line. We're opening ourselves to ridicule and rejection and pain. And in the case of our Lord, to death. But the important thing to remember is that His death wasn't the end. It was the beginning.

"My dear friends, that's what Easter is all about. The lessons of this day are many, but a key one is that we must live what we believe, not just think about it. We must follow our Lord's example of complete and un-selfish love. Sometimes that means we have to take chances. That in order to grow in our faith, and in our lives, we have to be willing to trust our heart with other people. To share what we believe, knowing that not everyone will treat us kindly. Knowing that we can become discouraged and afraid. But unless we let go of our fear, unless we follow the example of our Lord and reach out to other people with our love, we can never move forward or fulfill His plan for us.

"So on this Easter Sunday, as we celebrate new life in Christ, I ask Him to bestow the gift of His grace on all of us, and to give us the courage to trust in Him and to love as He did…completely, selflessly and without reservation. And now let us pray.…"

Clare felt tears welling up in her eyes at the beauti-ful message in Reverend Nichols's sermon. Uncon-sciously she looked to Adam, wondering if the message had special meaning for him, as well.

But he was turned toward Jack. And as she watched, a brief, knowing look passed between the two brothers.

Feeling like an eavesdropper, Clare quickly turned

back toward the front. But she couldn't help wondering what that look was all about.

"Do you think Dad will be surprised?"

Clare turned toward Nicole, who was setting the table. Fresh flowers were arranged in a glass bowl in the center of the snowy-white cloth, and there was a festive feel in the air. "Absolutely. I think he's convinced we've forgotten his birthday entirely. I didn't say a word to him about it this morning."

"Me, neither."

Clare flipped the switch for the oven light and checked the meat thermometer. "Looks like we're about ready. Now let's hope the guest of honor is on time."

As if on cue, they heard the sound of crunching gravel as Adam's car pulled up the driveway to the garage.

"Showtime," Clare said with a smile.

Nicole nervously wiped her hands on her oversize apron. "I hope he likes everything."

"Pork tenderloin, potatoes au gratin, green beans almondine—and a killer birthday cake—what's not to like?" Clare said encouragingly.

"Yeah. I guess."

A moment later they heard the door open. Adam strode into the room—but then stopped abruptly as his gaze fell on the beautifully set table, then traveled to the Happy Birthday banner and balloons that decorated the room.

"Happy birthday, Dad."

He heard the barely suppressed excitement—as well as the touch of uncertainty—in Nicole's voice, and gave her his full attention. "I thought everyone had forgotten."

She giggled. "We wanted to surprise you. That's why we didn't say anything all day."

Adam looked at Clare. "So you were in on this, too, huh?"

She smiled. "Guilty. But it was mostly your daughter's doing. In fact, she cooked most of the dinner."

"It smells wonderful."

"Well, it's all ready. Go ahead and sit down, Dad."

Adam did as instructed, and while Clare and Nicole set out the food, he couldn't help recalling last year's birthday. There had been no celebration. Nothing at all to mark the occasion. If Nicole had even remembered that the day held special significance, she had chosen to ignore it. His childhood memories weren't much better. The only concession to birthdays in his father's house had been a cake for dessert. Even during his marriage, he and Elaine had simply gone out for dinner—usually to a restaurant of her choosing. He had never had a birthday like this, in his own home, with decorations and a dinner cooked especially for him. He felt his throat grow tight, and there was an odd stinging sensation behind his eyes.

"Would you like to say grace, Adam?"

At Clare's gentle voice, he looked up, noting that she and Nicole had taken their places. Forcing himself to swallow past the lump in his throat, he nodded and bowed his head.

"We thank You, Lord, for this wonderful meal, and

for the gift of special people in our lives. We thank You for the many blessings You give us, for Your comfort and companionship in times of trouble, and for the joy and peace that comes from knowing You are always with us, in good times and bad. I ask Your special blessing today on Nicole and Clare, who have given me a birthday to remember. Please watch over them and keep them in Your care. Amen."

When he finished, the wistful look in Clare's momentarily unguarded eyes told him that his words had touched her deeply.

Adam couldn't remember when he'd enjoyed a meal more. The food Nicole had prepared was wonderful—thanks, he was sure, to Clare's close supervision—but even better was the company. Nicole chatted animatedly throughout the meal, and the easy banter among the three of them was in marked contrast to the silent, strained meals he and Nicole had shared prior to Clare's arrival. He had only one word to describe the transformation that had occurred in his relationship with his daughter: *miracle.*

Which was exactly what he'd prayed for. Thanks to an unexpected nanny. Adam thought back to his early conversations with Clare, how her surprising offer hadn't been exactly the kind of help he'd had in mind when he'd asked the Lord for assistance. But he also recalled reminding himself at the time that God's ways weren't always our ways. And that maybe Clare was the answer to his prayer.

As he regarded the lovely woman sitting across from him, he suddenly knew there were no maybes about it.

Recalling Jack's advice, he also knew exactly what he was going to wish for when he blew out the candles on his cake.

"I can't eat one more bite," Adam groaned as he finished off a second slice of the split lemon torte.

"So it was okay?" Nicole asked anxiously.

He grinned. "It was more than okay. It was the best birthday cake I ever had."

She smiled, and the pleasure in her eyes warmed his heart. "Cool!"

He reached over and gave her shoulder a squeeze. "You can cook for me anytime."

"Well, I couldn't have done it without Clare. She showed me how to make all the stuff."

"Then my hat is off to Clare, too," he acknowledged.

"And did you like your presents?"

Adam smiled. Nicole had given him the latest detective novel by his favorite author, and Clare had knitted him an incredible fisherman's sweater. He couldn't even begin to guess how many hours it had taken her to complete it.

"They were wonderful." His compliment encompassed both of his dinner companions, and a becoming flush spread over Clare's cheeks.

His response obviously satisfied Nicole, too. "I guess we did okay, huh, Clare?"

She smiled. "I guess we did."

Nicole turned back to Adam. "So do you have to work tonight?"

"Not unless someone calls."

"Good. Then we can play a game before I do my homework. You're supposed to have games at parties."

Adam grinned. "I don't think I'll be very good at pin the tail on the donkey."

She gave him a what-planet-are-you-from? look. "Dad, that is prehistoric! Nobody does stuff like that anymore. I borrowed a game from Candace that we played at her slumber party. It's called Revelation."

He wasn't sure he liked the sound of that. "How does it work?"

"Well, everyone draws ten cards, and each card has a question. Like, 'What's your middle name?' or 'What are you most afraid of?' Stuff like that. And you write your answers down. Then all of the questions get put in a pile, you draw them one by one, and everyone has to guess who wrote what answer. The person who guesses right most often wins."

Adam shifted uncomfortably. The game sounded a little too personal to him. He was trying to be more open about his feelings, but he wasn't sure he was up to something this potentially revealing. Even though he could almost hear Jack telling him to loosen up, he just wasn't there yet.

Adam was literally saved by the bell when his pager went off. Trying not to look too relieved, he reached for it and read the message. "I need to call the exchange," he said when he finished.

Nicole made a face. "But it's your birthday."

"People still get sick." He stood and put his hand on her shoulder. "Why don't you start that homework, and we'll try to fit the game in later?"

She sighed. "Okay."

"Hey." He leaned down. "Even if we don't get to the game, this is still the best birthday I ever had."

She searched his eyes. "Really?"

"Really."

A smile lifted the corners of her mouth. "I'm glad."

"Now you scoot, and I'll take care of this call." He stood and looked over at Clare. "I'll be back in a few minutes."

"Take your time. I'll get the dishes started."

Adam took as long as he possibly could with the call, and by the time he returned Clare had restored the kitchen to order.

"Everything okay?" she asked.

"Yes. Is there any coffee left?"

She checked the pot. "Looks like a couple of cups. Would you like some more?"

"I'll get it." He helped himself, then glanced toward the hall.

"I mentioned to Nicole that you were probably tired after working all day and might not be up to the game," Clare told him.

He shot her a grateful look. "Thanks."

She dried her hands on a dish towel, then folded it carefully and set it on the counter. "You didn't seem too anxious to play."

He took a sip of coffee. "I'm not sure it's my kind of game."

She looked at him. "That's what I figured."

What else did she figure, he wondered. Even though he'd been careful not to reveal too much about himself, this insightful woman seemed to understand things about him that he barely understood himself. Which was more than a little disconcerting.

But also encouraging. Because she hadn't backed off at his reticence, nor had she seemed put off by any negative conclusions she'd come to. Adam had told Jack that he trusted Clare. But he hadn't actually done anything to prove that. Maybe tonight was the time to see if he could live what he said he believed, as Reverend Nichols had suggested in his Easter sermon four weeks before.

"I thought I might sit on the porch for a while. It's a beautiful night. Would you like to join me?" he asked, striving for a casual, conversational tone.

Clare looked at him in surprise. The porch, with its wicker furniture and its restful view of blue-hazed mountains across the valley, was one of her favorite spots. But Adam rarely had the time—or took the time, she corrected herself—to enjoy it. She was glad he wanted to take advantage of it tonight. It would be a nice ending to his birthday.

"Sure. Let me grab a sweater."

He waited until she reappeared from the mudroom, a light sweater slung over her shoulders, then followed her to the front porch. Clare sat on the settee, assuming Adam would choose the matching chair at right angles. But to her surprise he settled in beside her, their bodies just a whisper apart. As the faint but heady scent of his aftershave filled her nostrils, her pulse suddenly vaulted into overdrive and her breath lodged in her chest.

Clare was completely taken aback by her reaction to

Adam's close proximity. And she was more than a little frightened when a surge of longing swept over her, so strong it stole the breath from her lungs. Trying not to be obvious, she discreetly attempted to put a little more distance between them. But she was already wedged against the unyielding arm of the settee. Short of getting up and calling attention to her predicament, she had no choice but to remain where she was.

"Jack really enjoyed this spot while they were here for Easter," Adam remarked, clearly oblivious to her dilemma.

Clare swallowed. It had been a long time since she'd had a reaction like this to a man. Visceral, powerful—and ill timed. She wasn't ready to get involved with any man. Especially this man, who was struggling with his own demons. Get a grip! she admonished herself, drawing in a long, steadying breath.

"I know you guys spent a lot of time out here one evening," she replied, struggling to keep her voice even. "He and Theresa are really a nice couple."

"They have something special," Adam agreed. "And I'm happy for them, of course. But sometimes…well, I guess I'm a little…envious."

She could relate to that. Watching Jack and Theresa interact over the holiday had been a bittersweet reminder of the good times she'd enjoyed with Dennis. "It's hard to be alone," Clare said quietly.

He shook his head. "It's not just that. I don't even have happy memories to fall back on, like you do. Even when we were at our best, Elaine and I…we never related the way Jack and Theresa do. We were never that much…in sync."

Clare had a feeling that they were moving on to untried ground. Though she had on occasion glimpsed deeply felt emotions in Adam's eyes, he had never before spoken of anything this personal. The closest he had come was the day of Nicole's party, when he'd alluded to his emotionally bleak childhood.

"Maybe you and your wife just weren't compatible," she ventured cautiously.

"That was certainly part of it," he conceded with a sigh. "We got way too serious way too fast. And that was my fault." He paused, and his voice was more halting when he resumed speaking, as if he had to dig deep to find the words. "I had…very few friends growing up. And I didn't date much. So I was completely blown away when Elaine took an interest in me. Later, when things started to fall apart, I realized that she…she had always been more interested in being married to a doctor than to me."

Knowing what a tight rein he kept on his feelings and emotions, and how carefully he protected his heart, Clare could only imagine what that admission had cost him.

"It sounds to me like there was fault on both sides," she said gently.

"Mostly mine. When I was growing up, my father…he made fun of us if we showed emotion—of any kind. He thought it was a sign of weakness. Jack was able to get past that and march to the beat of his own drummer. That's probably why he has such a happy marriage. But I…I wasn't as strong as he was. I cared what my father thought and tried to please him. Though I never did, of course. So I gradually closed up. And eventually I…I lost the ability to express emotions and to…connect with people."

Clare frowned. "That's not true, Adam. I've seen you with your patients. They love you. You have a wonderful bedside manner."

He dismissed her comment with a frustrated shake of his head. "That's different. It's all one-sided. They teach you how to listen and be sympathetic in medical school. But on a personal level, when you're trying to establish a relationship with the people you love, it has to be a two-way street. Listening isn't enough. You have to share with them, too. Let them see what's in your heart. I've never been able to do that."

He expelled a long sigh, and when he took a sip of his coffee Clare noticed that his hand wasn't quite steady. "Eventually, that's what turned Elaine off. Despite the fast courtship, despite the fact we married for the wrong reasons, maybe we could have worked things out if I'd been willing to let her in. But I couldn't. Instead, I began focusing more and more on the one area of my life where I felt capable—medicine. Which only made matters worse. And over time, any love between us died quietly, gradually slipping away, until one day it was simply gone."

"But you stayed together a long time," Clare pointed out.

He gave a short, mirthless laugh. "Yeah. But not for the noblest reasons. The one thing Elaine and I had going for us was…" He paused and shifted uncomfortably. "I guess chemistry is the right word. On a physical level. If it hadn't been for that, we would have separated far sooner. So I'm a bit wary of…physical attraction. Because it's not enough to sustain a marriage over the long haul."

"I agree."

"Anyway, I'm just not good at opening up. Of letting people get close. And you can't connect with people if you don't. My relationship with Nicole is a good example."

"But that's improving. You two are getting along better all the time."

"Thanks to you."

Clare shook her head. "I might have helped set the stage, but you had to step into the role. And you've done a wonderful job. In fact, I'd call it remarkable, now that I know more about your background. Because you didn't have a lot of tools to work with."

Adam set his mug on the coffee table and turned to Clare. How did she always know the right things to say, he wondered. "You know something, Clare? I love the sweater you knitted for me. It's a wonderful birthday gift. But what you just said is the best gift of all. I just wish I could believe it was true."

The sincerity in her eyes was unquestionable. "Trust me, Adam. It is."

There was that word again. *Trust.* He angled his body toward her and, without stopping to think, reached for her hand and brushed his thumb across her silky skin. "I prayed for help with Nicole," he said, his voice not quite steady. "And I've come to believe that God sent me you. And maybe not just for Nicole."

At the intense, undisguised yearning in his eyes,

Clare's heart stopped, then raced on. And all he was doing to kindle that reaction was holding her hand. Gently. Tenderly.

Adam studied Clare. She hadn't pulled away from him, but he was well aware of her conflicting emotions: confusion, yearning, panic. The same things he was feeling.

Adam hadn't expected his birthday to end this way. He'd asked her to join him on the porch to see if he had the courage to begin the process of opening up. But he'd ended up sharing far more than he'd planned. Which was odd, considering how emotionally distant he'd always been. Yet he didn't feel distant from Clare, whose loveliness and goodness and strength had not only touched his heart, but refreshed his parched and weary soul.

It had been a long time since Adam had kissed a woman. There had been no one after Elaine. And he'd keenly felt the loss of that human connection. Sometimes the loneliness left him aching for something as simple as a gentle touch or a tender look. But he'd ruthlessly stifled such needs, knowing he didn't have the right stuff to sustain a long-term relationship, and unwilling to settle for less—or to hurt someone else by trying.

Yet Jack seemed to think he had changed, that he was now better able—or willing—to establish the kind of rapport that made a marriage not just work, but flourish. So did Clare, if he was reading her correctly. And he wanted to believe them. Desperately. Because he was tired of being alone. Tired of holding up the No Trespassing sign that blocked his heart. Tired of being cautious. And afraid. And second-guessing.

Adam knew he was heading toward shaky ground. That maybe he was being foolish, that he might regret his actions later. But right now, at this moment, with Clare only a whisper away, he didn't care. He needed her.

And so he decided to do something that could change their relationship forever.

Chapter Ten

Adam slowly reached over and touched Clare's face, tracing the elegant line of her jaw with a whisper touch. Her skin was just as he'd imagined it—silky and smooth and soft—and his mouth went dry as he struggled to get his heart rate under control.

Clare seemed to be faring no better. A pulse hammered in the delicate hollow of her throat, and he reassuringly stroked her hand—though he wasn't sure if that gesture was for his sake or hers.

Adam's fingers trailed from her cheek down the slender column of her throat, then around to the back of her neck. He cupped her head gently, and as he gazed into her deep-blue eyes, he signaled his intent, giving her a chance to pull away. When she didn't, he slowly, deliberately closed the gap between them and leaned down for a kiss.

When he finally broke contact his hands were trembling and he reached up to brush a stray strand of hair off her forehead.

"Are you okay?" he asked her unsteadily when he could find his voice.

She stared at him solemnly and blinked once. "I don't know."

He gave her a shaky grin. "Me, neither. Let's just sit for a minute, okay? I think we both need to regroup. Doctor's orders."

He kept one arm around her shoulder and pressed her head into the protective curve of his arm, letting his cheek rest against her silky hair.

Clare could hear the thudding of his heart against her ear. She knew her own heart was in no better shape. She wasn't quite sure what she'd anticipated from their kiss, but she hadn't expected it to leave her wanting more. She wasn't ready for more, though. And she wasn't sure Adam was, either. So where did they go from here?

As Adam held Clare, he had his own questions. Had he changed enough to make a relationship work over the long-term? Was he willing to trust his heart—completely—to another person? He'd shared a lot with Clare tonight. But it had been hard. Very hard. Opening up didn't come naturally to him, as it did to Jack. Could he sustain that kind of sharing long-term? Or would he eventually fall back into old patterns—and wind up hurting Clare?

He didn't know the answers to those questions. So as he stared at the blue-hazed mountains in the distance, he put the matter into greater hands.

Lord, please show me the way to proceed. I'm falling in love with Clare, and I'm not sure I can let her go when the nanny job is over. But I don't want to hurt her. Please help me to know Your will, to do the right thing. Help me to choose wisely and not make a decision that satisfies only my own selfish needs. Because as much as I want Clare in my life, I also want what's best for her. Even if that means letting her go.

"I wondered where you guys were."

At the sound of Nicole's voice, Clare abruptly straightened up and Adam withdrew his arm. She felt hot spots of color burning in her cheeks, and she averted her face on the pretense of arranging her sweater, feeling as guilty as a teenager caught necking in her parents' living room.

"I guess it's too late to play a game, huh?" Nicole said.

Clare risked a glance at Adam, wondering if he felt as embarrassed as she did. But if the twitch at the corner of his mouth was any indication, he seemed to find the whole thing humorous.

"Probably," he said. "Besides, I think you ladies should make an early night of it, considering all the hard work you did for my birthday."

"Yeah. And I still have some homework to finish."

"I'll be in to say good-night a little later."

"Okay. 'Night, Clare."

"Good night, Nicole. You did a great job on the party."

"Thanks." Nicole turned to go, but paused at the door to look back. "It's okay if you want to put your arm back around Clare's shoulder, Dad. I think it's kind of cool."

With that she disappeared inside, letting the screen door slam behind her.

Adam turned to Clare and chuckled. "So much for being discreet."

She gave him a wry look, her color still high. "Kids are smart. And attentive. They don't miss much. Listen, I'm sorry if this…well, I hope you weren't embarrassed."

"Not nearly as much as you were."

Nervously, Clare adjusted her sweater. "It's just that…well, I'm not sure I'm ready for anything…serious. I still have…issues."

"I do, too. And I've learned from experience not to rush things. So let's just take this really slow, okay? I don't want anyone to get hurt."

She nodded and glanced toward the house. "Including Nicole. She and I have gotten pretty close, and she's asked me a couple of times about leaving. I don't want to build up any false hopes."

"I've thought about that, too," he replied. "I know she has a tendency to read too much into things sometimes. But I do agree with her about one thing."

"What?"

He draped his arm loosely around her shoulders and grinned. "I think this is kind of cool."

Clare smiled, but she didn't respond.

Because even though she didn't want to get her own hopes up, and even though she still had issues to resolve, she couldn't contain the glow that suddenly suffused her heart and spilled over, radiating warmth right down to her fingertips.

"Adam? I think you better take this call. It's the police."

Adam's head snapped up and he stared at Janice, who had just returned from maternity leave. "What?"

"It's the police. They said there's been…an accident. Line two."

Adam felt his heart stop, then race on as he glanced at his watch and reached for the phone. Clare was supposed to drive Nicole to a friend's house for a Friday-night sleepover about an hour ago. *Dear God, let them be okay!* he prayed.

He punched the number and tried unsuccessfully to speak, then cleared his throat and tried again. "This is Adam Wright."

"Dr. Wright, this is Lieutenant Stevens, Highway Patrol. Do you have a daughter named Nicole?"

"Yes."

"There's been a car accident. She's been taken to Memorial Hospital in Asheville."

Adam's grip on the phone tightened, turning his knuckles white. "How bad is it?"

"I wasn't at the scene myself. I only have a notation that it was a head injury."

Adam closed his eyes and tried to breathe. "What about Clare?" he asked hoarsely.

There was a sound of rustling paper. "I don't see anyone named Clare on the accident report. The driver was a Kathleen Foster. Her daughter, Jennifer, is also listed. They have minor injuries."

Adam frowned. "Are you sure?"

"That's what the report says."

"All right. Thanks. I'm on my way." Adam replaced the receiver, grabbed his briefcase and headed out the door. Janice gave him an anxious look as he strode past the desk, but he hardly paused, speaking over his shoulder in a clipped, rapid-fire tone.

"Cancel all my appointments for the rest of the day. I'm heading to Memorial Hospital in Asheville. Nicole was in a car accident. She has head injuries. And see if you can track down Clare. I'll call when I know something."

Adam didn't remember the drive to the hospital. All he knew was that he broke every speed law in the books. And that he prayed more fervently than he had in a long, long time.

When he reached the hospital, Adam parked his car illegally right outside the emergency room and almost ran inside. A woman who looked badly shaken, her arm in a sling, stopped him inside the door.

"Dr. Wright?"

He turned to her with an impatient frown. "Yes?"

"I'm Kathleen Foster. We met at the holiday concert at school. I'm so sorry about this." She was close to tears, and her face had an unhealthy pallor. "The truck crossed the median and I…I did the best I could."

Her voice broke, and despite his own panic, Adam shifted into doctor mode. "I'm sure you did. Look, Mrs. Foster, why don't you sit here for a few minutes?" He guided her to a chair. "I'm going to check with the doctor in charge. Is someone coming to be with you?"

She sniffed and nodded. "My h-husband is on his way. M-my daughter's still back there, but I w-wanted to catch you when you arrived."

"You just take it easy for a few minutes."

Adam left her, then made his way to the receptionist. "I'm Dr. Adam Wright. My daughter was in the car accident. I'd like to speak to the attending physician. Stat."

At his authoritative tone, the woman nodded and pressed a button, releasing the door to the emergency room. "Come in, please. I'll get her."

Sixty eternal seconds later, a tall, slender woman with short-cropped dark hair joined him inside the door and held out her hand.

"Dr. Wright? Ellen Grady. First, relax. I think your daughter will be fine. She hit the side of her head against the window when the car turned over, and she was unconscious for a few minutes. She's alert now, and there's no sign of serious trauma. Just a mild concussion, and some pretty colorful bruises on her right arm and leg."

Adam felt the coil of tension in his stomach ease slightly, and he wiped a shaky hand down his face. "Thank God!" he said hoarsely.

"Your daughter has been asking for you. But before I take you back, do you have any questions?"

He forced himself to take a deep breath, then slowly let it out before asking a series of concise, pointed questions to verify that the appropriate, comprehensive battery of tests had been performed. When he was satisfied, Dr. Grady led him down the hall to Nicole.

She was lying on an examining table in one of the small rooms, holding an ice pack against a rapidly discoloring bump on her right temple, her French braid in disarray. And she looked scared. Adam quickly moved beside her, reaching down to gently brush the hair back from her face.

"Hi, sweetie."

She reached out and grasped his hand tightly. "The truck was c-coming right at us, Dad," she said, her voice catching on a sob, her eyes still wide with terror. "I—I thought we were going t-to die."

He leaned down and pulled her slight, angular body close, burying his face in her hair. "It's okay, sweetie. Everything's okay now."

He held her for a long moment, and when she finally spoke again, her voice was muffled against his chest. "Can we go home now, Dad?"

"I think so. Sit tight and I'll check with Dr. Grady."

He found the woman in the hall outside, and she confirmed his assessment. "Normally I might want to keep her for observation, but you certainly know what to look for," she said. "And frankly, people are generally better off at home, anyway. I'll sign the release and you can be on your way. Someone will be in to help Nicole dress."

"Thanks. What about the others? I saw Mrs. Foster in the waiting room, with her arm in a sling."

Dr. Grady nodded. "Dislocated collarbone. Her daughter has a sprained ankle. According to the police, it's a miracle all three of them weren't killed."

"Is there someone who can tell me exactly what happened?"

The doctor snagged the sleeve of a passing aide. "Are any of the officers who came in with the car accident still here?"

The young man nodded. "There's one in the coffee room. I'll get him."

While Adam waited, the receptionist came over to him. "Mrs. Foster asked me tell you that she and her daughter went home, but she left her phone number if you want to call her." She held out a slip of paper.

"Thanks."

"Dr. Wright? Officer Parisi."

Adam turned and took the man's proffered hand. "My daughter was in the accident. Can you tell me what happened?"

"Near as we can tell, a truck in the oncoming lane lost control. The driver of your daughter's vehicle was alert and had good reflexes, so she was able to swerve out of the way and avoid a collision. Unfortunately, she slid off the edge of the highway and her vehicle fell onto its right side. It's pretty much totaled, but at least no one was badly injured." He shook his head. "This could have had a whole different ending if there'd been a head-on. Those three people were very lucky."

Adam didn't think it was just luck. But he let that pass. "Thank you, officer."

"My pleasure. I wish all of my calls ended this well."

Before he returned to the examining room, Adam stepped outside to phone Janice. After he gave her a quick update on the situation, he asked about Clare.

"I've been trying steadily since you left to reach her, but there's no answer at your house or in her apartment."

Adam frowned. "Okay. Thanks. Any urgent calls that I need to return?"

"Nothing that can't wait."

"All right. See you Monday."

As Adam rang off and made his way back to the examining room, his frown was still in place. Where was

Clare? Kathleen Foster might know, but she was on her way home. That left only Nicole.

She looked up when he rejoined her and started to get off the table, but Adam moved swiftly beside her. "Hey, not so fast! You've got one big lump on that hard head of yours, and you might be a little dizzy."

She clung to him and closed her eyes when she stood. "Yeah," she said faintly.

Once he had her buckled into the car, he slid behind the wheel and backed out. As he edged into traffic he glanced over at her. She had her head back and her eyes were closed.

"Nicole?"

"Hmm?" she said sleepily.

"Do you know where Clare is?"

"Home, I guess," she mumbled.

He frowned. Not according to Janice. "Sweetie, why didn't she drive you to the party?"

Nicole didn't answer, and he glanced over. She'd snuggled into the corner, her lashes dark against her pale cheeks, and her even breathing told him that she was asleep. So he didn't disturb her with more questions. Because in less than forty-five minutes they'd be home. And he'd find his own answers.

Clare's car was in the garage.

As Adam set the brake on his own car, he frowned. She was obviously home now. But where had she been earlier? What had been so important that she couldn't take Nicole to the party?

As Adam carefully unbuckled his daughter and lifted

her gently in his arms, his tension began to give way to anger. She'd suffered only minor injuries in the accident, but according to the officer, the outcome could have been far worse. Nicole could have been killed. His gut clenched painfully, and he had to blink rapidly to clear his suddenly blurred vision. When he thought how close he'd come to losing the daughter he was only just beginning to find…. His mouth settled into a grim line. Clare better have a rock-solid reason for putting his daughter's welfare into someone else's hands, he thought angrily.

As soon as Adam had Nicole settled in her room, he headed to the garage. He took the steps two at a time, then rapped sharply on the door. As he waited for Clare to answer, he tried to think of an excuse that he would consider acceptable. He couldn't come up with one, short of a death in the family.

He prayed that wasn't the reason.

But he knew that anything less would represent a betrayal of the trust he'd placed in her when he'd given her responsibility for the care of his daughter.

It was a no-win situation.

Someone was using a jackhammer in the next room.

Clare struggled to raise her heavy eyelids. No, it was the door, she realized. Someone was knocking on her door. Though pounding might be a better description, she thought with a groan, when the noise intensified. And it didn't sound as if they had any intention of going away.

With a supreme effort, she swung her feet to the floor and stood dizzily. Holding on to furniture for support, she made her way unsteadily to the door, where it took several fumbling tries before she managed to slide the lock back and pull it open.

Clare stared at Adam on the other side. At least she thought it was Adam. But she'd never seen that look on his face before. His eyes were cold and angry, and his mouth looked hard and tense. She tried to think clearly.

"Is something wrong?" she asked.

His eyes blazed. "Yes, something is wrong. Where have you been?"

"Here."

"You never left the apartment today?"

"No. I've been sleeping."

His frown deepened and his eyes grew even colder. "So there was no emergency?"

She stared at him blankly. "What?"

She saw a muscle twitch in his jaw. "Okay, look. I don't have time to discuss this now. But there's been a car accident. Nicole has a concussion. I brought her home from the hospital and I need to sit with her. We'll talk about this later."

He turned to go, and Clare clutched his sleeve, her eyes wide with shock. "Is she okay?"

Adam looked back at her. "No thanks to you," he said tersely. "She could have been killed. You said you were going to drive her, Clare. I counted on you. I didn't expect you to abdicate your responsibility and palm her off on Jennifer's mother."

Clare felt as if she'd been slapped. She recoiled slightly, her shoulders slumping as her eyes filled with tears. "Adam, I…I'm so sorry," she whispered. "Please… let me sit with her."

"I can take care of my own daughter," he said stiffly, his eyes like ice.

And with that he turned away and disappeared down the steps.

Slowly Clare closed the door, numb with shock. Tremors ran through her body, and she wasn't sure her wobbly legs would support her as she haltingly retraced her steps. But she didn't crawl back into bed. Instead, she opened her closet and reached for a small box on the shelf. She set it on the bed and, with shaky fingers, gently lifted the lid.

The photo she wanted was right on top, and for a moment she simply stared at it, tracing the edge of the frame with her finger. Dennis and David smiled back at her from the frozen moment in time, so achingly familiar, so much a part of her, so alive—and yet gone forever. She'd snapped the photo a couple of weeks before the accident that had cut their lives far too short.

The accident she'd caused.

Just like today.

As she lifted the photo, Clare's legs suddenly gave way and she sank to the floor. She put the photo against her chest and huddled into it, wrapping her arms around her body. She'd been here before. Felt the same crushing guilt. Over the past few months she thought she'd begun to deal with that burden, to gradually let it go. But now it came back, as sharp and intense and painful as ever. Thank God this ending had been different! But she could claim no credit for that. Once again, she'd shirked her duty and disaster had followed. Would she never learn?

For two long years, Clare had held her tears in check. But now they refused to be contained. For several moments they ran down her cheeks silently, and then a sob rose in her throat. And another. And still another. Until finally her body was wracked by them. Deep sobs filled with pain and regret and sorrow.

Clare had often felt alone since the accident. There had been times when the loneliness tunneled to the very depths of her soul, leaving her feeling hollow and empty. She didn't want to go there again, she thought in anguish. *Couldn't* go there again. Not if she wanted to survive.

Clare closed her eyes and rested her forehead on her knees. She desperately needed compassion. And kindness. And understanding. Thanks to Reverend Nichols, she'd found her way back to the ultimate source of all of those things. The One who didn't need words. Who could read what was in her heart and know what was needed.

And so Clare didn't even try to articulate the complexity of her emotions, the intensity of her distress, the depth of her despair. She just sent a simple, heartfelt plea.

Lord, I need You! Please help me!

With an effort, Adam forced his face to relax before he stepped into Nicole's room. But it wasn't easy. He was more angry than he'd ever been in his life. Clare had offered no explanation, no excuse for shirking her duty. He had trusted her with his most precious gift—his daughter—and she'd betrayed that trust. He found that hard to forgive.

Nicole looked at him when he entered the room. She was still far too pale, and the bump was now a garish purple, but the terror had faded from her eyes. He sat down on the bed and took her hand.

"How are you, sweetie?"

"My head hurts."

He reached into his pocket and pulled out a small penlight. "I'm not surprised. You might have a headache for a few days. Let's have a look at those pupils." He flashed the light in each eye, getting the response he hoped for. "Looking good. You just need to rest. I'll be close by."

She snuggled deeper into the bed and let her eyelids drift closed. But she opened them as he started to rise. "Dad? How's Clare?"

He looked down at her with a frown, wondering if her thinking was still a little muddled. "She wasn't in the accident, sweetie."

Nicole gave him an exasperated look. "I know that. She stayed here because she was sick. That's why Mrs. Foster took me. Is she okay?"

The twin furrows on Adam's brow deepened. Clare had finished her stint as a temporary receptionist the prior week, and he'd hardly seen her the past few days as he struggled to deal with an unusual spring outbreak of the flu. He tried to replay the encounter he'd just had with her, but he'd been so upset and angry that his powers of observation hadn't exactly been at their peak. Now that he thought about it, though, she had looked a little flushed. And her eyes…hadn't they seemed a bit dull and slightly unfocused?

"Dad?"

Nicole's voice brought him back to the present, and he reached down to give her hand a squeeze. "I'm going to run over there right now and check on her. I'll be back in a few minutes, okay?"

"Okay."

As Adam strode back toward the garage, a queasy feeling began to grow in the pit of his stomach—along with a growing certainty that he'd been way out of line, that he'd jumped to conclusions and wrongly berated Clare. After all these months, didn't he know her well enough to know that she'd never do anything to endanger Nicole? How could he have been so stupid? Even though he'd been upset about the accident and his nerves had been stretched to the breaking point, that didn't give him the right to take out his stress on the woman who had given him back his daughter in the first place.

Adam took the stairs two at a time, lifted his hand to knock—and froze. The muffled sound of raw, heart-breaking sobs came through the door, and he closed his eyes, feeling as if someone had kicked him in the gut. *God forgive me,* he prayed, his hands balling into fists.

Adam didn't even knock. He tried the door, found it open, and stepped into the dimness. The sound of Clare's anguished sobs led him to the bedroom, his stomach clenching more tightly with every step. And the sight of her huddled miserably on the floor, her head bent, her slight shoulders heaving, made him feel physically sick.

He went down on one knee beside her and laid a gentle hand on her shoulder. "Clare?"

She raised dull, bleary eyes to him, but it seemed to

take a moment for his presence to register. She was clutching a picture frame to her chest. "I—I'm so s-sorry, Adam," she said hoarsely, repeating her earlier apology.

His drew a ragged breath. "I'm the one who's sorry." Then he reached for her and gathered her slender, shaking body into his arms.

Adam felt her misery at the deepest level of his soul, and the incoherent snatches of phrases that were interspersed with her sobs tore at his heart.

"My fault… Selfish… My responsibility… Accident… no…! Not gone…! Nicole, please… So alone…"

"Shh, it's okay, Clare. It's okay." He stroked her back gently and pulled her closer, his chin dropping to graze her forehead. But when his skin made contact with hers he quickly backed off in alarm and stared down at her. She was burning up! Her face was flushed, and not just from crying. He placed a cool palm against her fiery forehead and tried not to panic as he reached for her wrist to check her pulse. She had been trembling before, from emotion, but suddenly her whole body began to shake with bone-jarring chills.

"Clare." When she didn't respond, he tried again, more insistently. "Clare!"

She lifted her head and tried to focus on him.

"Clare, how long have you been sick?" he asked, speaking slowly.

"Since l-last night," she whispered hoarsely, her teeth chattering.

"Have you been throwing up?"

He wasn't surprised when she nodded. He'd treated

enough cases to recognize the symptoms and instantly diagnose the problem. But this was one of the worst cases of flu he'd seen. She needed immediate—and constant—attention. And so did Nicole. Which meant there was only one solution.

"Clare, you have the flu," he said. "Since I have to care for both you and Nicole, I want you to come over to the house, okay?"

He wasn't quite sure she understood, but she nodded.

He reached over and pried her hands from the frame, glancing at the photo as he stood. And once more, he felt as if someone had delivered a punch to his stomach. The two smiling male faces in the photo had to be Clare's husband and son. The ones who'd been killed in a car accident. Just as Nicole almost had been today. He could only imagine the nightmare memories, and the pain, that today's scenario had evoked for the woman who now sat slumped at his feet. And his insensitive behavior had only made things worse.

He closed his eyes and bowed his head. *God forgive me,* he prayed again. *And please console Clare.*

Adam gently set the photo on the chest of drawers, then reached down and drew Clare to her feet in one smooth, easy motion. She wavered and gripped his arm, closing her eyes.

"I—I think I'm going t-to throw up again," she said faintly.

With Adam half carrying her, they made it to the bathroom just in time for her to be violently sick. When the retching finally stopped, she was so spent that she couldn't even stand without his support.

"I—I feel like I'm dying," she whispered miserably.

"Not if I can help it."

Adam guided her out of the bathroom, but when she stumbled he reached down and swept her up, cradling her against his broad chest. She was too weak to do more than lie passively in his arms.

"I'm sorry for the trouble," she whispered, her eyes huge in her pale face. Tears pooled in the corners of their blue depths, then spilled onto her cheeks. "It's all my fault."

Adam didn't know whether she was talking about the accident or about being sick. But it didn't matter. Neither was her fault—despite the blame he'd harshly laid on her during his first visit.

As he made his way carefully down the narrow staircase, Adam recalled that he'd asked God earlier to forgive him.

But as he looked down at the devastated face of the woman in his arms, he wasn't sure Clare ever would.

Chapter Eleven

The next twenty-four hours were a blur for Clare. She was alternately burning hot or freezing cold. Every muscle in her body ached. Her restless sleep was filled with heart-pounding nightmares that woke her abruptly, shaking and gasping for breath. And every once in a while something unpleasantly cold was insistently pressed to her chest.

But if she was aware of the bad, she was also cognizant of the good. The cool cloths on her forehead. The strong arm supporting her shoulders while she greedily drank great quantities of water. The gentle fingers massaging her aching muscles. And the soothing voice that always seemed to be there when she awoke from her bad dreams, reassuring and comforting her.

Clare lost all track of time. But when her eyelids flickered open after one of her frequent naps, she somehow knew she had turned a corner. Though she felt limp as a rag doll, her muscles no longer ached with such fierce intensity. Nor did she feel too hot or too cold. Just drained. And absolutely exhausted.

Clare turned her head toward the window, a simple action that seemed to require an extraordinary amount of energy. The shade was drawn, but faint light showed around the edges. Which meant it was either morning or evening. But she had no idea what day it was.

A movement on the other side of the room caught her eye, and she summoned up the energy to turn her head back in that direction. Nicole had cracked the door and was peeking in.

Clare managed a weak smile. And an even weaker greeting.

Instead of responding, Nicole turned and called out excitedly. "Dad! She's awake!"

A moment later Clare heard rapid footsteps on the stairs, and then Adam appeared in the doorway. "Wait out here," he instructed Nicole as he strode into the room. "I don't want to have to put you back on the patient list." He sat on the edge of the bed, then looked at Clare assessingly. Her eyes were clearer and more focused, and when he laid a hand on her forehead it was blessedly cooler.

As he reached for the stethoscope around his neck, Clare spoke. "You should warm that thing up before you use it. It's a form of torture."

Her voice was scratchy and almost unrecognizable, but he caught the faint teasing tone. For the first time in more than twenty-four hours, he felt the tension in his shoulders ease. "Welcome back," he said quietly. Following her advice, he warmed the stethoscope between his palms for a moment, then leaned over and slipped it inside the V-neck of her sweatshirt. "Just breathe when I tell you," he instructed.

While Clare followed his instructions, she assessed Adam. He looked as if he'd aged ten years, she realized with a pang. Twin furrows were etched deeply in his brow, and there were lines of tension and strain around his mouth and eyes. He looked utterly weary...and utterly wonderful, she thought, her throat contracting with emotion.

As he withdrew the stethoscope and looped it around his neck, fragments of the past twenty-four hours began to fall into place for Clare. "Adam...the accident... Is Nicole okay?"

He nodded. "The only remnants are a nasty bump on the head and some bruises."

"I'm so sorry," she whispered. "I should have..."

Adam silenced her by pressing a gentle finger to her lips. "This was not your fault, Clare," he said firmly. "If anyone should apologize, it's me. But you're in no condition right now to even think about everything that happened. You need to focus on getting well."

"What day is it?"

"Saturday night."

"And the accident was..."

"Yesterday, late afternoon. Now, I'm going to heat some soup and try to get something a little more solid into you. Do you need anything first?"

She blushed. "I...uh...need to go to the bathroom."

He nodded. "Good. Up till now, your body has been burning off the liquid almost as fast I could get it into you. If your fever hadn't dropped within the next couple of hours, I would have had to hospitalize you and get you hooked up to an IV."

She made a face. "Hospitals aren't my favorite place. No slight intended to your profession."

He smiled. "They're not my favorite place, either. I do everything I can to keep people out of them."

He rose and drew back the covers, then reached down to help her sit up. "Take it slow and easy. Just let your feet dangle over the side of the bed for a minute before you try to stand."

Clare did as he advised, almost frightened by her extreme weakness. "Wow!" she breathed softly. "This is weird. I feel like every ounce of my energy has been drained off and my muscles have gone on strike."

"A bad case of the flu will do that to you."

"But I never get sick! And I've never had the flu."

"You've never worked in a doctor's office before— especially one overflowing with flu patients. Trust me, you just made up for all the years you escaped," he told her, and though his voice was light she heard the serious undertones. And knew she had been a lot sicker than she could even imagine.

"Ready?" he asked. At her uncertain nod, he reached down and eased her to her feet. She grasped his arm tightly, then clung to him as he guided her slowly down the hall and into the guest bath. "Can you manage on your own?" he asked, giving her a worried look.

She nodded, not at all sure she could but equally sure there was no acceptable alternative.

"Okay, I'll wait out here."

By the time she opened the door a couple of minutes later, she had to hold on to it for support. Her legs had grown wobbly, and her hands were shaking. "You'd think I'd just run a marathon or something," she tried to joke, but she was too weary even to smile.

Without giving her time to protest, Adam reached down and tucked a hand under her knees, then swept her into his arms. He grinned at her as he started back down the hall. "I want you to know that I don't give this kind of service to all my patients," he teased.

As Clare looked up at him, she was overcome by his kindness and tender care, and she felt tears leaking out the corners of her eyes. She tried to avert her face, embarrassed at her uncharacteristic loss of control, hoping Adam wouldn't notice.

When he reached the bed, he gently laid her down and tucked the covers around her. Then he sat beside her and tenderly traced the line of one tear down her cheek, dashing her hopes that she had successfully hidden them.

"It's okay to cry after all you've been through, Clare," he said softly. "When you're stronger, we'll talk. Right now, you just need to rest. Physically and mentally." He rose. "I'll get that soup."

As Adam disappeared out the door, Clare thought about his advice. She could easily comply with the instruction to get physical rest. She really didn't have much choice.

But she wasn't so sure about the mental part.

Because the feelings and emotions Nicole's accident had awakened were far too powerful to ignore. Even though she'd managed to suppress them for nearly three long years, she sensed that this time she'd have to deal with them.

Once and for all.

* * *

Clare's recovery took far longer than she expected. For the first few days she could hardly drag herself to and from the bathroom. By the end of the week she felt strong enough to get dressed, but even the smallest chores tired her out. Adele had been a huge help, bless her heart. She'd dropped off several home-cooked meals and had come to stay with Clare the first couple of days when Adam had to go back to work. Nicole had been equally attentive. All in all, Clare couldn't have asked for better care.

But even though everyone kept a close eye on her, she still had plenty of time alone, with nothing to do but pray. And think. About mistakes and guilt and grief. About how dramatically her life had changed nearly three years ago. And about how dramatically Adam's might have changed just a few days ago. Thanks to her.

Intellectually, Clare knew that the circumstances of this accident were different than the one that took the life of her husband and child. Her abdication of responsibility this time hadn't been brought about by selfishness, but by sickness. Yet the outcome could very well have been the same. And how could she have lived with that? How could she live with it even now, knowing what might have happened?

"I'm on my way to the hospital, but I called and found out the Bluebird has meat loaf today. How does that sound for dinner?"

Clare turned toward Adam as he joined her on the porch. He'd run himself ragged looking after her in addition to taking care of Nicole and keeping up with the demands of his practice. And it showed in his face. He looked worn out. Luckily it was Saturday and he'd have a chance to rest a little.

"Why don't I make something tonight?"

"Not yet."

"Adam, I'm not an invalid."

"Not yet," he repeated firmly. "Doctor's orders."

She sighed and let her head drop back against the wicker chair. "You're spoiling me."

When he didn't respond, she turned her head, and the expression in his eyes made her breath catch in her throat.

"Impossible," he said quietly.

She forced herself to look back at the mountains as her heart filled with tenderness for this special man. A man she wanted to spend the rest of her life with. A man she hoped felt the same way about her.

But first she needed to take care of some unfinished business. Because until she dealt with the debilitating grief and guilt locked inside, until she released them from her heart, there was no way for love to get in. And she wanted to let love in. She wanted to let Adam in.

She took a deep breath. "Adam…I need to go back to Kansas City."

When he didn't respond, she turned to look at him again. His eyes were guarded—but she saw fear lurking in their depths.

"I thought you were staying for three more weeks," he said carefully.

She gave him a startled look, realizing he'd misunderstood her intent. "I am!" she reassured him quickly. "I just have to…take care of some business."

"Then…you're coming back?"

"Of course." She saw the tension ease in his shoulders. "I'm sorry…I didn't mean to imply I was leaving for good."

He smiled, but it was clearly forced. "Good. I was afraid that maybe the medical care wasn't quite up to par."

"No one has ever taken such good care of me," she told him quietly.

After a long moment, Adam broke eye contact and glanced down at his watch. "I need to get rolling. As soon as I do rounds, I'll be back. Nicole is going to a barbecue, so I thought maybe you and I could eat out here. The weather's been great, and you can't beat the view!"

"That sounds lovely."

"Nicole is upstairs if you need her."

"I know. I'll be fine." When he hesitated, she smiled. "Really, Adam. I'll be fine. I'm feeling stronger every day."

He nodded slowly. "Okay. But don't get too ambitious. You're not back to full speed yet. When were you thinking of going back to Kansas City?"

"Next weekend."

He frowned. "That's a long trip."

"I'll take it slowly."

He hesitated. "I'm not sure you should go by yourself. Would you…like me to come with you?"

She looked at him in surprise, touched by his unexpected offer, but shook her head. "No. This is something I need to do alone. It will only take a couple of days. But thank you, Adam."

With a nod, he reentered the house to prepare for his hospital visit. But his mind wasn't on his patients. It was on Clare and her upcoming trip. She'd assured him that it would be a quick visit, and he believed her. But it reminded him that time was running out on the nanny assignment. In three short weeks Clare would be gone. Permanently.

Unless he gave her a very good reason to stay.

"I moved back into my apartment today."

Adam looked across the wicker table at Clare. He couldn't really argue about her decision. She was perfectly capable now of taking care of herself. But he would miss having her living under his roof. "I suppose it was time," he concurred.

"More than time. I was way too lazy way too long."

"You were very sick, Clare."

She toyed with her garlic mashed potatoes. "But I'm fine now."

He glanced down at her half-eaten dinner. "Your appetite still isn't back to normal."

"It's coming along."

"You can't afford to lose any more weight."

She couldn't deny that her clothes were starting to hang on her. "I'll gain it back."

Adam laid his fork down. "Clare, I'm still worried about you making this trip to Kansas City. I'm not sure you're strong enough."

"I will be by next weekend."

He expelled a frustrated sigh. "Is this something you have to do now? Can't it wait a little longer?"

She shook her head. "I need to go at that particular time, Adam."

The resolute look in her eyes told Adam that she wasn't going to be dissuaded. So he didn't argue. Besides, he had an even touchier subject to discuss with her. He reached for his iced tea and took a sip, trying to figure out how to begin. Clare didn't seem to harbor any ill will toward him since his insensitive treatment of her the day of Nicole's accident, but he'd learned enough since then to know that she should. As he'd held her, comforted her through countless fever-induced nightmares, he'd been able to piece together some details about the accident that had killed her husband and son. Enough to know that Clare blamed herself for their deaths. That she felt she'd reneged on her obligations and let them down.

Exactly the things he'd accused her of with Nicole.

None of which were true.

Just as he was sure they weren't true with her own family. And he needed to convince her of that, to relieve her of the torment that she still carried in her heart over that accident. He had felt her deep-seated pain, and though she'd hidden it well before her illness—as she was hiding it well now—he knew it was still there. He wanted to release her from that suffering and help her heart heal, just as he'd helped her body heal.

"Clare, does your trip have anything to do with Dennis and David?" he asked carefully.

After a moment of silence, she nodded. "Yes."

He set his iced tea down and leaned over to capture her delicate hand in his. "Tell me about it, Clare."

His sun-browned fingers were so strong, yet so gentle, she reflected. Just like the man. She drew a ragged breath. If she harbored any hopes of creating a future with Adam, he deserved to know about her past. Even if he thought ill of her because of the terrible decision she'd made on that fateful day nearly three years ago.

"You talked a lot about them when you were sick," Adam spoke again. "And I had the feeling that you somehow think you were responsible for their deaths."

There was a long moment of silence while she tried to swallow past the lump in her throat. "I was," she finally whispered.

"Why don't I believe that?"

She looked over at him, her eyes raw and bleak. "It's true, Adam. If I hadn't been so selfish, they'd still be alive."

"Tell me," he coaxed again, his own eyes gentle.

So she did, haltingly at first, then more quickly, until finally the words came out in an almost incoherent rush. And in among the cold, hard facts, she wove her feelings of selfishness and guilt and pain and all the reasons why she felt responsible for the tragedy that had cut short the lives of the two people she loved most and changed her life forever.

When she finished she took a deep breath. "I thought I was making progress, that I was learning to let go of the guilt," she said brokenly. "And then the accident happened with Nicole. She could have been… She could have died, Adam! And it would have been my fault!"

He reached over with his other hand and cocooned hers protectively in his warm clasp. He'd thought a lot about the accident, too. And had come to a completely different conclusion.

"Let me tell you something, Clare. If anyone should feel guilty about recent events, it's me. Because I think you *saved* her life. And all I did was berate you for it."

Clare gave him a confused look. "I don't understand. You were right to be angry. It was my responsibility to take care of Nicole."

"And that's exactly what you did."

She shook her head, as if to clear it. "I'm sorry. I must be missing something."

"You are. And here it is. After the accident, I spoke with an officer who was at the scene. He told me how fortunate it was that the driver of Nicole's car was alert and had good reflexes, because she was able to swerve out of the way and avoid a collision. He also said things could have turned out very differently if there'd been a head-on crash. Clare, that's exactly what might have happened if you'd been driving. You were so sick that your reflexes were sluggish at best. By using good judgment and asking Mrs. Foster to take Nicole, you might have saved her life. And your own."

Clare stared at him, then closed her eyes and drew a deep breath. *"Thank you, God!"* she whispered.

"I made that same prayer, once rational thought prevailed. And I also prayed that you would forgive me. Because you have every right to hate me for the way I treated you," Adam told her quietly.

Clare opened her eyes. "I never held it against you, Adam. I've been there," she said fervently. "I know what it's like to lose people you love. And to be angry at those responsible. Because that's the same feeling I have against myself, for what happened to Dennis and David." She paused, and her eyes filled with tears. "Maybe I made the right decision this time. But I didn't the last time. Because I was too selfish."

Adam stroked her hand. "May I tell you something, Clare? At worst, you made a mistake. You did something out of character. But it was the type of mistake that would normally have no consequences. We all make those kinds of mistakes every day. That's just being human. But selfish? Never."

"That's what Reverend Nichols said. But I can't seem to let go of the guilt," she said with a sigh. "That's what this trip to Kansas City is all about. I need to deal with it. To try and put it to rest. And to let myself grieve." She ran her finger down her iced-tea glass, the beads of moisture damp against her finger, like teardrops. "Do you know, until the night I got sick, I had never cried for them?" she said softly. "I couldn't. I was afraid that I'd break apart if I did. But now I know that there is a time for tears. And a time for mourning. I need to get past the grief and the guilt so my soul can start to heal. Otherwise I'll never be able to move on. May fourteenth is…is the third anniversary of the accident. That's why I want to go back then."

Adam drew a deep breath. "I hate for you to have to deal with this alone."

She looked at him with quiet confidence. "I won't be alone, Adam. Thanks to Reverend Nichols, I've reconnected with the Lord. He'll be with me. But I could use your prayers."

"That goes without saying." He paused and squeezed her hand. "We'll miss you."

"I'll miss you, too. But I'll be back to finish out my assignment."

For the last three weeks.

The words were unspoken, but they hung in the air between them.

As Adam picked up his fork once more, he mulled over Clare's decision. She had made it clear that she was trying to tie up the loose ends of her old life so she could move on to a new one. By courageously confronting old demons, she was making a conscious effort to let go of the past so she could embrace the future with hope and peace.

Adam knew how hard that was. And he knew something else, as well.

The ball was now squarely in his court.

Clare stepped out the door of the motel into the blazing sun and almost recoiled from the hot, humid air that hit her in the face. Over the past few months she'd grown accustomed to the cooler climate in the mountains of North Carolina, and the unrelenting heat of Kansas City was a shock to her system. If it was already this bad at only nine-thirty in the morning, she knew it would surely be a sauna later in the day.

Resolutely, Clare straightened her shoulders. She wasn't going to let a little heat change her plans. Nor a little tiredness. Okay, maybe more than a little tiredness, she conceded. She'd assured Adam that she felt completely up to the trip, but the long drive had taken far more out of her than she wanted to admit. Though she'd tried to sound bright and perky when she'd called him last night to let him know she'd arrived safely, he'd seen through her pretense immediately, quickly discerning the underlying note of weariness in her voice. His own voice had been laced with worry when he'd spoken to her.

"Clare, I want you to get something to eat and go to bed. And promise me you'll sleep late tomorrow."

She'd been too tired to argue. "I will, Adam."

"And don't push yourself."

"I won't."

His sigh of frustration came clearly over the line. "I wish I was there."

"I know, but I need to do this alone."

"You also need to take care of yourself."

"That's exactly why I'm here, Adam."

"I mean physically."

"I'll do that, too."

There was a slight hesitation. "All right. I'll pray for you, Clare."

She replayed his promise in her mind as she locked the door of her motel room and headed for her car. She was going to need his prayers, she thought grimly. As well as her own.

Please, Lord, help me get through this. Let me feel Your steady, healing presence throughout this day. Give me the strength to confront the past and put it to rest.

Clare had carefully mapped out her route. Each place represented a significant part of her old life, starting with the house she had shared with Dennis and David.

As she pulled up across the street from the brick Colonial and put the car in Park, she let her gaze trace the contours of the stately home. The basketball hoop Dennis had installed was still visible above the side-entry garage, she noted, and a wistful smile tugged at the corners of her mouth as she pictured him unwinding after a long day by shooting baskets and, later, showing David how to play.

As she shifted her attention to the front of the house, she thought about the day Dennis had first brought her to see it, recalling the excitement in his eyes as he showed her around. Though she'd been suitably impressed, she'd found her greatest joy not in the house, but in the happiness it had given him.

She took a moment to replay in her mind the day they'd moved in. Dennis had insisted on carrying her over the threshold, and then they'd eaten a picnic dinner on the floor in the bare dining room while he described what the room would someday look like, promising to fill it with beautiful furnishings. A promise he had proudly kept.

When she looked at the window of the second-floor master bedroom her throat constricted with emotion. That room had been filled with love and laughter and sharing—a sheltered, special place where time stopped and the fears and concerns of the world disappeared.

David's room wasn't visible from the street, but she could picture it in her mind. Cluttered, filled with little-boy treasures like rocks, an occasional multilegged creature in a glass jar and shelves of soccer trophies. It had been right next to the master bedroom, and sometimes she and Dennis would stand in the doorway late at night, hand in hand, watching as David slept—and dreaming of the day when other childish voices, other childish treasures would fill the remaining empty bedrooms.

It was a dream that had never come true.

Clare blinked rapidly and swiped a hand across her eyes. She let her gaze once more sweep lovingly over the house and tucked the memory carefully in her heart. Then, with a final lingering glance, she drove away.

Her next stop was Dennis's office. She'd only gone inside the modern, mostly glass building a couple of times, when she'd met him for lunch. Today she remained in her car, looking at it from across the street, counting the floors until she could pick out the window of his spacious, tenth-floor office, with its command-ing view of the city. Clare knew what that space repre-sented to him. Beating the odds. Overcoming his background. Proving that he had the right stuff to succeed in a competitive, high-stakes world. Right or wrong, his success had helped him feel more worthy somehow. It had validated him. As a man of strong faith, Dennis had tried to keep worldly achievements in perspective. But he had still relished his success. Clare had understood that, given the poverty of his youth. And when she'd seen him here, in this world she only shared vicariously, she had been happy for him.

Her next stop was David's school. She didn't drive in, but stopped at the entrance gates. Which was where she had typically left him in the morning. He'd gotten to that age where having his mother drive him right to the door wasn't cool anymore. But she'd always waited while he walked up the curving driveway. And sometimes, as he'd trudged along, his knapsack slung over his back, she'd think ahead, to the day when life would take him much farther from her arms than a simple walk to the school door. She had wondered, back then, how she would cope when that time came, when she had to set him free to test his wings in the world. And she'd always dreaded that day.

She'd give anything now if she still had that to look forward to.

Struggling to contain her tears, she drove to the house where she'd attended the pool party. She hadn't known the host very well, but the party had been for a good friend of hers from her teaching days and she'd ended up having a wonderful time. The rambling, contemporary home on the corner lot looked exactly the same, she thought, as she slowly pulled to a stop. The pool was clearly visible behind a decorative iron fence, and though they weren't in use today, the lounge chairs were arranged much as they had been the day of the party. She'd been sitting in one along the far edge of the pool when the hostess had sought her out, portable phone in hand.

Clare had known right away that something was wrong from the expression on the woman's face. As she'd taken the phone, alarm racing up her spine, her heart had begun to thump heavily in her chest. And as she'd listened to the officer on the other end, who had apparently tracked her down from the pool party number Dennis had scribbled on a scrap of paper and tucked in his pocket in case he needed to reach her, she'd felt as if she'd been sucked into a vacuum, the party sounds fading away, the scene distorting before her eyes.

After that she'd switched to autopilot. She'd thrown a cover-up over her suit, and someone had driven her to the hospital. But it was already too late. Dennis had died at the scene. David had lingered briefly, but by the time she arrived at the hospital he was gone, too. All because she stayed too long at the party.

Clare hadn't been near a swimming pool since.

And she wasn't sure she would ever go to one again.

As she struggled to contain her tears, Clare realized that her hands were shaking. It was well past noon, and she knew she should stop and rest. Maybe get some lunch. Adam would insist on it if he were here. But the thought of food made her queasy. And with the most difficult part of her day still ahead, rest wasn't an option. So she resolutely headed for her next stop.

The church she and Dennis and David had regularly attended was just as she remembered it, Clare noted, as she pulled into the adjacent parking lot. It had been almost a year since she'd set foot inside, and she prayed it would be open.

Luck was on her side. The door was unlocked, and Clare quickly understood why when she entered. There had obviously been a wedding a short time before. White bows still adorned the pews, and beautiful flower arrangements stood on the altar, filling the air with a sweet, fresh fragrance. She slipped into a pew near the back, letting the peace and beauty seep into her soul.

As she looked around the familiar interior, it struck her how many pivotal moments in life were celebrated in this holy place. The moments that mattered the most, if one took the eternal view. People came here to celebrate birth into new life through baptism. They came to celebrate the union of a man and woman in marriage. They came on Christmas to celebrate the birth of Christ—God's great gift to humanity. And on Easter, to commemorate His glorious resurrection, which forever destroyed the power of death. Finally, they came at the end of an earthly life to mark the transition to eternal life. People came here for so many important events.

But they also came for personal reasons. To seek solace. And guidance. And grace. They came to share with the Lord their sorrows. Their joys. Their uncertainties. In other words, they came to pray. Not necessarily in a formal way. But in conversation. Or, as Reverend Nichols had so simply put it, they came to talk to the Lord.

Clare closed her eyes and took a deep, steadying breath.

Lord, please help me to know Your forgiveness. Please relieve me of the burden of my grief. Help me to fully and completely put my life in Your hands, confident that You will show me mercy and understand my sorrow and regret. I need to move on, Lord. I need to let go of the past. But I need Your help to do it, once and for all. Please help me, so that I can find the peace that comes from total surrender to Your will. And please help me as I make this last, most difficult part of my journey. Please be by my side.

She lingered for a few more minutes in the peaceful

refuge, drawing strength from its tranquility. But finally she rose. It was time.

She made just one brief detour, at a florist, on the way to her final destination. She hadn't mapped out this last leg of her trip, but even though she'd only been to the cemetery once, the route was etched indelibly on her mind.

As she slowly drove through the entrance, her last trip here came back with startling intensity. She recalled glancing out the window when the limo turned into the gates, noting the long line of cars behind her. The church had been packed, and apparently many had chosen to come to the graveside service, as well. A.J. and Morgan had sat on either side of her, gripping her hands tightly throughout the service and now, again, in the car. They hadn't spoken much. But their very presence, and the look in their eyes, had told her how much they cared, how deeply they grieved for her. She couldn't have made it through those terrible days without her sisters.

Clare pulled to a stop at the curb and reached for the flowers. She recognized the headstone, about twenty yards away, from the picture in the catalogue at the monument company. Slowly she got out of the car and forced her feet to move toward it. As she approached, the names on the stone gradually came into focus. Seeing them etched in granite, so permanent, so final, caused her breath to lodge in her throat, making it difficult to breath.

Dennis J. Randall. Beloved Husband.
David L. Randall. Cherished Son.

Then the dates…indicating lives cut far too short.
And finally, the Bible verse she had chosen.

For He has freed my soul from death, my eyes
from tears, my feet from stumbling. (Ps 114: 8)

The words began to swim before Clare's eyes, and
she sank to her knees beside the headstone, then
dropped back on her heels. Unsteadily she reached
over and let her fingers run lightly over the names,
feeling the ridges and the valleys of the letters and the
smooth, polished granite in between. The afternoon
sun beat down on the back of her head and threw the
letters into relief, each name casting a shadow that
extended beyond the actual letters. Just as their lives
extended beyond the grave, she thought. Dennis and
David would always live in her heart, in a special place
reserved only for them, cherished and loved for all
time. And they would always live in heaven, in the
loving care of the Lord.

Clare let one hand rest on top of the headstone, and
with the other she reached for the flowers she'd set on
the ground beside her. Tears began to roll down her
cheeks, but she made no attempt to stop them. Not this
time. Carefully she laid a red rose, then a yellow one,
on the grave. One for love, one to say she would never
forget them. The age-old language of flowers.

"I came today to say goodbye," she whispered, her
voice choked. "And to say I'm sorry. To ask your forgiveness. To tell you that there hasn't been one day in
the past three years that I didn't wish I could turn

back the clock and make a different decision. I miss you both so much! When you left, the sunlight went out of my world. Everything turned dark, and I lost my way. I existed, but I didn't live. I knew that wasn't what God wanted for me, but I couldn't find my way back to the light."

Her voice caught on a sob, and she took a steadying breath. "Then, through Aunt Jo, God gave me a job to do. I've been trying to help a father and daughter create the kind of family we had. And I think I've succeeded. But something else happened along the way. I began to realize that I wanted to be part of their family. I knew I couldn't do that, though, until I made my peace with you. And until I grieved. That's why I came today. To tell you how much I love you. How much I'll always love you. And to tell you that just because I want to let other people into my heart, they will never take your place. There's a special spot that will always be reserved just for you."

She rested her cheek against the stone, and her tears made dark splotches on the polished surface. "I wish I could talk with you, could know for sure that you forgive me and that you're okay with me moving on. But I'll just have to trust that you know what's in my heart, and that you understand."

Slowly she slipped the ring off her left hand and carefully tucked it in her purse. Then she let her fingers once more lovingly caress their names. "Goodbye, my loves," she whispered.

For several minutes Clare remained in that position,

the tears running freely down her face. Healing, cleansing tears of grief. Of closure.

When at last she straightened up, drained and weary, she was startled to find a cardinal staring at her from the ground, a few feet away. Oddly, the bird didn't seem a bit frightened by such close proximity to a human. Its scarlet head was cocked to one side as it regarded her quizzically. When Clare didn't move, it hopped a bit closer. Then closer still. There was something in its beak, but she couldn't quite make out what it was.

All of a sudden, the bird hopped onto the grave, dropped its cargo, then lifted its wings and soared into the air. Clare watched, mesmerized, as it rose against the clear blue sky, circled once and disappeared among the trees.

When she looked down, the bird's offering lay next to the roses she had placed there. Curiously she reached for it and set it in her palm. For a moment she couldn't figure out what the triangular object was. One edge was ragged, as if it had been torn, and what looked like part of a number was visible. She turned it over…and her breath caught in her throat.

A large heart filled the small piece of cardboard.

It was the corner of a playing card.

Clare wasn't a great believer in heavenly signs or messages from beyond the grave. But as she stared down at the sliver of cardboard in her hand, a profound, abiding peace spread throughout her. And in the deepest recesses of her soul, she felt as if she'd been given two precious gifts.

Absolution.

And permission to move on.

Tears once more filled her eyes, and she raised her face toward Heaven. "Thank you," she whispered.

Chapter Twelve

"It sure is quiet around here without Clare."

Adam's hand stilled for a moment, then he continued dishing out the Chinese food he'd brought home for dinner.

When he didn't respond, Nicole looked over at him. "Don't you miss her, too, Dad?"

He handed her a plate. "Yes. But she'll be back tomorrow."

Nicole sighed and glanced disinterestedly at her food. "Yeah, but not for long. She'll be leaving in two weeks. For good."

Adam was well aware of Clare's impending departure. It had been on his mind constantly. He'd prayed about it, asked for guidance, listened to his heart. He knew what he *wanted* to do. But he still wasn't sure it would be fair to ask Clare to commit to a man who had major problems with intimacy. Yes, they'd already connected and communicated on a deeper level than he ever had with Elaine. But could he sustain that? Or would he end up disappointing Clare? He didn't know the answer to that question. And he wasn't sure how to find it.

He'd struggled with another question, as well. He knew Nicole had come to care deeply about Clare. But was she ready to have someone move into a mother's role? Or would she resent another woman trying to take the place of the mother she had loved? Adam had been wanting to bring the subject up with Nicole for weeks, but he'd never found the opportunity. Or the courage. But time was running out. And there would be no better opportunity than now.

Adam forced himself to take a steadying breath and made a pretense of eating. "You're going to miss Clare, aren't you?" he asked, striving to keep his tone casual and conversational.

Nicole sighed. "Big-time. She's cool. I kind of hoped…"

Her voice trailed off, and Adam looked over at her. "Hoped what?" he prompted.

She shrugged. "I don't know. You put your arm around her once, out on the porch. And I see the way you guys look at each other, usually when you think the other one isn't watching. I'm not a kid anymore, you know. I thought maybe…well, that maybe you and Clare might fall in love or something. If you guys got married, she could stay."

Adam stared at her, stunned. "You hoped we'd get married?"

Nicole flushed. "Yeah."

"But…what about your mom?"

"What about her?"

"Well, I wasn't sure how you'd feel about someone taking her place."

Nicole shrugged unconcernedly. "Clare wouldn't do that. Clare is…Clare. She and Mom are a lot different. I love them both."

Adam stared at his daughter. She had honed right to the essence of the situation, which he had obviously made far too complicated. And he couldn't argue with her logic. Elaine and Clare *were* different. Completely.

"So are you going to?" Nicole asked.

"What?"

"Ask her to marry you?"

He hesitated. "I don't know," he said slowly.

She tilted her head and studied him. "How come you're not sure?"

Because I don't want to hurt her. Because I'm still not convinced I'm husband material. Because I'm scared she'll say no.

But his spoken words were different. "I don't know if she loves me."

Nicole rolled her eyes. "Good grief, Dad! How can you be so dense! Of course she loves you!"

"How do you kr‹

"I told you. I see the way she looks at you."

"Could you be a little more specific?"

"You know. Her eyes get kind of…soft or something. Like she thinks you're really special."

"Yeah?"

"Yeah. So are you going to ask her?"

"I guess I will."

Nicole grinned. "Cool! Then she can move into the house and we can be a real family."

As Nicole attacked her meal with sudden enthusiasm, her last words echoed in Adam's heart.

A real family.

That had a nice sound. A hopeful sound. And he wanted it more than he could say.

He just prayed Clare felt the same way.

"You didn't have to go to the Bluebird, Adam. I would have been happy to make dinner."

Adam glanced over at Clare. Since her return from Kansas City a few days before, she'd seemed tired and a bit too pale. He'd known the trip would take a lot out of her, physically and emotionally, and he'd been right. So he'd insisted that she take it easy for a couple of days.

"You can cook tomorrow if you really want to."

"I really want to."

She turned to look at the mountains then, and as he studied her in the twilight, he was grateful to see that tonight there was more color in her cheeks. She hadn't talked much about her trip, except to say that she was glad she had gone. But in her eyes there was a quiet serenity that hadn't been there before. And he had noted the absence of her wedding ring. So he knew the trip had done what she'd hoped—released her from the past so that she could build a new future.

A future he hoped included Nicole and him.

Adam felt his heart begin to thud heavily in his chest and he turned to look out over the distant mountains.

He'd been waiting for the right moment to propose, and this seemed to be it. It was a beautiful evening, the stillness broken only by the song of birds. Nicole had gone to dinner at a friend's house and wouldn't be home until much later. It was the perfect time.

Adam swallowed and looked over at Clare. She was still focused on the mountains, her face placid and at peace, her legs curled up under her. She looked so right sitting there on his porch, he thought. As though she belonged with him. For always.

He cleared his throat, and Clare glanced at him expectantly. Suddenly he wished he was sitting beside her instead of in the wicker chair at a right angle to the settee. But maybe this was better. From here, he had a better view of her face, a better angle from which to gauge her reactions.

"We missed you while you were gone," he began.

"I missed you both, too."

"Nicole said it just wasn't the same around here without you."

A smile tugged at the corners of her mouth, but she remained silent.

"She was right," he added.

Again, Clare remained silent, her eyes inviting him to continue.

Adam leaned forward and clasped his hands between his knees. "The thing is, Clare, we don't want you to leave when the nanny job is over."

She waited a moment, as if she expected him to say more. When he didn't, she spoke. "I have a job waiting for me in Kansas City."

"But there's a job for you here, too."

The tiniest frown creased her brow. "I never planned to be a nanny permanently, Adam."

"I don't mean that job." He sighed and raked his fingers through his hair. "I'm sorry. I'm really making a mess of this. I've never been good at this kind of thing."

"Just tell me what's in your heart, Adam," she encouraged softly.

He looked over at her, suddenly afraid. Afraid to do as she asked. And just as afraid not to. If he told her what was in his heart, he would be completely vulnerable. But if he didn't, how could he convince her to stay? He fought against his doubts, but fear knotted his stomach and made it difficult to breathe.

When he spoke, his voice was taut with tension. "I'd like you to stay, Clare. As my wife."

For a long moment she searched his eyes. Then she spoke. "Why?"

It was a simple question. And the answer should be equally simple. But he couldn't say the words he knew she wanted to hear.

"I'd like us to be a family," he said unevenly. "You've been wonderful with Nicole, and she doesn't want you to leave. Neither do I. I think we could have a good life together, the three of us."

He knew his response was lame. He knew it even before he saw the flicker of hope that had initially sprung to life in her eyes change to disappointment, then to sad resignation. Nevertheless, she waited silently for a moment, giving him a chance to say something else. But he couldn't find the words.

Finally she spoke again. "Thank you for the offer, Adam," she said quietly. "But I'm not in the market for that kind of job. You and Nicole will be fine now. I've done what Aunt Jo asked me to do. It's time to move on."

Adam felt something inside him break.

Once more she waited. But when he didn't speak, she rose and looked down at him, her eyes sad—and hurt. "I'm pretty tired, Adam. I think I'll go back to my apartment and turn in early."

A moment later he heard the screen door close gently but firmly behind him.

Adam let his head drop into his hands. *Lord, what am I to do now?* he pleaded desperately in the silence of his heart. *I can't let Clare leave. She means more to me than life itself. Please help me find a way to convince her to stay. Give me the courage to fully open my heart to this special woman, to overcome my father's bitter legacy once and for all. Please give me another chance!*

Suddenly the words of Reverend Nichols's Easter homily came back to Adam. The minister had said that in order to grow, we have to be willing to trust our heart with other people. That unless we let go of our fear, we can never move forward or fulfill God's plan for us. And that we need to love as Christ did—completely, selflessly and without reservation.

Adam believed that in his heart. But putting it into action required tremendous courage. A courage he was afraid he didn't have.

"Dad? What's wrong?"

Adam lifted his head from his hands and looked up

at Nicole from the shadows. He wasn't sure how long he'd sat on the porch, but the sky had grown dark.

Nicole moved closer. At the sight of his face, her eyes widened in alarm. "Is Clare sick again?"

Adam forced himself to straighten up. "No. She just went to bed early."

"So what's wrong?"

Adam sighed. "Sit down a minute, sweetie."

Nicole moved to the spot on the settee that Clare had vacated earlier and perched on the edge. When Adam didn't immediately speak, she leaned forward impatiently. "Dad?"

He wiped a hand wearily down his face. "Remember what we talked about the other night? About Clare staying? I asked her tonight. She said…no."

Nicole stared at him incredulously. "You asked her to marry you?" At his nod, she frowned. "But she loves you! What did you say to her?"

"I asked her to stay. As my wife."

Nicole's frown deepened. "What else?"

"I told her that I wanted us to be a family, and how much she meant to you, and that we didn't want her to leave."

She waited, much as Clare had waited earlier, as if expecting him to say more. When he didn't, Nicole leaned forward. "Is that it?"

"Pretty much."

Nicole rolled her eyes. "That is so unromantic! It makes it sound like the only reason you want her to stay is because of me."

"But that's part of it," he said defensively.

She looked at him with a wisdom far beyond her eleven years. "Dad, no woman is going to marry a guy because his kid likes her."

Adam felt his neck grow red. "It's more than that."

"Than what?"

"I like Clare."

"Like?" she practically shrieked.

"Okay, okay. I love her."

"And…"

"And what?"

"Come on, Dad! What else? Tell me how you feel about her." When he hesitated, she leaned over and laid her hand on his knee. "It's okay. You can tell me. This is the kind of stuff you share with people you love," she said gently.

Adam drew an unsteady breath, digging deep for the courage he hoped was there. "I—I can't imagine my life without her anymore," he said quietly, his voice slightly unsteady.

"That's better," Nicole said encouragingly. "Keep going."

"Sometimes…sometimes it scares me, but the fact is…I need her. Because she makes me a better person. And she makes my life so much richer. When she walks into the room, it's like…like the sun coming out after a gray, rainy day. Everything seems so much better and brighter. I love her so much sometimes that…that it hurts."

There was silence for a moment, and when Adam risked a glance at Nicole she was staring at him in awe.

"Wow!" she breathed. "Did you say any of that to Clare?"

"Not exactly."

Nicole leaned forward. "You need to use those exact words, Dad! Man, she'll melt!"

"But she already said no, Nicole."

"So? You can't give up! But the next time you need to do this right. The words are important, but you also need to be more romantic."

Adam gave her a helpless look. "Romance isn't my specialty."

She dismissed his comment with a wave of her hand. "I have lots of ideas," she said confidently. "Do you want to hear them?"

Adam was pretty sure he wouldn't be very comfortable with Nicole's suggestions. But he didn't have any other brilliant ideas. And if she could help him figure out a way to change that look of sad resignation in Clare's eyes to one of love and acceptance, he was willing to give them a try. "I guess I don't have anything to lose at this point."

Nicole leaned forward eagerly. "Okay. Let's start with roses...."

Clare sat cross-legged on her bed, sorting half-heartedly through a box of printed material she'd accumulated since arriving in North Carolina. School schedules and phone numbers and driving directions and brochures about various points of interest in the area that she thought might someday make nice outings. She really didn't need any of it now, she thought, her spirits drooping.

Clare rested her chin in her hands and propped her elbows on her knees. This wasn't the way she'd hoped her time in North Carolina would end, she thought with a melancholy pang. Thanks to Aunt Jo, she had found a new family to love—and a wonderful man to spend the rest of her life with. She'd dealt with her guilt and her grief. She was ready to move on. To start a new life.

Unfortunately, the wonderful man wasn't.

Clare sighed. She knew that Adam loved her. Knew that his feelings for her ran deep and strong. But she also knew that unless—or until—he was able to express those feelings, to admit that he loved her and needed her just as much as she loved and needed him, the relationship would be out of balance. A marriage in which one party held back, withholding trust at the deepest level, was not the kind of marriage she wanted.

Clare knew that Adam's demons were powerful. That his father's legacy had made it difficult for him to show emotion, to let people get close. But she had thought that over the past few months he had begun to overcome that hurdle, to trust her enough to share what was in his heart.

Unfortunately, she'd been wrong.

And as much as she loved Adam, as much as she wanted to be part of this family, she wasn't willing to settle for anything less than a marriage in which both spouses shared fully in each other's lives—their joys and sorrows, doubts and hopes, dreams and fears.

And Adam wasn't there yet.

Maybe he would never be.

The sharp ring of the telephone interrupted that disheartening thought, and Clare padded to the kitchen to pick it up.

"Clare, it's Nicole. Are you busy?"

"Not really. Just going through some papers. What's up?"

"I was going to make some chocolate chip cookies, but I can't get the mixer to work."

"I thought we agreed you wouldn't do any baking unless I was there."

"I know. But you're leaving soon, and I need to figure out how to do it by myself."

"Is your dad around? Maybe he can look at the mixer."

"He's busy. I don't want to bother him."

Clare frowned. Adam had called earlier and left a message with Nicole that he wouldn't be home in time for dinner, and not to wait. So Clare had left him a plate in the oven. She'd heard him pull in about an hour ago, but he must be tied up with some emergency.

"Okay. I'll be right over."

Clare shoved her feet into a pair of canvas shoes and tucked her T-shirt into her jeans. She'd already taken her hair down for the night, so she simply ran a brush through it. This shouldn't take long.

She ran quickly down the narrow stairs. But when she opened the outside door at the bottom, prepared to dash over to the house, she pulled up short, her eyes widening in surprise.

At her feet lay a single long-stemmed red rose.

With a note attached.

Slowly Clare reached down and lifted the fragile blossom, letting her fingers trace the outline of the velvety petals. She looked around. There was no one in sight, but a flutter of the kitchen curtains told her Nicole was in on this. She glanced back down at the rose and flipped open the folded sheet of paper that was attached to the stem.

"Dear Clare, I have never been very good with words or expressing what's in my heart. Last night is just the latest dismal example. I know I can never make up for botching what should have been a beautiful moment between us. But at least I can try. If you can find it in your heart to give me one more chance, please follow the trail of roses. I'll be waiting at the end to meet you. The next rose is at the end of the driveway. Yours always, Adam."

Clare read the note a second time, then carefully folded it and slipped it into the pocket of her jeans. She tried to remain calm, to tell herself this might be another false start that would end just as badly as the first one. But somehow her heart wasn't listening. A buoyant sense of hope welled up within her, and she lifted the rose to her face to inhale its sweet, intoxicating fragrance.

"Thank you, Lord!" she whispered.

Slowly she made her way down the driveway, the gravel crunching beneath her feet in the stillness of the twilight. And just as Adam had promised, another rose lay at the end, pointing to the right.

Clare picked it up and continued her journey, following the quiet country lane until she came to another rose, which pointed down a barely visible, overgrown footpath that veered off into the woods. She picked that one up as well and set off down the path.

Clare had never been this way before. The path was on private property, so she'd never explored it. And in the rapidly deepening dusk it was harder and harder to see the trail markings. But whenever she began to wonder if she had lost her way, she came upon another rose, confirming that she was still on the right track.

Clare counted the roses as she picked them up, and as she reached for the eleventh one she realized that it was pointing away from the path. With a frown she straightened and peered into the twilight. In the distance she could see a faint, indistinct glow, and she set off in that direction, weaving in and out among the trees.

When at last Clare emerged from the forest, her eyes widened in wonder at the enchanting scene before her. A white lattice arbor stood in a small, moss-covered clearing, backed by a clear, placid jewel of a lake. Inside the arbor were two chairs and a tiny table, draped with white linen. A plate of chocolate-covered strawberries stood in the center of the snowy expanse, with two crystal goblets beside it. The romantic strains of a classical string quartet drifted softly through the air. And there were candles. Dozens of candles. On the table. On the ground. Beside the lake. On stones and tree stumps and fallen logs. Illuminating the scene with golden, ethereal light.

It was magic.

But most magical of all was the man. Adam stood beside the arbor, impeccably dressed in a dove-gray suit, white shirt and silver-flecked tie. He was holding the final rose and gazing at her with an expression that could only be described with one word.

Adoring.

Clare melted.

For a moment the world stopped as their gazes connected. Clare saw in Adam's eyes exactly what she had always hoped to see. Love. Absolute, complete, unguarded love. He was holding nothing back.

Slowly she moved forward, until she was only a whisper away from him. He handed her the final rose, then lifted her hand to his lips.

Clare's throat constricted with emotion, and she felt tears of joy sting her eyes. Even though Adam hadn't yet said a word, she knew that the setting he had created tonight—with help from Nicole, she suspected—had taken him way out of his comfort zone. And gave her hope that he had, at last, found the courage to escape the bitter legacy of his father.

Adam saw the glimmer of tears in Clare's eyes and reached over to gently lay his palm against her cheek.

"I didn't plan to make you cry," he said huskily.

She blinked, then reached up to wipe the back of her hand across her eyes. "Adam, this is…" She gestured around the setting. "I can't even…" Her voice choked, and she had to stop and take a deep breath. "It's like something out of a storybook."

"When a man is blessed with a second chance to ask the woman he loves to marry him, he wants to do it right."

He took her hand and led her to one of the small white chairs, then gently urged her to sit. The heady perfume of the flowers that filled her arms was something Clare knew she would remember all the days of her life. She would never again inhale the fragrance of a rose without remembering the sweetness of this moment.

Adam went down on one knee and reached for her free hand, his warm brown eyes only inches from hers. "Let me start with an apology, Clare," he said softly. "Last night was a fiasco, and if I could erase it from your memory, I would. I knew I'd done a poor job, but Nicole pointed out in no uncertain terms just how badly I'd blown it. She read me the riot act, then kept after me until I finally told her what I should have told you. When I got done, she made me write it down so I would be sure to say it correctly tonight."

He reached into his pocket and withdrew a folded sheet of paper. "But you know something? I don't need this after all. Because these words were in my heart all along. I was just too afraid to say them. I was afraid I'd be rejected or made fun of, which is what my father did whenever I tried to tell him how I felt. That's a terrible legacy to give a child, and it has been a very, very difficult one to overcome.

"But I finally realized something last night. As long as I let what he did to me continue to affect my life, he still had control over me. And I decided I'm not going to give him that power anymore. Because I also realized that holding back doesn't protect your heart—it only alienates you from the people you love. It makes you isolated and lonely and empty."

He paused and drew a deep breath. "Clare, I told you last night that I'd like us to be a family. And that Nicole had come to care for you deeply. Those things are still true. But the main reason I want you to stay is far more selfish." He looked at her steadily, offering a clear view directly into his heart. "I love you, Clare. I love you more than life itself. And I can't imagine my future without you. Until you came, I existed in the shadows. I lived life, but only at the edges. I could never find a way to step into the sunlight. But you brought brightness and warmth to my world and gave me the courage to love."

He paused and reached into his pocket to withdraw a small square box, then flipped open the top to reveal a dazzling, heart-shaped diamond. "I chose this cut because I wanted it to symbolize my promise to you, Clare. For as long as I live, my heart will be yours. And I promise to always do my very best to share and to care and to love. Will you marry me?"

Clare stared at the sparkling diamond as the tears ran freely down her face. "Yes," she whispered. "Oh, yes!"

With unsteady fingers, Adam removed the ring from the box and took her left hand in his. Slowly he slid the band onto her finger. Then he stood and reached for her, drawing her to her feet. For a long moment they gazed at each other, and then his lips closed over hers in a kiss so tender, so full of promise, that she thought her heart would burst with happiness.

And in the moment before she lost herself in his embrace, Clare uttered a simple, silent expression of gratitude to the woman whose loving bequest had given two lonely people a second chance at love.

Thank you, Aunt Jo.

Epilogue

❦

"Clare, have you talked with Seth Mitchell recently?"

She turned from watering the fern on the front porch to look at Adam, who had just retrieved the mail. "Yes. I called him a couple of days ago—the day after you gave me this." She held up her left hand with a smile and wiggled her fourth finger. "I told him that I'd completed the nanny assignment but that I was staying to take on a more permanent job."

Adam returned her smile, and the warmth in his unguarded eyes made her breath catch in her throat.

"That must be what this is about, then," he said, holding out a letter.

She put the watering can down and reached for the slim white envelope. When she slit the flap, a note fell out, as well as another envelope. Clare quickly scanned the note.

"Dear Mrs. Randall: Your aunt asked that I forward this to you after the six-month period stipulated in her will. My congratulations again to you and Dr. Wright. I wish you great happiness."

Clare set the note aside and turned her attention to the smaller envelope, which was addressed to her and Adam in her aunt's flowing hand.

"Adam, this is for both of us. From Aunt Jo."

He stopped sorting the mail and walked over to her curiously. "Let's sit on the settee and read it together," he suggested.

Adam stole a quick kiss before he draped his arm around Clare's shoulders, and she gazed up at him longingly. "If we keep this up, we'll never get to Jo's letter," he teased.

Clare smiled. "Luckily we have a good chaperone."

Adam chuckled. "Too true. But I'm counting the days until you're living under our roof. In the meantime, my daughter is doing her job very diligently."

Clare nudged him playfully, then turned her attention back to the smaller envelope. Carefully she withdrew the single, folded sheet, then held it out so they could both scan it.

My dearest Clare and Adam,

If you are reading this, it means that Clare's nanny assignment has turned into something far more permanent. As I hoped it would.

Clare, you are a loving, sensitive, kind-hearted woman who has always had her priorities in order. The people you love have always come first in your life, and I greatly admired and respected the wonderful home you created for Dennis and David. I know their tragic deaths shattered your world in more ways than you ever spoke of. My heart ached for you, and I wanted desperately to help you find a way to recreate the kind of family you had lost.

That's where Adam came in. He has been a great friend to me for many years, and I have always considered him to be a fine man, with a tender heart and a great capacity to love. But because he carried his own scars, that capacity has never been realized. I knew it would take someone very special to reach him and to help him unlock his heart.

As I made the final revisions to my will, knowing that my earthly life was soon to end, I wanted to give you both a lasting gift. But what you needed most, Adam—help with Nicole so that the two of you could become a family—was not in my physical capacity to give. So I sent you Clare. I knew that her warm and loving heart could work miracles in your troubled relationship with Nicole. And I hoped, as time went by, that it would also work miracles in you so that, in the end, she would choose to give you a gift of her own—her love. In doing so, she would also fulfill my dearest wish for her—she would find a new home and a new family to love.

I cannot tell you how pleased I am that my wish came true. May your life together always be filled with joy, peace and hope. God bless you both. Aunt Jo.

As Clare finished reading the note, she reached up to brush the tears from her cheek. When she glanced at Adam, his eyes were suspiciously moist, as well.

"Did it ever occur to you that Aunt Jo had an ulterior motive for sending me here?" Clare asked softly.

Adam shook his head. "Never."

"But how could she have known this would happen?"

"Jo was a very astute lady. I guess she knew what we needed even better than we did. And you can't argue with success."

Clare smiled up at him tenderly. "I can think of lots better things to do than argue, anyway."

His eyes darkened, and he reached over to trace the elegant curve of her jaw. "Where's the chaperone?" he murmured.

"Cleaning up her room."

"Then we have plenty of time," he said.

"For what?"

"For this."

He drew her close, and as his lips claimed hers, Clare prayed that Aunt Jo knew the outcome of her carefully laid plans.

Because the ending wasn't just happy. It was, as she had hoped, a miracle.

Dear Reader,

As I write this letter, I am still enjoying the fragrance and beauty of eighteen long-stemmed roses that my husband sent me for my birthday. And I have to admit they helped inspire the last scene in this book! I am so very blessed to be married to a wonderful man who never hesitates to tell me how much he loves me, and who demonstrates that love in countless ways every day.

As Adam learns in this book, love can't exist in a vacuum. It must be nurtured constantly, and it requires sharing at the deepest, most intimate levels. That isn't always easy. But only when we let people into our hearts do we experience love in the fullest sense.

And that's true for any kind of love. Between man and wife, parents and children, brother and sister, and between friends. Love is a precious gift, one that far transcends the value of any material object. That's why Aunt Jo wanted to leave this enduring legacy to her three great-nieces. And as each comes to realize, love is the best gift of all.

In the meantime, may all of you find the courage to open your hearts to love, and may your days be filled with joy and hope.

Irene Hannon

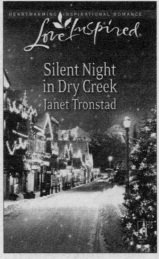

Love Inspired®

For private investigator Wade Sutton, Dry Creek holds too many memories—and none of them fond. Yet he can't say no when the sheriff asks him to watch over a woman who might be in danger. Getting to know lovely Jasmine Hunter just might give Wade a good reason to call Dry Creek home once more....

Look for

Silent Night in Dry Creek

by

Janet Tronstad

Available October wherever books are sold.

Steeple Hill®

www.SteepleHill.com

HEARTWARMING INSPIRATIONAL ROMANCE

Get more of the heartwarming
inspirational romance stories that
you love and cherish, beginning
in July with SIX NEW titles,
available every month from
the Love Inspired® line.

Also look for our other
Love Inspired® genres, including:

Love Inspired® Suspense:
Enjoy four contemporary tales of intrigue
and romance every month.

Love Inspired® Historical:
Travel to a different time with two powerful
and engaging stories of romance, adventure
and faith every month.

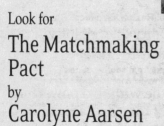

REQUEST YOUR FREE BOOKS!

2 FREE INSPIRATIONAL NOVELS
PLUS 2
FREE
MYSTERY GIFTS

Love Inspired®

YES! Please send me 2 FREE Love Inspired® novels and my 2 FREE mystery gifts (gifts are worth about $10). After receiving them, if I don't wish to receive any more books, I can return the shipping statement marked "cancel". If I don't cancel, I will receive 4 brand-new novels every month and be billed just $4.24 per book in the U.S. or $4.74 per book in Canada. That's a savings of over 20% off the cover price. It's quite a bargain! Shipping and handling is just 50¢ per book.* I understand that accepting the 2 free books and gifts places me under no obligation to buy anything. I can always return a shipment and cancel at any time. Even if I never buy another book, the two free books and gifts are mine to keep forever.

113 IDN EYK2 313 IDN EYLE

Name	(PLEASE PRINT)
Address	Apt. #
City	State/Prov.	Zip/Postal Code

Signature (if under 18, a parent or guardian must sign)

Mail to Steeple Hill Reader Service:
IN U.S.A.: P.O. Box 1867, Buffalo, NY 14240-1867
IN CANADA: P.O. Box 609, Fort Erie, Ontario L2A 5X3

Not valid to current subscribers of Love Inspired books.

Want to try two free books from another series?
Call 1-800-873-8635 or visit www.morefreebooks.com

* Terms and prices subject to change without notice. Prices do not include applicable taxes. Sales tax applicable in N.Y. Canadian residents will be charged applicable provincial taxes and GST. Offer not valid in Quebec. This offer is limited to one order per household. All orders subject to approval. Credit or debit balances in a customer's account(s) may be offset by any other outstanding balance owed by or to the customer. Please allow 4 to 6 weeks for delivery. Offer available while quantities last.

Your Privacy: Steeple Hill Books is committed to protecting your privacy. Our Privacy Policy is available online at www.SteepleHill.com or upon request from the Reader Service. From time to time we make our lists of customers available to reputable third parties who may have a product or service of interest to you. If you would prefer we not share your name and address, please check here. ☐

LIREG09

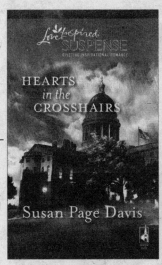